A Bit of Earth is an imaginativel[...] novel. Lim's clever fusion of fiction and history, [...] supple, and controlled diction, enriched with occasional humour and a spattering of sparkling imagery, make the novel brilliant, stimulating, and a compelling read.

Mohammad A. Quayum
Professor & Head Department of English Language and Literature
International Islamic University, Malaysia

A Bit of Earth is important both as a literary masterwork as well as a historical document telling in fictional terms the social history of Perak's Kinta Valley. It also has the virtue of being un-put-downable—a sure sign of a master storyteller, but over and above this, the novel affirms Suchen as one of the most important writers to have come out of Malaysia.

Wong Phui Nam
Poet, Malaysia

A Bit of Earth chronicles the visceral and cultural struggle of a young Chinese immigrant to survive in an equally struggling Malayan nation. His experience reminds us of the significance of origins, how it defines us as individuals and as members of our community. Likewise, this experience confirms how difficult and confusing it is to locate a liminal ethnicity within the diasporic and postcolonial contexts. The immigrant earns his bit of earth only by continuously re-inventing himself and by negotiating with the forces of history.

The novel makes history personal. It is a joy to teach and a riveting read.

Lily Rose Tope, Ph D
Professor, Department of English & Comparative Literature
University of the Philippines

Astonishing tour de force. You have created a physical and social landscape and peopled it with characters with real human feelings on issues of political import as well as on the everyday strains of personal and social survival.

Martin Marroni
Poet, Scotland

I was very impressed by the range and scope of the novel—how you pack in so much very fascinating history. Also how you deal with the conflict within families as it relates to a political situation. Tuck Heng is a wonderful character and I was totally hooked on his particular story. And you bring the whole thing to a splendid climax. I enjoyed learning so much about other cultures and was sorry to get to the end of the book!"

Diana Hendry
Poet & Writer
United Kingdom

Her novel brings into sharp relief conflicts over colonization, nationalism, and community. The central question explored by *A Bit of Earth*—how individuals transform and yet maintain feelings of belonging in a rapidly changing world—is as relevant in Singapore and Malaysia today as it was during the time in which the novel is set.

Philip Holden
Associate Professor
Department of English Language and Literature
National University of Singapore

Suchen Christine Lim's *A Bit of Earth* depicts the emergence of national consciousness in nineteenth-century Malaya amid the engrossing, complex relations between multi-ethnic characters and their families. A compelling and dramatic novel that draws the reader easily into the life of its main protagonist Tuck Heng, the immigrant from China made good, *A Bit of Earth* deserves to be read for giving us a sense of a past not usually experienced in contemporary Singapore fiction and for provocatively getting us to question the way we make sense of history, what we remember and what we forget.

Angelia Poon
Assistant Professor
English Language and Literature
National Institute of Education
Nanyang Technological University

A BIT OF EARTH

A BIT
OF EARTH

SUCHEN CHRISTINE LIM

Marshall Cavendish
Editions

Extracts from *A Bit of Earth* were previously published in *More than Half the Sky: Creative Writings by Thirty Singaporean Women*, Times Media ("Bandong"); *Virtual Lotus: Modern Fiction of Southeast Asia*, University of Michigan Press ("Two Brothers"); *WLT World Literature Today*, University of Oklahoma ("Clash of the Clans")

First published in 2001 by Times Books International. Reprinted 2002.
MCIA edition published 2009

This edition published 2023 by Marshall Cavendish Editions
An imprint of Marshall Cavendish International (Asia) Pte Ltd

Other Marshall Cavendish Offices
Marshall Cavendish Corporation, 800 Westchester Ave, Suite N-641, Rye Brook, NY 10573, USA • Marshall Cavendish International (Thailand) Co Ltd, 253 Asoke, 16th Floor, Sukhumvit 21 Road, Klongtoey Nua, Wattana, Bangkok 10110, Thailand • Marshall Cavendish (Malaysia) Sdn Bhd, Times Subang, Lot 46, Subang Hi-Tech Industrial Park, Batu Tiga, 40000 Shah Alam, Selangor Darul Ehsan, Malaysia

Marshall Cavendish is a trademark of Times Publishing Limited

National Library Board Singapore Cataloguing in Publication Data

Name(s): Lim, Suchen Christine.
Title: A bit of earth / Suchen Christine Lim.
Description: Singapore : Marshall Cavendish Editions, 2023.
Identifier(s): ISBN 978-981-5084-44-3 (paperback)
Subject(s): LCSH: Malaya--Fiction. | Immigrants--Fiction. | Families--Fiction.
Classification: DDC S823--dc23

Printed in Singapore

To my grandparents who came from Tangshan, the land beyond the mountains of Perak, and to my farsighted mother, who made sure that I was sent to school.

And lest we forget where we came from, this novel is also dedicated to the descendants of Chinese immigrants—Tay Kok Leong, Tay Kok Kiong, Lim Chi Minh, Lim Chi Sharn, and Shannan Wong, and to the descendants of Straits-born Chinese—Ophelia Ooi, Ngiam Gek Kim, Juliana Lim, and the late Aileen Lau.

ACKNOWLEDGMENTS

I thank the Fulbright Foundation for giving me the time, space and solitude to rework *A Bit of Earth*. Special thanks to Professor Peter Nazareth and his wife Mary from the International Writing Program, University of Iowa, and Professor Shirley Geok-lin Lim, University of California, Santa Barbara, for being such wonderful supportive hosts during my 1997 sojourn in the United States.

On the Singapore home front, my special thanks to our poets and prose writers Lee Tzu Pheng, Leong Liew Geok, Rasiah Halil, Catherine Lim, Edwin Thumboo, Robert Yeo, Kirpal Singh and many others whose public readings and conversations on writing and literature kept the little creative fire in me burning bright.

I also thank my friends Chen Chong and Liang-yue, who translated the two fragments on pages 11 and 386 into Chinese.

CONTENTS

I

SLASH AND BURN
1874

FIRST FRAGMENT

我叫王德兴，生
于咸丰七年七
月十五日。我的
故乡是广东省
三河村。先父是
王天庆，乃村里
的一名大夫。

I, Wong Tuck Heng, was born on the fifteenth of the seventh moon in the seventh year of Ham Fung, in my native village of Sum Hor, in the Canton Prefecture of Kwangtung Province. My father was Wong Tin Keng, the village physician ...

Chapter One

*H*e went over one more time what he had composed inside his head when he was tossing in the middle of the South China Sea, in the *tongkang*, the barge which had brought him to this part of the world.

> *When I was thirteen years of age, my father, Wong Tin Keng, the village physician, was imprisoned and tortured upon the orders of a corrupt magistrate. This vile slave of the Manchu devils accused my father of being a member of the Heaven and Earth League, a noble society founded by the loyal sons of the Chinese earth to overthrow the Qing dynasty and restore the glory of the Ming throne. Because my father was a loyal son of the Chinese earth, he was tortured to death. Soldiers torched our family home. I was the only one who escaped death.*

Then he shut his weary eyes against the splinters of sunlight bouncing off the waters of the Bandong River. Once again he heard his mother yelling, "Run! Tuck Heng, run!" She pushed him out the door. "Aiyee!" A fiery beam crashed down upon her. Instantly she was engulfed in flames.

Screams and the odour of burning flesh had pursued him for the next two years, turning his sleep into nightmares. Manchu devils had hounded him by day, and Memory Ghosts had devoured him by night. He had to watch his mother, brothers and sisters burn to death, night after night. Rough hands had stifled the screams that rose from his throat—hands of his parents' friends and relatives. If they had been caught shielding him, these brave souls and their entire families would have been killed. "Pull out the weeds, destroy their roots!" That was the edict issued by the Qing emperor for those who dared to oppose the Son of Heaven. To avoid the destruction of their families, many Chinese scholars had had to serve the Manchu invaders, his father had told him. "But not your great-great-grandfather. He left the capital and returned to our village, and we, his descendants, became doctors instead of scholars." This knowledge had lodged like a gold nugget in his heart ever since. Even as he had scuttled like a gutter rat, hiding in dark dank holes while making his way to the coast. After the fire, his sole duty to his parents was to stay alive, and this had sustained him and given him the tenacity to endure squalor, hunger and danger.

His dark eyes searched the Bandong River now for the silent lords—the harbingers of death. A large black log was floating perilously close to their sampan. Chan Ah Fook had warned him to look out for those evil beady eyes.

"It's the eyes; they're the only signs which give them away," he had whispered. "If not for their eyes, ah, you won't know they're crocodiles! And only a Malay boatman can bring us up the river safely. They've got special prayers and charms. But remember, once we're on the river, don't ever say the word 'crocodile'. You'll offend the beast. This land is full of jinns and spirits. Hill, rock, valley and river—all have guardian spirits. Newcomers have to be careful not to offend them. Understand or not?"

And he had nodded as he listened to the old coolie in silence.

Their lone sampan inched its way up the river, pushing against the current. The boatman's oar sliced through the muddy waters in stroke after stroke, his eyes on the riverbank, ever watchful for the slightest movement in the thick foliage which fringed the river. The jungle guarded the water's edge. For miles there was nothing but an impenetrable wall of green, broken occasionally by a few brown huts built on stilts. Tuck Heng wiped the sweat from his face with the sleeve of his coolie tunic. The heat was oppressive. The silence on the river was beginning to weigh heavily upon him. River, sky and jungle for mile after mile. River, sky and jungle. He had come to the land of foreign devils.

White-skinned and brown-skinned devils had crowded the pier where Chan Ah Fook had met him. What a babble of tongues and noise then! And now this unbearable silence, as though they were in a cavern never before traversed by man. He muttered a prayer. Hidden eyes were watching them as he untied his queue, mopped his brow and rewound the length of hair round his head. Clutching his cloth bundle, he pressed it hard against his chest. His thin hard face looked older than his fifteen years. His brows were creased in a dark frown against the shafts of light bouncing off the river. The afternoon sun hung in the sky. Implacable like a god.

He fixed his eyes on the back of the Malay boatman. By the power of my ancestors, Malay devil, row faster, faster, he kept thinking and wished that the acute pain in his chest would stop. Let him live through whatever ordeal Fate had in store for him in this land of the brown-skinned devils. He pressed his cloth bundle against his chest. Harder, harder. He would cut off an arm or a leg if that could ease his pain. Curse this oppressive silence! Curse the Manchu dogs! The bastards! May they die without a place to lay their bones! Without descendants to mourn them!

"Psst!" Chan Ah Fook's weather-beaten face came up close to his ear, his square jaw jutting out as he strained to keep his voice low.

"Throw this red packet into the water. Sweeten the guardians' mouths with sugar. Pay your respects and tell them you're new."

Tuck Heng flung the red packet into the river and watched it sink into the murky depths. A sudden rustle of leaves. He started, his eyes searched the shadows. A monkey screeched. Then a flock of birds rose from the trees. The air was cool at this stretch of the river which was shaded by the jungle trees. The sun had dipped behind the dense wall of green by now. An uneasy silence settled upon the river with the onset of the tropical twilight.

"Watch out!" Ah Fook hissed. "Hakka dogs might set a trap for us here!"

His shoulders stiffened at this hint of danger. His nose sniffed the air like a dog on the alert. When a bright blue kingfisher dived into the water, his hand reached for the knife in his belt. But he relaxed when he saw that it was only a bird.

"Quick, quick!" Ah Fook hissed at the boatman in a tongue which sounded like gibberish.

But the boatman understood Ah Fook's heavily accented Malay, and the sampan moved faster upriver.

"Nearly there. Keep your eyes on the riverbank." Ah Fook switched to the familiar Cantonese dialect of their native Sum Hor and then, back to Malay, "Stop here!"

"You speak very well, Uncle."

"In these parts you must speak the Malay tongue. Don't fear shame. Open your mouth more. Soon you'll be speaking like me."

Their sampan slid to a halt.

Night had fallen by this time, and the riverbank was a mass of shadows. Tuck Heng thanked his gods and ancestors for his safe arrival. Clutching his cloth bundle, he stood up eagerly and jumped off the sampan. Down he sank, knee-deep into the soft mud. Fool! He cursed his own stupidity. He clambered up the riverbank. Slipped. And climbed again.

"Shit up to your knees. Shit and mud. Symbols of wealth."

"Shut your mouth!"

"Curb your tongue! Wait for Uncle here. I will lead the way. Show you where the dungholes are."

The boatman's laugh and Ah Fook's words stung him. He loathed mistakes. They were signs of weakness. How could he have been such a fool as to mess up his first step on the new land! And he had fallen upon it. Bowed before it. A good omen?

"Humbled by the guardian spirit of this place, that's what!

Be patient, young dog. Those who are too hasty, like your father, get killed. Follow me. I know this place like the back of my hand."

Chastened, he followed Ah Fook down the path to the settlement. The moon had risen, and he could make out the dark shapes of the huts and the patches of yellow light beyond the bushes. There were many questions inside his head as they plunged into the wilderness. Before he could ask them, the night was shattered.

"You're in luck, young dog! They're going to drown the bitch tonight! Come!"

Chan Ah Fook raced ahead. The gongs grew louder. When they reached the village square, it was swarming with hundreds of miners and a sprinkling of women. Everyone had gathered in front of a temple, and the air was thick with Cantonese curses and obscenities.

"Drown the bitch!"

"Let the whore die!"

The men were pushing and jostling to get to the centre of the square. A miner swung his lantern above the heads of the crowd. "Throw her into the river!" he yelled.

"Not so fast!"

"The bitch must die a slow and painful death!" the men on the other side of the square roared.

"Whip her! Whip her!" the crowd chanted.

He shoved and elbowed his way to the front. Kneeling before the temple, hands tied behind her, the object of the crowd's wrath was splattered with mud and dung, and bleeding from several lacerations on her face and arms. She had been whipped, and the lashes had cut deep into her flesh. A purple gash on her temple had left a trail of blood on one side of her face. Miners, bare to the waist and sweating like workhorses, were pelting her with lumps of dung.

"Slut! Whore!"

But the woman showed no sign that she had heard. Her eyes were glazed and fixed on a point above the heads of the mob. Her impassive face was oblivious of her tormentors. A miner went forward and gave her a violent kick. She fell onto her side. No sound escaped her lips. She lay where she had fallen, an inert figure that drove the men and the few women in the crowd into a frenzy. More lumps of pig's dung flew through the air. One of them hit her in the eye.

"Ancestors, open your eyes! See the shame she has brought upon our village! We women of Sum Hor have a good name! But this she-fox has soiled it! Let me dig out her eyes! Her heart!"

A big-boned woman rushed forward and seized the bound victim by the throat. If the men had not pulled her away, she would have strangled her.

"Good, Ah Lai's mother! Kill her with your own hands! Your no-good daughter-in-law!"

"She's no daughter-in-law of mine! I curse the day she crossed my threshold!"

"Didn't you buy her for your idiot boy? Didn't you?"

"I was blind at the time! By the gods, I swear I was blind!" the big-boned woman shrieked, her eyes blazing with rage.

Throughout this exchange, the victim maintained a stoic expression. Is it strength or indifference? he wondered. He had never witnessed the punishment of an adulteress before, although he had heard stories of how such women were drowned in rivers and lakes back home in Sum Hor. He peered at the woman as he would a trapped rat. Even a rat would shriek when tortured, but she neither cringed nor whimpered. Her silence incensed the mob.

"Whip the bitch! Whip the lust out of her!"

The women started to flail her with bamboo poles. The louder their men urged, the harder the women hit. It was as if they had to prove their own fidelity to moral law.

"Kill her!" the men ordered.

"Stop! By our ancestral laws, she must die by drowning!"

"Who's that?" he asked.

"Tai-kor Wong Fatt Choy, Lodge Master of the White Cranes in Bandong. The man you must obey." Chan Ah Fook had emerged suddenly at his elbow. "I will bring you to him when this trouble is over."

Tuck Heng studied the broad unsmiling face of the thick stocky man. Big Brother Wong had a high forehead. His queue hung down his back like an emblem of his authority, unlike the coolies who had wound theirs round their heads.

"Brothers! We, the White Cranes of Bandong, are faithful to the laws of our clan and village—laws laid down by our forefathers in Sum Hor, laws obeyed by hundreds of generations. An adulteress shall die by drowning in a pig basket!"

His foghorn Cantonese voice rose above the cacophony, the voice of ancestral authority and continuity in the new land. The miners, uprooted from home and hearth, clung to that voice and obeyed it.

"Drown her in a pig basket!"

"Let me scratch out her eyes first!" Ah Lai's mother lunged forward.

But the men yanked her away. One of them brought out a large cylindrical rattan basket used for ferrying pigs. Two miners held the basket firmly, while two others thrust the bound woman into it. The mob jeered and pelted her with stones. The pig basket offered her scant protection since there were large gaps through which the men could see her.

"Big Dog! Big Tree! Take her down to the river!" Tai-kor Wong ordered.

Two burly miners, heavier and taller than most of the men, stepped forward. Using thick twine, they secured the pig basket to a bamboo pole and hoisted the pole onto their broad shoulders, the basket swinging between them.

"To the river!" Tai-kor Wong barked.

"Drown her! Drown her!" the mob started to chant.

There was a carnival air about the procession. Some men carried paper lanterns, some were beating gongs and tin pans, and the rest were cursing and swearing at the top of their voices.

"The sow slept with a Hakka dog!"

"Throw her into the river! No burial for her! Let her be a nameless ghost!"

No fate is worse than this, he thought. Dead and clanless. What could be worse?

Several miners poked and jabbed the woman in the basket with the sharp ends of their bamboo poles, hooting with wicked glee as she writhed in pain. The basket swung wildly between the carriers.

"Take this! Stick it into her!" A miner handed him a bamboo stick.

"Do it, young dog!"

"Give her a hard one!" Ah Fook's voice ripped the air, yelling with the rest of them. A devilish fever had swept through him.

The woman in the basket let out a piercing squeal like a pig being slaughtered.

"Good, good!"

They whooped and hooted like fiends from hell. A grizzled old miner thrust his hand into the basket and ripped off a piece of the woman's clothing. He flung it into the air, and his mates roared and guffawed. They surged towards the pig basket. Eager calloused hands, starved for the touch of a woman's breast, thrust through the gaps in the rattan. They squeezed and pinched and groped. The basket swung wildly. Shrieks pierced the night's foul air. They'd broken her silence! The mob hit their gongs and tin pans in reckless glee, mad malice glittering in their eyes.

The men plunged into the river with their victim. More men waded in. They beat the water with bamboo poles to keep the crocodiles at bay. Those on shore kept banging on their gongs and tin pans, calling on their ancestral gods and spirits to witness their righteous punishment of the adulteress.

As the pig basket was dropped into the river, a wild cheer rose from those on the riverbank. The gongs clamoured and clanged. Above the din, he heard a thin shrill cry. It sliced through his heart like a blade, and bleeding, he staggered back to shore, pushing his way through the mob.

Chapter Two

*T*he village square was deserted. Only the temple was aglow with oil lamps and candles. Inside the thatched hut, some women were laying out bowls of food on the altar. He caught a whiff of boiled sweet potatoes. Heaven would be eating a piece now!

"What're you doing here?"

The sharpness of the woman's voice startled him. But he stood his ground, shoulders braced and eyes alert. The gaunt woman had a face like a bittergourd left to dry in the sun. Her coarse brown skin and deep furrows spoke of long hours in the harsh tropical sunlight. Looking at her, he was suddenly reminded of China. Peasant women, similarly dressed in shapeless garb, had given him food and shelter when he was on the run.

"Auntie," he murmured.

"Never seen you before. Who are you?" Her voice was hard as nails.

"I'm Wong Tuck Heng."

"Who brought you here?"

Another woman came towards him.

"Are you a Hakka dog sent to spy on us?"

The stout woman advanced, a meat cleaver in her hand.

He backed away.

"Aunties, I'm Cantonese, not Hakka! I'm from the village of Sum Hor!"

His eyes darted from one woman to the other. Six or seven of them. One was clutching a meat cleaver. Two had poles in their hands. Swiftly he assessed the danger. No chance of escaping unhurt if there was a fight. He had to convince them that he was not an enemy. Beg them to believe him if he had to. Pride and arrogance counted for little if he were to die before his time. That was the one thing he had learned during his two years on the run.

"Aunties, I beg you, please listen to me! Uncle Chan Ah Fook brought me here. Ask him. If you kill me before finding out the truth, you'll regret it for the rest of your lives!"

The women laughed till tears rolled down their cheeks. They shook their heads and wagged their fingers at him.

"What a talker! A dead man listening to him will come back to life!" the stout woman with the meat cleaver exclaimed.

"Stupid boy! Once you opened your big mouth, we knew you're our clansman from Sum Hor!"

"It's your accent. You can't run away from that. And your thick black brows and those eyes. Just like your father's. But ha!" the gaunt woman scoffed. "He was fair as a scholar. You? Brown as a coolie."

The twinkle in her eyes and the smile on her face made him feel welcome. He gave a broad sheepish grin. The mob and the drowning had put everyone on edge, he thought.

"It's all right. Just your anxiety, this being your first night in the new land."

"I've been expecting you all day. Here's a sweet potato. Your belly must be aching."

"Thank you, Auntie."

"Call me Wong-soh. Like everyone else."

"Do you know who she is?" a woman, big with child, asked him.

He shook his head.

"You'd better respect her. She's the wife of Tai-kor Wong."

He put down his bowl and executed a kowtow.

"Wong-soh, please forgive my ignorance. I, Wong Tuck Heng, pay my deepest respect to you."

"Get up, get up!"

Wong-soh laughed, her deep furrows bunching up at the corners of her eyes, which were half-closed like curtains to hide the great pleasure she took in his kowtow.

"Our village doctor, the gods bless his spirit, has a respectful son," the woman with the meat cleaver said. "Your father cured my father once. You can call me Aunt Loh."

"My respects to you, Aunt Loh."

"No need to be so polite!"

"But it shows what book learning can do for a boy. So different from the hooligans we've seen tonight."

"Let the boy eat! We've got work to do. You sit there." Wong-soh pointed to the bench.

He sat down beside the big-boned woman. She was sobbing quietly and took no notice of him.

The others returned to their work. They set out plates of boiled pork, chicken, sweet potatoes and yams before their patron saint, Lord Guan Gong, and their ancestors, whose names were carved on tiers of wooden tablets.

"Lord Guan Gong, hear my prayers! My heart is broken to bits! Ah Lai's father, forgive me! Your good-for-nothing wife has no eyes!" The big-boned woman fell upon her knees before the altar.

"Ah Lai's mother, you can't be everywhere," Wong-soh consoled her. "How could you have known?"

She tried to pull Ah Lai's mother to her feet.

"Let me be, Wong-soh! Spirit of Ah Lai's father, I kowtow before you. My fault! My fault! My fault!"

She banged her head upon the leg of the altar with each shout of "My fault!" The other women tried to restrain her.

"It's the sow's fault! She brought shame upon our village," one of the women said.

"Lee-soh is right. Not your fault."

"It's your son's fate. So many chickens in the coop and you chose this one for him."

"Lee-soh, you're so right! I chose the chicken so I brought the shame!" Ah Lai's mother hit her breast.

"Let me die! Let me join Ah Lai's father!"

"How can you say that?" Aunt Loh quickly brushed aside her ill-omened sayings. "Who is going to look after Ah Lai if you're gone?"

"Ah Lai's mother, do you have the heart to leave your son alone in this world?" Wong-soh asked her. "Men can fly off like the wind. But we women must remain to look after our flesh and blood."

Wong-soh glanced at the boy on the bench. Her heart was aching for him who was not of her flesh and blood. Not yet. Not yet.

"My life is cursed! Ah Lai's marriage was my reward for a lifetime of toil. His father's hope for someone to sweep our graves after we're gone. But that sow has cheated on our boy! Made him a laughing stock!"

"How much did you pay for her?" a young woman asked.

Ah Lai's mother lashed out at her as if she had been hit.

"Do you think I've been lying when I said I paid good money for her? That shameless daughter of a whore said to me, 'Ah Lai doesn't know what to do in bed. He's dumb.' 'Why do you think I bought you from the brothel keeper?' I asked her. 'A woman like you ought to know how to teach my son. I don't expect gratitude from you,' I told her, 'but I do expect to hold a grandson.' And if you think of the money I've spent on her, I've a right to expect something back, right or not?"

"How much?" the young woman persisted.

"Fifteen silver dollars, that's how much! Half of my life savings!"

"Aren't we like small frogs never out of the well?" Lee-soh exclaimed. "Fifteen dollars. Big as cartwheels to us. But loose change to the traders from Penang."

"I know, I know. But how could I buy a nice girl at this price? So I said to myself, don't worry. A girl from a good family might not want him, but a girl from a brothel will thank the gods if I offer her a good home. That was why I bought a used hen like her. Tell me, all of you, would you have paid more for her? Would you? Would you?"

"Calm down, Ah Lai's mother."

"No, Wong-soh! The butcher's wife insults me, and you ask me to calm down? Are you taking their side?"

"Ah Lai's mother, I'm on nobody's side. But as the saying goes, 'Once a whore, always a whore.' If we buy trash, we get trash, right or not?"

"Right! You're all right!" Ah Lai's mother screeched. "If I had more money, I would've bought him a good girl from China! But I'm a poor widow with an idiot son. Gods in heaven, I curse that bitch!"

"Ah Lai's mother, let the dead rest!" Lee-soh looked as if she had more to say, but she went back to trimming the lamps.

"Say what you want, Lee-soh! Say it to my face now! Not behind my back later!"

"Ah Lai's mother, did you know that Ah Fah used to cry her heart out? Each time we went to the river to wash clothes. 'I'll go mad soon,' she said to me one day. 'My mother-in-law is turning me into a madwoman.'"

The other women tried to stop her, but she pushed them away.

"Your son is twenty-eight this year. But inside his head, he's only six years old. When you locked him in the bedroom with Ah Fah, he kicked and bit her. She showed me the teeth marks. And the lashes. You caned her every night, she told me. A mother-in-law is the sky and daughters-in-law are the earth. You can do anything to her as long as she's under your roof. So she looked for another roof."

Ah Lai's mother was strangely quiet after that.

--∘≡◉⊂∘--

"Tuck Heng!"

He stumbled out of the temple.

"Where the hell were you?" Chan Ah Fook bawled at him.

"I'm sorry, Uncle Ah Fook. I was hungry so I went into the temple."

"Stay close to me from now on!" Ah Fook turned and yelled at his men. "Look out for Hakka dogs!"

Ah Fook's dark brows were drawn forward over his eyes as he scanned the crowd filling the village square rapidly.

"Some things never change," he said bitterly. "Thousands of *li* away from home and we are at war with the Hakkas again! Those blood-sucking parasites shouldn't even be here. We were granted the right to mine in Bandong Valley, you know that?"

He shook his head.

"We were the first in this valley! Then it was just jungle and death. The *menteri* of Bandong had begged us to come here. The chief minister owed us large sums of money. To pay off his debts, he granted us the mining rights in Bandong. Then things changed. Those wily Hakkas bribed him. As they say, 'Money can make the devil push your cart.'"

Tuck Heng cast a worried eye over the sea of faces. Hundreds of miners, thirsting for vengeance, could lead only to one thing, one huge almighty brawl before the night was over. People could be killed. He sighed. What an ill omen for his new life here! He'd hoped to find peace and safety among his clansmen in the new land.

"When do we begin?" a man yelled from the back of the crowd.

"Soon."

"How soon? My beard is turning white!"

"As soon as Tai-kor Wong says so, you swine!"

Ah Fook searched for the hecklers. But the oil lamps and paper lanterns around the square had thrown an ominous yellow light upon the faces of the miners. How could he tell friend from foe?

"Some Hakka dogs are among us!"

Tuck Heng reached for the dagger hidden in the folds of his waistband.

"Got a knife?" Ah Fook asked.

He nodded.

"Good! If you see any of the Hakka maggots, use your dagger! You understand?"

He nodded, numb with fear. Let there be no fighting, he pleaded with the gods. No killing. No burning.

"On your knees and kowtow!" a White Crane guard yelled.

Ah Fook pulled him down beside him. "Kneel and do as I do!"

Big Dog and Big Tree stood on either side of the temple door like sentinels at heaven's gates. Tuck Heng kept his eyes on the sea of kneeling men, his nostrils flaring as he sniffed out the miners' bloodthirst. Drowning the adulteress had not appeased them. A multitude of voices rose from the village square.

"Kill the Hakka dogs!"

"Kill those who defile our women!"

The temple drums boomed.

"Master of the White Cranes of Bandong!"

Men bearing blue flags with the white crane symbol flanked Tai-kor Wong. His square bronze-coloured face with its wide heavy jaws was unsmiling. He held three lighted joss sticks, their incense rising in white swirls above his head. He stood before the large stone urn in front of the temple and raised his joss sticks high above his head. The crowd in the square kowtowed three times.

"Lord Guan Gong! Hero of the Three Kingdoms! God of War! Protector of the poor and oppressed! Lord of courage! Prince of loyalty! Knight of integrity! We bow before thee!"

"Kowtow once! Twice! Three times! Rise and stand!"

Big Dog and Big Tree barked the orders in rapid succession in the time-honoured ritual of the White Cranes.

Tai-kor Wong stuck the joss sticks into the urn of ash, kowtowed three times and stood with hands clasped above his head.

"Lord Guan Gong, we kowtow before your lordship! We bow before you and offer your lordship our humble greetings! Please accept your humble followers' kowtows!"

His great voice resounded through the square of three thousand miners as he intoned in formal Cantonese:

"Your Honour, please hear us, your humble supplicants. Spirits of our revered ancestors! The Earth God of Bandong! We beg your lordships. Please bend your ears and listen to our report on the drowning of that shameless sow who has defiled our village! Before you we stand, your unworthy descendants! We beg of you to accept our deepest regrets and our abject apologies for this blight upon the good name of the White Crane *kongsi*! We vow before your eminence that we will never rest! Not until the honour of the White Crane is restored!"

"Until the honour of the White Crane clan is restored!" the crowd roared like a sudden thunderclap.

Roosting jungle birds shrieked in a rush of wings from the sleeping trees.

"Kill those Hakka dogs!"

The miners stamped their feet and punched the air. Vengeance fever was running high. Tai-kor Wong raised his hands for silence.

"My brothers, I know your hearts! The White Cranes have lost face! Not to avenge this loss is to invite the world to laugh at us! Like dung invites dung flies. The White Cranes will fight back! But not tonight!"

"Tai-kor, what are you waiting for?"

"Are we White Cranes scared of dogs?"

The voices had come from the far end of the square. Tuck Heng scanned the faces of the crowd.

"Quiet!" Tai-kor Wong bellowed. "Those sons of whores will not escape death! If I, Wong Fatt Choy, fail to restore our honour, chop off my head! I swear before the gods!"

"Fight now or we'll have your head!"

Ah Fook leapt onto a crate to get a better view of the hecklers. Tuck Heng clutched his dagger.

"My brothers, listen to me," Tai-kor Wong went on, reason creeping into his voice. "The Hakka dogs are waiting for us to rush into battle unprepared tonight. But we White Cranes are no fools! We will show the Hakka dogs that we have the patience of a python. We strike at the right moment. Then we'll swallow our enemy. Guts, bones and all! My brothers, return to your quarters. Your elders will plan the next move."

Chapter Three

An air of self-satisfaction hung about him as he strolled through his large compound, trailed by a group of sycophantic retainers who kept a discreet distance between him and their lowly selves. The menteri of Bandong was known for his swift hand and quick temper. Many a man had had his throat slit or his face slapped because of an ill-considered remark. But that had not discouraged the young men who came from miles around seeking employment in the minister's service, for Datuk Long Mahmud was the wealthiest chief in these parts.

A strikingly handsome man in his late thirties, he was aristocratic in his bearing, with a high forehead and an aquiline nose with a neat black moustache beneath it. He carried himself like a warrior prince, demanding unquestioning obedience from his followers. Like his father before him.

As he strolled down the path leading to his residence, his eyes were coolly assessing the men putting the finishing touches to the *balai*, the audience hall he was building. His brown face gave nothing away except the impression that he would not tolerate fools easily. Strong men had been known to quake before him when he was angry. His reputation as one of the dashing hot bloods of Perak's nobility and his prowess in the Malay martial art of *bersilat* had spread as far north as Kedah, where younger warriors uttered his name with awe.

Before his father's death, he had been a rake and a wayward wanderer, travelling to Penang, Malacca and

Singapore, gambling away hundreds of silver dollars a night. Rumour had it that he often made up for these gambling losses by robbing a European vessel or two. It was no secret among those who knew him that he detested the English and the Dutch sea captains who had branded his Bugis relations as pirates and outlaws and had handed them over to the British navy for punishment. He was apt to remind his listeners that before the arrival of the Dutch and English, the Bugis were kings of the seas of Southeast Asia. They were the warriors and kingmakers, not the beggars and brigands the Dutch and English had made them out to be. However, such things no longer preoccupied him. Ever since his father's untimely death, the responsibilities of government and trade and the cares of looking after his family and clan had turned him away from all that. Now a territorial chief, he realised that a warrior's prowess was not enough. He must cultivate allies through sweet talk and wily deeds if he were to survive the intrigues in the sultan's court and maintain his hold on the Chinese miners in his district.

Two men were coming to see him that night. One was the son of the menteri of Larut, chief of the richest province in Perak, and the other was the Lodge Master of the Black Flag clan. And I'm ready, he thought, pleased with the figure he cut. He was dressed formally to receive his guests. His maroon jacket of stiff Kelantan silk woven with fine gold thread shone in the evening light. The row of ornate gold buttons down the front of his jacket and the diamond rings on his fingers spoke of his wealth and good fortune. His trousers of stiff black silk, made tight round the ankles, were partially covered by a handsome sarong, which hung in graceful folds from the waist to the knees. Emerald green, peacock blue, gold and silver threads were cunningly woven into an intricate weave of ever-changing shimmers. His headdress was no less striking. It was a kerchief of stiff cloth, tied above his brow, folded over his head and arched up on the left, with a border of gold leaves. It was often reported that the menteri's attire was richer and grander than the sultan of Perak's.

Needless to say, every *penghulu*, every chief in the country had heard of Datuk Long Mahmud's wealth, and his power was reputed to be second only to that of the menteri of Larut. It had even been whispered that the sultan himself feared the Datuk and was beholden to him for numerous gifts of money and jewellery to the royal purse.

His swift ascendancy in the Perak court was naturally a worrying affair to the other chiefs, who suspected that there was more to his generosity than met the eye. His bloodline was impeccable. The descendant of a long line of noble families in the Celebes and Aceh,he was linked, on his mother's side, to the legendary Tun Perak, the greatest chief minister of the Malacca sultanate. This connection alone would have been sufficient to gain him the support and respect of all the common people.

And Datuk Long Mahmud was fully aware of the advantage of his noble lineage in times of trouble. He knew that his fellow chiefs feared his undue influence over the heir to the throne. Fools, he thought, such influence was empty without the backing of wealth and weapons! And he was not ready to make his move yet. First he had to build upon and expand his father's gains. Thanks to Allah's most gracious mercy and compassion, his late father had succeeded in persuading the sultan to cede to the family, in perpetuity, the whole of Bandong Valley, a feat repeated by only one other chief, the menteri of Larut. It was a legacy he had to preserve, he thought. And his eyelids drooped like a veil over his dark eyes, hiding all signs of what he might be thinking.

After a long time in which he seemed plunged into deep thought, he raised his handsome profile and sniffed the fragrance of jasmine perfuming the air in his compound. His eyes travelled to the distant hills surrounding his beloved valley. Bequeathed to him by his father. Bequeathed to his father by His Royal Highness. The land of his children and *Insya Allah*, God willing, the land of his children's children and all their descendants. Not just an acre of earth for digging and planting, or measuring and selling by the white men and the Chinese.

He stopped at the foot of the stone steps.His home was an impressive building of white stone and teakwood, raised a few feet above the ground by stone pillars. It was a beautiful Malay-style house built on a much grander scale than the kampong hut on stilts. The only building of brick and teakwood in the country,it boasted a sloping roof of red tiles and eaves of carved wood. At the top of the steps was a spacious covered verandah fronting the main entrance. Elaborately decorated with carved beams of teakwood, it had a balustrade with an intricate floral design. Rich wall hangings and carpets from the Middle East, bamboo mats from Malacca, and silk cushions from India had turned the verandah into an audience chamber in which the Datuk received and dined with his guests.

Slaves and servants hovered about him. When he moved, their eyes followed him.When he stopped, they waited for a word or an order, their eyes anticipating his wishes. When he stopped at the foot of the steps, one of his female slaves descended in haste and knelt before him with head bowed and eyes lowered.

"Pardon, my great lord and master! Your most unworthy slave welcomes you home. Please pardon your unworthy slave for her slowness in greeting your lordship. May His Most Merciful and Bountiful shower His blessings on you!"

She removed his sandals with the reverence of one touching a sacred object. Then, using a polished coconut half-shell, she scooped water out of a stone jar and gently washed away the sand clinging to his feet. She knelt to dry them with a soft cloth, her lips brushing his feet lightly. He admired the suppleness of her body and the roundness and fullness of the breasts beneath her cotton blouse.

"Enough," he murmured and rewarded her with one of his rare smiles which she caught when she raised her eyes at the sound of his voice. But she hastily lowered them again and backed away with bowed head, profound salaams, and as many words of self-deprecation as demanded by custom.

"Come and serve me tonight."

"Your unworthy slave hears and obeys you."

More slave girls awaited him when he entered the verandah. One came forward with a towel for his face. Another brought a silver basin of rose-scented water for the washing of his hands before the evening meal. Two slave girls stationed themselves behind him, fanning the air with palm leaves as he reclined on a cushion. When their lord and master had rested sufficiently, more slaves came in. A rich meal of *nasi lemak*, rice cooked with coconut milk, and spicy curries of beef, chicken and vegetables was set before him. Oil lamps were lit and a rich warm glow flooded the verandah.

He ate slowly, relishing each bite as was his habit. Five or six slave girls fanned the air, while others waited on him in silence, discreet and alert to his wishes. It was said that among the chiefs of Perak, he owned the largest number of debt slaves and indentured labourers. So numerous that he himself had lost count. Thousands of peasants in Bandong Valley owed their livelihood to him and looked up to him as their lord and protector. When the rice harvests failed, he lent them goods and money. When they could not settle their debts, they offered him the services of their wives and daughters, who would then work as his slaves in his household.It was a practice sanctioned by law and tradition, and he had never questioned the rightness or wrongness of it. If fate had blessed him, he was obliged to provide for his peasants and collect what was owed to him. No more, no less.

"Good evening, my most honoured and respected Father. May Allah's greatness and mercy always watch over you."

"May He who sees all things watch over you too, my son."

Ibrahim had the makings of a fine warrior. Fifteen years old, the son of his first wife.

"Come, share the evening meal with me. We're expecting visitors."

"Who are they, most honoured Father?" Ibrahim asked as he moved across the room with the padded stealth of a tiger.

He was a tall noble-looking youth with the same proud eyes as his father. His high forehead and smooth sun-browned face belonged to his Celebes ancestors, but the dignity with

which he conducted himself was his mother's, the daughter of
a noble family of chief ministers.

"The chief of the Black Flag is coming to pay his respects
and taxes. After that, the son of the menteri of Larut and his
matchmaker. He wishes to marry your sister. Sit with me and
learn. Insya Allah, you will take my place one day."

"My most honoured Father, I thank you for your kindness
and trust."

"Is your mother well?"

"My mother asked me to let you know that she is well."

He fumed in silence at the arrogance of his first wife. No
greeting or words of respect for her lord. Just a message that
she was well. Arrogant, wilful and headstrong, Tengku Saleha
was the daughter of the chief minister of Pahang.

"Tell your mother that I wish her well," he growled.

"Greetings, my lord! May His Most Gracious and Merciful
bless you and your family! Your humble slave awaits your
lordship!"

His face lit up when he saw the Kedah trader. Musa Talib
was kneeling at the top of the steps, reeling off a string of
salaams and other words of respect.

"Musa, my dear friend, come over here. Please sit." He
indicated one of the cushions. "You're just in time to join us
for the evening meal."

"O my lord, you honour me. Please accept my thanks and
gratitude. May Allah in His most gracious and bountiful mercy
continue to bless your lordship and your lordship's son!"

"May His great compassion bless you too," both father and
son replied.

"But first let this slave make his report. The Tuan Hakka of
the Black Flag and his men are camped outside your lordship's
compound waiting to come into your presence. If it so pleases
your lordship, of course," Musa Talib added hastily. He knew
full well that all the Malay chiefs were very touchy about their
dependence upon the Chinese miners for their income, and a
go-between like him had to tread with great care if he valued
his life.

"Ah, Musa, my friend. This evening it so pleases me to let the Chinamen wait a while. A little anxiety is not such a bad thing for our friends in the Black Flag, don't you agree?"

He turned to Ibrahim.

"Remember this, my son. We can ask the Chinese miners to leave our land any time we please. Keep them waiting now and then. Otherwise they'll think that they're more powerful than us. Might they not, Musa?"

Caught off-guard, Musa could not hide the slight quaver in his voice.

"Your ... Your lordship certainly has a point there."

"Your Hakka friend is Tuan Yap Kim How, isn't it?"

"Yes, my lord ... no ... I mean no, my lord. Not friends. No, no." Musa Talib shook his head emphatically. "That Hakka is an associate. Business and trade only."

"Good, Musa, I'm pleased to hear that. You've done very well in your trading with your associate."

"His Gracious Merciful has blessed me, my lord."

"Come, my friend, let's eat. Then we'll talk to the infidels."

"Thank you, my lord, thank you. Your unworthy slave thanks his lordship. May Allah bless you. You're most kind to this unworthy slave."

Musa Talib bowed low as he waited for the slave girl to fill his plate with fragrant rice. He kept his eyes on Datuk Long Mahmud's face as he scooped up a ball of white rice with the stubby fingers of his right hand and put it into his mouth. He ate delicately and sparingly despite his great bulk. He was a big-boned man with chocolate brown skin. Everything about him was broad and generous, from his wide face to his flat nose and thick brown lips. His dark eyes were watchful as he ate, his jaws masticating upon a piece of beef, like a buffalo chewing cud. He had grown up together with the Datuk in those far-off days, before the Datuk's father had acquired land rights, tin mining rights, revenue collection rights and trading boats to sail up and down the coast of Perak. In those early days, Musa's father, the Indian-Muslim trader, gave credit and loans to the Datuk's father. Musa and Datuk Long Mahmud were carefree young bucks then, out to have a good time together. But things had changed ever since the Datuk became menteri. These days, it was not often that Musa was invited to dine with the Datuk. He wondered what lay ahead for him this evening.

Datuk Long Mahmud's face was a mask in the lamplight. It betrayed none of his thoughts about Musa, whom he referred to as the *Mamak*, when talking to his advisors.

But Mamak Musa would never betray that he was affronted by the derogatory name. Why should he be such a fool? Years of serving the Malay chiefs had taught him to be servile in words and wily in deeds. He was not ashamed of his own lineage. His Indian-Muslim ancestors had settled in Kedah more than three hundred years ago; Musa had even claimed with the pride of a rooster that his forebears had once exercised a strong influence over the affairs of state and trade in the royal court of the Malacca sultanate. But that, Datuk Long Mahmud mused, was typical of Musa's hyperbolic stories.

"Musa, my friend. You're pensive tonight. Your face is full of thoughts."

"Must be the heat. I've been walking too much, and this fat body of mine is tired."

"Give our honoured guest some lime juice."

A slave girl quickly poured out a tumbler of lime juice for Musa Talib who drank it gratefully.

"I've asked Ibrahim to meet you tonight. My son, Musa Talib is my friend. He and I have been through much together when we were young, reckless and fearless. Is it not, Musa?"

"Aye, those were the days, Datuk." Then lapsing into the more familiar tone of friendship, he went on, "The days when our kris and swords were swifter than the thunderbolts from heaven. We banded together to drink the blood of those English dogs who plundered our land."

They laughed at the memory of their exploits.

"'My beloved land and home!' you used to bawl at the top of your voice when you had one toddy too much, and I had to lug your fat body home." And then, in a more serious tone, the

Datuk went on, "So you see, Ibrahim, it's important to have a few good friends in life. One like Che' Musa here."

"You do me a great honour, Datuk, to consider me a friend still."

"Why, Musa, I've always thought of you as my friend. And because I consider you a friend of my family, I'm going to seek your advice on Ibrahim's education."

"Your lordship honours me. Your slave is not worthy of the honour. But as always, I'm at your lordship's service. But please keep in mind that I'm only a humble trader, and this is something new," Musa murmured, caution in his voice.

"No, no, not new. I've given the matter much thought. I intend to send Ibrahim to Penang. For a year or so. Insya Allah, he might learn something valuable from the white man."

"Learn from the English dogs in Pulau Pinang?"

Too late! He had dared to question the Datuk's judgement and violated the rules of *adat* or custom.

"Pardon, my lord! Pardon your slave!" Beads of anxious perspiration covered his forehead.

"How many times have I told you that it's called Penang now?" the Datuk chided him gently. "I'm told by Baba Wee that the English dogs even call it Prince of Wales Island after one of their princes."

"Aye, begging your pardon and forgiveness, my lord! Your slave craves your pardon! As Allah is my witness, I am a Kedah man, and I can never bring myself to call our island by the white man's name. Please forgive me, my lord!"

"Musa, as always you take things too much to heart." Datuk Long Mahmud shook his head. "Come, my friend, let's look ahead. That's the way to go. Now about Ibrahim's education. I'm thinking of sending him to the English school to learn the language of the white man."

He went on talking as if he was unaware of the shock and surprise on the faces of his audience. Ibrahim would have protested vehemently had he been less well-bred. His face was impassive. But Musa Talib was vulgar. He questioned the wisdom of sending away the heir to the seat of Bandong. The

Datuk's second and third wives and his other sons might misread his intentions and create trouble for him. Besides, what could the boy learn from the white men who had robbed the Malays of their land? Land that is Allah's gift to those born in this country? Sending the boy to Penang to be taught by Englishmen might make him half-white and half-brown.

"So you disagree with me, Musa."

"No, no, no, my honoured lord! Please forgive your unworthy slave who has chatted like a silly mynah bird. This unworthy slave has spoken far too much. I forgot myself. Please forgive me, please forgive me!"

Musa Talib beat his chest and bowed his head several times in abject fear. His distracted eyes wandered to the Datuk's hand. He might kill him with a single thrust of the kris hidden in the folds of his sarong.

The room was strangely quiet. No one spoke. The slave girls, sensing the gravity of their master's mood, kept very still. For a moment or two, Musa did not know whether he would be allowed to live.

"I will think about what you have said. Send for the *munshi*. We will listen to what the teacher has recorded in the annals on the founding of Bandong. Will you stay and listen too, Musa?"

"You do me a great honour, my lord."

Musa Talib kept the smile upon his face, but inside his heart, he was fuming. He had failed to see the trap in time. Like a half-submerged crocodile in the river, the Datuk had been waiting for him to stumble before grabbing him in his jaws. Stupid, stupid fool! he scolded himself. He knew that before the evening was over, he would have to pay dearly for having spoken so boldly out of turn, and it would cost him a goodly sum. A sum that would pay for Ibrahim's English education. But what good would an English education do for the future menteri of Bandong?

Chapter Four

*T*ai-kor Wong paced to and fro outside the miners' shed as he questioned Ah Fook, his chief waterman.

"What about the waterwheel?"

"My men will fix that. We've also strengthened the east wall."

Ah Fook had a good head for waterwheels and earth works. Luckily for him, years of tinkering with water, tin cans and bamboo pipes in Sum Hor had made him an expert on changing water courses and diverting water supplies to the mines.

Born with a good head on his shoulders, Ah Fook was unlike the thousands of ox heads and mule heads who came out here. A wave of pride tinged with regret swept through Tai-kor Wong. If not for fate, he too would be one of these indentured mules, his youth sold to the highest bidder. For the price of a ship's passage from China, a tin mine owner could buy several years' worth of a coolie's labour. Then the poor mule would be worked till his strength and life gave out. Unless of course he was blessed like Ah Fook and himself. He frowned and squinted in the glare of the noonday sun. Ah Fook's account of yesterday's troubles was disturbing.

"Act quickly Tai-kor, or else the hot bloods will scream for your head."

"We meet tomorrow morning. Bring that young pup to see me."

The young pup was out in the tin mine, at the foot of the craggy grey hills, stripped to the waist, his back blistered by the sun.

The opencast mine, a large shallow basin, was bare of trees, bush and grass. The earth was exposed to the unmitigated glare of the sun, which hung above in a blaze of blue. It beat down without mercy upon the backs of the miners. Like keringa ants, they scaled the slopes and clambered up the narrow steps cut into the sides of the earth walls, their baskets of gravel balanced precariously on the ends of bamboo poles slung across their shoulders.

Tuck Heng hauled his load of sand and stones. A straw hat on his head afforded some protection from the sun, but the rest of his body was being roasted slowly in the open fire. As the sun rose higher and higher, the heat became more unbearable. He mopped the sweat from his brow and wiped off the cloying dust on his body.

A pale orange dust spread by a warm dry breeze covered the men and huts, and settling, it formed a film over the coolies' water urns. Dust entered their nostrils and choked their lungs. It scratched at their throats and made them cough incessantly. The older coolies spat upon the parched earth and cursed. Tuck Heng went on shovelling. A coolie snarled at him, "Your belly's full, ah? Not starving like us?"

"He is new, potato head! Still full of the fat of our homeland," another coolie called out.

"I spit on our homeland! Hunger and death! That's what you find there!"

"The Thunder God strike you dead! How dare you talk like this about home?"

The two men glared at each other. Tempers were short. The miners' backs were whipped by the heat. The men around the pit stopped digging. Tuck Heng felt their stares upon his back.

"Mule head! Showing Big Rat that you can work harder than the rest of us?" Potato Head advanced menacingly. His hand shot out. Tuck Heng staggered backwards. The other men in the pit crowded round.

"What's going on?" Big Rat, the head of the work gang, called out. "Are you fed three bowls of rice a day so you can hit a pup?"

"Our bellies are growling!"

"We can't eat a newcomer! Take him!"

One of the miners shoved him towards Big Rat.

"Eat him! Suck him! See if I care!"

Big Rat stalked off in a huff.

The coolies guffawed and slapped their neighbours' backs. The tension eased and the men were grinning at him.

"Give the whelp a good suck," a miner hollered from the top of the pit. "He's starved for a tit!"

Tuck Heng grinned, relieved. He didn't mind being the butt of the older men's jokes. It showed that they had accepted him at last after ignoring him for days. He tramped down the path to the eating sheds with the rest of them. They traded dirty jokes and told stories with the punch typical of the Cantonese of Sum Hor. He felt at home among them. They were the clansmen of his homeland. The homeland he tried not to miss. If he closed his eyes, shut out the jungle and just listened to the men's talk, he could imagine himself back in Sum Hor and ease the lump lodged in his chest.

He held out his tin basin. The cook doled out generous helpings of sweet potato porridge into it. Like every miner, he had been given a tin basin, a pair of bamboo chopsticks and a tin mug when he joined the work gang. The tin basin was his eating bowl and his wash basin. If he lost it, he would have to buy another one, and the cost would be deducted from his miserable pay.

He had joined the work gang on his second day in Bandong. "Watch and learn," Ah Fook had said before he left.

And learn he did. The work was backbreaking. He was not used to the long hours in the sun. He longed for water and a bit of shade, but he dared not stop digging for too long. The leaders of each work gang had the power to whip laggards and idlers. Their job was to see that the men filled their quota for the day. As a new miner, he had to dig and carry the baskets of gravel to the *palongs*, the troughs where the gravel was washed for tin ore. A *changkol* for digging, two rattan baskets and a bamboo pole were his tools. For the rest, he had to use brute strength.

Brute strength was the engine in the mine. It sank shafts into the earth and burrowed tunnels under the hills. Brute strength climbed rickety scaffolding up the cliff faces, hundreds of feet above the ground. It toiled from sunrise to sunset, struck at the granite and hammered at the unyielding earth until, bit by bit, the earth yielded its lode of tin. Sometimes in a fit of spiteful vengeance, an avalanche of rocks buried the miners. It was a daily struggle, pitting strength against strength, men against rocks. But neither showed mercy. And none was expected.

"Get to work, rice worm!" Big Rat shouted at him.

Startled, he resumed digging. Water. He longed for water. The monotonous chug-chug-chug of the water pumps constantly reminded him of his thirst. A sip. A drop. Just one cool drop of clear liquid. The clang of hard steel against rocks rang through the valley. It had been hours since the midday meal, and his water gourd was empty. But he dared not stop work to fill it. The older miners had told him earlier that a blazing afternoon sun was a sure sign of a thunderstorm below the horizon. He looked up. There was no sign of rain.

Bastards! They must have tricked him again. Then he became deeply ashamed. His thoughts and conduct these days were not befitting a doctor's son. But he was not going to be a coolie forever. His ancestors expected him to make good in this life.

"You lazy son of a pig! Do you want a whipping?" Big Rat yelled at him again.

"Dig. Don't dream," the wiry miner beside him hissed.

Tuck Heng quickly picked up his hoe and struck the rock face again and again.

"Don't think I can't touch you just because Uncle Chan Ah Fook brought you here." Big Rat growled, flexing his thin bamboo pole menacingly. "You're in my charge, and I can hit you good and proper, do you hear?"

He nodded. He had seen him hit the miners. But he knew too that Big Rat was bullying him to impress the others.

"Don't let me catch you idling again! Even a doctor's son must work for his bowl of rice, do you hear?"

"I heard you, Tai-kor," he lowered his voice.

Taken aback, Big Rat seemed mollified. Even a little embarrassed. No one had ever addressed him as Big Brother. He sauntered off, not sure whether he had been mocked or respected. The other miners grinned and winked. Tuck Heng knew he'd made some friends that day.

Chapter Five

"Your Honour, please accept my respects."

Tuck Heng got down on his knees and kowtowed to the Master of the White Cranes again and again.

"Enough! Call me Tai-kor Wong. Wait till the Malay king appoints me *Kapitan China* of Bandong. Then you and everybody can address me as Your Honour!"

"*Aiyah!* The boy doesn't know what you're talking about!"

Wong-soh's smile was wreathed in wrinkles. She was obviously very glad to see him again.

Tuck Heng's sun-browned face had turned a dull red. He wanted to make a good impression on the man who had paid for his passage out here. But now he wondered if there was something amiss. "Ka-pee-tan Chee-na." What did it mean?

"Ah Fook, you'd better teach him the laws and customs here. Tell him what's a Kapitan China."

"Listen and learn, young dog," Ah Fook began in the half-mocking, half-serious tone which he had used throughout their journey upriver. "The Malay kings don't know how to rule us sons of China. So they appoint kapitans. It's the highest position for us Chinese."

"And a kapitan passes an examination?"

"No! Even an illiterate like me can be a kapitan. That's what's so great about living in this new land. A man can be poor and unschooled. But he can rise and become rich."

"No learning is required?"

"None."

He turned to Tai-kor Wong. The Lodge Master nodded. So Ah Fook was not pulling his leg. But what kind of land was this? Learning was at the heart of the world he had left. Even a poor village doctor had to have knowledge of the Classics. How could a man progress without examinations?

"Work hard. Use your head. When you have money, people will listen to you. And if the clans listen to you, the Malay kings will respect you."

"Grow rich first! Then even the foreign devils in Penang will respect you," Tai-kor Wong growled.

"Marry a *towkay*'s daughter. Become the son-in-law of a rich merchant. Fastest way to be rich."

Wong-soh's voice was unusually bitter. But before anyone could say another word, she had disappeared into the kitchen. Tai-kor Wong turned to him.

"We've all tasted more salt than you've eaten rice, young man. Listen to Ah Fook. He's Chief Waterman, Incense Master and Captain of the Guards. Have you paid him your respects, Tuck Heng?"

"Forgive my ignorance, Uncle Ah Fook!"

He kowtowed again and again. It had never crossed his mind that he had been under the personal protection of the captain of the White Crane guards!

"Your kowtow's a bit late," Ah Fook chaffed him. "Humility in a young man is a good thing. But I must say you've got a poor eye. Didn't even know a dragon when you met one."

"I was blind."

Then he saw the pot of tea on the table. Seizing one of the bowls, he poured out a bowl of steaming hot tea and offered it to Ah Fook.

"Forgive my poor eye. Please accept this bowl of tea and my apologies, Uncle."

"Enough, enough!" Ah Fook laughed. But he accepted the tea.

"I can do with a bowl of tea too!"

"Loh Pang! Come in!"

"My head's about to explode! Couldn't sleep these past few nights. Each time I close my eyes, I see those hyenas, and I hear their vile sneers! We've got no face left, Tai-kor!"

"Butcher, that's why we're here. To plan our revenge," Ah Fook answered. "Calm down so the good doctor's son can pay his respects to you. Greet Uncle Loh Pang."

"My respects to you, Uncle Loh Pang."

"I've great respect for your father. His Big Character Poem on the village wall. That's courage, my boy! I can't read. But people say it tells those Manchu bastards that we Chinese are not dead!"

Tuck Heng poured out more tea and served his elders a bowl each with both hands. His father's poem had cost the lives of his entire family. His father's moment of glory was his family's hour of death. Everyone spoke of his father. But who recalled his mother, his brothers and his sisters? He tried not to be bitter.

As the men talked, his eyes wandered round the hut. It was a plain one-storey structure of wood with an *attap* roof or thatching of palm leaves. Behind the wooden partition of the front room were the kitchen and the bedroom. Judging from the clanging of pots and ladles, Wong-soh was preparing food.

"You in there! Quiet!" Tai-kor Wong shouted.

The clanging stopped.

"The men want revenge. Drowning the adulteress is not enough," Loh Pang reported.

"Not enough!" A big man with a loud voice came in.

Tuck Heng recognised him at once as Water Buffalo. He had been given the nickname after winning a tug-of-war with a half-starved water buffalo in a padi field. As the story went, the Malay farmer had been so incensed at the humiliation suffered by his prized beast that he chased Water Buffalo with an axe and threatened to sever his thick head with a single blow. Only Ah Fook's intervention in halting Malay had prevented the tragedy.

"Tai-kor, I don't have to tell you what the young hotheads are saying every day to Lee Peng Yam."

"Piss on you, Water Buffalo!"

An intense wiry man came into the hut. A homemade cigarette dangling from the corner of his mouth gave the impression that he wore a perpetual sneer.

"Tai-kor, good morning. This is the third morning, and the men are still waiting."

"Right, Brother Yam! I didn't sleep a wink these past few nights."

"*Chieh*, Loh Pang, I slept. I know our Tai-kor will come up with a plan to fight those bastards. A plan with the cunning of crocodiles."

"I'll leave crocodiles to you. We all know how you killed one of them. Single-handed."

"Wah!"

"Young dog, blind again?" Ah Fook grinned. "This dragon is commander of the White Crane guards. Greet Uncle Lee Peng Yam."

"Uncle Lee, please accept my respects."

"Revenge! We want revenge!"

Big Dog and Big Tree stomped into the hut. Tuck Heng remembered them as the guards who had trussed the adulteress into the pig basket. They were burly tin smelters who had come to Bandong after their parents were killed in a clash between the Cantonese and the Hakkas. It was said that they hated the Hakkas with such vehemence that they fought like raging bulls in clashes with the enemy.

"Tai-kor, double vengeance. That's what we want," Big Tree declared.

"Do to their women what they've done to one of ours," Big Dog urged. "Mothers! Wives! Sisters! Daughters! Let me get my hands on the bitches!" He cackled and wiggled his hips so there was no mistaking his vengeful eagerness to show off his sexual prowess.

"Good, ah!" Lee Peng Yam applauded.

"Back in the Year of the Rooster, those bastards did exactly that to the wives of our brothers in Larut. Rode the women like horses. After that, the good ones drowned themselves in the mining pool. Thirty of them. Bloated like drowned pigs. I don't ever want to see that again."

"We do what we have to do, Loh Pang. You want us to be the laughing stock in this land?" In the silence that followed, Lee Peng Yam's eyes mocked his listeners as he puffed on his cigarette.

"Tai-kor, strike while our bellies are on fire!" Big Tree stood up, one foot upon his stool. He was growing restless. "We must fight!"

"Old Bull is not here yet. Wait for him," Tai-kor Wong said.

Just then Old Bull, the oldest and most respected White Crane elder, burst into the hut, flushed and irritable.

"Damn those farters and potato heads! Every son of a mother was hogging a hut this morning! And what a bellyache I got, waiting for one of them to come out! 'Swine! Come out if you've got no dung!' I shouted myself hoarse, but not one of those pigs came out!"

The men roared, for no matter how many pits were dug, there were always not enough toilets in the settlement.

"Have some tea to settle your bellyache," Tai-kor Wong soothed his old friend. "Tuck Heng, pay your respects to Uncle Old Bull. He knew your father very well."

"When your father was still wet behind the ears, lad! You should call me Granduncle."

The old man took his face between his rough miner's hands and looked into his eyes. "Make your parents proud so that their death is not in vain. Your mother was a good woman and your father a brave man."

The room swam. Mute with pain, he could only nod.

"The good doctor saved my mother's life once." Wong-soh, who had come into the room with a kettle of water, had tears in her eyes too.

"No more tears. The lad is here now. To work. Not to cry like a woman." Tai-kor Wong waved her away.

"Young dog, go into the kitchen and help Wong-soh with breakfast."

Now that Old Bull was there, the men were impatient to

begin their discussion. Their young dog went round the table, pouring out mugs of scalding hot tea from a tin kettle. Then he helped Wong-soh to bring out a large basin of steaming rice porridge with bits of sweet potato swimming in it. Plates of salted eggs and vegetables were placed on the table. And there was a pork stew, a luxury for the miners. Only Tai-kor Wong could afford to eat pork on ordinary days. Several pairs of chopsticks plunged into the stew. The men ate ravenously, but none of them thanked Wong-soh. Nor did they show any appreciation. Wong-soh handed him a large bowl of porridge. To his surprise, there were several pieces of pork in it.

"Thank …"

"Shh!" She placed a finger on her lips.

He ate his porridge, squatting in the doorway between the front room and the kitchen so that he would not miss out on the men's talk.

Wong-soh could not take her eyes off him. He was the son she had dreamed of for years.

"Tai-kor Wong, this is not the first time we've had trouble, and it won't be the last," Loh Pang was saying as he helped himself to a piece of pork fat. "Everything happens in cycles of three or five. That blasted dam two years ago was the first time. The adultery this year is the second. Sure to be a third."

The others went on eating.

"It's the truth!"

"Ha!" Old Bull scoffed. "Year in, year out, you say the same words!"

"I've said this many times at council meetings, and I say it again. A man's deeds can change his fate and the course of his life."

"For generations, we fought the Hakka dogs. Back home in Sum Hor, we fought them. Here in a new land, we still got to fight them! Old Bull, this is the fate of the White Cranes!"

"Butcher, we've had trouble ever since we hacked our way through this jungle! Didn't the Datuk send over his medicine man to chase away the evil spirits in you once?" Big Tree teased him.

"I had belly worms. Then swamp fever hit us."

Chan Ah Fook shook his head and flicked off a pesky housefly with his chopsticks. "Our White Crane brothers dropped like flies singed by the candle. Those were terrible days. Before your time, Peng Yam."

"And what have you got in return?" Lee Peng Yam threw his cigarette butt onto the floor and rubbed it into the bare earth with his foot.

"The Datuk is a smart one. He collects taxes and grows fat," Big Dog muttered.

"And Tai-kor, your friend, that Mamak Indian, Musa Talib," Lee Peng Yam's mouth curled in a smile as he rolled himself another cigarette, "I heard he's getting those Hakka swine upstream to pay higher rents to the Datuk. And that means more mines for them and fewer for us!"

"I spit on the Hakka dogs!" Old Bull banged a hard fist upon the table.

The rough-hewn table wobbled at the impact, and the others had to hold on to it to keep it on its legs.

"Old Bull, not so hard. I don't have time these days to make another table for the old lady."

"Wong-soh, I didn't mean to destroy your table! I'll build you a better one when we lick those bastards. Those Hakka dogs bring nothing but misfortune. The year they dammed our river was the year of the worst drought in Sum Hor."

"Then we had the locusts. Ate up all the crops left in the field after the drought …"

"Loh Pang, we've heard about the old days in Sum Hor a thousand times!" Lee Peng Yam cut him short. "If we go on like this, we will never see Sum Hor again!"

"Curse your mouth! Don't expect Loh Pang and me to stop talking about Sum Hor! Born in Sum Hor. Raised in Sum Hor. I'm going back to die in Sum Hor!" Old Bull put down his chopsticks and glared at the wiry man who was half his age. "When I was fighting Hakka dogs back in Sum Hor, you weren't even born yet!"

Lee Peng Yam lit another of his homemade cigarettes

and went on addressing the rest of the council. "We're not in Sum Hor now. We're in a new dunghole called Bandong. With newbattles to fight. A new history to make. If you want to talk about fighting, talk about Bandong Valley five years ago. Thosebastards destroyed our water courses and killed twenty-five of our brothers! Have you forgotten them? And when we wereslow in fighting back, who came in the night to burn our houses?"

The men were silenced, even Old Bull. He picked up his chopsticks and his bowl and started to eat ferociously. The younger men in the council began to talk about battle plans.

"Fart to you all!" Ah Fook burst out. "Can't you let Old Bull have his say? Have you forgotten the old country?"

"We've lost face. So we've got to do something about it. Talking about Sum Hor won't help," Peng Yam insisted.

"I say we attack the bastards' village tonight! Kill those sons of whores!"

"Big Dog, eat up first. Then we plan," Tai-kor Wong stopped him. It was clear to Tai-kor Wong that the younger men looked to Lee Peng Yam for leadership.

"Tai-kor, I'd rather die fighting than have the dogs push us ..."

"You think I'm slinking away? My tail between my legs?"

Lee Peng Yam laughed and waved his hands in protest.

"Tai-kor, please accept my most sincere apologies! I didn't mean to offend you. But we must strike while the furnace is hot."

"Right! What are we waiting for?" Water Buffalo jumped up from his seat.

"Sit down!"

Tai-kor Wong pulled out a dagger and plunged it into the table. The blade stood upright, proudly displaying its ivory handle carved in the shape of a crane. The men stopped arguing. They lay down their chopsticks and waited for him to speak. But he remained silent, his eyes on the younger members of the council.

One by one, Big Tree, Big Dog and Water Buffalo looked

away. Only Lee Peng Yam was bold enough to keep his eyes on his chief. The two men were like animals with their eyes locked in battle. The room became unnaturally quiet. Tuck Heng dared not move. Wong-soh came and crouched next to him. Finally Lee Peng Yam backed down and looked away. Only then did Tai-kor Wong speak, his voice low and smooth.

"I do not doubt your loyalty to the White Cranes. But remember that I am Tai-kor. I'm responsible for the security of this village."

After a short pause, he went on, "Peng Yam, tell us your plans. How are you going to attack the Hakka village? Do you know how the enemy is armed? Are you sure that they are not lying in wait for us?"

When no answer was forthcoming, he went on, unhurried and ruminative, as though he was thinking deeply about the whole issue of an instant attack.

"If I were the Tai-kor of the Black Flags, I'd send out spies. And I'd spread rumours. Then I'd fortify and prepare my men for a big battle with the White Cranes. To fight a good battle, the general must plan well. Now Peng Yam, tell us your battle plans."

Tai-kor Wong picked up his chopsticks and reached for a piece of pickled cucumber. He chewed upon it thoughtfully with no sign of impatience or anger. Seeing this, the others began to eat again.

Lee Peng Yam's face was a scowl.

"Just think. If we fight the Black Flags, will the Datuk stand by and do nothing? War means no mining. No mining means no taxes. If we attack first, he will slap a heavy fine of several thousand silver dollars on us. And he might kick us out of here. I'm not saying that he will. But if the Black Flags are looking for an excuse to urge him to kick us out, then we'll have given them one."

"Why didn't I see that?" Loh Pang exclaimed.

"We didn't think that far," Big Tree muttered.

Lee Peng Yam was scowling again.

"Think again," Old Bull joined in gleefully. "If we fight,

we'll be paying for the trouble started by those dogs in the first place."

"Fight we lose, don't fight we lose!" Lee Peng Yam raised his lone dissenting voice again. "Fight we pay, don't fight we lose face! Is our Tai-kor saying that we do nothing?"

"What're we going to do, Tai-kor?"

"This way, we die! That way, we also die!"

Several voices spoke at once, and Tai-kor Wong called for order again.

"Tai-kor!" Lee Peng Yam leapt to his feet. "Measure for measure! Do to all their women what they did to one of ours!"

"We've never done such an evil thing before!" Ah Fook protested.

"This is war, Tai-kor! Hit back twice as hard, or else those dogs win!"

But Tai-kor Wong was not convinced. The older men looked troubled.

Tuck Heng glanced from one group to the other. Wong-soh gripped his arm as the two of them held their breath and listened to the debate round the table.

"Look, Tai-kor. The traders in Penang expect us to make a profit," Lee Peng Yam persisted. "If we lose out to those dogs, where're we going to hide our faces?"

"Peng Yam is right, Tai-kor!"

Now it was Ah Fook's turn to stand up. Lee Peng Yam's nostrils were quivering as he lit another cigarette. His foxy face showed that he could smell victory. The White Cranes had to strike back twice as hard if they did not want to be ousted by the Black Flags, Ah Fook said. But the Black Flags were not the only source of trouble for the White Cranes. Those red-haired English barbarians were eyeing the rich tin deposits in Bandong too. English merchants and adventurers were buying up large areas of land from the Malay chiefs. It wouldn't be long before they reached Bandong Valley. The White Cranes must protect their mines and their rights.

"Tai-kor, it's not going to get easier, this mining business. We should be clever like the followers of General Meng

Yuanjun. Didn't he say, 'While the cock crows, the fox steals'?"
Lee Peng Yam asked. "Give me thirty young bulls, Tai-kor,
and I will do the rest!"

"Lee Peng Yam, I respect you as a warrior. But as long as
I'm Tai-kor here, I give the orders. I will pay the Datuk a visit.
Ah Fook, Old Bull and Loh Pang will come with me. You wait
till I return."

Chapter Six

Outwardly he looked like one of them. He behaved like them, crouching on his haunches on the bench to eat his meals, shoving food into his mouth with his chopsticks, his hand reaching out for another piece of meat even before he had swallowed what was in his mouth. But he was not one of them, he told himself. He was a poet's son. A doctor's son. Yet the more he got to know them, the more he felt an affinity with them.

Ignorance and fear in a new land had made them even more communal. Each coolie suppressed what made him different from others. The nail that stood out must be hammered down; otherwise it would scratch others. "Be like them," Ah Fook had advised him, "don't show off your learning." But he was a descendant of scholars. He had learning and yearnings different from theirs. He had to leave this dunghole! But in the meantime, he would have to fit into the White Crane community as best as he could.

Already his boyhood days were fading fast in his memory, glowing like a distant star. He felt at home and yet not at home in the new land. He inhabited a borderland with the same gods of his ancestors, followed the same communal laws of his clan and lived in huts like those back home in Sum Hor. And yet, this was Bandong Valley, the land of brown-skinned people.

All around were the mountain ranges and brooding hills, the silent jungles of green shadows hiding strange beasts and spirits which pressed upon the borders of his consciousness, a constant reminder that he was no longer in Sum Hor even though the miners talked and lived as though they were still in China. Except Lee Peng Yam and the younger ones. They were willing to confront this new land head-on. But the older coolies kept harking back to their home village. No wonder Lee Peng Yam had exploded at the elders' meeting. Young though he was, and new to the land, Tuck Heng found himself agreeing with the obnoxious man that they were indeed in a new dunghole with names like Bandong and Perak. Names which sounded strange to his ears. Names which meant nothing to him. Not like Sum Hor—a name that stirred his heart and made him think of mother, father and home. A name that brought tears to his eyes and a dull ache in his chest. He longed for the familiar landscape of flat plains and placid streams. He yearned for the songs of the village girls washing their clothes at the well. O Sum Hor, Sum Hor.

"Young dog, dreaming again?" Big Rat called out to him. "Lee Peng Yam is calling a meeting. If you want to live, you'd better come along!"

The shed was packed when he got there with Big Rat. The young men thumped each other's backs. The excitement of an impending hunt gripped them. They smelt blood, and like hounds, they were raring to go. Faces were flushed as mugs of *samsu* were passed round, the cheap Chinese rice wine going to their heads. Some broke into a raucous song about Hakka maids and Hakka men.

"Where's the village?" he asked.

"Upstream, close to the hills," Big Rat replied.

"Where the land is more fertile. They grow more vegetables than us," a coolie told him.

"It's the Hakka sows! They can make anything grow. Even in the poorest soil," another miner joined in. "My old Ma used to say those Hakka sows were good for rearing pigs and growing vegetables. Strong as oxen. They can work in the field right up to the day they give birth."

"That's why, brother, you can pound them, squeeze them, ride them! As hard as you like!"

"We like our women soft," Big Rat snorted.

"Chieh! If you're offered one of those Hakka Ah Soh, don't tell me you're going to say no, not delicate enough for me!"

Big Rat scowled at his tormentor. His mates roared.

"Who can afford to be choosy? Who among us can afford Sum Koo's girls every day?"

"Who's Sum Koo?"

"You don't know Sum Koo?" a young coolie hooted.

"He doesn't know Sum Koo! This one is green!"

"Big Rat, are you his godfather?"

"Are you guarding his manhood?"

"Money is guarding young Tuck's manhood!"

"Opium's a cheaper mistress!"

"That's so, Big Rat?"

"You're such an earnest fool! Who except me, your big brother, will tell you about such things and make a man of you?" Then in a more serious tone, Big Rat added, "There are three thousand of us in this dunghole. Only twenty or so have wives and families. The rest of us make do with the occasional runaway Malay slave and Sum Koo's girls."

"Silence!"

Lee Peng Yam's voice rose as he listed all the wrongs the White Cranes had suffered at the hands of the Black Flags.

"Remember, my brothers! 1867! The year of the terrible riots in Penang! 1869! The year the dogs dammed our water course! 1872! When the wives of the White Crane heroes in the Batang mines drowned themselves! Because the Hakka dogs had defiled them! And what about those in Larut? Do you need any more reminders?"

"No!"

The men broke into angry yells.

"Our idiot boy wears the green hat of a cuckold! His shame is our shame!"

"We'll show the Black Flags what the White Cranes can do!"

Where Tai-kor Wong had counselled caution and patience, Lee Peng Yam was urging them to action. Heroes with courage in their hearts must uphold the honour of the White Cranes! They could not wait any longer. The longer they waited, the more cowardly they would appear to the world. He had a plan which required the services of thirty young dogs hungering for a bitch.

"We're here! Here!"

Pandemonium broke loose. It was several minutes before order was restored. Lee Peng Yam was grinning when he announced that he had to keep the number small because he had other plans for the heroes, which he was not at liberty to discuss with them just yet.

"But if you heroes want a fight to restore your good name, then fight we will!" He raised his clenched fist.

"Brothers in blood!"

The men cheered. They chanted and sang the White Crane song.

Then Big Tree reeled off the names of those chosen for the mission.

"Tuck Heng!"

Even Big Rat gave a start. Tuck Heng was sure that Big Tree had made a mistake. He was a newcomer, a nobody and only fifteen years old. There were many older than he who would give anything to be chosen.

"No mistake! I've chosen you because I don't want any soft-handed lily-livered son of a mother in the White Cranes. If you can't subdue a woman, what good are you?" Lee Peng Yam laughed his mirthless laugh, his unlit cigarette dangling from the corner of his mouth.

Tuck Heng hid his contempt. The others slapped him heartily on the back.

"Lucky dog!"

Chapter Seven

"Ah Mei! How's your old man?"

"Still the same. No better."

"Ah Loy-soh, where's she?"

"Don't know."

"She has gone out to her vegetable patch. To bring back a pumpkin for you to boil with the herbs."

"Where's Big Mole this morning?"

"Gone to the vegetable patch with Ah Loy-soh. Said her yams are ready for harvesting."

"Harvesting? Listen, my toes are laughing. Her yams are the size of my fingers."

The air was filled with the laughter of the Hakka women making their way to the river.

The heroes of the White Crane slithered like shadows in the undergrowth of the jungle. Only their dark eyes peered above the cloth that covered their faces. They were dressed like Malay peasants, in loose black tunics and long black cotton pants, with sarongs slung across their shoulders. Some had strips of cloth tied round their heads, while others wore kerchiefs to hide their long queues. Crouched in the thicket of bush and lallang, they were animal-like, alert and malevolent, waiting to pounce upon their prey. They had come upstream under the cover of darkness and had left their boats some distance away to avoid detection. Then they had made their way inland before doubling back in the early hours of the morning when the Hakka men had left for the mines.

All through the night, Tuck Heng had kept close on the heels of these White Cranes who seemed to know their way in the mysterious darkness of the jungle. He alone could not see beyond the dark. It was as if a thick blanket of shadows had engulfed him. He felt lost and afraid. Shapes were indistinguishable. He could not make out whether a shadow before him was a rock or a man. And so he had stumbled, guided only by the hisses and whispers of those in front of him. His ears picked up their sibilant noises, and his feet trod gingerly over unfamiliar ground. It was a relief when he finally found himself crouched among the rest of them, behind some bushes not far from the riverbank. His head, covered by a kerchief, was damp with dew and sweat. He felt extremely uncomfortable in his Malay attire. The sarong, slung across his shoulders, was a strange garment to him. A piece of cloth with the two ends joined together. He wondered how a man could wear that and be comfortable enough to move about.

As a vague greyness descended upon the river, he saw that Lee Peng Yam was crouched not far from him. The man had ordered them not to speak, not to kill, but they could do what they wanted with the Hakka women.

The sun was rising behind the trees, its light touching the tips of the coconut palms. The air was cool and still. All round him, the predators were taut with waiting. He could hear his own heart pounding as the sounds of the women's chatter and laughter drifted towards them. He felt the sudden rush of blood into his head when they came within sight. The masked warriors around him tensed, their bodies taut upon the approach of their prey. Fifteen, sixteen, seventeen. All of a sudden, Peng Yam's whistle pierced the air.

His heroes rushed out of the bushes in one body and pounced upon their helpless prey. Rough hands dragged them into the bushes, gripped the women's throats and stifled their screams. A rush of feathers took to the air. Jungle fowl screeched as the sun and earth spun in turmoil. The world was boiling over in wicked passion. Bushes shook and swayed.

Lallang was slashed, their sharp green blades flaying the bodies of their victims. Their clothes were ripped off. One victim let out a shriek, but she was swiftly silenced. Then as the woman slumped to the ground, the hero dropped his pants and took her as she lay there. Tuck Heng turned away. All round him, grass and bush shook and trembled as the White Crane heroes executed their orders, two or three men taking their turn with one woman.

He grabbed a handful of mud and leaves and stuffed them into the mouth gaping beneath him. His own eyes, frantic with fear, looked to the trees, the sky, and then directly at the sun which mercifully blinded him with its light. He fought his impulse to run. Clenching his teeth, he held down the writhing, thrashing body under him. His eyes shut tight, but he couldn't shut out the grunts of hogs on heat. He couldn't do it! Ma! His heart wailed for his mother. Like a lost and bewildered waif, he stumbled through the lallang, heading for the safety of the shadows. Still the grunts pursued him. He dived and buried his head under a mound of leaves, panting, his body shaking like an addict deprived of his opium.

⋆═◉◉═⋆

He woke up to a throbbing headache the next morning. A feeling of utter desolation swept through him. He wished he were dead. He could not bear to think of what he had become. Not man enough to do it. Not man enough to deny it. And to prove that he was a man, he had turned to drink. Bowl after bowl of the samsu he quaffed like the rest of the miners. Never had he drunk such heady stuff before. Egged on by the men, who were drunk with the hollow victory of their despicable mission, he had consumed far more of the rice wine than was good for his belly. Not because he had liked it, but because he was a coward. With each roar of "*yam seng!*" he had downed a bowl of rice wine to still the fear that someone might unmask him. He had failed Lee Peng Yam's test.

He groaned and felt himself at sea again, floundering and rolling with the motion of the waves. His head ached. He lay still, not daring to move in case he threw up. Keeping his eyes closed, he stretched out his leg. The cool hardness of his father's metal box steadied him and gave him comfort. It was still beneath his blanket where he had left it. If someone had asked him for it last night, he would have gladly handed it over if that could have saved him from shame.

He could remember little else of the night before. The wine must have knocked him out cold. How he got into bed and who helped him, he had not the slightest idea. To be dead to the world in drunken stupor was not something he liked. Two years of evading the Manchu dogs should have taught him that that was the way to death. With a feeling close to despair, he realised that this was yet another failure since his arrival in the new land.

His future appeared bleak. He, a poet's son, had descended to the level of vermin. He lived with vermin, ate with vermin and slept with vermin—a hundred of them cramped into a cowshed built to house only forty. Powerful vermin had bunks along the walls of the sheds, where cracks in the wooden partitions let in fresh air. Powerless vermin slept in the middle of the windowless shed, the warmest part of the room with the greatest number of bunks pushed close to one another. On every side, vermin bodies pressed against him. He could not stretch out his limb without touching another's. Most of the time, he slept huddled on his side, legs drawn together against his chest. Like an opium smoker, he thought.

He had to rise above this vermin level of existence. O gods of my father and mother, help me, he prayed. He lay still and thought for a long while. Before he could leave them, he had to live like them, be one of them. And in this strange new world, if he was not with the White Cranes, where could he be? How might it profit him to leave these vermin? He was vermin like them. He groaned.

Feelings rather than thoughts assailed his sickened heart. He was lonely and anxious. His need to be accepted by his fellow clansmen was far stronger than anything he had learned at his mother's knee. "Be honest. Be upright. Be filial," his mother had taught him. "An uncut jade will not a jewel make; an unethical act will not a righteous man create," his father had drilled into him. But where are his father and mother now?

Tears rolled down his cheeks. He lay with his eyes closed, waiting for his head to stop throbbing. When he opened them, there was a blankness in his gaze. A grey light was creeping into the shed. All round him, men slept, curled like prawns pressed together. He dared not move lest he should wake his neighbours. Below his bunk, others were stirring. He shivered a little in the chill air of a wet grey dawn. The coolie next to him stirred, yawned and scratched his armpits. Soon lusty yawns, loud as the bellows of an elephant, filled the shed as coolies in the top and bottom bunks woke up.

He got up too and coiled his queue round his head. Then he slid to the edge of his bunk.

"Pig head! Watch where you put your stinking feet!"

He peered down. It was the wiry man in his work gang. He had taken over the bunk below him, vacated by a miner who had died from opium poisoning the day before.

"So sorry, Uncle. Good morning, Uncle."

"He thinks he can get away with things just because he addresses me as Uncle. Bah! That's what all newcomers do. Scrape and kiss your butt. Then before you know it, he's standing on your head," the wiry man ranted to the empty air.

Tuck Heng tied a towel round his head to stop the throbbing at his temples.

"Very sorry, Uncle. If I have offended you, I didn't mean it. I've never drunk samsu before."

"Don't ever touch that evil drink again! Your uncle here had to lug your dead body back and put you to bed!"

"So you're the kind soul! Thank you, Uncle!"

He jumped down from his bunk and bowed.

"Are you trying to kill me with good manners? Call me Old Stick. Ready for the fire! Of no use to anyone!"

"Shut up, loud mouth!" a miner on the top bunk yelled.

"Ugh!" Old Stick coughed and wheezed like a tubercular patient and spat out a thick gob, which he promptly stamped on and rubbed into the floor of bare earth. All the coolies believed that phlegm accumulated in the lungs during the night would endanger their health and block their vital breath. They coughed and cleared their lungs lustily each morning with a vehemence close to religious fanaticism, in the mistaken notion that such a daily performance would lessen their aches and pains.

"Uncle Old Stick, you need a ginger drink to heat up your lungs."

"You're the son of Sum Hor's doctor. Pasted his poem on the village wall, didn't he? That cost him his head. The Manchus were crazy. What's a few words? So you know what's heaty and what's cooling, eh?"

Old Stick's mood seemed to have changed for the better after his coughing fit. He followed Tuck Heng out of the shed, and they went down a muddy path to the outhouses and wash area.

"Not much, Uncle. But enough to stop my headache."

"So the Hakka hens gave you a headache! How many of them did you take?"

Tuck Heng felt the hot rush of blood into his face and made no reply.

"Must be your first time!" Old Stick cackled. "A young cock!"

Several coolies, washing their faces at the water jars, guffawed and hooted.

"We had our fill, scholar boy! Did you?"

Tuck Heng made no reply.

"Quawk! Quawk! Quawk! What a shy young cock!" a miner with a foxlike face and sly eyes remarked in a loud voice to his companions.

"Quawk! Quawk! Quawk! Shy young cock!" they echoed.

Encouraged, the fox-faced miner continued to taunt Tuck Heng about his sexual ignorance, lack of prowess and even the size of his manhood. Words and phrases he had never heard before made his ears burn with shame. The ribaldry of the men unnerved him. The eyes of the young coolies mocked him.

Through their eyes, he saw that he was a foppish, priggish rich man's son who had come down in the world. He was crawling like the rest of the vermin, except that he was stupidly denying it, even to himself. Their derision rang in his ears. Hot tears rushed into his eyes and brought on more hoots and howls. But they were nothing compared to the whoops of that sharp-faced fox.

The fox was doing a song and dance around him, and before he knew it, his fist had shot out and the fox was yelping in pain, hand cupped over a bleeding nose. Then a hard kick in his belly sent him flying across the yard. He hit his head against a water jar. But he picked himself up immediately and fell upon his attacker. The two of them wrestled to the ground. The fox's friends joined in the scuffle, and several blows rained on him before he broke free and let out a kick which left one of his attackers sprawled on the muddy ground.

"Good, ah! Good, ah!" the other miners shouted.

By now the wash area was full of coolies waiting to use the latrines. The fight was a great entertainment for them. Several others joined in the fray. Old Stick tried to stop the fight, and when he could not, he hauled up a bucket of water from the well and flung its icy contents on the fighting dogs.

"Do you want to die? These are Lee Peng Yam's men."

"But I'm his man too! Didn't I go with him to the Hakka village?" Tuck Heng protested.

"But who's served him longer? Who's got more friends? Fool!" Old Stick pulled him away from the wash area. "Move! Don't look back. And don't return the stares, or they'll fight you again."

"I can take care of myself, Uncle Old Stick."

"That you can, scholar boy! Didn't you just give those curs a beating? Best fight I've seen in years!"

It was no use trying to explain to Old Stick that he was not a scholar, just a boy who could read and write a little. It was just as useless to try and explain why he did not and could not rape a woman. None of the coolies would understand. They would simply reject him, and Lee Peng Yam would kick him out of the White Crane. He was so sick thinking about this that he did not catch what Old Stick was saying at first.

"What?"

Old Stick hitched up his cotton pants, which had slipped, and retied them round his thin waist with a bit of cord. On his face was a wide grin, and the lights in his eyes were dancing with glee. His teeth, blackened by years of opium and a poor diet, were in a state of rot.

"Now that you've proved yourself to the young bulls in the White Cranes, the big man is going to make you a White Crane warrior."

"Aren't all of us warriors?"

"All of us are water buffaloes. The warriors are defenders. They get higher rank, better food and a better sleeping place. I was a warrior once."

He was so relieved by what he had heard that his face must have been an open book to Old Stick, for the latter immediately cautioned him.

"Don't look so happy yet. They'll work you hard. Then when they're finished with you, they'll cast you aside. In my day, I've done enough bad things to be sent to the Eighteenth Level of Hell. Those horse-headed guards will throw me into a cauldron of oil and deep-fry me. The gods know how many times I've tried to repent. To pray that I may go home one day to see my son. He's about your age. Maybe you know him. His name is Kum Loong. He was born in the Year of the Dragon."

Old Stick's eyes searched his face eagerly. But he shook his head, and Old Stick, disappointed, continued, "If I live to see my son—he was born after I left Sum Hor so I've never seen him—but if I live to see him, I will fall on the ground and kowtow to the gods till my head cracks! And I'll slaughter ten pigs to thank them."

Old Stick fell into another fit of coughing and wheezing.

"I'll make you a herbal brew tonight. It'll ease your cough, Uncle."

"You're full of fire in the belly. Are you a dragon like my son?"

"I was born in the Year of the Goat."

"They say a goat is smart up here." Old Stick tapped his head. "One look at your face, I can tell you'll go far. But don't rush. Learn all you can about this dunghole." He waved his hand impatiently at the thatched huts of the settlement.

"We are all from Sum Hor, all relatives. But this village is no different from the world. Big fish will eat small fish. Remember, not everyone you call Uncle is your friend. We see a man's mouth and a man's face, but we can't see into his heart."

Old Stick sighed and shook his head. They had left the huts behind them and were walking towards the riverbank.

"When I was a young man, I thought, a few years in Nanyang, and then I'll be home! I'll be rich, and I'll repair my hut in Sum Hor and be a farmer again. That dream vanished in opium smoke!"

They had reached the riverbank and were heading towards the jetty. A large riverboat and several small sampans were tied to its posts.

"Whose boat is that?"

"The rich trader from Penang. Since Tai-kor Wong and Ah Fook are not here, our young master, Lee Peng Yam, is trading with them and lining his pockets."

"Tai-kor Wong has gone downriver to pay his respects to the Malay emperor. They say he goes there three or four times a year."

"Who told you that?"

"I overheard some people talking."

"What do they know?" Old Stick scoffed. "Number one, there's no Malay emperor. Tai-kor Wong has gone to pay respects to the Datuk of Bandong. Number two, he does not pay respects three or four times a year. Only once. With money. The other times he goes to Penang to pay respects to his father-in-law, Baba Wee, the richest towkay on the whole island. Our Tai-kor Wong married Baba Wee's fifth daughter, and because his second wife is from a rich and powerful family, she is now Tai-kor Wong's first wife. Wong-soh can't say a word because she's childless."

"She must be very sad."

"It's her fate."

Old Stick coughed again, a deep racking opium smoker's cough which made him retch. He clung to the jetty's wooden post for support. Then he straightened up and wiped his mouth with the back of his hand. When he spoke again, his eyes had a faraway look.

"Umbrellas have different handles, people have different fates." He sighed. "Tai-kor Wong was once poor and hungry like me. Now he's rich, and I'm still poor. Like you, he's got a honeyed mouth and a fast tongue. After a few years in this dunghole, he learned to speak like the Babas and the foreign devils. And ended up working for Baba Wee. That made his fortune."

His coughing started again. His whole body shivered as though he was freezing. He retched as each spasm coursed through him. Weak and exhausted, he made a sign that Tuck Heng should leave him.

Tuck Heng pitied the thin figure with his singlet so worn out that it was futile mending it. Through its tears, he could see that Old Stick was just skin and bones. An opium addict's body, he thought.

He walked to the end of the jetty. His eyes travelled across the brown placid water of the Bandong River to the dense green wall on the opposite bank. There was no sign that a woman had drowned here. No sign that the beastly lords of the river had devoured her. No sign that a mob had raped and killed women on its banks. The river looked the same as when he had sailed on it a thousand years ago. Nothing had changed. Nothing. And yet, for him everything had changed.

Chapter Eight

Sunset—the Hour of the Tiger's Prowl—was deemed the most auspicious time for the initiation ceremony.

"Lucky dog! I've waited nearly two years for this. But you! Here for a month only and you're initiated."

Tuck Heng grinned. "Born lucky."

Ah Loy boxed his ear, and the two of them wrestled playfully round the empty shed.

Ah Loy was a poor landless peasant who dreamed of returning to Sum Hor one day with enough money to buy a piece of land for his parents. The older miners laughed at him. "On twenty-four dollars a year? Not in your lifetime. Maybe in your next life!" But Ah Loy smiled and went on dreaming.

"Put these on." Ah Loy handed him a white cotton jacket, white cotton drawstring pants and a length of red cloth.

"Why are they initiating us when Tai-kor Wong is not here?"

"Don't know."

"But you've been here longer than me. Why are we initiated so fast? And why the two of us?"

"I told you I don't know."

"But I know." Old Stick came into the shed. "For you."

He thrust a pair of straw sandals into Tuck Heng's hands.

"But Uncle Old Stick, I ... I can't accept this ...!"

He looked down at Old Stick's bare feet, deeply touched by the gift.

"You look down on me?"

"No! Uncle Old Stick, please forgive my bad manners!"

"Wear them for the ceremony. In my time, all new recruits must wear straw sandals. To protect the feet. To remind us that we're travellers in this world."

He put on the straw sandals.

"Tie that red cloth round your head. And let your queue hang down. Something for your feet. Something for your head. All things must have a top and a bottom, a beginning and an end. From today onwards, you're both White Crane warriors." Old Stick grinned as though he was their benefactor. "Go forth and fight. Don't let that gutter rat push you around."

"You want to die, ah? These walls have ears," Ah Loy hissed.

"That rat has already flung me onto the dung heap. What do I care?"

"You've been drinking again."

"Not your business."

"Who said he'd chop off his hand if he lifts another bottle to his mouth? Who said he'd stop smoking the poisonous weed? Who, eh?"

"Why, you! You son of a bitch!"

Old Stick lunged at Ah Loy but missed.

"Winded warrior! Can you blame Lee Peng Yam?"

"Bastard! You've drunk his spittle! That's why you're licking his arse!"

Old Stick lunged forward again, but Ah Loy skipped out of his way.

"Stop it, Old Stick! I'm not hitting you only because of your age!"

"Pig brain! So you think you'll be a somebody soon?"

"Say what you like!"

"What do you know? Who's ever heard of an initiation ceremony for just two recruits? Do you think your grandfathers own the White Crane? We are about to go to war with the Black Flags, yet Lee Peng Yam has time to initiate you two pups? That son of a rat is using you! He wants to act the big brother in the White Crane. Impress all the young fools here!"

"Old Stick, get out of here before I bash your head!" Big Dog yelled at him from the doorway."Recruits! Follow me!"

Blue flags and red banners billowed in the breeze in front of the temple. The flag with its distinctive white crane was the symbol of their brotherhood. The ground in front of the temple was adorned with hundreds of these flags marking out the gateway to the Walled City, the home of the White Crane brothers. The red flags of Lord Guan Gong and the Revered Ancestors, the Banner of Victorious Brotherhood and the Flag of Universal Harmony lined the path leading to the temple, the symbolic Walled City. Only those worthy of being warriors were allowed to enter and join this elite band sworn to defend the White Crane.

"Can you remember what to say?" Big Tree asked the two of them.

"We can."

Warriors dressed in blue with red bands tied round their heads lined their path which was strewn with rocks and broken stones. Behind them was the crowd of coolies who had come to watch this unusual ceremony of inducting two recruits.

A loud roll of drums sounded.

"Strangers at the gate!" a warrior bellowed. He spoke in formal Cantonese according to the prescribed ritual. "Whence comest thou?"

"From the east!" the recruits answered.

"What seekest thou?"

"We seek the honour to serve Lord Guan Gong, Master of the White Cranes, and our Revered Ancestors!"

"Proceed on your knees up the Path of Stepping Stones to Honour!"

There was another roll of drums. They went down on their knees and moved step after agonising step over the broken stones, till their knees bled and their white pants were stained with the blood of their endeavour. A gong was beaten after each step taken by the recruits. When they reached the door of the temple, there was another drum roll. Another warrior opened the door.

"What seekest thou?"

"We seek the honour to serve Lord Guan Gong, Master of the White Cranes, and our Revered Ancestors!"

"If you have the courage to serve, follow me!"

The drums sounded a deep low rumble followed by several rapid beats. The warrior and the two recruits marched briskly round the temple three times. They stopped at intervals to bow to the Guardian Spirit of the East and the Lord of the West. They bowed to the Guardian Spirit of the White Cranes, the God of Thunder and Lightning and the Goddess of Mercy. Then they faced the setting sun, knelt and kowtowed three times to the Earth God, the guardian of all life on land, a deity depicted as an old man with a white beard, dressed in white flowing robes. The white crane, symbol of longevity, was said to be his companion.

The drum roll stopped when the warrior led his recruits back to the temple entrance. The crowd cheered as the Master of Initiation, Lee Peng Yam, and the Council of Elders emerged, dressed in white with red bands round their heads. Lee Peng Yam recited the history of the White Crane in a loud voice.

The crowd, especially the older men, nodded knowingly as Lee Peng Yam called out name after name of the heroes and places marking the battles of the clan. When he ended, the two recruits prostrated themselves on the ground and begged the Master of Initiation and the elders to accept their unworthy selves as warriors. They pledged their lives and their undying loyalty. The Council of Elders nodded, and the Master of Initiation ordered the recruits to kneel to receive the secret passwords.

A roll of drums and loud beating of the gongs informed the gods and the ancestors that the new warriors were about to be tested for courage and loyalty. They were led to an area marked by a red banner bearing the legend "Gateway to the Valley of Swords".

Behind the banner, two rows of White Crane warriors stood facing each other, their swords drawn to form an arch.

Two warriors dressed in black, known as the Executioners, confronted them at the head of the arch.

"Halt! Who dares to enter the Valley of Swords?"

"We who have come to serve Lord Guan Gong, Master of the White Cranes, and our Revered Ancestors!"

"Are you pure of heart?"

"We are!"

"Are you stout of heart?"

"We are!"

"Do you dare walk through the Valley of Swords?"

"We have nothing to fear!"

"What are the swords for?"

"For beheading traitors!"

The drums rolled and then fell silent. Night had fallen upon the settlement. Tuck Heng, followed by Ah Loy, walked slowly under the arch of swords and entered the temple. Oil lamps and red candles burned brightly. Shadows larger than life loomed among the warriors and elders. The air was thick with incense smoke. He and Ah Loy knelt before the altar as the Master of Initiation and Guardian of Oaths and Discipline read out the thirty-six rules of the White Crane. Then the thirty-six oaths were administered.

"We swear never to reveal the secrets of our brotherhood.

"We swear to serve with unerring obedience our Tai-kor and elders in the council.

"To help a brother in need.

"To help a brother's family in need.

"Respect at all times a brother's property.

"Respect at all times a brother's wife and female relatives."

And the list went on till his head ached. The pain in his knees was agonising. After the last oath, they kowtowed three times. A large yellow sheet of paper, filled with red characters, known as the Document of Honour and Loyalty, was burned at the altar so that word would ascend to heaven and Lord Guan Gong would be informed about the new warriors' oath of allegiance. When the last bit of yellow paper had turned to ash, Water Buffalo took a pinch of the ash and mixed it into two cups of tea. The tea was then given to the new warriors who drained the contents in one gulp.

"From this moment onwards, let courage and loyalty, good faith and integrity, duty and filial piety course through your veins and bring you and your descendants a good name in the White Crane!" Lee Peng Yam intoned.

"Let the gods and our ancestors be witnesses to your solemn oath!" the other elders added.

"Bring in the cockerel!" Lee Peng Yam ordered.

Two warriors brought in a white cockerel and a large china bowl half-filled with water. One of them held the bird's throat firmly over the china bowl and used a knife to slit its throat. Thick blood dripped into the bowl. His finger was pricked. A few drops of his blood dripped into the bowl and was mixed with that of Ah Loy's and the cockerel's.

A gong sounded. Lee Peng Yam said a short prayer and handed him the china bowl. He took a sip and handed the bowl to Ah Loy who in turn took a sip and handed the bowl back to Lee Peng Yam.

"You have drunk the blood of the brotherhood. That which has been sealed in blood will remain sacred forever. From today you are warriors sworn to defend our brothers in the White Crane."

Chapter Nine

He had finally made some progress in the new land. His head felt light. He left Ah Loy and went immediately to the house of Wong-soh. He must pay his respects to the wife of the Master of the White Cranes. He had not seen Wong-soh since the White Cranes' victorious ambush upriver, he thought. And the thought startled him. How quickly his mind had adjusted to events! Like all the young miners, he was already using the same euphemistic phrase to refer to the mass rape of the Hakka women upstream. "Victorious ambush upriver." There was an unmistakable ring of triumph in the phrase, even a blast of vengeful glee over their enemy's shame.

He knew that he ought to rejoice, but his heart was void of gleeful feelings. It was torn between loyalty to the White Crane and faithfulness to the teachings of the ancient scholars. "To be a man is to uphold humaneness and lawfulness," his father had taught him. To be a White Crane warrior is to protect, defend and fight for the brotherhood. That was his oath. How could he juggle the two without compromising one or the other? How did his father do it? He longed for someone to guide him.

The lateness of the hour made him hesitate. Ah Loy had already returned to the sleeping sheds. And yet he could not rest that night till he had seen Wong-soh and let her know that he had been initiated in Tai-kor Wong's absence. Old Stick might be right. Lee Peng Yam might be using him and Ah Loy to show off his authority during Tai-kor Wong's absence. The more he thought of it, the more uneasy he felt. He knocked on the door.

"Wong-soh! Wong-soh!"

The door flew open, and a whole bucket of urine was flung into his face. He was drenched from head to toe. Sputtering, he shook the foul liquid out of his eyes and tried to open them. Wong-soh came out with the chamber pot in her hands.

"Animal! Don't you dare step across my threshold!"

He could only gape at her like an idiot.

"I've no eyes for the likes of you! You filthy gutter rat!"

"Wong-soh, I'm sorry I was initiated without Tai-kor Wong's permission. But I'm loyal to him! I swear it!"

"Depraved gutter rat! You talk like a scholar! But act like a beast!"

"Wong-soh, please listen!"

"I've no ears! What did those wives and mothers do, ha? Answer me! Answer me!" She shook him till his teeth chattered. "Why didn't you animals fight man to man? Heartless cowards! And you of all people! You! Son of the learned doctor!"

"But Wong-soh, I didn't do it! I didn't!"

He was jumping up and down in his utter relief. Here was someone who wouldn't think less of him for not doing what the young bulls did.

"I begged and pleaded for you to be sent out here! To save the last drop of your father's blood! Aiyah, I should've let those dogs behead you! It would've saved your father's name! Saved your mother's ghost from eternal shame!"

"Wong-soh! Wait!"

He caught hold of her arm, but she shoved him aside and grabbed a thick bamboo pole. Eyes blazing with fury, she hit him with the pole, ignoring his loud protests of innocence.

"Beast! Animal! Out of my sight! Out! Out!"

"I've been wronged!" He fled in the direction of the temple.

Then Wong-soh sank to her knees, her weatherbeaten face

crumbling under the strain, but she was beyond caring who saw her cry.

"Gone, all gone."

"What happened?"

Aunt Loh pushed past the crowd of curious neighbours.

"I flung a pot of urine at Tuck Heng!"

"You never change. Always hands first, mouth last!"

They were childhood friends who had sailed to this godforsaken dunghole together. In a voice choked with grief, Wong-soh told Aunt Loh that she had been fuming ever since she had heard what Lee Peng Yam and his young bulls had done upriver. But there was nothing she could have done to stop them. The men were in charge. But she had not expected young Tuck Heng to join those animals.

"To think that I pleaded with Old Wong to let me adopt him. Loh-ma, what hope have I now? He was my last hope for a son."

She choked on the words. The bitter barren years welled up in her eyes. She shielded her naked grief with her arms. But she knew that this was a useless gesture. Everyone in this settlement knew that she was barren and had had to settle for the status of a minor wife when Tai-kor Wong married the daughter of the wealthy Baba Wee.

"Look at me," She gripped her friend's arm. "Am I not cursed? Remember the day we arrived? That was the day Old Wong told me that he had a wife in Penang and that she's his number one wife. Other wives got a welcome. I got a dead cat stuffed into my mouth. Forever silenced. Because I'm barren!" Her eyes besieged her friend's.

"Our faces were smooth, and our hair was black when we first came out to this jungle," Aunt Loh muttered.

"But you have sons and daughters now. What do I have?" Wong-soh's voice was bitter. "Even the little I've begged for is gone."

Aunt Loh shook her head and sat down on the doorstep beside her friend. Wong-soh had always been different. No woman in the settlement, no one except Wong-soh, would punish a boy for doing what men do. No one else felt that there was anything wrong with the men's "victorious mission upriver". An enemy was an enemy.

She patted Wong-soh's arm. It was useless trying to make Wong-soh see the mission in the way everyone in the settlement saw it. Wong-soh had always been strong-headed. Which was why she was caned more often than any other daughter-in-law in their village. What was worse in the eyes of the village elders was that Wong-soh had accepted her caning with the stoicism of a man. She did not cry or beg for mercy like the rest. Aunt Loh admired Wong-soh's strength.

They had grown up together and had been child brides of thirteen married into the village of Sum Hor when the world was young and green and full of grain. Then in the year of the second great drought, their menfolk had left their village forever, leaving behind aged fathers and mothers, grieving wives and hungry children. The next year many of the young wives left behind were blessed with their husbands' seed which bore fruit after ten months. The village elders shook their heads and thought that the Wongs and the Lohs were better off with their childless daughters-in-law. Then the seasons returned to normal. The elders began to sing a different song, and the childless daughters-in-law were scorned. Life was bleak and desperate.

But Wong-soh refused to succumb to her bleak fate and secretly encouraged Aunt Loh to do the same. They hired themselves out as labourers and night soil collectors, working for anyone who could pay them a few coppers.

After fifteen backbreaking years, they had saved enough money to leave their village and sail across the ocean to join their menfolk. During that fateful voyage, their world became as wide as the sky above and as huge as the ocean below. They saw themselves as woman warriors who braved the tumultuous seas to catch up with their future. In their imagination, they were like the heroic swordswomen in *gongfu* tales who could fight demons as well as men.

When they arrived in Singapore, they travelled in another

boat to reach the settlement in Bandong. A year later, Aunt Loh was blessed, and a son was born. In the third year, a daughter followed. Then there was a second and a third girl. Wong-soh, however, remained barren year after year. In the sixth year of her arrival, when she was considered past childbearing, she conceived. But her joy was short-lived. The child died in her womb, and Wong-soh was devastated.

"I must've been a murderer in my past life, and now I'm being punished!"

"Don't give up so quickly. Pray to the gods. I will talk to young Tuck."

Chapter Ten

An uneasy air of expectation settled on the men in the mines. The euphoria of their "victorious ambush upstream" had given way to a sense of wariness and unease. Lee Peng Yam was worried. What if his young bulls had failed to pass themselves off as Malays during their attack on the Hakka women?

"Be prepared for those dogs! Keep a sharp lookout!"

In the opencast mines, the still air and the sweltering heat pressed heavily upon the men. The fierce rays of the sun and the constant chug-chug-chug of the water pumps dulled their minds. They moved with the silent mechanical energy of oxen in the field and plodded with sure-footed tread among the rocks. They hauled baskets of gravel up the slopes to the wooden channels of rushing water, where the gravel would be washed for ore.

Old Stick stood in the shadow of one of these raised wooden channels. The heat and the work were punishing. All that morning, he had been wheezing like a winded horse. With great effort, he lifted his hoe only to let it fall heavily to the ground again. The smallest movement of his limbs drained his fast-ebbing strength. He tried to raise his hoe again, but a sudden wave of darkness washed over him. He felt himself sinking into the earth and pulled himself up with an effort. His hoe dropped from his hands and hit the hard earth in a cloud of dust. He wheezed and gasped for air.

"Uncle Old Stick, are you all right?" Tuck Heng rushed up to him.

He pounded Old Stick's back to ease his wheezing, but spasm after spasm of coughing shook his emaciated body.

"Sit over there. I'll get you a drink."

Tuck Heng left him leaning against the stakes which supported the wooden channels. Old Stick was shivering even though the day was unbearably hot. An afternoon storm, the kind that built up whenever the heat was intolerable, was brewing beyond the hills. Old Stick tied a dirty rag round his head to stop his temples from throbbing. His throat was parched and his eyes were bright with fever. He drank some of the water which Tuck Heng brought him. Another spasm shook his thin frame. His face was flushed a dull red when the uncomfortable wetness oozed down his legs, soiling his pants yet again.

Tuck Heng avoided Old Stick's eyes. The stench from his pants was unmistakable. The man had lost control of his bowels, and the dysentery was gaining ground. But Old Stick had insisted on coming to the pit with his mining gang.

"Who'll feed me if I don't work? You think Lee Peng Yam will bother with me? He's my punishment. Done too many vile things in my young days."

Old Stick's frame shook uncontrollably as yet another spasm coursed through him. Tuck Heng tried to shield him from the sun with his straw hat.

"Let me tell you. I killed my own daughter. She ruined her marriage, and I ruined her and the whole family. That's my life. Full of vile useless deeds! Useless, useless, useless," he moaned as the pain coursed through his twisted bowels.

"Back in Sum Hor, I lost my land. Land my family had farmed for fifteen generations. I couldn't pay the rent. Years of drought! A wife and ten useless daughters! I buried the tenth when the piglet was born. What could I do? Tell me, you people, tell me!"

Ah Loy and one or two miners came over to see what was wrong with him. But when they heard him moaning about his useless life, they quickly returned to their work.

"Can you smell it on him?" Ah Loy hissed.

"His shit?"

"His death. The horse-headed guard is here for him."

The superstitious miners moved away. When a man started to recall and confess his past misdeeds, it could only mean one thing—his time had come.

"Only those about to die remember their bad deeds and confess," Ah Loy muttered. "You'd better get back to the pit."

"Don't go," Old Stick held on to Tuck Heng's hand. "I had to sell off some of them. Why should I slave like a water buffalo? So that other people's sons can carry them off to work on their farms?"

Old Stick's voice rose to fever pitch. He would not let go of his hand.

"Sold off three girls to the brothel keeper. You people out there! Don't pretend you haven't done the same. Why else would we call our daughters Thousand Taels of Gold? Because they're for selling! Right or not? Right or not?"

None of the miners answered him. "To rant like Old Stick is to invite bad luck. He will be claimed by the Bandong spirits," the miners whispered to one another and prayed that these spirits would not claim them too. But in their hearts they knew that Old Stick was not the first and would not be the last among them to go the way of the sick and desperate. Thousands had died in the Bandong earth without ever seeing their homeland again.

"Don't go."

"Uncle Old Stick, please, you must rest."

"I married off my Thousand Taels of Gold to the old pawnbroker. My number four was his fifth concubine, and the pawnbroker offered me a very good sum for her. Enough to pay the rent on the farm for that year. But my number four was an ass! A stubborn mule! Do you hear me, Number Four? Even if your ghost haunts me, I'll still say you're a stubborn ass!" Old Stick spat. "If you'd stayed with your husband, you could've saved all your sisters and your parents! But you had to run away. He beat you so you ran away. What's a few beatings to a woman? Which woman has never been beaten? Go away, Number Four! Don't stare at me!"

Old Stick coughed and sputtered. Tuck Heng signalled to the miners for help. But no one came.

"Listen to me! Not her!" Old Stick was tugging at his hand. "'Return to your husband!' I yelled at her. But her voice was even louder than mine. 'Pa, he bites me like a dog! He wants me to be a dog in bed!' She screeched like a she-devil. I locked the door and refused to let her in. She drank poison and died in my pigsty."

Old Stick broke into a cold sweat and his teeth started to chatter. He pulled his ragged tunic tightly across his chest. Then he glanced miserably at the mess between his legs and turned to Tuck Heng.

"She died with her eyes open. And blood oozing out of every hole in her body. Her eyes, her ears, her nose. She cursed me with her death! She's after me!"

"Tuck Heng! Back to work!" Big Rat hollered from the pit below.

"Go, go!" Old Stick seemed to have returned to his senses.

"I'll bring you some food later."

He left Old Stick seated in the shade of the wooden channel and hurried back to his digging in the pit below. Moments later, there was a roar like the crack of a thunderbolt.

An avalanche of gravel and water gushed out from the collapsed channel above Old Stick. The more he tried to claw through the debris, the more he fell and sank into the mud. His body lay inert. Then it moved feebly, his head lolling from side to side as the merciless mud and gravel poured all over him, filling his gaping mouth, his distended nostrils, and his eyes wide with fear and shock. Powered by the water pumps above, the gravel rushed down the wooden channel and ran in rivulets between the legs of the coolies who had rushed up from the pits. They saw Old Stick's arm, brown and bony, shoot up an instant. It clutched at the empty air, then fell limp and prone. In another minute, the grey sludge had covered it.

"Uncle Old Stick!"

Tuck Heng was the first to reach him. The coolies pried his body free from under the rocks and pulled it out from the wreck.

"Stop the water pumps!" Lee Peng Yam shouted.

"Hurry, hurry! Over this way!"

"More poles! Over here!"

Old Stick's body was pushed to the side as the miners worked feverishly to shore up the collapsed channel.

⊷≡◎⊂≡⊷

The coolies have a saying, "The richer the man, the more elaborate his funeral." Since Old Stick was very poor, his funeral was very simple. He had no family and no friends. His only official mourner was Tuck Heng. Wong-soh was hastily summoned to perform the last rites on behalf of Old Stick's wife and daughters. She burned incense and joss papers at the site of his death to ease his journey into the Underworld. That over, Old Stick's body was prepared for burial the same day.

"Wong-soh, so sorry to rush you," Big Rat apologised. "But Lee Peng Yam said we got to bury him quickly, and let the others get back to their digging. No sense in losing our wages."

"I understand."

"Big Rat, I'll go with Old Stick to the grave."

"Choy, Tuck Heng! Say you'll be the mourner! Not go to the grave with him!" Wong-soh chided him. Then she turned to Big Rat. "Luckily you ordered him back to the pit. If not, he too would've joined the ancestors. You saved Tuck Heng's life today. May the gods bless you, Big Rat."

"Thank you, Big Rat," Tuck Heng muttered dutifully.

But he was really in no mood to thank anyone. Everybody appeared callous in their unseemly haste to bury poor Old Stick. Didn't Sum Hor's traditions and customs demand some sort of mourning for the dead? Especially if the dead was a White Crane warrior? He looked at the coolies who had returned to their digging in the pits. He was disgusted. The White Cranes followed tradition only when it suited them—

when dealing with adulterous women. But tradition was cast aside for money and wages.

"Young dog, if you want to be foolish and give up your day's wage, that's all right with me. And you don't get free food tonight, you hear me?"

"Tuck Heng, come to my hut for dinner."

"Wong-soh, I don't want to be hard on the boy, but I've got to see that everybody obeys the rules."

"Big Rat, I understand. Tuck Heng, come for dinner."

He nodded, too surprised for words. One minute he was assaulted with urine and the next he was invited for a meal.

"Aunt Loh told me everything," Wong-soh whispered, keeping her voice low so that no one else heard her. "No one else knows about it. Just us two old women." Then raising her voice, she said, "It's going to rain. I've got to go."

The sky had indeed darkened suddenly. Tuck Heng's thoughts were in a whirl. All he could think of was what Wong-soh had told him, and he was relieved. At last Wong-soh believed that he was an honourable young man, and that was more important to him than anything else at that moment.

"Young Tuck, over here! We're tying up the body!"

Two men returned with Old Stick's bedding. They wrapped his mud-covered body in a blanket and straw mat. The mat was folded over the body from one side to the other, and the whole bundle was tied and secured with cord, ready for removal to the burial ground. Old Stick's shoulders were tied to one bamboo pole and his feet to another. Then the four bearers hoisted the carrying poles onto their shoulders, two men to a pole.

"Make way! Make way!"

Tuck Heng ran ahead of the men as they trotted up a slope with the corpse swinging between them. In his right hand, he held three lighted joss sticks to lead Old Stick's spirit to the burial ground. When they reached a junction where the mud track split into two paths, he stopped to burn some gold and silver joss papers, to bribe the jungle jinns and other spirits to let Old Stick's soul pass through their territory.

The burial ground was on a hill reached by a cart track.

The track was hemmed in on both sides by thick bush and jungle. The bearers, with the corpse swinging between them, laboured in the still air under an overcast sky. Not a leaf stirred among the trees. The heavy silence of death swung between them, and thoughts of the Other World were not far from their minds. Tuck Heng stopped to burn more joss papers under an ancient tree.

Rumbling dark clouds, heavy with rain, came over the Bandong Hills. A sudden blinding flash split the overcast sky, followed the next instant by a thunderous clap. The sun was eclipsed, and in the sudden gloom, a windy blast tore down the cart track. It ripped the leaves from the trees. The change was so sudden that the coolies shuddered even though they knew that this was the nature of tropical storms in Bandong Valley. A second flash of lightning split the heavens. Another crack of thunder. Then the storm broke over their heads. Pallbearers and corpse were pelted with the full force of the rain. Water poured down in torrents, accompanied by strong gusts that blew sudden and furious, flinging gravel and stones before their faces. Tuck Heng and the pallbearers bent their bodies as successive flashes of lightning raced across the darkened sky and thunder cracked the heavens above. The pallbearers dropped their burden in the middle of the cart track and raced for the protection of an overhanging rock which housed a shrine to the Earth God.

"Come back! You can't leave Old Stick here!" Tuck Heng yelled. He was completely drenched in the sudden deluge, but he could not and would not leave Old Stick's body to the mercy of the storm. The horror of the ragged bundle lying in the middle of the flooded track brought hot angry tears to his eyes. He tried to drag the poor corpse onto higher ground, but the entire track had turned into a stream of rushing water. There was not a piece of dry ground anywhere. The flood waters ran up against the dead man's head, veered and divided into two streams that swirled round his sides, sweeping leaves, twigs, pebbles and sand in their path. Old Stick's body lay stiff as a rod in its wet shroud, exposed to the full force of the thunderstorm with its electrifying flashes of lightning. Then a sudden flash rent the gloom. Old Stick's body sat bolt upright!

Tuck Heng let out a yelp and fled in the direction of the pallbearers. He was shivering with shock and fear as he crouched close to the shrine of the Earth God.

"Old Stick's spirit is unhappy! His body sat up!"

"Lord Buddha protect us! God of the Earth protect us! Forgive us, Old Stick! We didn't mean to drop you!"

Tuck Heng and the four coolies chanted over and over again a prayer to the Lord Buddha as the thunderstorm unleashed its fury upon the earth.

"Old Stick, please forgive us," Tuck Heng prayed. "We don't mean any disrespect. We'll bury your body when the storm stops. I promise."

Tuck Heng peered through the thick sheet of rain and caught a sudden gleam of metal. His heart stopped. Men with knives and guns were hiding in the bushes. Hakka Black Flags! He had to warn the others.

"Old Stick, protect me!" he yelled and sprinted towards the corpse.

Chapter Eleven

*H*e kept on running in the rain, past the hideous corpse of his friend, sprinting down the cart track. He veered and stumbled into the thicket, plunging knee-deep into the rain-soaked bush and lallang which cut his arms as he swept aside their knife-sharp blades. Behind him, not far away, he could hear the sounds of fighting and pursuit. On reaching the open stretch of scrub near the tin mines, he raced down the path towards the settlement, splashing through streams of mud. He did not slip. He did not stumble. He now had an unerring sense of direction and an acute sensitivity for the changing terrain under his feet. He leapt over rocks and boulders with the agility of a deer. Years of eluding capture by the Manchu guards had armed him well.

"Black Flags!" he bellowed.

The White Cranes sheltering in the sheds heard his warning at once. They grabbed their poles and whatever they could lay their hands on and raced after him towards the settlement. Gunshots rang out behind them. His first thought was for Wong-soh, the other women and their children.

"Wong-soh!" he hollered.

Bullets whizzed past his head. Old Stick's spirit was shielding him from the gunfire, he thought. Old Stick had been warning him about the snakes in the bushes. That must be why his body had sat up in that preposterous manner! To scare off the enemy waiting in ambush! Thank you, Old Stick!

"How many dogs?" Lee Peng Yam stopped him. His voice was hoarse from shouting. All round them, the White Cranes were racing to the food stores and ammunition sheds with rifles, choppers, axes, parangs and whatever they could grab in the confusion.

"Don't know! Didn't see!"

More gunshots rang out. Hordes of Hakka miners were streaming down the slopes towards their huts.

"Take the women and children down the river!" Lee Peng Yam pushed him towards the jetty.

There was no time to lose. Big Rat led a small group of men and ran towards the Bandong River. The White Crane warriors would be able to hold off their attackers for a while. Tuck Heng followed them and they sped down the lanes of the settlement, yanking the cowering women and children out of their huts.

With each passing minute, the sounds of gunfire grew louder. The children tumbled after the adults, wailing for their mothers in the noise, smoke and confusion. Spears carrying balls of fire hissed through the air. Several huts burst into flames despite the rain. He rushed into Wong-soh's hut, grabbed her by the hand and pulled her into the safety of the bushes. Then they ran through the thick undergrowth till they reached the river. Not once did he let go of her hand despite her protests that she could look after herself. His sole thought was to get her to the boats. He had lost one mother before, and he was determined not to lose another.

"Into the boats!"

He shoved Wong-soh into the water and helped her into one of the boats. Then he waded back to shore to help the other women and their children. He pulled Aunt Loh and shoved her into the water too.

"Take her! And this one! And this one!"

He flung child after child into Aunt Loh's arms. When he saw Big Rat, he grabbed another child and flung him into Big Rat's arms. He was tireless as he swam back and forth between the boats and the shore, his arms making a grab for each woman or child floundering in the treacherous waters. Behind him, the settlement was on fire. The storm had eased into a drizzle, and thick columns of smoke rose from the burning huts. The fighting reached the riverbank. Several gunshots rang out in unison. He turned and saw White Crane warriors pitch forward and fall on their faces. The Black Flags closed in on them. A moment later, a violent blow hit his left arm. A bullet tore through his shoulder. He staggered and fell heavily into the water, gasping as more gunshots were fired into the river. Balls of fire hit the boats. Warriors fell like dominoes. He thrashed about in the bloodied water, flailing his arms as darkness threatened to swamp him. Blindly he struck out for the boats that were moving downriver with the current. He felt himself being pulled along, gasping and choking as water rushed into his nostrils and lungs. Then he knew no more.

When he opened his eyes again, he found himself gazing into the weeping face of Wong-soh.

"Thank the Lord Buddha, you're alive! Two days and two nights! You slept as one dead!"

He asked about the children.

"All safe, all safe! Drink this."

His throat felt parched. He was burning with a high fever and his whole body ached.

"Aunt Loh and I pulled you out of the water."

"What about Big Rat? He was beside me."

"He's in the next boat. He's trying to get us to Penang."

He touched the bandage on his left shoulder and grimaced with pain.

"Is the bullet still inside?"

"No, I cut it out. What you need now is some good medicine to close the wound."

He remembered his father's medicine chest. His one and only link with China had been left behind. He groaned and closed his eyes.

"Tuck Heng! Tuck Heng! Don't die!" Wong-soh shook him violently.

He opened his eyes and gazed up at her tearful face.

"Don't worry, Wong-ma, I won't die."

"Did you hear that?" Aunt Loh asked the women crowding inside the boat. It was one of those large flat-bottomed riverboats with an attap hut serving as the main cabin. Twenty women and children were sheltering inside it.

"We heard," the women replied.

It was then, and only then, that it struck him that he had inadvertently called her Mother Wong.

"The gods know how many times I've prayed for this!" Wong-soh was in tears. "Thank you, Lord Buddha! Thank you, Lord Guan Gong!" She clasped her hands and bowed to the heavens.

Aunt Loh turned to him, but he was just as surprised as she was at the turn of events. "You two are of the same fate. One with no children and the other, no parents. Two lives floating like leaves in the ocean with no blood relations in this part of the world."

"Wong-soh, why the tears? Adopt him," the butcher's wife urged.

By now everyone in the boat had edged closer.

"When we reach Penang, you can do it formally in the temple and give thanks and prayers to the gods. But who knows what tomorrow will bring! Today we're safe. Tomorrow? Who knows?"

"Choy! Let's talk about happy things! Wong-soh has found a son!" Aunt Loh chided the woman.

"Call her Wong-ma, Tuck Heng!" the women urged him, eager to be part of something joyous. "Let your joy dispel bad luck."

"Greet your adopted mother, Tuck Heng," Aunt Loh pressed him.

"Wong-ma," he croaked.

The butcher's wife thrust a mug of water into his hands. "No tea, so water will do. The gods in heaven will understand. Ah Tuck, kneel and offer your Wong-ma three kowtows."

He knelt and kowtowed.

Wong-soh accepted his mug of water and wiped away the tears streaming down her face. Her deep wrinkles creased into a broad smile as she took a sip of the sweetest water she had ever tasted.

"Sleep, my son. You've got a mother to take care of you now."

He lay down and turned to face the wall so that no one could see his tears. It had been such a long time since someone had called him Son.

Chapter Twelve

When Tai-kor Wong's boat docked at the jetty of Kuala Bandong that fateful day, the whole river front was full of men and animals.

"How are we to get through?" Ah Fook groaned as he signalled to the boatman to bring their boat closer to the jetty steps.

Eager hands made a grab for the boat's ropes and pulled her in. But the small jetty was overcrowded with *prahu,* rafts and numerous small sampans. Their owners swore at each other in a babble of tongues as they made way for the larger riverboat of the White Cranes.

"Faster! Old tortoise!"

"How fast can I go? His tub is blocking the way!"

"Whose sampan are you calling a tub?"

"Out of the way!"

Men clad in sarongs and naked to the waist raced down the jetty with sacks of rice, slabs of fresh meat and bunches of coconuts, bananas, rambutans and vegetables, their progress impeded by several bleating goats and cackling hens running frantically between their legs. Some Malay boys were trying to catch the animals. An old Indian coolie in a white dhoti shouted at the urchins, who dodged in and out among the adults, laughing and revelling in the noise and chaos of the river front.

"Looks like the whole village is preparing for a festival," Tai-kor Wong muttered.

"Good! There will be food and women. My belly needs food and my old bones, a massage." Ah Fook chuckled at the thought of supple feminine hands kneading his tired flesh.

"You old fox! Thinking of your Malay woman again?"

"You've got yours. So I've got mine. Right or not?"

Tai-kor Wong's face broke into a grin.

"Right, you old fox! We'll rest here for a few days."

Then he spied the ungainly figure of Musa Talib lumbering down the jetty like a water buffalo.

"Our Mamak is coming. Just look at how he's dressed. In cheap cotton *baju*. Like a poor farmer!"

"Malay folks, what do you expect them to wear?"

"The outside world judges you by your clothes."

"Your fat trader, he's fated to be rich. So he's rich, even if he wears rags! If a man's not fated to be a prince, he won't be one even if he wears yellow silk."

"Che' Wong!" Musa Talib clambered up the gangplank.

"My friend, what news?" Tai-kor Wong called out in fluent accented Malay.

"The news is good, but the noise is killing me! Everyone shouting like quarrelsome mynahs! Pushing this way that way! Like maggots in a dead goat!"

"What're you people celebrating?"

"Che' Wong! You don't know? Kuala Bandong will see the grandest wedding tonight. The Datuk's eldest daughter is marrying the son of the menteri of Larut; the two most powerful families in Negeri Perak will be united. And if your humble slave may say so, I had a hand in the arrangements. There's going to be a feast for the whole of Kuala Bandong! Thousands are coming for the wedding! You and your men are invited. Your father-in-law has also been invited, but he cannot come. He has sent a big present. Very big," Musa gushed without pausing for breath.

"Stop screaming like a cat on heat! I'm breathless just listening to you. I'd better bring a gift. From the White Cranes. It'll have to be substantial, no?"

"Yah, my friend. Very substantial."

Musa rubbed his palms together as he drew closer to Tai-kor Wong. They made their way down the jetty and Musa lapsed into the more intimate Baba-Malay patois spoken by Tai-kor Wong and his relatives in Penang. It was an indication of the closeness between the two men.

"My friend, please don't forget your other gift. For the Datuk. More important than the gift for the bride and groom, yah?"

He gave Tai-kor Wong a playful jab in the ribs.

"Have I ever forgotten about such things? A man must first pay his dues before he sits down to eat, right?"

"Right! 'Always pay your dues and give tribute to the lords on high,' my father used to say, 'then you'll be welcomed by all the lords of the land and the royals of this country.' Tribute saved my head more than once!"

Musa Talib grinned and tapped his temple.

Tai-kor Wong cocked his head and looked at his partner's dark sweaty face and even darker oily neck.

"Yah, your God gave you a thick head."

And they slapped each other on the back as if they had just heard the most outrageous joke. Ah Fook and the other Chinese miners, who were walking behind them, found their behaviour utterly incomprehensible. But the two partners neither noticed nor cared what the others thought about them. They had been trading partners up and down these parts for several years, from Bandong Valley to as far away as Larut and Kinta; both knew very well the danger that could befall many an unwary trader doing business with arrogant and petulant Malay chiefs, whose hands were quick to draw the kris and slit a trader's throat.

"I've got a very thick skin round my throat too. Like leather."

"Mine is not as thick as yours. More like the turtle's neck. Tell me, what's the gossip from Pulau Pinang?"

"The *Sayed* from Pulau Pinang said that the price of tin has gone up in the white man's country. So now the English want to dig for the tin themselves and they're swindling every sultan and raja in Malaya to get mining concessions."

"Bad sign, my friend, bad sign. These royals know nothing about mining."

"That's why they find a man like me useful! We Mamaks have served the Malay sultans since the Malacca sultanate. At one time, our word could make or break a raja's chance to sit on the throne."

"But those days are over, Pak Mus. The English dogs are the kingmakers now."

"The bastards! They eat up our land! Swindle our chiefs! I can't wait for the day, Insya Allah, when they'll be out-swindled!"

Tai-kor Wong shook his head and resigned himself to listening as Musa Talib launched into his favourite topic. The Indian-Muslim trader was obsessed with some vague notion of vengeance against the English, not unlike his own feelings against the Hakka scum, he thought. This was what he liked about Musa. The man had guts and passion and spoke his mind like a patriot whenever the mood struck him, although he was also rumoured to be a double-headed snake who would bite off the hand of his own brother for an extra bag of rice. But he, Tai-kor Wong, was not one to heed gossip and rumours fuelled by rivals, and Musa Talib had plenty of rivals and enemies. He himself had plenty too.

Besides, he had always admired Musa Talib's ability to serve several masters at the same time. Being a shrewd man, he appreciated Musa's nimble mind, which could switch from one master's demands to another's agilely, serving men as different as the Datuk and himself, and the Hakka scum. Musa had served each one faithfully as a purveyor of information and a supplier of goods and services, advising, placating and humouring each in turn. A faithful servant. A trusted friend. But he knew that the wily trader had also used others for his own gains. Not that Tai-kor Wong minded. He would've done the same had the opportunity presented itself. A man's fingers are not all of the same length, and one has to take the good with the bad in any relationship. Particularly a trading relationship, he thought.

He had met Musa Talib in Penang when he was looking for a local trader who was familiar with Bandong Valley and could bring rice and other supplies to the miners in the White Crane mining settlement. At that time, Bandong Valley had just been opened up for tin mining and trade and the area was so infested with river pirates that no Chinese trader wanted to go in. Musa had agreed to undertake the venture, provided Tai-kor Wong shared the risks and profits with him. Since then Musa had kept his word and despite the attacks of river pirates and the monsoon rains which capsized some of his boats, he had kept the White Crane settlement well-supplied with food and weapons.

From this venture, the two men had branched into the trade for buffalo and deer horns, hides, rattans and canes. With Musa as his partner, Tai-kor Wong soon became one of the few Chinese traders who knew the ways of the Malays in the interior and spoke their language fluently. Musa also initiated him into the pleasures provided by the Malay ladies and he was particularly grateful to Musa for getting him a good woman in Kuala Bandong. "It's no good, Che' Wong, for a man to be alone," Musa had said to him one day. "The Almighty Creator made women for men's enjoyment and we men have to show appreciation by taking pleasure in them." Tai-kor Wong thought that the Indian-Muslim's view of women was not so different from his own. As he told Musa then, women were teacups and men, teapots. "One teapot can pour into many teacups. Never one teacup into many teapots." Musa had laughed at the image. "It shows that you Chinamen have wit like us Malays. Let's drink to that, my friend!" That night Musa had brought him to the house of the beautiful Che' Dah. Today he was eager to see her again and breathe in the fragrant oil she used to massage his body. His loins tingled with longing. But resolutely, he turned away from such frivolous thoughts. Not till he had settled this business of the taxes which was vital to the White Cranes.

"My friend, I heard that those Hakka dogs came earlier than usual to pay their taxes."

"No use for me to deny what you already know."

"Tell me, how much did the Hakka pay the Datuk?"

"Che' Wong!" Musa protested and looked as if he had been pushed against the wall by such bluntness. "There're three who can answer you truthfully. The first is His Most Gracious, Most Merciful and Compassionate who knows everything. The second is the Datuk who knows most things. The third is Inche Yap Kim How himself who paid the money."

"And you, the monkey, know nothing!"

Musa Talib's swarthy face broke into a broad grin as he rested his fleshy arm on his friend's shoulders.

"That's why we're partners, Che' Wong. We're alike. That's why we understand each other."

"So?"

"Alas, I'm only a small pond. I'll bring you to the Bandong River. To the lord himself. Then you can fish to your heart's content, yah?"

They entered the compound of the menteri of Bandong.

Chapter Thirteen

The courtyard of Datuk Long Mahmud's house had been transformed into a vast open stage with a raised platform to seat more than a hundred guests. Young coconut palms and cut banana trees laden with bunches of half-ripened fruit lined the sides of the platform. Long garlands of coconut fronds, intricately woven with white jasmine, pink frangipani and red hibiscus, were strung between the trees, their scents mingling with the bold pungency of curry and spices. Large earthern pots of spicy beef *rendang*, lemony fish *assam*, peppery chicken *soto* and rice were being cooked over open fires.

The day before, the courtyard had been the scene of a mass slaughter of goats and fowl, with the women shooing away eager curious children. Kampong folk from miles around had come to help in the wedding of the Datuk's daughter, pounding chillies, chopping onions and grinding spices. Now they were stirring cauldrons of curries and fragrant rice, all the while chatting with friends and neighbours, joking with the menfolk and screaming at the urchins. Young maids, teased by young men, fanned the fires and sweated over vats of hot oil frying banana fritters and other savouries.

Glints of the morning sun danced among the coconut fronds as a warm breeze wafted through this busy happy scene in the compound. The women's chatter and the children's shouts of boisterous laughter danced up the steps of the Datuk's residence, waltzed through the doorways and down the wood-panelled corridors, wriggling through the wooden shutters, till the sounds of their merriment brought a smile to the Datuk's lips. His bedroom was an oasis of peace and quiet compared to the rest of the house. He had completed his morning prayers hours ago when the muezzin's call to prayer rang out from the mosque.

"Allah is great. Allah is merciful. Blessed be His name," he murmured under his breath, thinking what a great match he had made for the daughter of his first wife.

"Send for Datuk Ibrahim," he ordered the maid kneeling patiently by the doorway. "For you," he added, handing her a trinket of gold for her services the night before.

"Thank you, my lord! Thank you for your generosity! Your unworthy slave thanks her lord and master!" The girl, overwhelmed by his gift, kissed his hand and hurried off to search for Ibrahim.

He leaned back against the cushions on the matted floor with an air of complete satisfaction. His daughter's wedding to the son of the menteri of Larut would be the start of a grand alliance. Insya Allah, may it lead to an increase in his influence in the royal court for the good of Perak!

From the window of his bedroom, the future of Bandong Valley appeared bright and sunny, filled with the bounty of the land. The fragrance of aromatic spices wafted in on a light warm breeze. His satisfaction was immeasurably heightened at the sight of Musa Talib walking into the compound with the headman of the White Cranes. The handsome sum he was about to receive from Tai-kor Wong would defray the cost of the wedding and pay for his own ambition. He was worried about the intense rivalry between the White Cranes and the Black Flags. These Chinese leaders were no fools, he thought. Like the barbaric white men, they would grab what they could for themselves. He felt the pressure to do the same, or else he would lose out to other chiefs. Yet he was a descendant of Bugis warriors, not a man of greed. He hoped Bandong Valley would continue to prosper in peace with the tin mined by the Chinese, the taxes collected by his penghulus and the harvests brought in by his farmers and slaves, every man knowing his place under the sun so that the English would have no excuse to take over his beloved valley.

Reports had reached him from the south about how English gunships had bombarded the forts of many Malay chiefs, to stop them from collecting taxes from English-owned vessels passing through their stretch of the river. He had no intention of letting those thieves and their mighty cannons rob him of his heritage. A chief had the right to collect taxes as he pleased, where he pleased and from whom he pleased. A right granted by the sultan! Which almighty spirit had given the English thieves the right to interfere in this country? To take over the land in the name of peace?

By the time Ibrahim entered the bedroom, the Datuk's air of satisfaction and contentment had fled.

"Honoured Father, please accept your unworthy son's greeting. May Allah shower His blessings and grace upon your lordship." Ibrahim's lips lightly brushed his extended hand.

"Thank you, my son. May Allah bless you. Sit down. I've something important to tell you, because one day, Insya Allah, you'll take my place."

"My honourable Father will live for many years, I hope," Ibrahim murmured, his dark eyes following his father.

Datuk Long Mahmud took out a rolled parchment from a wooden chest and handed it to Ibrahim.

"Read it before you accompany your sister to Larut tomorrow."

Ibrahim unrolled the document which bore the seals of the sultan of Negeri Perak and his heir, the *raja muda*.

Be it known that, after due consideration and deliberation with our princes and chiefs, we confirm our bestowal of Bandong Valley, a Province of this Negeri Perak, which we had previously bestowed upon his father, and which we now bestow upon Datuk Seri Long Mahmud and his heirs, to be governed by them and to become their property.

Ibrahim looked up and saw that his father was watching him closely.

"Read on so that you'll know that this valley is ours forever."

A cockfight was about to begin in the compound, and his friends were waiting for him. His cockerel, a ferocious male with the talons of a killer, was going to win the fight today. But a well-bred warrior should never reveal his feelings. So Ibrahim hid his impatience, finished reading and handed the document back to his father.

His father rolled up the document and returned it to the chest. Then he spoke in a soft measured voice, like an old seer who had just seen the future.

"I fear there will be unrest in our land. Blood will be spilled and honourable men will die. It's bound to be so when more than one covets the throne of our land. But I didn't call you in here to speak to you about trouble. I wish to speak to you about learning."

Ibrahim fixed his dark eyes upon his father's face. The Datuk had never spoken to him like this before. He sensed the portentous nature of this talk and listened intently.

"Our world is changing, my son. Ever since the Portuguese set foot on Malacca, the white men have spread like a white disease up and down our land. The Portuguese and the Dutch have departed, but the English predators have taken their place. Their traders are full of greed and lies, and they've ships armed with guns and cannons. Many chiefs had to give up their rights to land and mines before such a mighty power. The sultan will not and cannot fight the white predators. My son, we have the blood of warriors and chiefs coursing through our veins. This land is our land. Even if the world changes, this will not change. But a menteri these days cannot hold his own against the white predators. Many have learned to speak our tongue and turn our words against us. My son, I would like you to learn their tongue and read their writings. So we will know for sure that what they say to us in our tongue is the same as what they write into their books in their own tongue."

"Where will I learn this?"

"In Pulau Pinang. Musa Talib and Che' Wong of the White Cranes are our good friends. They will take you there. Che' Wong's father-in-law, Baba Wee, will make all the necessary arrangements. You'll stay with his family and attend school with his grandchildren. He's given me his word that he will look after you."

"Sparrows live with sparrows; hornbills live with hornbills. If it pleases my honoured Father, your son would rather stay here with you and his own people. Pulau Pinang belongs to the white men now."

"But it's important for my son to learn the ways of the white people so that he can guard the land of his forefathers."

"Honoured Father, your son understands you completely," Ibrahim answered with a sinking heart.

"May Allah bless and protect you always. We'll receive our visitors. Come."

They went out to the airy covered verandah and settled down on the cushions. Ibrahim, his heart heavy with the news he had just received, longed to run off and join the other boys in the compound. He could see that his younger stepbrothers were already up to their monkey tricks, kicking up the dust and chasing one another. How he envied them!

He was going to miss Bandong Valley. The valley with its jungles was his playground. He knew every pond, stream and river by name. Every aged teak or jelutong tree, every big rock or promontory had a story which he had heard from childhood. He had grown up knowing every jinn and spirit that might harm or help him. With one or two companions, he had often pursued the thrill of the hunt, joined in the singing of the winds from the hills and crouched with the silence of the bush waiting for his prey.

"I know you will miss home, my son," Datuk Long Mahmud said softly.

He turned to watch the antics of his younger sons by his two young wives who were commoners of no consequence; for them he need not plan anything. They and their kind would depend on the generosity of the future menteri, like so many others before them. He did not give them another thought and laughed heartily when one of the boys fell to the ground.

"The boy's never still. Like a monkey."

The boy who had fallen was soon howling for vengeance. He punched one of his brothers, and a fight broke out. Ibrahim stood up.

"Let them fight, my son. These boys fight one another as often as they play."

Like their mothers, he thought. These commoners would squawk and scratch like fowl in a coop, but not the daughter of a raja bendahara. Her blood was noble and her breeding superior. He had to admit that his first wife had brought up Ibrahim well. Ibrahim would never roll in the dust with the other boys. His mother had taught him to carry himself like a leader and a warrior of noble blood. His heart swelled with pride when he thought of how, one day, Ibrahim would speak to the English in their own tongue and hold his own against their scheming and plotting.

"Come, let's eat."

He gave the serving girl a smile and was pleased when she lowered her eyes most becomingly and blushed. Slave girls appeared charmingly delicate from afar, like a bloom up in the tree. But when one had picked them, their charm wilted, and they turned coarse like his two commoner wives, who quarrelled daily over their sons.

A sudden crash in the next room cut short his musing. He looked up, his face an ugly scowl.

"Who dares make such a racket while I'm eating?"

Before any of his slaves could reply, there were screams and shouts in the compound.

"The Chinese are killing us!"

Ibrahim sprang to his feet. He had caught the gleam of metal through the bushes. "Run!" he yelled at his siblings.

"Guards! Guards!"

Ibrahim sprinted down the steps of the verandah. Women were rushing around in the compound like hens gathering chicks before an attacking hawk. Ibrahim spied Musa Talib and Tai-kor Wong running towards his father just as the crack of a gunshot rang out from the bushes. Musa Talib lurched forward, ran a few steps and fell, arms and legs splayed out.

Tai-kor Wong plunged into the dense vegetation for cover. Then he ran into one of the nearby houses and out again through the back, yelling at the top of his voice in Malay.

"Black Flags! The Hakka Black Flags are attacking us!"

He dived for cover again just as a spear whistled inches from his face. He fell to the ground and crawled on his belly through the thick lallang. Another spear found its mark and a Malay guard crashed heavily onto him.

Armed Hakka miners were smashing through the Datuk's defences and swarming into the compound. The Malay villagers and guards were fighting back with whatever weapons they could lay their hands on.

The White Crane miners, caught by surprise, were joining in the melee. But in the noise and confusion, it was hard to tell White Cranes and Black Flags apart. In their panic, the Malay villagers were hacking at all Chinese in their path.

Down by the river, a group of the Datuk's warriors were storming through a Chinese mob, their gleaming parangs slicing the grass shields of the miners. But a boatload of Black Flag coolies soon outnumbered and overwhelmed the Malay soldiers. They fired volley after volley of gunshots from the boat and set fire to the jetty.

In the village centre, another Black Flag mob surrounded Kuala Bandong's only police station. The beleaguered police guards tried to fend off their attacks, but a fiery arrow hissed through the air and landed on the station's attap roof in a burst of flames. The policemen fled. More Black Flags fanned out and set fire to several houses along the waterfront.

"Kill the rapists!" the Black Flag leader roared.

"Kill the pigs!" the captain of the Malay guards rallied his soldiers as they fended off their attackers valiantly.

Swords and parangs clashed amidst the overturned pots of curries and open fires. The leader of the Black Flags charged up the steps to the verandah. Without a moment's hesitation, the Datuk pulled out his dagger and hurled it in an arc. It hit the Black Flag leader in the neck and he fell, rolling down the steps. Two other fighters immediately leapt up the steps to take their leader's place. They lunged at the Datuk with their swords. He leapt backwards out of their way, but not before one of them had stabbed him in the shoulder as he fought off the other with his long kris. Ibrahim rushed to his father's aid. The Datuk shoved him aside.

"Go save your mother and sister!"

Several Black Flags were climbing over the balustrade. The Datuk swung around with the sharp instinct of a warrior. Swiftly he threw himself to one side of the sword coming at his throat but was knocked off balance. An arrow ripped into the Black Flag's back. The Datuk tried to scramble away, but the fallen fighter caught hold of his leg and brought him crashing to the ground. With a violent kick, he broke free. A second Black Flag lunged at him with axe held high. Another arrow whistled through the air and hit him in the chest. The man dropped his axe and howled with rage and pain as he tore at the arrow's shaft. A second arrow pierced the Black Flag in the throat. Blood gushed out of his mouth. Eyes wide with fear and shock, he choked and crashed forward. A third Black Flag jumped into the battle and slashed the Datuk on the arm. His kris fell out of his hand. The Black Flag hacked downwards, but a timely spear pierced him in the belly. Tai-kor Wong pulled the Datuk out of the way.

"Follow me!" he shouted in Malay.

A roar of gunfire burst forth from the mosque. Hundreds of Malay warriors poured into the compound. The Black Flags, seeing that they were outnumbered, fled from the scene.

"Praise be to Allah, Che' Wong! These are the soldiers of my son-in-law!"

Chapter Fourteen

"*B*ring back any wounded Black Flag. Shoot those who are dying. Allah has been merciful."

Soldiers and villagers cheered.

"Victory is ours! We'll expel the Black Flags from our valley, Che' Wong."

"This is great news for the White Cranes, your lordship."

"Che' Wong, it's the least I can do. You risked your life to save mine."

"The Black Flag is my enemy too."

"Honoured Father, Che' Musa Talib is alive!" Ibrahim announced.

Several soldiers staggered in under the weight of the fat trader, who was lying on a makeshift carrier.

"Praise be to His Most Compassionate! Your unworthy slave lives to attend the wedding of your heroic son-in-law and daughter!"

"You ox! I thought you'd gone off to your Creator when I left you lying in that lallang patch!" Tai-kor Wong laughed.

"I was shot in the leg, but I did not lose the use of my head. So I just lay where I fell, and the Black Flags ignored me. But my lord, I didn't forget to pray to His Most Compassionate to protect my friends."

"While you were praying, Che' Wong was like a brother to me. He risked his life to save mine. Che' Wong, my blood brother!"

Datuk Long Mahmud clasped Tai-kor Wong's hand. It took everyone by surprise for he was a reserved man. The person most surprised naturally was Tai-kor Wong himself. He bowed again and again, modestly disclaiming any extraordinary effort on his part.

"Your Lordship, thank you, thank you!"

"Tonight we celebrate our victory and friendship! Tomorrow I will expel the Black Flags and you, Che' Wong, will go with Musa to the land by the Bandong River and select a site of ... let's say ... one thousand acres to build your house."

"I ... I don't know what to say."

"No need to say anything. We're brothers now, and I will be a White Crane too."

"Is everyone in the family safe, my lord?" Musa called out from his stretcher, gesturing impatiently to the men to put him down, which they promptly did, glad to be relieved of their load.

"Thanks be to Allah! Everyone is safe. The Black Flags failed to enter the women's apartments. And Musa, one hundred acres of land is yours for praying for my safety."

"Thank you, my lord! Your unworthy slave pledges his loyalty to you forever!"

"My lord! We've caught a Black Flag!"

The captain of the army knelt before the Datuk. "Three hundred men dead. One hundred of them are Black Flags. We killed another sixty-one who were dying. Then we found this dog hiding in the lallang."

He pushed the Black Flag forward. The young man, aged sixteen or seventeen, lay on the ground, bleeding from several knife wounds and a gunshot wound in his shoulder. He made no answer when the captain questioned him. Enraged, the Malay captain caught hold of his queue and pulled him to his feet. He drew out his kris.

"Answer! You dog!"

"Wait!" Tai-kor Wong intervened. "With your lordship's permission, allow me to question this dog in his own tongue."

"Proceed."

"Listen carefully, dog," Tai-kor Wong said in Cantonese. "These Malays are worse than the Manchu dogs back home. They whip their enemies with a bamboo dipped in the juice of a poisonous plant. First you'll itch as if bitten by a thousand ants. Then you'll burn with a thousand fires, and your flesh will rot away. They will not send you to your ancestors straightaway unless you tell them why the Black Flags attacked them. Speak and I'll see to it that you will not be whipped with this poisonous bamboo."

The wounded man blurted, "They raped our women! We want to avenge the honour of our women!"

"What did he say?"

Before Tai-kor Wong could answer the Datuk, Ah Fook came running into the compound with several White Crane miners.

"Tai-kor! Our men raped some Hakka women. And the Black Flags attacked our village and burned everything! Lee Peng Yam and several elders have been killed! The rest have scattered or are dying!"

At this, Tai-kor Wong turned and killed the wounded man with a thrust of his dagger.

II

STRIPPED AND SHORN
1875

Chapter Fifteen

It was the hour before dawn when the sky was still a dark slate grey over Penang island. The muezzins in the mosques were summoning the faithful to prayer, their grave tonal voices trailing over the rooftops of the sleeping town. As the Muslim immigrants from Kedah, India, Sumatra and Arabia knelt upon their prayer mats facing Mecca, the aged caretaker of the Goddess of Mercy Temple was planting joss sticks in the urns of ash on the altar, while a grey-robed monk bowed his shaven head and chanted prayers for the souls of the nameless thousands who had left China to work but had died on this island.

Along the sea front where the towkays had built their great houses, the lamps were lit in Baba Wee's study in the upper storey of his mansion and he was already at his desk going through the business of the day. About sixty, he was the quintessential Baba from an old Malacca family who spoke Baba Malay and Hokkien with ease, as well as a smattering of Cantonese, English and Thai. He wore a queue and was dressed like a Chinese from China. He was, however, educated in the Malay language like his brothers and cousins and wrote his letters in a fine flowing Jawi script. He took great pride in the *Berita Peranakan*, the first Baba newspaper in the Straits Settlements published and edited by his younger brother.

Although of Chinese immigrant stock, Baba Wee regarded himself a native son. He was born to a family of prominent merchants whose forebears had settled in the Malaccan sultanate before it was conquered by the Portuguese in 1511. They had planted their roots in the Malay Peninsula, married Malay and Batak women and raised their children in their new homeland. Their bones and the bones of their descendants were interred not in China but in Bukit China, the hill overlooking the Portuguese fort in Malacca. His great-grandfather and grandfather had held high positions in society and had been appointed the agents of several Malay rajas and princes. The Wee family, like many great Baba families, had joint ventures with these rajas, and from its base in Malacca it had branched out into other parts of the Malay Peninsula. Twenty years ago, Baba Wee had moved his family to Penang where he owned several large plantations. His business had expanded north into Kedah and Perak. He was also the agent of the raja of Batung and the menteri of Bandong. His advice was often sought by the Malay princes, as well as by the lieutenant governor of Penang, who regarded him as a leader of the Chinese community.

A light knock on his door made him look up from his papers.

"Good morning, Father-in-law, and good health to you."

Tai-kor Wong made a deep bow as a mark of his great respect.

"Sit down. Many things I want to talk to you about. You came back only one, two months ago?" He spoke rapidly in Hokkien with the distinctive lilt of the Malaccan Babas.

"About three months ago, Father-in-law."

"All kinds of rumours are reaching my ears these days. Things I didn't hear from you. So I thought I'd better hear from you first before we go into town."

Tai-kor Wong's heart sank. He wondered what the old man had heard. But his father-in-law had returned to his papers and did not look up for a long while. He was left standing like a schoolboy before his schoolmaster. He swallowed hard and wondered if this was a subtle display of ill humour. Humbly he remained standing, even though he had been invited to sit down on one of the high-back chairs. He had never felt at ease in this room, which was furnished in the English style, with furniture imported from London. The walls were lined with shelves and cabinets of sombre wood, and the large Victorian desk before which he was standing marked the great divide between him and his father-in-law, benefactor and employer. He thought of his utter dependence on his father-in-law's good graces and chaffed at being so tied to the old man. And yet, had it not been for Baba Wee, who gave him his first break as a petty trader, he would still be a penniless coolie labouring on the wharf like the thousands now crowding into town ever since the troubles broke out in the tin mines. After giving him a job as a foreman in his shipping company, Baba Wee sent him into the interior of Perak to do some trading with the Malays. After he had successfully organised the riverboats, with the help of Musa Talib, to send supplies to the miners in Bandong, Baba Wee had picked him to be his son-in-law. Shortly after that, he was appointed Tai-kor of the White Cranes in Bandong. He knew that his appointment had rattled many people, among them Baba Wee's first wife and her sons.

When Baba Wee finally looked up from his papers, his face was grave and his manner formal.

"Our friends in the English courthouse told me that the Black Flags sent another petition to the tuan besar governor. They accuse us, the White Cranes, of conspiring with the menteri of Bandong to destroy their tin mines and plunder their village. Making thousands homeless and jobless. Worse, they named your trading partner, Inche Musa Talib, as a gunrunner. That Che' Musa, in violation of Penang's laws, supplied you and the menteri with arms and ammunition secretly purchased here. They've asked the tuan besar governor to stop him."

Tai-kor Wong smiled, relieved it wasn't about Wong-soh and Tuck Heng. Fat Musa must've enjoyed himself making a fool of the English navy, he thought. English gunships were far too heavy and large. Musa's boats must have given them the slip in the shallows of the Dindings. Good! That fat ox could always be depended on to run an English blockade.

"Father-in-law, Che' Musa would be unable to buy guns and ammunition if English merchants didn't bring them in without their government's knowledge."

"I can't tell the tuan besar governor that. How can I let him lose face?"

"Then we have to remind him that the Black Flags attacked first. Our men were killed off like flies! Our women who were left behind were captured by the Black Flags and raped! We were defeated because we didn't have enough guns and ammunition. I'd warned Lee Peng Yam earlier but that fool didn't listen!"

Tai-kor Wong paused to control his anger which threatened to rise each time he mentioned the scoundrel. That vain cock's ambition had cost lives and started a major war in Bandong Valley. He'd found out too late about the assault and rape of the Hakka women. Upon reaching Penang, the first thing he did was to swear all the Bandong White Cranes to silence. Not even Baba Wee was told. If news of the dastardly act leaked out, not only would the White Cranes lose face, but Baba Wee would lose his high standing with the governor.

"Father-in-law, we also have to remind the tuan besar governor that the menteri of Bandong tried to expel the Black Flags because they attacked Kuala Bandong. Ever since I saved his life, the Datuk has provided the White Cranes with arms and soldiers to fight the Black Flags. This is not a conspiracy. It's help given by one brother to another."

"My friends in the English courthouse told me that the Black Flags attacked the Datuk because his men ambushed and raped their women. Now is this true?"

A long pause.

"Father-in-law, the truth is this: Lee Peng Yam's men disguised themselves as Malays and raped the Hakka women."

"What?" Baba Wee could barely control his rage. "Why didn't you tell me?" he bellowed.

Tai-kor Wong was sure that the entire household must have heard him. But he kept his own voice low and calm.

"I wanted to protect you. What you don't know, you can't tell the tuan besar governor. Then he can't accuse you of condoning Lee Peng Yam. The scoundrel acted against my orders! I know other people say I'm a scoundrel too. That

I hide things from you. Let them say! I shut my ears and do what I think is right!"

Baba Wee permitted himself a smile. Once again he felt that he had made the right choice in choosing this blunt-speaking China-born as his son-in-law. He disliked men who tried to be subtle in speech and long-winded in coming to the point, even though well-bred Malays and Babas considered it a sign of ill-breeding if a man spoke bluntly.

He took a different view of things. The shrewd old Baba knew that a lowly China-born he raised to a high position in the family business would be utterly grateful and loyal to him, even more loyal than his own sons, the spoilt brats he was cursed with. Tai-kor Wong could be entrusted to safeguard the family's fortunes. His own flesh and blood took more interest in bird-rearing and cockfighting. He sighed inwardly at the thought of his pampered sons.

"Sit down. Tell me everything. From head to tail."

Relieved that his father-in-law's mood had changed for the better, Tai-kor Wong sat on one of the high-back chairs, looking quite uncomfortable as he reported on Lee Peng Yam's despicable act.

"A man can't trust his underlings fully. Right or not?"

"Right, Father-in-law. I must return to Bandong."

"The tuan besar governor is calling for a meeting in a few days' time. Wait till this is over."

"Are they sending soldiers into Bandong then?"

"Who knows? Every clan leader and Malay raja from Perak has been asked to attend this meeting. But the Datuk won't come. He has asked me to represent him. If the Datuk finds out the truth about the rape, then all our good relations with him will be lost. You're right to swear your men to secrecy."

There was a light knock on the door. The head servant came in to inform them that the rest of the family was waiting in the ancestral hall.

"You go down and tell Tua Neo I'm busy."

Chapter Sixteen

*T*ua Neo, first wife of Baba Wee, was already in the ancestral hall. Stern-faced and hawk-eyed, she watched the amahs and maids bringing in trays of food and vases of fresh flowers for the monthly thanksgiving feast, which was Tua Neo's delectable reminder to the spirits to continue to shower their blessings on Baba Wee, his family and his enterprises. She was a strong believer in the efficacy of wining and dining the gods in order to win favours from them.

"Protect them, Lord Buddha! Please let young and old leave home without fear of harm or misfortune!"

She was meticulous and exacting about her offerings to the gods. If a dish was not well-cooked or if it was sloppily presented, she would ferret out the offender, be it cook, amah or bondmaid, and have her caned without mercy. Sloppiness might offend the gods and ancestors and cause them to withdraw their blessings from the family.

A handsome Nonya from a rich Baba family, she cut a striking figure in her elaborately embroidered *baju panjang* of thin voile which reached below her knees. It was worn over a rich batik sarong, and pinned down the centre, holding the folds of the baju together, were three large gold and diamond *kerosang*, brooches, of a floral design. Her dark well-oiled hair was combed back and fashioned into a *sanggul sipot*, a snail-shaped chignon, held by three gold claw-shaped hairpins. Diamond earrings and gold chains and bracelets adorned her person, and on her feet she wore a pair of *kasut manek-manek*, beaded slippers, made by one of her daughters-in-law.

"Tua Neo, good morning," Baba Wee's second wife greeted her and bowed in deference to her authority in the household. "I hope all the dishes are pleasing to you this morning."

"Hmm."

She listened attentively while Ee Neo dutifully reported what went on in the kitchen wing, prattling as was her habit about this and that in the singsong patois, stumbling over the Hokkien and Malay words because, as Tua Neo had sniffed to her own relations years ago, the conniving little witch was a Cantonese China-born who had been very poorly brought up and could never speak properly.

Ee Neo was not a highborn Nonya but she wore a baju panjang too, though it was a plain one befitting her lower status. The daughter of a poor trader, she had no dowry and was dependent on the generosity of Tua Neo. Ee Neo's pinched face hinted of suffering despite the smile on her face. Her movements as she cleaned the oil lamps on the altar were small and quick like a bird's, eager to please and quick to hop out of harm's way.

"And so I said to cook, 'Look and see properly lah,' I said. 'Use your eyes and taste-taste a bit! Not that I want to make trouble for you,' I said. 'But if you can't get the chicken curry right, not too hot, not too oily, the way Tua Neo wants it, then I can't keep quiet about it. I'll have to tell Tua Neo about it,' I said," she prattled on as she rubbed the brass lamp till it shone. Then she lit the wick and placed the lamp on the altar, making sure she left no fingermarks on its stand.

Tua Neo's three daughters-in-law came in, attended by their personal bondmaids. By then the sky had lightened and Tua Neo's face had darkened.

"A filial daughter-in-law rises before the sun to serve tea to her parents-in-law." Tua Neo's voice was loud enough for all to hear. "Properly trained and properly brought-up daughters rise before dawn. That was what I did when I was a daughter-in-law."

"Tua Neo, good morning and good health. Please accept this cup of tea," First Daughter-in-law murmured soothingly as she bowed and served the matriarch, showing by manner and voice that she was pliant and obedient and was not offended at all by her mother-in-law's remarks.

Gratified, Tua Neo sipped the hot fragrant tea and handed the cup back to First Daughter-in-law, who took the cup and handed it to her bondmaid. Second and Third Daughters-in-law greeted Tua Neo in turn, murmuring the same words of greeting and respect, and served her a cup of tea too, re-enacting the ritual they had observed every morning since they crossed the threshold as wives of Baba Wee's sons. After they had served Tua Neo, they turned to Ee Neo and greeted her respectfully. They did not serve her tea, for Tua Neo had insisted on the strict observance of tradition, which decreed that difference should always be maintained between first and second wives.

Moments later Siok Ching came in with Tai-kor Wong and their three sons.

"Tua Neo," she greeted Tua Neo first before greeting her own mother. "Ee Mak, good morning."

Her sons followed her example and greeted First Grandmother before greeting Second Grandmother. Tai-kor Wong did the same and gave Tua Neo a deep bow as a sign of his great respect for her. When he turned to Ee Neo, he adjusted the tenor and tone of his greeting so that it conveyed politeness but not warmth or deep respect. He was mindful of not offending Tua Neo while they were enjoying her hospitality. It would be months before his own house could be repaired and made habitable again. He cursed the Black Flags. If not for them, he wouldn't have to watch his words and actions quite so carefully.

"Good morning," he greeted his sisters-in-law. He tried to sound as courteous as he could, enquiring after their husbands who were sleeping late as usual. Despite his attire and courtesy, they had never accepted him as a Baba gentleman. Damn it, he thought, he always felt like a labourer's son in Wee Mansion no matter how he behaved or what he wore! His maroon silk tunic and black silk pants, worn at Siok Ching's insistence, discomfited him. Their silky softness and the tunic's row of hand-sewn frog buttons with pearls down the front made him feel like the proverbial *Sar Sum Siew*, the rich spoilt brat, especially now that his queue was well-oiled and neatly plaited. Siok Ching had insisted he wear the black velvet shoes worn by the men in her family. "They're towkay shoes and you're a towkay now," she'd reminded him. "Don't forget, your surname is the same as Father's. Same character. Different sounds. In Hokkien, we say Wee. In Cantonese, you say Wong." She had sounded very pleased with her discovery for it implied that her husband was almost a son of Baba Wee.

As always, she was trying to make the best of their marriage. After all, he was the illiterate son of a half-starved peasant and she was the daughter of Baba Wee. Although Siok Ching's mother was just a concubine, she still counted for something as the secondary wife of a rich man. Siok Ching herself had been taught to read and write. Being no scholar, the Chinese characters were too much for his head although he realised their importance in society. He was not a learned gentleman like the Wee brothers. In Bandong, among his coolies and miners, he did feel like a gentleman. But not here. Not next to his brothers-in-law. He knew that his lowly origins pained Siok Ching sometimes. So when she insisted on being accorded the status of first wife, even though he had married Wong-soh earlier, he had agreed readily, feeling that somehow he had to make it up to her for marrying a coolie. Not that she had had a choice. It was Baba Wee's decision.

"Son-in-law, is something worrying you?" Tua Neo was solicitous.

"No, no, Tua Neo. I must apologise for being a little late in coming down. I was talking with Father-in-law."

"No need to apologise for talking with your father-in-law. I wish my own sons were talking with their father too! But what to do? They are not as clever as some people in using their tongues."

"Brother-in-law, no need to apologise for being late. Important people can come late, only not so important ones must come early." First Sister-in-law gave everyone a saccharine smile.

"How right, our First Sister-in-law! My eldest brother must be the most important man in the family. He doesn't come down at all. Not even when Father is here," Siok Ching's saccharine sweetness matched her sister-in-law's.

"If we followed tradition the way we've been taught by Tua Neo," Second Sister-in-law drawled with a slight toss of her head, "we'd all know the proper thing to do. In some families, things are so confusing we don't even know who's the first wife or second wife, who's the son and who's only adopted."

Tai-kor Wong started. He glanced at Second Sister-in-law. The witch smiled at him like a cat toying with a mouse.

"What're you talking about?"

"Nothing, Tua Neo, nothing! My words came out before I could stop myself. It's something I heard from my relatives and it concerns our family."

"Second Sister-in-law, you'd better say it here, otherwise other people will accuse you of talking behind their backs," First Sister-in-law advised her.

"What have you heard? Tell me," Tua Neo ordered.

Second Sister-in-law glanced furtively at Siok Ching's impassive face. Then, lowering her eyes, she spoke in a soft voice that had a hint of mockery. "Please forgive me, Siok Ching, and I apologise to our brother-in-law too. My tongue was faster than my thoughts. Yesterday I went to the Goddess of Mercy Temple to pray and I met my relative who told me that the first wife of our brother-in-law had just brought her adopted son there. I was shocked! Our Siok Ching is the first wife of Tai-kor Wong. So how can there be two first wives?"

"Liar!"

"Wait, Siok Ching!" But she had already run out of the ancestral hall.

Tua Neo glared at Ee Neo as if it was all her fault for having such a daughter.

"Forgive us, gods in heaven! It's the day of thanksgiving! A prayer day, a good-luck day! And your daughter runs away!"

"Ee Neo, don't just stand there. Light the joss sticks!" First Sister-in-law ordered. Then turning to Tua Neo, she said sweetly, "Neo, please don't wear yourself out with worry. Take care of your health. I'll call the children to come in and we can begin prayers."

As soon as prayers were over, Ee Neo slipped upstairs to Baba Wee's room. Closing the door behind her, she stood silently, waiting for her husband to notice her, marvelling at her own boldness these days. When she was younger she wouldn't have dared to enter Baba Wee's room without being summoned. But over the years, she had gained courage as Baba Wee and Tua Neo had mellowed and she was used more kindly by both. For this, she was grateful to the gods who had heard her prayers. Let them hear her prayers for her daughter now!

"What is it?" Baba Wee finally looked up from his papers.

"So sorry to trouble you, Ba, but it's … it's about my daughter … I mean … your daughter, Siok Ching, who married Tai-kor Wong," she spoke in a quick nervous voice, tripping over her words.

Her eyes reddened as she tried to press down the rising pain in her throat. She feared that her only daughter might soon be relegated to the lowly position of a second wife if Tai-kor Wong's China-born wife were to stay on the island. Then remembering how Baba Wee disliked weepy women, she blinked away her tears and pushed aside the painful memories of the indignities she had suffered as a young concubine of little consequence. She forced a smile upon her face and couched her request in words carefully chosen not to offend Baba Wee.

She started her speech by expressing her gratitude to Baba Wee for taking her away from a poor family to raise her to great heights in such an illustrious household. She would never have attained such a high position in this world if Baba Wee hadn't looked kindly upon her unworthy self, and she was eternally grateful to Baba Wee for making her his second wife. Then she thanked him for clothing her in silk and jewellery.

"Go on, go on. What is it?" Baba Wee shook his head impatiently.

"Begging Ba's indulgence respectfully, I've to point out that Siok Ching is born and raised in the lap of luxury as befitting the daughter of a man of great wealth and prestige. And so," she hesitated just a moment before putting it to him bluntly, "how can she be known as second wife of Tai-kor Wong? Our family and relatives know that Siok Ching is not a second wife but other people will gossip about her. That barren woman has even brought her fifteen-year-old adopted son along!" She stopped when she caught her voice rising higher than usual. She glanced at Baba Wee, expecting a sharp rebuke.

No word came from him. He seemed to be deep in thought, his eyes on the paper on his table. He glanced at the bowed figure of the mother of his child. Dark anxious eyes peered out of her pinched sallow face. The pale lips were tremulous. With great difficulty, he recalled that the trembling woman before him was once a young girl with soft lips, soft arms and a yielding body. He had made the mistake of summoning her to his bed once too often in those early years and an incensed Tua Neo had whipped Ee Neo after each night in his bed. After several whippings, he had felt so sorry for Ee Neo that he stopped asking for her and went to the houses of pleasure instead.

"I'll speak to my son-in-law. Go. Tell the syce to bring round the gharry." He dismissed her with an impatient wave of his hand.

Tai-kor Wong's heart sank when he was summoned. He knew that the onus was upon him to resolve the matter of his two wives.

"Father-in-law," he began, "my China-born woman is here. She came with the rest of the Bandong miners a few months ago. I did not ask her to come."

He paused and waited. When Baba Wee remained silent, he went on, "Siok Ching is my first wife. I've always said so and I've not changed."

He paused again and waited. But Baba Wee remained adamantly silent as if waiting for something more.

"Father-in-law, I truly regret any unhappiness I've caused the family. I've already made plans for her to return to China. On the next junk which leaves for Kwangtung in two days."

"Good, Son-in-law. My heart is ten times lighter now." Baba Wee smiled. "But there's one more thing. People say this boy, Wong Tuck Heng, is your eldest son."

"I recognise no sons! Except the three boys your daughter gave me!"

"So what I've heard is totally wrong."

"My China-born woman adopted the boy without my permission! She has been doing far too many things behind my back! It's only out of respect for my parents that I keep her!" Tai-kor Wong did not try to hide the anger rising in him.

"If a man's house is not in order, he won't have the peace of mind to go about his business. Every home should have only one head. Father and husband. Every kitchen also should have only one head, and that is the first wife, mother of all his children and the children of his other wives. Otherwise there'll be no peace."

"Father-in-law, I've always considered Siok Ching my first wife."

"We'll not talk about this again. Come, we have to leave after breakfast. We must talk to the other White Crane elders before I meet with the tuan besar governor."

Chapter Seventeen

*T*emple Street near the docks was the meeting place of the gainfully employed and the desperately unemployed. Hundreds of miners who had fled from the troubles in Bandong Valley, Larut and elsewhere, had converged on the area. The back lanes and side lanes were choked with idle men. They squatted beside the open drains, shoved their way along the five-foot paths, overflowed onto the roads and blocked the progress of pushcarts, rickshaws, buggies, gharries and bullock carts inching their way through the heart of the trading district. All were hoping to earn a few cents to buy the day's bowl of rice. But jobs were scarce.

Traders and merchants were jittery about their investments in the turbulent Malay states. The town was full of rumours. To the few policemen patrolling the area, mainly Sikhs and Amboynese employed in the colonial police department, the babble of Chinese tongues was incomprehensible. They walked through the throng, unseeing and unhearing. They did not see the knots of coolies swelling. Neither did they hear talk of murder and slaughter nor rumours of impending war between the Hakka and Cantonese miners.

"Tai-kor Wong was killed in bed! His head chopped off and flung out the window!"

"The gods have eyes!"

"Let the White Cranes taste our sword of vengeance!"

"Kill those sons of pigs! How many of our brothers have they killed, eh? How many, I ask you?"

As the morning wore on, the talk grew more virulent and strident. Tales of past battles were recalled and relived. Venom and rage spread among the coolies, smiting the knots of men huddled in the shadows. The sun rose higher in the cloudless sky and soon not many patches of shade were left. More coolies squeezed into the covered walkways of the shops. Tempers ran short. A word here, a word there; a few words overheard and repeated; an imagined insult, a stare, a push and a jab in the ribs, and before anyone knew it, something had ignited the tinderbox. A scuffle broke out just as Baba Wee's gharry swung into view.

A young coolie was pushed into its path. The two horses neighed and reared up. The Indian driver was nearly knocked off his seat.

"Whoa! Whoa!"

"Look out!" Other gharry drivers fought to control their horses too. Shouts and curses rang out on all sides.

Baba Wee's Indian driver swore at the startled coolie and raised his horsewhip in a threatening gesture. Men started running towards the gharry. The horses grew jumpy and tremulous. They pawed the ground nervously as the coolies swarmed round them.

"Back off! Back off!" The Indian driver raised his whip again.

Several coolies yelled at him and threatened to beat him up for insulting their friend. They advanced with poles in their hands. More coolies joined them, swelling the crowd. The gharry was hemmed in on all sides. The mob jostled and pushed, rocking the vehicle from side to side.

Inside the covered gharry, Baba Wee froze in his seat. He couldn't understand the Hakka words spoken but he knew that the coolies were Black Flags.

"Get us out of here!"

"Can't!" Tai-kor Wong hissed. "The dogs have surrounded us!"

The two men conferred rapidly in Hokkien. "Run!" Tai-kor Wong shouted to the Indian driver as he pulled Baba Wee out of the gharry and pushed his way through the crowd.

"Hoi! That's the White Crane head! Catch the bastard!"

A thunderous roar rose from the mob. They set upon the two men. Passers-by fled. Stalls were overturned and some rickshaws were smashed. Fifty White Crane warriors emerged from their headquarters down the road. Armed with bamboo poles, they fended off the mob's attack on their leaders.

Tuck Heng, his arm still in a bandage, plunged into the fray. He swung his bamboo pole and knocked the teeth out of two Hakka coolies blocking his way. He grabbed hold of Baba Wee just as a group of pole wielders surrounded the frightened old man. Tuck Heng lunged at them and cracked several heads. Then he pulled Baba Wee after him and sprinted towards the White Crane building. Several blows, aimed at Baba Wee, landed on Tuck Heng's shoulders. But he managed to pull Baba Wee up the steps and hustled him into the safety of the clan's hall just as shouts of "Police! Police!" sent the attacking mob scattering down the street.

Within minutes, the crowd had melted. Temple Street and all its side lanes and back lanes were emptied of people. A force of thirty uniformed policemen, many of whom were burly turbaned Sikhs, marched down the road, armed with *rotans*, canes and rattan shields. No one knew whether it was the sight of the white man leading the group or the Sikhs which had miraculously dispersed the mob of several hundred.

Baba Wee, pale from the shock of his experience, emerged from the White Crane building accompanied by Tai-kor Wong and Chan Ah Fook.

"Sergeant Thomson!"

The Englishman hesitated. Then a look of recognition came into his eyes. Baba Wee was well-known for the grand party he held for the Europeans in Penang every year.

"I hope no harm has come to you, sir."

"Thank you, Sergeant Thomson. You and your men have

saved my life," Baba Wee replied in his best English as he shook hands with the young man.

Tai-kor Wong, standing beside his father-in-law, was aware that keen eyes behind the wooden shutters of shophouses peering through the slits of the windows in the upper storeys were taking in everything, especially the handshake between Baba Wee and the representative of British authority in Penang. The significance of the handshake was not lost on Tai-kor Wong. He stuck out his hand and murmured in his best English, "Tank you, Kapitan Tomsen."

Chan Ah Fook, taking the cue from his leader, repeated loud enough for all to hear, "Tank you, Kapitan Tomsen!"

"Tank you."

"Tank you."

"I shall call upon the lieutenant governor and thank him personally for maintaining such an effective police force on the island. As a member of the trading community here, I'm very grateful to your men and I shall see that your effort does not remain unknown."

"Why, thank you, sir, that's most kind of you." The young sergeant blushed.

His youth, his inexperience, being a recent arrival to the colony, and his background as the son of a poor clergyman made him susceptible to their courteous bowing and respectful mutterings of "Thank you, thank you." The young sergeant was so overwhelmed by the old man's courtesy and gratitude that when the Indian driver returned with his gharry and horses, he promptly helped Baba Wee into the vehicle. The dignified old Baba smiled and thanked him before driving away, leaving the Englishman completely oblivious of the way he had been manipulated into demonstrating support for the White Cranes. For the sight of an English officer from the colonial police force shaking hands with an elder of the White Cranes and helping him into his gharry could not fail but leave an indelible impression on all the watchers. Tai-kor Wong and Chan Ah Fook could hardly suppress their smiles. The prestige of the White Cranes had risen as high as the heavens.

"Did you see that? Your father-in-law, nobody can match him in cunning. Those Hakka swine will think twice now before they attack us."

"Right, right!" Tai-kor Wong chuckled. "My old fox led the red-haired devil like a puppy on a string. Did you see how the puppy danced? These barbarians are so stupid!"

"Tai-kor, don't look down on them. I used to think they were stupid too. But I've heard their queen is cunning as a fox spirit! She's got more guns and ships than our Empress Dowager. If our Old Buddha is like their queen, then she can throw all the foreigners out of China!"

"Watch your tongue, old man!"

"It's true. The Old Buddha is senile!"

"Enough, old man! One day you'll go home and the Manchu dogs will sniff you out and kill you!"

Tai-kor Wong shook his head. Ah Fook's heretical ideas could land him in trouble, even death by beheading. Spies were always on the lookout for anti-Manchu elements, especially in the city of Kwangtung. He himself was no supporter of the Manchus, but his Chinese soul believed that the Son of Heaven was indeed superior to all other rulers in the world. He recoiled instinctively from the thought that the red-haired queen of the foreign devils was cleverer and wiser than the Empress Dowager of China. Impossible! If it was true, it'd turn his world upside-down. He was shocked by Ah Fook's irreverence. Yet, at the same time, he was drawn irresistibly to it. The blood of generations of rebellious Cantonese flowed strongly through his veins. Heresy attracted him and heretical ideas once uttered could not remain motionless in his mind. They rocked and agitated his thoughts. Rumours, gossip, bits of news of recent events in China crowded into his head as he listened to Ah Fook's argument that the Manchus were losing ground to the red-haired foreign devils. Chinese ships had been sunk by the English navy off the coast of Shanghai two months ago. The Germans had landed in Shantung and defeated a Chinese army led by a great Qing general. The imperial eunuch, Admiral Ying Min, had just lost an important naval battle to the foreign devils because there were not enough ships and ammunition. The news startled him.

"So … ah … so…" He struggled to accept the fact that Ah Fook's view was not so untenable in these troubled times.

"Tai-kor! Is the Manchu court a Chinese court? The Empress Dowager and the emperor are not Han Chinese. Have you forgotten the glory of Ming?"

"Not so loud, old man!"

"What's there to be afraid of? Death? Thousands have died. If I don't die today, I'll die tomorrow. But one day we'll restore the glory of Ming and the Han people! "

"Old friend, be careful with your tongue!"

"This is Penang, not China! Do I talk like this to every son of a dog? Except to Tuck Heng. The boy's a hero now."

"Tuck Heng! Tuck Heng! I've heard nothing but Tuck Heng!"

"What're you complaining about? Look, he's cured my bad leg." Ah Fook pulled up his trousers and showed him the patch of black herbs Tuck Heng had plastered on his old wound.

Tai-kor Wong swore under his breath.

"Save your curses for later, Tai-kor! Wong-soh is waiting for you. She's adopted Tuck Heng."

"Let her wait! That bitch always does things first, then tells me later! Now she's gone and adopted the boy and expects me to accept him as my son too! Did I say I needed a son? Did I?"

Poor Wong-soh, Tuck Heng thought. Increasingly of late, she had sounded more combative in her speech as though she was looking for a quarrel. Several of the women and their children had already had a taste of her acid tongue. He felt her pain. Away from Sum Hor and China and without the support of her village elders, Wong-soh was a woman of no consequence. In the new land, her clansmen were powerless immigrants like her, entirely dependent on Straits-born Chinese like Baba Wee.

"Tuck Heng!" Ah Loy bounded up the stairs. "Prepare yourself for the worst. Everyone is saying that Tai-kor will never agree."

"I only pray that our Tai-kor has a big heart. More for Wong-ma's sake than mine."

"But she has acted very rashly. Everybody said so."

He had no answer to that. What Ah Loy said was true. But what had been done before the gods could not be undone.

"They're in the hall now. Don't raise your hopes. You're going to fall."

"'If you fall, grab a handful of mud when you rise,' my mother used to say. Some good can be wrested from even the worst of circumstances." He smiled, putting on a bold front. "Worse things have happened to me before. Yet I've survived. The gods will protect me."

It did seem to him that the gods and ancestral spirits had crossed the ocean with him to protect him. Wong-soh, he believed, had been chosen by the spirits of his ancestors to be his adoptive mother. If all had been planned by the deities and fated to happen, then a man would have to learn to accept whatever life lay before him. If it was his fate to be Tai-kor Wong's son, then so he was; if not, nothing he did would make a difference.

Voices rose from the stairwell; before they knew it, Tai-kor Wong, Chan Ah Fook and Wong-soh had entered their room. Ah Loy slipped out but Tuck Heng remained standing by the window. No one noticed him. Tai-kor Wong was sputtering with rage as he spoke, not to Wong-soh, but to Ah Fook who

Chapter Eighteen

Tuck Heng withdrew from the shuttered window. Destiny was coming up the steps. If Tai-kor Wong refused to accept him as his adopted son, he would die of shame. The whole White Crane kongsi knew that Wong-soh had adopted him during their flight down the River Bandong.

The murmur of voices along the passageway rose higher. Other members of the White Crane clan were also waiting to hear what Tai-kor Wong would say. Their headman had not uttered a word concerning the adoption. Feigning work and illness, he had studiously avoided stepping into the White Crane building since Wong-soh's arrival. All his meetings with the White Crane elders had been held in Baba Wee's mansion. This had fuelled gossip and many unsavoury comments. "You think he's not scared of Old Man Wee, ah? Can't even shit without his father-in-law's approval." The laughter was cruel. Poor Wong-soh had to pretend that she was not aware of the talk that portrayed her husband as being not man enough to stand up to his wealthy in-laws. Some women had even hinted with a tinge of glee that their headman was henpecked by his Straits-born wife, which was why he dared not visit Wong-soh. Others pointed out with worldly cynicism that wealth and power could command obedience even from the spirits; in deference to his wealthy in-laws, Tai-kor Wong had to make it clear to everybody in Penang that Baba Wee's daughter was his number one wife.

turned first to one, then to the other as he tried to play the peacemaker.

"Ah Fook! Such things are not for a wife to decide without first consulting her husband!"

"How can he decide when he hasn't even stepped into the building? Ah Fook, I waited! I waited for his lordship! But he refused to come here!"

"This is not the first time she's defied me! Which woman dares to sail the oceans and come out here without her husband's knowledge? Which woman dares to adopt a son without her husband's permission? She has scratched off my face!"

"Tai-kor, let's talk over this calmly."

Ah Fook looked from one to the other.

"How can I be calm? The whole island is laughing at what the bitch has done to me! Gave me a son without my knowledge! She's just out to ruin my name!"

"Our Wong-soh is not vengeful. Let's talk this over."

But Tai-kor Wong was in no mood for talk.

"Get them out of here! Back to Bandong!"

"But there's a war in Bandong," Ah Fook reminded him.

"Then go elsewhere! Go back to China!"

"Is he out of his mind, Ah Fook? The boy's wanted by the Manchu dogs in China! Even if he doesn't recognise him as his adopted son, he should have a heart! Even dogs have hearts, right or not, Ah Fook?"

"Right, right, I beg you, Wong-soh, sit down."

But she remained standing while Tai-kor Wong paced round the room like a caged tiger.

"Ah Fook, she knew the rule! I allowed her to stay in Bandong on condition that she was not to step onto this island!"

"There's a war in Bandong, can you please tell the heartless fiend?"

"Leave and go elsewhere then! Why come here with a son I've never asked for? Why make more trouble for me?"

"You! You! You! That's all you think of!"

Wong-soh blocked Tai-kor Wong's way, forcing him to look

at her haggard face. It appeared to Tuck Heng that something inside her had finally broken.

"You listen to me, Wong Fatt Choy!" she screeched at him. "I was here for months, waiting! But you didn't care whether I was dead or not! All you think about is your name! And your family here! But don't you forget, Wong Fatt Choy! You had a family in Sum Hor too! I might be your accursed barren wife, but I was also your parents' filial daughter-in-law! I didn't leave our village until I had buried them! What did you do, filial son?"

"Wong-soh! Wong-soh! What's in the family, keep in the family! Too many ears are listening."

"Let the walls hear! For years I said nothing because I gave him nothing! But is faithfulness nothing? Is loyalty nothing? Who fed his parents during the drought? Who fed his parents during the flood? Who sold her labour to buy them a coffin and a grave? Even now their spirits are waiting for their filial son to return to build a headstone for their grave!"

"You tell the bitch!" Tai-kor Wong pulled Ah Fook towards him. "She should return to Sum Hor and build my parents' headstone!"

"He thinks I was born yesterday? Even the stupid pig knows that he's getting rid of me! Not to build a headstone! But to please an important old man!"

"You hollering bitch! What important old man?"

"Your god! Baba Wee!"

"You watch your words, woman!" Tai-kor Wong strode across the room. His face was an ugly scowl and his fist was raised.

But Wong-soh stood her ground and continued to taunt him. Ah Fook tried to stop her but she pushed him aside.

"Can't even say the great name aloud without shitting in your pants, ah?"

He slapped her hard across the face and almost went berserk in his rage and shame as he seized her hair and banged her head again and again on the table.

"Wong-ma!" Tuck Heng flew across the room. Before Ah

Fook could stop him, he had flung his body on top of Wong-soh's to shield her from further blows.

"Tai-kor Wong! Baba Wee has sent for Tuck Heng! He says Tuck Heng saved his life!" Big Tree rushed in.

Chapter Nineteen

*T*hree days later Tuck Heng was still dazed. Standing on the crowded wharf, he heard the clanging of bells to signal the arrival and departure of ships and tongkangs. A thousand million strange voices were screaming. The wharf seemed like a boiling cauldron of clamouring coolies. His tunic was soaked as he hoisted the metal trunk onto his shoulders and started up the steps.

"Tuck Heng! This way!" Lee-soh, the butcher's wife, called after him.

Like one in a dream, he turned and followed her, oblivious of the sea of Indian coolies lumbering past him with sacks of cloves and other spices from the Celebes and bales of cotton cloth from India. Neither did he see the Chinese coolies, barebacked with towels swinging from their necks, bowed under sacks of rice and sugar. Shouts of the vendors, traders and merchants did not reach his ears. Nor did the curses of the sailors.

"Slowly! Watch where you're going!" Lee-soh yelled. "Be careful with that trunk! Her whole fortune is in there!"

Like a mute, he followed Lee-soh up the tongkang gang-plank. Hands reached out and took the metal trunk from his shoulders. On deck were the women who had come to bid Wong-soh farewell. The only male besides himself was Ah Fook who carried Wong-soh's second metal trunk.

Mute and grim-faced, he stood next to Ah Fook. Memories of his own vile voyage out here assailed him. He couldn't rid his mind of the stench of corpses in the dark hold, the filth of unwashed men and the buckets of human soil. He had had to sleep between two corpses for several days before they were removed and thrown overboard. When a typhoon smashed into their tongkang, every son of a mother fought for himself as their ship rose and fell with dizzying suddenness in the howling gale and tons of water cascaded down the holds and galley. Like drowning rats, he and his fellow passengers clawed at one another, trying to reach for safety. Their tongkang rocked and twisted like a matchbox in the gale, its timbers groaning and shuddering as though they would split. Down in the holds, plunged into sudden total darkness, they retched and cowered among the crates and barrels, howling like mongrels in pain, nearly crazy with fear. Many died on that voyage, some by their own hand; others, too weak to defend themselves were knifed by fellow passengers for something as petty as a pair of cloth shoes. Barefaced greed and fear had reduced the men to the lowest level of scum. He shuddered as he remembered the hell he had glimpsed on that ship and feared for Wong-soh's safety.

"She's a paying passenger. They get better treatment," Ah Fook assured him. "Usually the return voyage is not the same as coming out here, quite pleasant they say."

"Which of us can afford to pay for the voyage home?" Aunt Loh sighed. "Me, I'll never see Sum Hor again."

Wong-soh patted her friend's arm. "I'll visit your family and let them know that you're well."

That brought tears to Aunt Loh's eyes. She had not seen or heard from them for twenty years. She might as well be dead as far as they were concerned. The thought of never seeing their homeland again cast a pall upon the group. Many of the women choked back their tears.

"All is fate, and we must accept it," Wong-soh comforted them. "Look at me. For years I wanted a son. Got one finally, only to part from him. It's fated, right or not?"

Tuck Heng turned away. Must fate always rob the little we have? Was it fate when Old Stick and those killed in Bandong lay unburied in a strange land? Was it fate when Ah Lai's mother was raped? "Retribution!" she was heard to cry before plunging the knife into the belly of her idiot son.

"Tuck Heng!"

He turned and faced the teary-eyed women again.

"Go to Wong-ma. Say what you want to say quickly. We don't know when we'll be seeing her again!"

"Lee-soh, no unlucky words!" Aunt Loh stopped her. "We will meet Wong-soh again."

Wong-soh, smiling through her tears, took Aunt Loh's hands in both her own, but she was too overcome to say anything. Even Chan Ah Fook dabbed his eyes.

"Take care of your health, Wong-soh!" Ah Fook's gruff voice was choked.

"You too, Ah Fook, be in good health. Keep an eye on my boy. He's my life now. And Son, listen to Uncle Ah Fook's advice."

Tuck Heng nodded but still no words came to him.

"All of you, stop crying! You're alive and I'm alive. And as long as we're alive, we can always make things better, right or not? The emperor has ordered me to go. So I go. The emperor has ordered me to build a proper grave for his parents. So I will. As long as he does what he's promised for my son, I will be his loyal subject. But let him harm a single hair on Tuck Heng's head and he will see a different me!"

Her anger kept her spirits buoyed up.

"I won't abandon you, Son."

"Wong-ma, take care of your health."

He looked at her as if about to say something more but the ship's bell rang. There was a flurry of movement on the decks. They were ordered to get off the tongkang. He knelt and kowtowed three times before he was pulled to his feet and led away by Ah Fook.

Chapter Twenty

*H*e was an orphan again. At the insistence of Baba Wee and Tua Neo, he moved into Wee Mansion. But he was neither elated nor saddened at the turn of events. If he was fated to remain an orphan, so be it. If he had to live in a new land by his wits and skills, then he would be alert and learn.

Three days after he moved in, Baba Wee hosted a grand dinner for two hundred guests, the members of the White Crane who had fought off the Hakka mob in Temple Street.

"Friends and brothers, by your courage and prowess, you have upheld the name of the White Crane! I drink to your honour!"

The men rose from their seats and yelled in unison, "Yam seng!"

Servants went round the tables to refill the empty glasses with more brandy.

"Friends and brothers of the White Crane! I would not be standing here tonight if it weren't for this brave young man beside me. He is the adopted son of my son-in-law, Tai-kor Wong, and so he's my adopted grandson. Brothers of the White Crane! For those of you who don't know him, allow me to introduce my adopted grandson, Wong Tuck Heng!"

Tai-kor Wong's wife made it clear that she would have as little as possible to do with Tuck Heng. He shrugged off her dislike and tried his best to fit into his new family. But that wasn't easy to do. The family was large and unhappy. There

were many things which he, as a newcomer, was just beginning to discover. He had to learn a new dialect, Hokkien, to
understand what they said to him. Before long he noticed that
Tua Neo took a perverse pleasure in using him to taunt her
stepdaughter. Siok Ching's face grew dark with suppressed
anger whenever Tua Neo sang his praises.

Three months later, when the durian season arrived, he
discovered even more things. The season brought hot dry days
and huge quantities of a thorny pungent fruit from the orchards
and jungles in the outlying areas of Penang island. Nobody, it
seemed, not even the British governor or the newly appointed
British Resident of Perak, could displace this king of tropical
fruits, and during the season of its reign, everyone rejoiced
and revelled in the consumption of the rich ambrosial fruit of
the gods.

In the Wee household, masters and servants alike craved
the fruit. Being the "new guest from China", as he was known
among the Wee relations, he had not the faintest notion what
all the fuss was about.

"It's like a drug, as potent as opium. The more you eat,
the more you want. Some Malays claim that the best durian is
found in elephant dung. The elephant knows how to pick the
best fruit. It swallows the durian, thorns and all, and it comes
out whole. So the fruit inside the shell is clean. Now that type
of durian is prized by the Malay rajas."

Unfamiliar with the ways of these Straits-born Chinese, he
was not quite sure whether they were pulling his leg. He had
always known the lychee was supreme. The fruit was prized
by the Chinese emperors, praised by the poets and immortalised
by the artists. But wisely he kept such thoughts to himself and
did not seek to contradict his new relatives.

The Malay gardeners in the Wee mansion claimed that the
wild jungle durians were superior to the cultivated variety in
Baba Wee's orchard. One evening they slipped away, and at
dawn returned with a sackful of durians picked from trees that
grew to a height of twenty feet or more in the jungles around
Penang Hill. Their young masters paid a handsome sum for

these durians and had them brought into the men's wing secretly so they could feast on the wild fruit without insulting their grandfather, who claimed that his orchard produced the best durians on the island. Swearing him to silence, these grandchildren and grandnephews inducted him into the pleasures of the durian feast behind locked doors and closed windows.

"So the smell won't go outside. If Grandfather knows, he'll be so angry."

"Eat up, Chinaman. Durian will help you speak Malay. Even a little English if you're smart."

Boon Leong and Boon Haw collapsed onto their bed, howling with laughter. He detested those two stuck-up little asses.

"Papa said he's our brother," Boon Pin reminded them.

"Brother, my foot!"

"Shut up, Boon Leong! Let Tuck Heng eat!" An older cousin cuffed him on the head. Boon Leong made a face.

"Pumpkin head!" he hissed.

The next day, Baba Wee held a durian feast for the family in their holiday bungalow in Ayer Itam.

"Eat, Tuck Heng! Everybody loves it! Except the Englishmen. Their tongues are too blunt and their noses too stupid!"

Hoots of laughter greeted his remark. The family was seated in a circle on the floor of their spacious verandah. A pile of the thorny fruit was in the middle of the circle and the men of the family were prying them open with knives.

Tuck Heng scooped a yellow fruit out of its thorny shell.

"Use your fingers. Like this! Don't dirty your palm or else Grandmama will scold you." Little Boon Pin instructed him in the art of eating the creamy fruit.

"Like this?" He took a bite. Then, breaking into a boyish grin, he declared, "Very good! Very tasty!"

"Grandmama, look! Tuck Heng Kor is eating his durian!" Boon Pin called out to Tua Neo.

"First time eating, and he likes it!"

The boys howled, "Yah, yah! The very first time!"

Tua Neo smiled indulgently at her grandsons.

"Tuck Heng likes durian! That means he'll stay here. All the China-born who like durians don't go back to China."

"Mak, how can you be so sure?" Siok Ching carefully scooped another yellow fruit out of its thorny shell. "Most China-born want to return to China when they grow old."

She glanced at her husband, seated opposite, but Tai-kor Wong said nothing, intent only on helping Boon Leong pry open another durian.

"Papa, are you going to China?" Boon Leong asked.

"Your father will return to China. But only for a visit. And Siok Ching, you can go with him. Right, Son-in-law?"

"Right after I've made my fortune. Let me see to the opening of the new mines first."

The family elders nodded approvingly and Baba Wee looked pleased.

Tuck Heng followed the conversation of the adults with great interest. His mastery of Penang Hokkien had improved and he could understand all that he heard around him. And more. Because he could hardly speak the dialect, he was forced to look more closely at gestures and facial expressions. He saw more than was revealed in speech and came to know more about the unhappiness around him. Being sharp and knowing, he valued this information which seemed to give him a sense of power. Baba Wee's daughters-in-law were unhappy about their husbands' pursuits outside the home, the gambling dens they frequented, the debts they accumulated and the prostitutes they kept as mistresses. They feared that if their husbands' gambling habits and sexual peccadilloes were made known to Baba Wee, the stern patriarch might disinherit them. So they tried to cover up their own husbands' misdeeds by revealing those of other people's husbands. This led to much bickering and squabbling in the women's quarters.

His self-assurance grew as his knowledge of the household expanded. But he kept his thoughts and discoveries to himself. He confided in no one and made himself useful to everyone, especially to Tua Neo, the one with the most influence in the house. He impressed the old lady with his knowledge of the Three-Character Classic and Four-Character Classic. Being illiterate, Tua Neo did not realise that these were mere primers for children and she often called upon him to recite these in front of her friends, Nonya ladies just as illiterate as herself. Sometimes he was asked to recite them to her grandsons, most of whom were enrolled in St Xavier's, the Christian Brothers' school. These boys scoffed at his learning. "Chinaman!" They stuck out their tongues at him as soon as their grandmother had left the room.

He went out of his way to be useful to Siok Ching, the one most threatened by his presence, and Boon Pin, her youngest son. Without prompting from anyone, six-year-old Boon Pin had addressed him as *Kor*, Elder Brother, much to his mother's chagrin. After that, Boon Leong and Boon Haw were forced to address him as Kor too.

"Boon Leong, take a fruit from this shell here and give it to Tuck Heng. A bit overripe, but it's not heaty."

"Mak, please eat it yourself. Tuck Heng has more than enough." Siok Ching masked her displeasure with a smile.

"Grandmama, please eat it! I've got enough!"

He was shrewd enough to know that the more obliging he acted, the more petty Siok Ching would appear to others. He took a shell with two pieces of creamy fruit nestling in it and offered it to her.

"Eat it yourself."

"Siok Ching, take it," Wee Thiam, her uncle, urged her. "Your adopted son is trying his best to please you."

Defeated, Siok Ching accepted his durian. Baba Wee's brother was a blunt-speaking man who brooked no nonsense from anyone. The owner and editor of Penang's only newspaper in Baba Malay, he was highly respected in the family.

Knowing that Wee Thiam was very interested in stories about corrupt Qing officials in Kwangtung, Tuck Heng started to tell him what he had heard about them. He was a good storyteller and the younger members of the family crowded round him.

"Let Tuck Heng eat his durian first! How can he eat and talk at the same time?" Tua Neo exclaimed. "Come, Tuck Heng, try this fruit. It's the Kedah variety."

"Tuck Heng has more than enough," Siok Ching protested again. "Give it to the other children."

"Sister-in-law, let Tua Neo indulge the boy. Everyone is saying that as he's Tai-kor's adopted son, he's also Tua Neo's grandson. And the elder brother of your children."

First Sister-in-law's eyes had a mischievous glint that worried Siok Ching.

"Come, eat more, Tuck Heng! Poor boy, you'll be shipped off to the wilds of Perak soon."

Second Sister-in-law asked in an innocent voice, "Tua Neo, all my boys like Tuck Heng as much as Boon Pin. Can he come again?"

"What're you talking about? Tuck Heng is my grandson. So this is his home."

"Thank you, Grandmama. I'm a poor orphan. So I'm very grateful that I can call you both Grandmama and Grandfather."

He knelt on the mat and kowtowed.

"My child, no need, no need!"

Baba Wee and Tua Neo were beaming at him.

"The gods sent you to protect Grandfather. How can we ever forget that? Every year on the anniversary of that street fight, I'll go to the temple and thank the Goddess of Mercy for her blessings."

The talk soon turned to the arrival of the new Resident of Perak.

"The Arab Muslims, the Hindus, the Sikhs, the Gujeratis and all the Europeans and Malay princes will be there to meet him," Wee Thiam announced.

"They say that this Mr James Birch is high up there. Even more powerful than the sultan. The treaty says the sultan must listen to him."

"The exact words go like this." Wee Thiam took out his pocketbook and read from it. "'The Resident's advice must be asked and acted upon on all matters except those touching Malay religion and custom.'"

"The Malays see Raja Abdullah as God's representative on earth! I can't imagine him asking the white man for advice on everything," Baba Wee said.

"I agree. I know Raja Abdullah. And our friend Musa Talib ..."

"Musa Talib? Is he back?" Tai-kor Wong was amazed.

"The Mamak's here to get supplies. Safeguard the Datuk's interests and his own naturally." Wee Thiam laughed. "I brought him to see our lawyer, D'Rozario."

"D'Rozario?"

Such names were still strange to Tuck Heng's ears but he was learning fast.

"We need Eurasians like Charles D'Rozario these days. They know the English law much better than us."

"Look, the ants are coming," the children cried, bored with the adults' talk.

"Ee Neo! Bring out the nasi lemak!"

Baba Wee's second wife rose from her mat and silently did as she was told. Siok Ching's unhappy eyes followed her mother but she quickly masked her pained look when she noticed Tuck Heng observing her.

"What's nasi lemak?" he asked.

"Rice cooked with coconut milk. Eat it with durian." Tua Neo handed him a plate of the steaming fragrant rice.

The children mixed the rich creamy durian into their rice, making a yellow mash which they scooped into their mouths with their hands.

"Eat with your right hand, not your left," Tua Neo admonished them.

He tried to use his hand, mixing the sticky rice with the yellow flesh of the durian before gingerly conveying a lump of it into his mouth. His grimace soon turned into delight.

"So good to eat! So delicious!"

His terrible accent threw his listeners into fits, for try as he did, he could not master the singsong intonation of Penang Hokkien.

"Chinaman!" Boon Leong sneered.

Chapter Twenty-one

Most honoured and respected Wong-ma,

Please accept your son's deepest regard, respect and greetings. It is hoped that this letter finds you in good health and good cheer. May the gods bless and protect your comings and goings. May good fortune accompany you every step of the way.

My adoptive father also sends his greetings. He is in good health. He wishes to know if the village stonemason has started work on the headstone for his parents' grave. He is most anxious about it since the auspicious date for its erection has already been set by the geomancer. "Hurry the stonemason," he said. "Pay him more if necessary. But complete the headstone before Lunar New Year."

Your son deeply regrets having to write the above. Please understand that it is written upon the instructions of my adoptive father. My duty is to write his letters for him so that he need not go to the letter-writer in Temple Street.

Because of this appointment, Madam Siok Ching resents me. However, this is something which cannot be helped. Her own sons, Boon Leong, Boon Haw and Boon Pin, are studying in a school run by the foreign devils and they read and write in a foreign tongue. They cannot read and write in the language of their father's homeland.

But do not worry too much. Your son knows how to look after himself. Please be assured that Baba Wee and everyone, both the elders and the young masters in the family, treat me very well. The only one who keeps aloof is my adoptive father's eldest son, Boon Leong. He is probably influenced by his mother. Your son, however, will continue in his effort to befriend all his brothers.

Last week my adoptive father and his family moved back into

their own house, rebuilt after the fire. It was a grand and joyous occasion. Two long strings of firecrackers were let off when the lion dancers arrived. My adoptive father and his wife hosted a grand dinner for all the leaders and important men in the White Crane kongsi as well as all their relatives.

The new mansion is like one of the grand houses of the foreign devils. Some relatives are jealous of my adoptive father and they say that his mansion is built with Baba Wee's money.

Three days ago, Baba Wee, his sons and my adoptive father went to the pier to welcome the English Resident of Perak, the new ruler in Perak. My adoptive father wore the official Qing robes and looked like one of the mandarins of the imperial palace. Some people say that one day he might be appointed the kapitan China of Kinta Valley by the new king of Perak! Everyone thinks that there will be peace and prosperity, now that the English great lord has made the Malay chiefs and all the Chinese societies sign what people call the Pangkor Treaty. The Hakkas have even named one of their settlements Taiping, Great Peace, to show that they truly wish to live in peace with us! There will be no more fighting, and everyone will be able to trade and live safely.

Perak Country is a strange land to me. And so are the Malay people and their language. When I leave Penang to travel to Kinta Valley after Lunar New Year, there will be many things to learn. My adoptive father is taking me and Uncle Chan Ah Fook and three thousand miners to open tin mines in Kinta Valley. We will travel first by boat and then by elephants through the jungle so that we can also visit other White Crane mines along the way. One of the first places we will visit is Bandong Valley. The elders in the White Crane have asked my adoptive father to bring a Taoist priest to the site of the last battle to say prayers for the repose of the dead. We must also comb the area for bodies so that we can give all the miners a proper burial ceremony. I intend to look for Old Stick's body and offer prayers to thank him for saving my life. I am looking forward to the journey and hope to learn many things.

In the meantime, your unworthy son pleads with Wong-ma to take good care of her health and not to worry too much. I will work hard and save up enough money to bring you back here to live with me.

Your filial adoptive son,
Wong Tuck Heng

Chapter Twenty-two

The sails of the tongkang flapped in the late morning breeze as it rounded the headland within sight of the swamps. As it came to anchor at the mouth of the river, Tuck Heng heaved a sigh of relief. Solid ground under his feet soon.

The tide had gone out, revealing a wide expanse of muddy flats, tangled tree roots and rotting vegetation along the banks. A small jetty of coconut trunks and bamboo poles bounded together by strips of rattan served as the landing place for the small sampans and other boats which came to call before going up the Perak River.

Several sampans came towards their tongkangs. Tai-kor Wong, brows furrowed and eyes squinting against the needles of sunlight bouncing off the rolling sea, barked out his orders. His Cantonese swear words and curses made Musa Talib roar with delight. The fat trader could swear as well as any Cantonese coolie.

"Are you sons of the tortoise? Faster!" he bellowed in Malay at his own boatmen. The broad sleeves of his white baju were flapping in the breeze. Like the wings of a fat gull. Tuck Heng smiled.

"Faster, faster! Are you eating wind or are you working?"

Half-scolding, half-cajoling, he spurred his boatmen to speed up the unloading and to steady their sampans in the swell of the waves.

"Steady! These Chinese miners can't swim! Fall into the

sea and they'll sink like rocks!"

"Tuck Heng! Get into the next sampan! Keep an eye on the unloading. Look sharp, you understand?"

"I understand, Wong-fu."

He'd almost swallowed the last word. The honorific *fu*, a formal term for Father, was stuck in his throat. He had yet to get used to Tai-kor Wong being his father.

"Pak Mus!" He leaned over the railing and called out to Musa Talib, who was squatting in the sampan like a fat Buddha. The boat was bobbing dizzily at the end of the rope ladder. "I'm coming down!" he shouted in heavily accented Malay.

"Come down!"

"But the sampan is moving!"

"You fall, we catch you!"

"Pak Mus! Save me …!"

A heavy swell rose, and the rope ladder swung out to the far left so that all he saw were the waves. Musa grabbed hold of his legs.

What a relief when his sampan reached the jetty and his feet touched land! The party which came on shore included Tai-kor Wong, Chan Ah Fook, Musa Talib, some of the crew and several miners. The village headman welcomed them.

"Are the animals ready?"

"All ready to leave, Insya Allah, Pak Mus."

More miners came on shore. Some would travel by land while several hundreds more were being transported by a flotilla of riverboats up the Perak River.

"Split into two groups. Safer. The English great lord's army can't be everywhere."

"Whatever you say, Tai-kor!"

"Why you call me Tai-kor?"

"The Bandong war has sealed us in blood. So now you know you can depend on me! And I, on you!" Musa Talib gushed and spread out his arms in a broad generous gesture.

Tai-kor Wong glanced up at the bright blue sky. "Looks like it might rain in the afternoon," he said. Then he fell silent.

What could a man say in the face of Musa's effusive

sentiments? Yet he was sure that the trader's feelings were genuine and, despite his embarrassment, Tai-kor Wong was touched. If only the fat fool would stop babbling about their partnership-in-blood and brotherhood to everybody! He had had to bite his tongue several times during the voyage to stop himself from blurting out what he knew. Curse Lee Peng Yam! Everything that Lee Peng Yam had done in the name of White Crane honour went against his sense of justice. But he was a member of the brotherhood sworn to secrecy and must never reveal what he knew to Musa Talib. Loyalty to clan and race demanded silence, a silence which Musa had interpreted as deep sincerity. All the more fool he! Tai-kor Wong thought bitterly and wished the fat ass would shut his big mouth.

"My brother! He saved the menteri's life but does he crow about it? So I've got to be the one to crow like a hen that has laid an egg!"

Musa Talib and the village headman laughed heartily.

"Coolies! All of you follow Chan Ah Fook! Except those coming with me! Ah Fook, lead these bastards and go by boat to Kinta. The other boats should arrive within the next few days."

"Tai-kor, leave it to me. I'll get these buffaloes moving."

"I'm not leaving these parts till I've paid one last visit to Bandong."

He paused and looked towards the wall of green beyond the river. Blood, rape and gore. The line marking the margin of existence for men was thin and fine.

"Will you be stopping in Kuala Bandong for a few days? There's a little … er … little favour I've to ask of you."

"Spit it out, old man!"

"It's my woman. If you've the time, please find out if she and her boy are alive, and if they are, give them some money."

"I'll see to it that they've enough to live on."

"Thank you, Tai-kor."

"No need. Between old friends, I understand. When times are better, you'll be able to save some money and bring out a woman from Sum Hor. Start a family."

In Kuala Bandong, Datuk Long Mahmud was thinking of family too. Ever since the Black Flags' attack on the day of his daughter's marriage, he had felt vulnerable, uncertain of his hold over the Chinese miners in his valley. And to add salt to his wound, the governor had summarily allotted the Bandong mines to his attackers. It was treachery of the highest order. The white men were trying to reduce his power and break up his friendship with the White Cranes. They feared his power. He could almost smell their cunning when he was on board their ship. He cursed them and vowed never to give up control over his sweet valley.

But these days, the air in his valley was no longer as sweet as it used to be. The signing of the Pangkor Treaty had fouled the air for him. Thank Allah that his daughter and son-in-law were unharmed and safely married in Larut. With the menteri of Larut as his in-law, he'd like to see what the white men would do about their alliance. Those crocodiles had the new sultan in their jaws now. They would never be satisfied till they'd eaten him. Curse the wars! They had littered the valley with rotting flesh and bones! Such a desecration of his ancestral land by the Black Flag murderers! He swore at them. And he swore at the greedy white dogs hot at their heels. The white men were using the Black Flags to rob him! He was sure of it.

A sudden anger at the turn of events seized him. He slipped the dagger from under the folds of his sarong and with a sudden movement, swift and silent, his deadly projectile flew upwards and sliced through the stem of a durian above him. The thorny fruit fell with a thud and split open. His followers under the tree sprang away like animals from a trap. But his young children by his commoner wives rushed for the fruit and fell upon it like vultures upon a dead goat.

"That is exactly what the white men will do to us when the sultan falls," he murmured, half to himself and half to Ibrahim.

Ibrahim watched his younger siblings scramble for the rich

creamy flesh of the durian. Gone was his boyish air. His dark-brown face had grown serious and watchful since the Black Flags' attack. His kris had tasted blood.

"Come, Ibrahim, you were about to ask me a question."

"If it pleases my honoured Father to speak of such things to his unworthy son, my cousins and I would like to know more about this powerful white man whose name is James Wheeler Birch."

"He's a spy of the white governor. He's going to turn our land upside-down."

"Begging my Father's pardon, my cousins and I are still puzzled. Why is he not challenged to battle then?"

The Datuk sucked in his breath. He was just as puzzled and exasperated as these young men. There was no precedent for what the new sultan had done. The word "fool" was not far from his lips whenever he thought of the new king installed by the British. But he was still a loyal chief and he could not bring himself to utter it in front of these young warriors.

"My honoured Uncle." Rahim came forward. "How can a white man tell his royal highness what to do? It's never happened before. Not without a great war."

"Not in Perak."

"True, my honoured Uncle. But it happened in Melaka," Nazri said softly so as not to sound as though he were contradicting an elder. He was a handsome warrior who could wield a kris as well as the Datuk himself. "When the Portuguese and the Dutch came, they fought openly! They were warriors! But these Englishmen! They just sit and talk."

"They're cowardly traders and shopkeepers, snakes and serpents who employ scribes to steal from us! Why aren't our chiefs fighting them?" Rahim's eyes blazed with a dark anger.

"The chiefs have no money to buy arms and weapons. The white governor in Singapore has taken away their right to collect taxes in their own land!"

"My honoured Father, we heard also that the white men use scribes to write lies into their books and made our sultan and chiefs sign the books in Pangkor. How do we know that what's written in their white tongue is the same as what's written in our own language?" Ibrahim asked.

"My son, I was there on the white governor's ship and I saw his scribe scribbling away in the corner when we talked. I too have my doubts."

And these doubts had plagued him day and night. He had watched those white barbarians on the ship—how they'd moved like water buffaloes across the meeting room, their weight making the ship's boards creak with each step, and how their hard leather boots had knocked against the ship's woodwork. The barbarians had shown no courtesy. They had neither bowed nor salaamed. They did not remove their footwear when they entered the meeting room. Their arrogant blue eyes had looked straight at his royal highness as though they were his equal. During the meeting, he had sat on the floor with his fellow chiefs and had maintained a stern silence throughout. But he had not been idle. He had watched the white men wilt in the heat as the meeting wore on. Their thick heavy clothes, too warm for the tropics, grew dark stains under the armpits. Their stiff collars had choked their thick necks and they'd had to mop their brows and red faces ever so often. They could not sit still. They'd shifted restlessly like peasants as the heat got to them. But what had offended him most was the stench from their bodies. It was almost unbearable. Like milk curdling in the sun. It had taken all his willpower and good breeding not to betray by look or gesture that he had noticed anything. Their speech was utterly incomprehensible— the mouthing of low guttural sounds followed by bursts of laughter or the shaking of the head, and the restless twisting of their whiskers. Red, brown and yellow hair covered their mouths and lips. The amount of hair on the faces of these white men had amazed him. Their beards and moustaches concealed their faces and intentions. But their blue and grey eyes betrayed them. Now that he had seen the white men up close, he knew them to be cunning creatures. One of them, called Swettenham, had even mastered the Malay tongue and had spoken to them sweetly on behalf of the white governor.

"Learn the white man's tongue as soon as you can." He turned suddenly to Ibrahim.

But Ibrahim looked at him as if he had been asked to do the impossible.

"The meeting at Pangkor was not a meeting among equals. None of us was asked to speak. Our silence was so loud, it should've told the white men something. But they're proud in their hearts. They can only hear if you make a noise." A fierce pride filled his heart when he said, "The white barbarians must be taught the laws and customs of our race and our land."

"Begging my Uncle's pardon, your unworthy nephew has something else to ask you."

"What is it, Nazri?"

"We heard that his royal highness and all the chiefs signed the Pangkor Treaty on board the governor's ship. Is that true, Uncle?"

"May His Most Compassionate and Merciful forgive us! We the chiefs signed away our god-given rights. We were the accursed coconut shells. Turned up, we fill with water; turned down, we fill with earth. What could we have done? Fight their cannons with our spears? So we signed the papers!" He groaned. "We're going to be paid like servants from now on!"

His warriors could hardly believe their ears.

"My honoured Father! Musa Talib and Panglima Sangor are approaching us."

The Datuk turned and greeted Panglima Sangor, a chief who lived near the official residence of James Birch.

"How are things with you? What's the news?"

"The news is bleak, my honoured friend." Panglima Sangor shook his grey head. "The times have changed."

"And my lords, permit this unworthy slave to add, it's a sad day for us when the white man's advice must be asked."

"Asked and acted upon on all matters except those touching Malay religion and custom."

"But Pak Mus, hasn't the Resident meddled with our tradition and custom already? He took away our chiefs' rights!" Nazri looked at his elders, seeking an answer and assurance.

But the Datuk said nothing.

"And this Inche Birch also interferes with our custom of keeping slaves and retainers," Ibrahim added softly.

"Tok Wang told us Inche Birch took away the women and forced them to stay in his house! He wants these women but he doesn't even have the courtesy to ask our chiefs!"

"He never asked! He forced the chiefs to surrender their weapons! Burned their houses when they refused! He even forbade them to wear their kris!"

"Doesn't he have any respect for our chiefs?"

"Are we going to let this infidel get away with this?"

"Are we worms or dragons in our land?"

Datuk Long Mahmud and Panglima Sangor ignored the outbursts of the young warriors. Such ill-mannered talk in their presence would have brought a sharp rebuke in normal times. But there were more important things to worry about than the manners of the young men.

"I bring worse news, my friends." Panglima Sangor's face was a wooden mask as he spoke. "A week ago his royal highness summoned some of us. He told us that he's forced to hand over the government of the country to Inche Birch. According to the terms of the Pangkor Treaty."

A howl of dismay rose from the warriors. They looked to their chief. The Datuk's voice was low and calm when he finally spoke.

"That Birch has gone too far! He's no right to take over our government. If we're not careful, by and by he will put more white men in charge. Then one day, these white men will drive us out of our own country."

"No!"

"His royal highness has been forced to hand over the government to Birch. No matter what we think of the sultan, we've got to stand by his royal highness."

The Datuk looked at each warrior in turn.

"We, the sons of Bandong, cannot spoil the good name of our forebears. We must never be disloyal to our sultan. Do you understand?"

As Ibrahim listened to his father's measured words, a fierce pride and a passionate guardianship for the land filled him. Bandong. Perak. These were immortal names. He was ready to do battle with anyone should his father give the word. But the Datuk remained silent.

For a while no one spoke. Even the garrulous Musa Talib was silent. Then Panglima Sangor broke the news which roused their blood and rage.

"I've been sent to tell you that Birch is coming here."

"Why?"

"His officers want to put up posters in your villages to tell the peasants about the new government and the collection of taxes. Maharaja Lela was the one who asked me to inform you."

No one, not even Ibrahim, dared to look in the Datuk's direction. The Datuk's voice was strangely flat, almost devoid of any feeling when he spoke.

"Please inform Maharaja Lela that the people of Bandong will do what the people of Kota Lama did."

Rahim, Nazri and the others turned to Ibrahim but he was just as puzzled by his father's words.

"My honoured Father, what did the people of Kota Lama do?"

At this, his father's eyes shone with an unmistakeable mirthless glint.

"The people of Kota Lama did what the mousedeer did! They teased the crocodile till it slithered away in shame! Praise be to Allah for their courage! When Birch went upriver to Kota Lama in his boat, the villagers lined the entire length of the riverbank, all armed and ready for death. Ready to uphold their pride and protect their land. Their chief sent a message. The villagers would fight to the death if Birch landed."

"What did the dog do?" Rahim asked.

Musa looked as if he would burst if he were to remain silent any longer.

"Nothing!" he roared. "The crocodile fled without setting foot on Kota Lama! Such is the courage of Inche Birch that his boat turned around and went the way it came!"

Ibrahim and his cousins cheered. No one could beat Musa in the telling of a tale. Even the stern-faced Datuk laughed.

"But why is this crocodile coming to Bandong?"

"He wants you to know that he's the new ruler." Panglima Sangor's voice was choked. He could hardly speak for the rage in his heart had been eating him for days. "I don't know how long we can tolerate the arrogance of this white man."

"I might be a Kedah man, my lords, but I don't like what the white men are doing in Perak."

"Nor I, Musa! I'm the menteri here. I will not allow any white man to post proclamations in Bandong Valley. I will never acknowledge the authority of this Birch. Not even if his highness has done so. And you, my friend, you can tell Maharaja Lela that I am of the same mind as him."

"Then come with me. Maharaja Lela and some of the chiefs are meeting to discuss this matter."

"But what about Che' Wong and his miners, my lord?"

"Musa, thank you for reminding me. Bring them here tonight. I'll meet my brother tonight before I leave. Ibrahim, be present tonight when I meet him. When he returns from his business in the Kinta, you'll go with him to Pulau Pinang to study the white man's tongue."

"Pardon my asking. Why're you making your son learn the enemy's tongue?" Panglima Sangor asked.

"I've seen how a white man has learned our tongue and used it to his advantage. Ibrahim can do the same for us by learning the white man's tongue."

Chapter Twenty-three

What's he saying?"

"He said not to worry. The footprint belongs to a tiger, but this one is a grandfather so it won't harm us."

"Inche', ah! How you know, ah?" Tuck Heng tried his fragmented Malay on Ibrahim. "How? Speak up!"

" Ibrahim scowled. The Malay warriors advanced menacingly. Confused, Tuck Heng backed away. Tai-kor Wong seized him by the shoulders and felled him with a blow.

"Why is he so rude to our young chief?"

"He doesn't mean to be rude. He's new here and his Malay is bad. He's stupid and doesn't know anything."

Then he turned to Tuck Heng, "Fool! You've offended a young chief! He could've killed you! Kneel and bow very low to that young man, potato head!"

Tuck Heng did as he was told. Tai-kor Wong turned to Ibrahim. "Begging a thousand pardons, my young lord! Compassion and mercy are yours! I thank my young lord for not killing my slave."

"Che' Wong, my father welcomes you like his brother so you're like an uncle to me. But tell your people that I know a tiger's print when I see one."

Ibrahim turned away abruptly and sprinted into the bushes, heading towards the jungle like an animal streaking home. He swung his razor-sharp kris to the left and to the right, lopping off leaves, stems, branches and vines to cut a path through the thick undergrowth. Dark, tense and unseeing, he strode into the greenness which swallowed him. Strange snakelike vines twisted above him like the hangman's rope. He stood still as a rock, his eyes growing accustomed to the dull green light filtering through the canopy of leaves above him. Gradually his calm forbearance returned. As his anger ebbed away, his sense of the jungle's strange ethereal beauty heightened. A purple bloom peeped from under an umbrella of brown ferns. A dark blue moth fluttered on a leaf. His eyes began to make out the different types of bush, fern and vine in the formless green that enveloped him like a mother's womb.

High-pitched cicadas at noon and the faint cries of the jungle fowl and gibbons soothed his troubled spirit. These were familiar sounds heard since his childhood. The rush of falling water in the distance lured him further and further into the greenness, till he reached the banks of the Bandong River flowing swiftly seawards to the wider world beyond. Away from the jungle and valley he loved and into a vast and unfamiliar terrain, which lay under the sun, beckoning yet threatening, a world his father had ordered him to explore. He crouched beside the river and fixed his troubled eyes on the far shore. O the inexpressible comfort of feeling safe in the green world of his forefathers in which he was king. He found another paw print in the soft riverine mud.

⊷⟶◉⟵⊷

Tuck Heng picked his way through the dank wilderness. Lallang and weeds covered the former settlement of the White Cranes. The remains of the charred huts on the riverbank were choked with mud and filth. Beneath the layers of moss, lichens and creepers lay the bones and half-eaten bodies of miners. Choked with the stench and foul air of rotting flesh, he plunged his hoe into the stubborn earth, ripping off the unyielding weeds. He dived into the waist-high grass and tore his way up to where the ambush had taken place.

"Old Stick! Old Stick!"

Silence answered him.

"Uncle Old Stick!" he shouted louder.

From far off, like an answer from another world, came the eerie echoes of his own voice ricocheting off the rocks, then fading away into the silence again.

He looked about him as he stood among the grass and bush, feeling a presence other than himself. A presence that had been there long before the Chinese came. And it had reclaimed the land when they left. Its silence hung like a thick veil over the valley in the noonday heat. Nothing stirred in the hot humid air. He moved forward, treading with great care through the shoulder-high weeds and lallang which cut his skin.

"Forgive my trespass, forgive my trespass," he murmured as he searched through the thick undergrowth, stopping now and then to clasp his hands instinctively and bow to the invisible guardians. Then he heard it. Like the distant rumbling of thunder.

"Tiger!" he yelled and fled.

Chapter Twenty-four

Ah Fook and his coolie miners stood on the banks of the Kinta River, gazing upwards at the wilderness towering above them. They were standing on the edge of the world, on land unpenetrated, untouched and unseen until their arrival. Dwarfed and hemmed in by jungles, silent with foreboding even in the brilliant sunshine, the coolies could see shadows slide and slither among the sullen trees. They shivered and uttered a prayer before plunging into the shadows. They moved warily, careful not to give offence to the invisible guardians of this virgin land. But they were hungry, tired and anxious to empty their bladders. Gingerly the men stepped forward, muttering the ritual apologies they had brought with them from China; mindful that these spirits might not understand Chinese, they bowed before each big rock or tree before urinating at its base, appealing to the jinns not to take offence at their watery intrusion.

The feeling that they had no right to be here was difficult to shake off even though the powerful English lord in Singapore had allotted this land to them. They knew the original owners must resent it. They could feel the presence of the guardians of the land, hovering somewhere in the dull silence which enveloped the entire forest. The miners spoke in hushed voices. Hidden eyes were watching them.

"Don't touch or move anything until after the prayers," Ah Fook said.

He was an old hand at this. He knew that the massive walls of greenery, untouched and unchanged through the centuries, held secrets buried deep in the land's memory. The jinns and guardian spirits frowned upon intruders. And rightly so, he thought, for he was a firm believer in the territorial rights of the spirit world.

When all their boats had been unloaded, the coolies donned their cotton jackets and untied the queues wound round their heads. Ah Fook led them in an old Chinese ritual to pay homage to the guardians of the Kinta earth and its mighty river. He lit a bunch of joss sticks and held them high above his head. Clasping their hands, the miners faced east, knelt upon the riverbank and kowtowed three times to the spirits of the east. Southwards they turned and kowtowed to the spirits of the south. Westwards they turned and kowtowed to the spirits of the west. Then northwards they bowed till they had paid homage to all the spirits of the cardinal points, male and female.

Ah Fook stuck joss sticks along the bank of the river, in front of a huge rock, and his miners knelt before the rock and kowtowed three times to the spirits of the river and the rocks. Holding the remainder of his joss sticks high above his head, he led his wary coolies into the jungle and planted joss sticks at the roots of several giant trees.

"Please accept our deepest respects and apologies. We mean no harm. Accept our humble offerings of incense. If we prosper, a feast will be laid out for your lords and ladies. We beg you to please let us stay and work in your valley in peace."

On their first night, the miners prudently slept in their riverboats. The next day Ah Fook sent several miners upriver into the riverine inlets to ferret out the tiny clusters of attap huts hidden in the rainforest. At each dwelling, the miners told the inhabitants that they required the services of many woodcutters and a spirit doctor. Then they returned and waited for word of their presence to spread to the interior.

After several days of waiting, a dugout canoe appeared one morning, bringing three Malays, one of them an old man bent with age.

"We bring Tok Simangi, the pawang," one of the young men said.

Speaking in broken Malay and aided by numerous gestures and grimaces, Ah Fook finally settled on the fee for the spirit doctor's services.

That same day Tok Simangi performed an ancient ritual on behalf of the Chinese miners and the permission of the guardian lords of the valley was sought.

"'You can work here now,' their lordships said."

Ah Fook greased his palm with some silver dollars.

Over the next few days, several boatloads of Malay wood-cutters arrived. Ah Fook quickly organised them into teams and told them to start work immediately. Like a general directing his army, he was eager to seize the advantage he had gained.

"Follow the Malays! Cut when they cut! Burn the weeds! Raze the jungle. But say a prayer before you do anything!"

More woodcutters arrived over the next few weeks. The ancient silence of the valley was shattered forever by the men's voices and the thuds of axe and parang against wood. Hundred-year-old giants crashed to the ground. Maiden bushes were ripped. The land was stripped of its centuries-old garment. Deeper and deeper the men penetrated, ripping open what had been closed, deflowering what had been untouched. Then they set fire to the fallen. Huge bonfires razed the jungle. Her dominion was pushed back, further and further each day to a safe distance, away from the proposed digging of the mines and the miners' quarters. Subdue her, or else she kills us, Ah Fook thought. He was a coolie miner with an instinctive enmity for the earth and her dangerous temper, which could erupt in a sudden landslide to kill men unawares. So he was not taking any chances.

By the time Tai-kor Wong, Tuck Heng and another three hundred miners arrived, vast tracts of virgin land had been burned. Taking advantage of the hot dry season before the monsoon rains, the trees were torched by the Malay woodcutters who were experts in the slash-and-burn method.

For weeks the charred land smouldered and belched dark columns of smoke which blocked out the sun. Soot and ash rained continuously upon the miners and the air turned grey. Land and sky joined seamlessly in a mesh of grey smoke and hot fumes cauterised the men day and night. Wood smoke had engulfed the entire valley, choking men and animals with its ash. Acrid smoke stung their eyes and dried up their throats and lungs. Tempers ran short in the blistering heat from the fires.

Fist fights broke out among the coolies and Tai-kor Wong had to wield the whip to restore some semblance of law and order in the logging camp, which had grown to a thousand men by then.

The scorching days stretched to weeks and the number of coolies dwindled. Scores of them fell like singed moths as they fought to control the raging fires. Every day some unlucky miners were burned by falling branches or blistered by hidden embers or killed by falling trees. In the eyes of the superstitious, the forest fires had acquired a life of their own. The men grew fearful. Shrines to the Earth God appeared mysteriously in various parts of the camp and the miners placed joss sticks, red candles and wild flowers before their images.

As weeks passed into months, many miners died from drinking bad water, while others fell victim to the deadly diseases spread by flies and mosquitoes. The hill slope to the east of the river was littered with their unmarked graves. Only the Malay woodcutters and the *orang asli*, the original inhabitants of the valley, seemed unperturbed and unscathed. The more enterprising among them had even started a lucrative trade in magic stones, amulets and tiger's teeth, which they sold to the Chinese miners who wore them for protection.

For Tuck Heng, the forest fires brought a return of his nightmares and he suffered nights of cold sweats and broken sleep. Ah Loy held him down each night as he shivered and cried to the ghosts of those he had lost in the fire back home in Sum Hor, but Ah Loy did not betray what he heard during the night, and for that Tuck Heng was extremely grateful. He was determined to forget the past. He did not speak about his terrible nights to anyone. To speak would give them life; silence was the act of forgetting and surviving. Having come this far into the strange wild country, he was determined to push ahead and get on with his life.

So he mourned his past quietly, confiding in no one. To lean on another's door was to depend on them for support. "The sky and the earth can be measured but the heart of a man cannot be gauged." That saying, heard in childhood, had stayed with him. He tried to recall other proverbs he had heard in his childhood, and in doing so he grew heartsick again for those bygone days in China.

Mourning made him careless. One day he was felled by a falling branch. He suffered a broken leg and was laid up in bed for several days. Time and memory being an immigrant's worst enemies, he fought them off resolutely. He refused to stay in bed. He hobbled out to the cooking sheds and helped the cooks. When his chores were done, he squatted on the bare earth with stick in hand and kept himself busy by writing five to ten pages of text from the Chinese classical primers he had memorised as a child. Part of every day for as long as he was unable to join in the heavy labour of sawing and cutting, he spent scratching on the dirt floor rows upon rows of Chinese characters.

"I didn't know you're such a scholar!" Ah Kow, the cook, was very impressed. He scratched his armpit. "Got you! You bloodsucker!" And flicked off the squashed bug from the folds of his jacket.

Tuck Heng grimaced. His brief sojourn in Baba Wee's mansion had spoiled him. He had become overparticular about dirt. These coolies had not the slightest notion of personal hygiene. Every son of a mother in the camp was infected with head lice and body lice including himself. Even Tai-kor Wong was not free of bugs. But no one seemed bothered except him. Lice, he was told, were part of living in a logging camp. When the new settlement was ready, the lice would disappear.

"What are you writing?" Ah Loy asked him.

"Words from the Thousand Character Classic."

"A learned man!"

But Ah Loy's remark brought him no pleasure. He felt like a fraud and a show-off. He was not learned. Merely literate. What he had written were disjointed words and phrases recalled with great difficulty and he was quite sure that some of the strokes of his characters were wrong. But who was to know? All the coolies were illiterate. Even Tai-kor Wong. So he was the scholar among them! The full force of his inadequate learning hit him. He choked back his tears. All that he had mastered were the primers for a child in China! And yet how he had strutted in these rags to impress Tua Neo and Baba Wee in Penang. His cheeks burned at the memory of his foolishness. He had stopped reading. And his writing was simply a desperate attempt to escape from the meanness and deprivations of his life in the logging camp. A camp without women was barbaric. Wong-ma and her friends would never have allowed the men to be so dirty and uncouth. They would have boiled vats of ginger and lemon grass water to delouse all their clothes and bedding. He heaved a sigh and gazed blankly at his sorry words on the dirt floor. They had carried him home to a China where he used to have a father, mother, brothers and sisters in a clean home filled with scrolls, books and writing brushes, and where life was comfortable and civilised.

Word of his writing soon spread through the camp and the coolies came round to the kitchen shed, especially young men his age who sat or stood around, smirking. No one said a word at first, then their whispers grew louder.

"Better than us, is he?" Small Rat nudged his neighbour.

"My feet are stuck in dung! What about you?"

"I was born a prince."

"You'll toil like an ox and die like one!"

"Everyone has to die! He forgets what he is! A buffalo like us! Even got lice like us!"

"A scholar with lice? What about his lily-white hands?"

They howled and hooted. He loathed their crudeness. And yet he could not bring himself to fight them as he once did in Bandong. Adopted grandson of Baba Wee he might be yet he was not Baba Wee's flesh and blood. He was a coolie. Like these louts. But these louts were not as ignorant as he once believed. They possessed a hard clarity that saw their world as it was. He was soft in the head, clinging to the past as though he were back home in China, where a student studying for the imperial examinations had status and respect. But out here, in this raw backward land, all men were equal to the scholar if not superior to him, because out here, a man who could neither dig nor labour was of no use to anyone.

"Can you eat books?" Ah Loy challenged him. "Did Tai-kor Wong gain a rich father-in-law because he can write or because he can use his mouth? He can talk like a Baba and a Malay. And look at Baba Wee! Talks with the red-haired foreign devil like a friend! That's why he's rich and respected. What use is your writing if you can't use your mouth?"

He gave up his writing as soon as his leg healed.

He was not unwilling to learn and adapt. When a man's horse dies, he must get up and walk, he told himself. His father had prized poetry above all else. "Poetry is true, sacred and wise; the vessel for the wisdom of the sages," his father had said, and impressed upon him that to be human, one had to learn to read and write the words of one's ancestors and the poetry of the philosophers. But poetry was the cause of his father's death.

The coolies were not so foolish. They had not his father's reverence for the word. At best the word was a tool for accounting purposes, the black ink marks one made in the ledgers of commercial houses.

He joined the coolies, slogging with them through the heat and fumes, sullen but uncomplaining, accepting the sudden turns of the tropical weather and the vagaries of wild nature. After each day's work was done, he joined the gangs who combed the burned-out parts of the jungle to scavenge for the roasted animals that supplemented their scanty diet of rice and tapioca. Like Ah Loy, he learned to eat whatever animal he could find—wild boar, deer, jungle fowl, tigers, squirrels, monkeys and even charred frogs and lizards.

"Eat it, Tuck. Monkey brain good for the body. Keeps the heat in you during cold nights."

"No thank you."

"To eat is good fortune. In Sum Hor, I starved. Here, plenty of food."

The two of them joined the Malay woodcutters to comb the surrounding hills for wild herbs and other medicinal plants. They gathered wild rosary peas and boiled these to treat miners afflicted with malaria. For a small fee, they also brewed a soup of monkey brains and wild ginger for those suffering from aches and pains. They gathered stinkwort when he learned from a Malay woodcutter that its leaves could be used to treat poisonous snakebites. Urged by Ah Loy, he also made a concoction of lallang roots, wild ginger, pepper and other weeds, which he sold to the miners as a remedy for fever and dysentery and to expel intestinal worms.

His reputation as a medicine man grew. The miners consulted him and bought his brews and concoctions. Soon his little jar hidden in the ground under his bunk began to fill up with coppers and silver dollars. His heart felt light and his vision of the future became a vast colourful canvas whenever his hand dropped another few coppers into the jar. "This is so much better," he confessed to Ah Loy, "than scratching characters on a dirt floor." Like a chance spark from the forest fires, the notion of enterprise had ignited a corner of his mind and there it burned with the iridescence of gold and silver.

Then the monsoon came, bringing rain and cool nights of blustery thunderstorms. Twenty elephants, with their Malay mahouts seated astride their necks, pushed huge sawn-off logs into the swollen river. The logs were floated downstream to the new mining settlement, where other elephants hauled them out of the river and left them to dry on the riverbank. When these were sufficiently dried, gangs of carpenters under the supervision of Loh Pang sawed the logs into planks for building huts and sheds. Rows of large sheds were erected in the new settlement and the miners left their flimsy lean-to shelters and moved into their permanent homes. The Malays called the settlement *Kampong Kinta Manis*, the village of sweet Kinta.

Tai-kor Wong and his elders in the White Crane established a hierarchy of command with Chan Ah Fook as the village headman, while elders like Loh Pang and Water Buffalo took charge of the warriors. Each warrior, like Ah Loy, headed a gang of twenty to forty tin miners. Much to his relief, Tuck Heng was considered too young at sixteen to be in charge of the older miners. Tai-kor Wong ordered him to assist in setting up the waterwheels, the ingenious Chinese-invented *chinchia* system used for pumping water to the mine shafts and channels.

That new assignment spelt the end of his brewing days. For weeks he tramped after Ah Fook, up the wooded hills and down the snake-infested valleys, trudging with a basket of tools on his back. Ah Fook, the master engineer, barked at him, scolded and cursed him for each mistake, for that was how an apprentice should learn from a master.

"Nothing can be learned without pain and humility!"

So he held his tongue and followed Ah Fook in sullen silence, hauling the basket of pickaxes on his back.

"Your book learning is no good here. Use your head! Your eyes! See those rocks over there? There! Stupid! To your right! That's where we'll build those palongs. Plunge a bamboo stake in there to mark the spot, thick head!"

Ah Fook was relentless in his teaching, conscious of his promise to Wong-soh that he would keep an eye on her precious and see that the boy learned and advanced. Building waterways was his craft. It was all he knew and this was what he was teaching the boy—something he was not doing for his own flesh and blood who was somewhere out in the wilds of Bandong with his Malay mother. The son he had fathered was growing up not knowing that his father was Chinese. The more he thought about it, the more his sense of distance widened between him and the Malay woman whose loins he had known for five years. He spat into the brilliant sunshine and yelled at Tuck Heng with more ferocity than he intended.

"Over here! To the east! You fool!"

After several weeks of scolding, Tuck Heng learned by trial and error how to gauge the lay of the land, the intricacies of its wooded terrain, its rocks and limestone, and the nature and force of waterfalls. He spent days hammering bamboo sticks into the rocky earth to mark the areas where the wooden palongs would be built.

At the end of each day, he lay exhausted in his bunk and dreamed of the medical hall he would own some day and of the rows of shophouses he would build in Kinta Manis.

"Stop dreaming! The supply boats are late. Our rice stocks are low. Tai-kor Wong is very worried." Ah Loy pulled him aside and hissed, "Keep this to yourself. Some people have been stealing from the rice sheds."

"But that's wrong!"

At once, he regretted the exclamation. It had a hollow and self-righteous ring even to his ears.

"When a man's belly is hollow, he will kill his own brother." Ah Loy looked at him squarely, his voice low and level. "We've left mothers, fathers, wives and children. What for? For a bowl of rice. And some dollars to send home, right or not? So when there's no rice to eat, men in the jungle go mad! My first mine in Larut, one year there was not enough rice in the camp. Only one bowl for dinner. One night some bastards attacked the warriors on guard duty in the rice shed. The Tai-kor of that camp and his warriors beheaded nineteen men the next day. Their heads were displayed on bamboo stakes."

"This stealing, what will Tai-kor Wong do?"

"If the thieves are caught, they'll be put in leg irons and left to die in the sun."

The next morning, five men bound hand and foot were left outside the supplies store. A large wooden board had a single Chinese character written in blood: "thief".

Chapter Twenty-five

*T*he wind and the weather being in their favour, their boat went down the Kinta River speedily. By evening they had reached a small village where Tai-kor Wong hoped he would find Musa Talib and the supply boats.

"I'll wring the Mamak's neck if he doesn't give me a good excuse," Tai-kor Wong muttered as he stepped ashore.

The sky had turned crimson with the sun sinking behind the bank of coconut trees beyond the wet rice fields. A lone buffalo turned lazily on its side in the soft grey mud. A cool breeze from the river sent ripples of darkening water across the flooded fields. The unfamiliar aroma of tropical spices wafted by as he and the White Cranes drew nearer to the attap houses.

"The Chinese are here!"

Half-naked children raced towards them, laughing as they shouted to their friends. The headman of the village and his men met them.

"Tok Penghulu," Tai-kor Wong spoke in formal Malay, "we're looking for the trader, Musa Talib."

"Why do you seek him?"

"Pak Mus is my trading partner, Tok, and his supply boats are late in bringing rice to Kinta Manis, the new mining village."

"Aaah." The penghulu's dark face broke into a smile. "You must be Che' Wong."

"I am, Tok Penghulu."

"Welcome, welcome! Come with me. Pak Mus is waiting for you."

They were taken to an open space of hard beaten earth in front of the penghulu's house. A big buttressed rain tree with a high canopy of dark aged boughs and thick green leaves arched over the courtyard like a huge umbrella. The penghulu's men squatted in groups of threes and fours beneath its spreading branches. Here and there, wood fires had been lit. The penghulu's female slaves were bent over the cauldrons of rice and spicy curries as their doelike eyes darted mischievous glances at the men.

"Please come with me, Che' Wong. Your men can stay in the compound. They will be fed."

"Thank you, Tok."

"Let's go to my house. Musa is there."

"My friend, I thought the pirates had gotten you this time!" Tai-kor Wong hollered when he saw Musa.

"Not the pirates. The white Resident's soldiers. Those pigs found out that I was the Datuk's trader and confiscated my boats and supplies!"

"Why would the English soldiers do this to you?"

"Always behind the news, my friend!" Musa slapped his forehead. "The whole of Perak knows that Maharaja Lela's men have killed Resident James Birch."

"We're cut off from the world in Kinta Valley. Not a single supply boat in the last three months! How to get news?"

"All Malay supply boats are not allowed to go upstream. Allah is my witness! Perak is in a state of war!"

"It began in Pasir Salak, the village of Datuk Sangor," the penghulu added in his low gravelly voice. "The Resident was killed in Che' Kong's bathhouse."

"The heavens, ah! A disaster! A terrible disaster!" Tai-kor Wong exclaimed in Cantonese, forgetting where he was in his distress. His agitated eyes travelled round the room. But the faces in the lamplight revealed nothing. He mopped his brow as the enormity of the deed sank in and he wondered if the White Cranes were implicated in the killing of the British Resident:

Ah Kong was a member of the White Cranes, the sole Chinese living in Pasir Salak. He had lived there for many years and could speak Malay like a native. He had even married a Malay woman.

"Che' Kong, did anything happen to him?"

"Don't worry, Che' Wong, His Most Gracious and Compassionate protected your friend. When the killing took place, your friend was inside his house," the penghulu told him. "He and his family are staying with his wife's relatives in a village not far from here. I've sent a messenger to bring him here. Insya Allah, you'll see him tomorrow."

"Thank you, Tok Penghulu."

The White Crane kongsi would be in serious trouble with the British authorities in Penang if it was implicated in any way in the killing of a representative of the British Crown. Visions of gunships and soldiers loomed before his eyes.

"How did Maharaja Lela's men get to the Resident? And how did the Datuk get mixed up in this? Is he well, my friend?"

"He's well."

"I thought I saw Ibrahim, his son, outside. Is the Datuk in hiding?" He looked at Musa.

"Come, my friend, let's have dinner and I'll tell you the whole story."

They sat on the mats in a circle. Some women brought in oil lamps.

"It's going to bring us misfortune. The pigs have already captured the honourable Siputam, one of the men involved in the killing," Musa Talib replied, shaking his head before lapsing into a long silence during which he fixed his eyes on the floor. When he spoke again, it was with a sigh. "To think that His Most Merciful had spared the Datuk's life and mine during the battle with the Black Flags! Was it for this? May Allah forgive me my regrets."

Tai-kor Wong looked at the solemn faces of the penghulu and the village elders. He had lived and traded in the region long enough to know that appearances often belie reality. He would have to wait and listen patiently to many formal and often flowery speeches before the truth unfolded.

"I hope—no, I pray, Tok Penghulu, that all will be well with the Datuk and Maharaja Lela. I'm just a Chinese miner and trader who knows little about your troubles with the white men." He turned to the village elders. "But honoured Tuan-tuan, together with my friend, Musa, I've gotten to know and respect the Datuk. And I know that the Datuk loves his valley. His heart is in the land."

The penghulu and village elders nodded so he knew he had said the right thing.

The slave girls brought in bowls of curries and rice heaped on banana leaves.

"Eat, my friend," one of the village elders murmured. "Any friend of the Datuk is also our friend. You're like a brother to him. And a brother to Musa. Praise be to Allah!"

May Lord Guan Gong protect me! Tai-kor Wong smiled and nodded as he prayed to his ancestral gods. This was what he had secretly feared. That his well-known friendship with the Datuk would implicate the White Cranes and get him into trouble with the English authorities. And yet, he thought, his astuteness as a trader battling with his conscience, how could he, in all fairness, abandon the Datuk who had been sorely used as a pawn by a rogue member of the White Crane? And yet … he struggled for a way out … and yet the pressing neces-sity of the present times and his responsibilities as the head of the White Cranes demanded that he distance himself from those whom the English authorities had deemed rebellious and treacherous. A sigh escaped him as he tried to swallow his rice. His thoughts and inclinations were swinging back and forth like a pendulum. The barbarians are the new rulers. To survive, a wise Chinese must work with and not against the new powers that be, he thought, his shrewd eyes darting from one Malay face to the other, seeking a clue as to what they expected of him.

"Honoured Tuan-tuan, forgive my frankness. But I fear that Maharaja Lela's deed will bring the wrath of the white governor upon your heads."

"Che' Wong, what choice do we have? Swallow it, the

mother dies; spit it out, the father dies. Poison has already entered our land through that Birch. The war has already begun. Many chiefs and their men have fortified their villages," one of the elders told him.

"If a tree has many roots and is firmly rooted to the land, why should the tempest be feared?" another village elder added.

"The Datuk and Maharaja Lela have many followers. They will fight."

"Pardon me, honoured Tuan-tuan. But I worry for the chiefs. How can they expect to win? The English have many guns and soldiers."

Silence greeted his question. He swallowed hard and tried again. "Honoured Tuan-tuan, I beg your indulgence and forgiveness. I don't mean to doubt the ability of the chiefs. But I worry because I come as a friend. I pray you won't take offence."

The men nodded encouragement so he went on. "Sultan Abdullah has signed the Pangkor Treaty and asked for a British Resident. The white men want to rule this land." More nods from the elders. "Now I speak as a brother and as a friend. Your spears, your poisoned arrows and cannons are not enough to secure victory."

"Che' Wong, what you've said is true. But the monkey and the mousedeer see things differently: the monkey from the treetops and the mousedeer from below. The white men want to rule this land but can you tell me," Tok Senik, the oldest of the village elders, asked him, "do you think the people of this land, the trees in the jungles and the beasts of the forest know the name of this white ruler? Do they care to know? Do they want to be ruled by the white men? In my aged heart and in my aged soul, I know that they don't. For thousands of years since the time of Solomon, the jinns of the forest, the people and the beasts of the land, and the birds of the air have risen out of our rich brown earth without the white man. Brown earth, not white, Che' Wong. This brown earth is ours. Defend it we must!"

Marked upon their sun-browned faces was the pride they took in the wisdom of Tok Senik, the most respected man in these parts. For a while, no one said anything. They concentrated on the excellent meal, savouring the sweet-sour pickles which went with the rice and beef curry. As they ate, a jingle sung by the young warriors in the compound drifted into the verandah and their words seemed to fill the room with a bittersweet irony.

> *If you have no guns, better hold your tongue;*
> *If you're without a kris, better be contented;*
> *Avoid your enemy if muskets and cannons*
> *you've none;*
> *Avoid a war if rice and padi you're without.*

"Sultan Mahmud of Malacca and his warriors died fighting the Portuguese," Tok Senik murmured under his breath at the end of the song. "We've warriors willing to shed their blood still."

The slave girls brought in silver pitchers of lime water for the men to wash their hands after the meal.

"Thank you, Tok Penghulu. Excellent dinner."

"You're very welcome."

"I beg your forgiveness if I've given offence."

"Nothing to forgive, Che' Wong. You spoke from your heart."

He was acutely aware that Malay custom demanded polite and carefully worded speech, especially on subjects that touched the heart.

He had long known that many of the Malay chiefs in that area had no love for the white intruders seeking trade and gold or tin ore. And yet the temptation had been too great. There was revenue to collect and money to be made, and their wealth had increased with the opening up of the country for trade and mining. But this very openness led to unhappiness, jealousy and rivalry among the chiefs. And this rivalry was cited as a reason to impose white rule. As a Chinese trader, he had come to view the white man's rule in Perak as a good thing—peace was good for trade and mining. Wisely he kept such thoughts to himself.

Musa offered him a rolled cigar. He lit it and inhaled its

pungent fragrance. Soon tobacco smoke enveloped each man seated on the matted floor and for a long while no one said a word. Tai-kor Wong smoked his cigar and waited patiently. After some time, Musa coughed and spoke in a low serious voice.

"My friend, we appreciate your frankness and we know that what you've pointed out is true. We're no match for the white men's cannons. But," he paused and flicked off the ash on his sarong, "who knows this land better? Our warriors can melt into the jungle like shadows but the white soldiers can't."

"Pak Mus has spoken well," the headman added. "But you, Che' Wong, have also spoken well and from your heart."

"Aye!" the village elders agreed.

They pulled at their cigars and each man seemed sunk in thought again. It was another long silence before the penghulu spoke again.

"Although we sons of the soil know this land from the time we were born, we cannot overcome the white men whose hearts are hard and greedy."

"Several lives have already been lost since this war began," Tok Senik added. "It has divided us. Some support Sultan Abdullah, some support Raja Ismail and some support Raja Yusoff. It's a sad day for this land of grace when brothers fight against brothers and chiefs against chiefs. May Allah forgive us all!"

"Maharaja Lela's men have fled Bandong Valley. But the Datuk and his men are still hiding in the jungles of Bandong. Their supplies are running out."

The penghulu turned to him and, looking straight at him, continued in his slow deliberate way, "You, Che' Wong, are a son of the land from a faraway country but you understand how we feel. We speak to you as a brother of the Datuk. He needs your help. Your boats can bring food to his men. Musa can't do it alone for the white men won't let him go up the Bandong River. We realise this is a grave matter. Give us your reply tomorrow. Perhaps after you've heard what Che' Kong, the jeweller, has to say. Insya Allah, your answer will gladden our heavy hearts, Che' Wong."

Chapter Twenty-six

"My heart dropped! Surely I will die! The fighting and gunfire! Like the battles in Bandong all over again!

"I knew trouble was coming. The Resident's boat. It was anchored near my place. You know, the day before my left eye was twitching the whole morning. I said to my wife, 'This twitching's no good. Not a good sign.' True enough, the very next day there was the Resident's boat and his policeman was coming towards my shop. My wife was so scared. She called out to me. The Malay policeman was a foreigner, not from these parts. Maybe from Singapore. He came into my shop and told me that his tuan besar wanted to use my bath hut by the river. Could I say no? I just nodded. But inside my heart, I said to myself, trouble. This English foreign devil would bring me trouble. The Malays hate him. People in Pasir Salak have been talking bad about him for weeks. And they talked openly. I heard what Datuk Sangor said and what Tok Pandak said. 'Dog,' they called him and all sorts of other vile names.

"That morning when I stepped out of my shop, a crowd had already gathered. Sixty or seventy men, all armed with spears and guns. They were shouting, 'Infidel! Dog! We don't want you here!' But the Resident was deaf! The crowd was yelling and there he was, just walking past them like he was the king of the deaf! His own guards were Indian sepoys, not from Perak. They didn't tell the Resident what the crowd was shouting about! And his Malay interpreter. He too didn't tell the Resident. I looked at the white man's face. Like a mask with a beard.

"I saw him walking towards my shop. He gave some papers to his Malay interpreter. And the fool pasted the Resident's proclamations on my shutters. They were written in Malay! So why did he choose a Chinese shop? He could've gotten me killed! The villagers were already armed. Now I know many of them and they know me. But still I was scared. They might think that I support the Resident! Angry men can't think straight. Right or not? The people were so worked up by these proclamations. Telling them to obey the Resident. Not their sultan. How can? The sultan is their king!

"Tok Pandak tore down the proclamations. He shouted to his men, 'We don't recognise white rulers here! If they put these up again, we'll kill them!' Tok Pandak was furious. His men smashed down my windows. My wife and I were shaking inside my shop.

"Now any fool would've seen the angry faces of the villagers and sensed trouble. Even if you couldn't see their anger, you could see their spears and knives and guns! Right or not? But the Resident was blind. And stupid! Before that day, I've always felt that the English barbarians were much cleverer than us! But no more! My eyes opened that day and saw how stupid and foolish an Englishman can be! Maybe he was too proud. He thought the Malays wouldn't dare to attack him. He ignored the threats. That's why he's dead."

-•⇒◎⇐•-

Berita Peranakan, a weekly paper written in Malay and published by Baba Wee's brother for the Malay-speaking Straits-born Chinese:

> We regret to report that the first British Resident
> in Negeri Perak, Inche J.W.W. Birch, has been killed
> in the village of Pasir Salak. It appears that Inche

Birch was killed by angry villagers while he was taking his bath. His Malay interpreter is reported to have been killed too, while four of his guards were wounded and two are missing. All the Malay chiefs and rajas are suspected of complicity in the murder and the British authorities are investigating the matter.

Raja Ismail is reported to be amassing his forces for the purpose of expelling the British from Perak. Last week the British residency in Bandar Bharu was besieged by Malay forces, but our correspondent reports that it has since been relieved by British troops. Other Malay chiefs are reported to have built stockades and fortified their villages. According to the servants of the late Inche Birch, the Malay chiefs have accused the British Resident of being high-handed in the matter of their runaway slaves and the collection of revenue. They have also accused him of trying to take over their country.

The *Straits Chronicle*, published by Englishmen for the British community in Penang:

The government has received further information about the murder of Mr Birch. The majority of the Malay chiefs are unshaken in their loyalty to us and the disturbances are confined to a limited area controlled by brigands and outlaws.

1,500 British troops are on their way from Calcutta and Hongkong to take part in further operations against the Malay rebels. The trading community here urges the government to take stern action against all those who disrupt the peace in Perak and to send a strong message to the Malays that all rebels and murderers will be severely punished.

Some of our men have already lost their lives in the fight to restore law and order in this troubled region. We regret to report that Major Hawkins was killed in action together with two sailors and one Gurkha guard during an engagement on the banks of the Perak River. Our troops, in retaliation, ascended the riverbanks and destroyed the village of Enggar. They burned the village and all the adjoining houses after the Malay rebels had fled.

Berita Peranakan:

> British troops are using guns and rockets to
> destroy several stockades in Bandong Valley in an
> attempt to dislodge the menteri of Bandong and his
> men. All mining operations in the area have ceased.
> No riverboat is allowed up the river. Chinese miners,
> as well as Malay villagers trapped in the valley, are
> in danger of starvation.
>
> We appeal to the authorities to permit our supply
> boats to go up the Bandong River to bring supplies to
> our starving miners who are caught in the crossfire
> through no fault of theirs.

⋯≡◎⋐≡⋯

From his corner of the supply boat where he sat plaiting his
queue, Tuck Heng was watching the impassive face of Ibrahim.
A stony silence hung between them. One chicken, one duck,
he thought, how to talk? And what could he say? The Malay
lord might flash his kris again. He wasn't going to risk getting
his arm slashed for nothing. Then again, why should he fear
him? His father, the big chief, is in trouble with the English
and needs Chinese help. Tai-kor Wong is surely going to earn
a huge sum of money or a large piece of land as a reward for
helping the chief.

He glanced at Ibrahim's mute brown face again. It
seemed to have lost its proud lordliness. Not wishing to
be unfriendly, he ventured a tentative smile. But Ibrahim
pointed to something coming towards them. Gods in heaven!
Moments later a small flotilla of light steam launches carrying
British troops and Sikh guards was passing by them. Ibrahim
squeezed between the sacks of rice, not daring to move. Tuck
Heng held his breath and prayed that the British officer, on
seeing the Chinese faces on board, wouldn't stop to search
their boats. The sigh of relief that they let out after the
launches had passed brought them closer in spirit, if not in
speech. They smiled at each other sheepishly.

On their second night on the river, they heard an exchange of fire on the riverbank. A loud explosion of rocket fire sent some of the boatmen scrambling into their boat shed for safety. They huddled among the sacks of rice and refused to continue rowing. It looked as if a mutiny might break out. When the rocket fire finally subsided, Tai-kor Wong had to promise the rowers more money before they would pole their boats upstream again.

"Money! Give!" Tuck Heng shouted in his fractured Malay.

Ibrahim nodded and smiled for the first time, and so began the painful process of nods and the exchange of fragments of Hokkien and Malay words accompanied by gestures, grins and more shouting.

After four days of rowing and poling, their boats finally reached Kuala Bandong. But only a few women, children and old men came out to meet the boats.

"Where's everybody?" Ibrahim raced towards his father's house. Several Malay warriors stepped out of their hiding places to greet him.

"Tell my father that Che' Wong and Pak Mus are here with the supply boats," Ibrahim said, his dark eyes eager and anxious. "Where's my mother? My sisters and brothers?"

"They're in a safe place, protected by His Most Compassionate, my lord."

Ibrahim raced up the steps of his home and entered the dim interior of his father's beautiful house. The first brick house in Perak. A house grander than the palace of the sultan. The pride of Bandong. He ran his hands over the carved teakwood, the ornate decorations of vines and flowers on the balustrades and pillars. His feet felt his father's handsome rugs from Persia and his hands touched his mother's curtains of stiff batik woven by the family's slaves. He walked through the house, going from room to room; beneath his look of lordly restraint was a gleam of pride and eagerness to reassure himself that what he held dear was still there. His honoured father's house. He walked over to the window and looked out at the green rice fields and the blue hills rising behind the thick belt of jungle in the distance. His land, he thought, dreaming of his own distant hills till sudden shouts sent him racing outside to the compound.

"My honoured Father!" Kneeling, he kissed his father's outstretched hand. "Allah be praised! You're safe."

"Allah be praised that you're safe too, my son. But you must leave with Che' Wong and Musa as soon as the boats have been unloaded."

"But your son would like to stay here with you to fight the infidels."

"I will permit no such thing, my son. Your duty is to the family. I'm counting on you to take care of them should anything happen to me. Your heart is known to me, my son. May Allah watch over you and guide you always. Insya Allah, we will meet again."

The Datuk turned away and started to give orders for the unloading of the boats. Ibrahim, head downcast, walked back towards the house.

"Tuck Heng! Help them!" Tai-kor Wong ordered. "Hurry! We must not get caught!"

The jetty was swarming with Malay villagers who seemed to have appeared from nowhere. Just as he flung a sack of rice onto the jetty, gunshots rang out. Speeding towards them were two steam launches carrying British and Indian troops. By the time they landed, the Datuk and his men had melted into the jungle.

He stood with Tai-kor Wong and the Chinese boatmen on the jetty, their hands above their heads. The British officer in charge came up to them and demanded in halting Malay, "What place is this?"

"Kuala Bandong, Tuan," Tai-kor Wong replied in Malay as he executed a low and humble bow.

The officer, his face flushed with heat and exertion, towered above him in his uniform of starched khaki cloth.

"What are you doing here?"

"We … collect rice supplies … for our miners in the tin mines upriver."

"Is this the village of the rebel chief?"

"So very sorry, honourable Tuan! We came to buy rice. We don't know the chief. So very sorry."

"Move aside!"

"Thank you, honourable Tuan."

The soldiers fanned out to search the huts and attap houses. They stomped up the rickety stairs with their guns and bayonets.

At one of the huts near the Datuk's house, six or seven young Malay men, armed with knives and parangs, blocked the soldiers' way and refused to move aside. Affronted, the Indian troops stormed the hut and a fierce fight broke out. Two Indian soldiers were killed and another two wounded. The Malay warriors fled into the jungle as the British troops opened fire.

"Round up everybody! Every stinking man, woman and child! Teach these damn brigands a lesson!"

The soldiers fired a volley into the air. The children started to wail. All the women, children and old folks were rounded up and herded into the forecourt of the Datuk's house.

"Burn down that damn building!"

Indian troops lit flaming torches and flung them onto the verandah of the house, setting the curtains ablaze. A breeze fanned the flames and the wooden walls soon caught fire. Suddenly a bloodcurdling cry silenced the soldiers' whoops.

"Infidels! Dogs!" Ibrahim ran out of the building and let fly his dagger. It struck one of the soldiers on the shoulder. Then he raced down the steps and charged at them.

Tai-kor Wong, Tuck Heng and the other Chinese men flung themselves to the ground as Malay warriors streamed out of nowhere and hurled themselves fearlessly into the mass of British and Indian troops.

From where he was crouching with Musa, Tuck Heng saw some of the soldiers running back to their steam launches. Minutes later rockets were fired into the jungle. Cries of pain and anguish filled the air. Another rocket was fired towards the house.

"Filthy dogs!" Ibrahim screamed as another part of his once beautiful home burst into flames. He lunged at the nearest white soldier with his deadly kris. Tai-kor Wong leapt up and tried to pull him back. Rapid gunshots were fired in their direction and in the ensuing confusion Tai-kor Wong was shot in the back.

"Father!"

Tuck Heng sprang up and raced towards the English soldiers.

"Kill them all!" he bellowed in Cantonese, hot tears streaming down his face. "Kill them! Kill them!"

He was berserk with anguish and fury. Another father had been snatched from him. Musa Talib grabbed his queue and pulled him to the ground. Then the buffalo sat on him. He kicked and struggled to free himself.

"Don't move, you fool!"

From where he was, pinned under Musa's body, he saw the Datuk and his men charge out of the jungle in full force. The Malays let off volley after volley of arrows and spears, wounding and killing several soldiers. In retaliation the steam launches fired round after round of rocket fire, killing the Malays like flies.

The Datuk raced up the steps of his residence in a desperate attempt to save his home from the raging fire.

"My house! My beautiful home!" was his last anguished cry before he fell on its stone steps, killed by rocket fire.

The Malays were surrounded and overwhelmed. Ibrahim was captured and bound. British and Indian troops set fire to every Malay hut in sight. The whole village went up in flames. From the billowing clouds of black smoke rose the wails of widows and orphans. Their cries filled the air. But to Tuck Heng's dismay, the gods in heaven were deaf that day.

He saw Ibrahim herded onto one of the steam launches. The young chief turned and watched, stony-faced, as the roof of his father's house crashed to the ground.

III

SPROUT AND SHOOT
1901

Chapter Twenty-seven

THE HUMBLE ADDRESS OF THE STRAITS CHINESE BRITISH ASSOCIATION, PENANG, S.S., PRESENTED TO HIS MOST GRACIOUS MAJESTY, EDWARD, KING OF GREAT BRITAIN AND IRELAND, DEFENDER OF THE FAITH AND EMPEROR OF INDIA, ON THE OCCASION OF HIS ACCESSION TO THE THRONE OF GREAT BRITAIN AND IRELAND, 1901.

May it please Your Majesty,

We the members of the Chinese community of Penang venture to approach Your Majesty and to offer our humble but earnest and heartfelt congratulations on Your Majesty's accession to the throne of Great Britain and Ireland.

Many of us have the great fortune to be the subjects of your majesty while others have come from far and wide to make a home in this colony. We venture to say that no class or section of the inhabitants of Your Majesty's widespread dominions have greater reason to rejoice on this occasion than we who live under Your Majesty's wise and enlightened rule.

As the representatives of the British subjects of Chinese descent in British Malaya, we rejoice in the opportunity which is now afforded us, of giving expression to the strong feelings of loyalty, devotion and attachment to Your Majesty's throne, as well as gratitude for the security and prosperity we enjoy under the aegis of the British flag.

*We pray the God who is Lord of all nations upon the
earth, that He may in His mercy bless Your Majesty's reign
and may your loyal subjects of all races and creeds continue
to live in peace and prosperity!*
And we, as in duty bound, will ever pray,

Ong Boon Leong, LL.B (Cambridge)
President, Straits Chinese British Association

Looking elegant in his formal attire of dark coat and dark grey
trousers, Ong Boon Leong waited for the applause to die down
before handing over to the governor the slim silver casket with
its declaration of loyalty to the newly crowned British monarch.
His speech in English had been impeccable, delivered with a
distinctly Oxbridge accent, of which he was extremely proud
for none in the colony could speak as well as he.

"But only so among Asians; only among us Asians," he
was usually quick to add in a soft self-deprecating murmur
whenever he was praised by a member of the English community. His modesty added to his charm, so he was generally
well-liked.

The Right Honourable Ong Boon Leong was a man of his
time in a world that had been tilting westwards ever since the
signing of the Pangkor Treaty at the end of the Perak wars, a
quarter of a century ago. He was not only English-educated,
but also the first Straits-born Chinese to cut off his queue and
have his hair styled like an English gentleman.

Like most boys from wealthy Straits Chinese families,
he and his two brothers had been educated by English
schoolmasters who were the elite staff of the first English-
language school in Southeast Asia, known ironically as the
Penang Free School. The young Boon Leong, a keen student
with an excellent ear for the nuances of the language of the
empire builders, was one of the very few boys in the colony
awarded a Queen's scholarship to read law in Cambridge
University. While at Cambridge, he stayed with the Reverend
Dr James Graves and his family, and under the tutelage of Dr

Graves, Boon Leong was inducted into the finer aspects of being an English gentleman.

Upon his return from England six years later, he had set up a law firm to help steer his Chinese clients through the maze of English laws and colonial regulations. He soon gained the confidence of the influential Straits Chinese and they chose him to be their leader and spokesman. This brought him to the notice of the governor. He was invited to serve in the colony's Legislative Council and became a well-known figure in public and civic affairs.

"Thank you, gentlemen, thank you! A splendid gift and a most gratifying display of your loyalty!" The governor was effusive in his thanks. The Straits Chinese British Association had paid for the celebrations to mark the accession of Edward VII and had organised a garden party for Penang's leading citizens.

"Thank you for your kind words, Your Excellency." Boon Leong bowed. Then he led his delegation of English-educated lawyers and merchants to the red-carpeted area, gratified that they were to stand next to the representatives of the European community. It shows the world how highly we Straits Chinese are regarded, he thought.

Watching him, Inspector Ian Thomson was reminded of Boon Leong's grandfather. That old Baba was a gentleman, he thought. Never before had he witnessed a grander funeral than the one Baba Wee's family had arranged for him. As the inspector-in-charge, he had rendered invaluable service during that funeral. Well, let's hope the Right Honourable grandson will remember that and find him a suitable position after his retirement from the police force.

The stocky man heaved a sigh as he mopped his shiny brow. Stout and red with too much beer and sun, he was no longer the young and dashing sergeant who had rushed headlong into a riot to save Baba Wee's life twenty years ago. Neither was he the courageous officer who had led his police forces upriver to attack the Malay rebels in Bandong.

Now he longed for ease and comfort, preferring to let

the young officers take charge while he busied himself with schemes to increase the size of his retirement fund. Officers in the colonial service were grossly underpaid; once a man was retired from the service, all his years of loyalty to the empire, his citations and decorations would count for nothing. A smart fellow had best look out for himself rather than depend on the big boys who ran the empire from London. A year or two in one of the rich Malay States would add a few more hundred pounds to his miserable pension, he calculated. And he would be able to provide for poor Molly in her twilight years and buy his long-suffering wife a comfortable cottage in Moreton Heath. That would be something to look forward to. He dreaded the empty existence of a retired officer from the colonies. On his last visit home, he had found the London clubs full of lonely grey men living in genteel poverty.

A roll of drums made him return to the festivities on the Padang. The huge lawn was thronged with loyal subjects of all races who had gathered to watch the royal regiments trooping their colours. Amid the gaiety and sunshine, the sudden realisation that he was going to miss such pomp and ceremony back home in the grey Midlands clouded his vision and dampened his pride. He blamed it on the heat that he was beginning to find unbearable. He took out a neatly folded handkerchief to soak up the beads of sweat gathering on his forehead.

The sun had dissipated the morning's coolness and the ladies were shielding their faces with their lace parasols. No one was listening to the governor's speech. He glowered at the shoving throng. Every goddamn race under the sun is fidgeting behind the rope, he thought. A good thing we used a thick rope. It wouldn't do to have them jostle about the governor like so many heads of cattle.

"Damn this blasted heat!" he muttered to the young subaltern next to him. "Look at those Asiatics. No idea of orderly behaviour. A good thing we got the cordon up. Self-restraint is not in their blood, you know."

He twisted the ends of his moustache and exchanged

brief nods with the officials from the Colonial Office and the Federated Malay States who were standing stiffly in the red carpeted area. Next to them were the colony's European lawyers, bankers, insurers, merchants and representatives of the major European trading houses. No cordon of rope kept this elite group away from the red carpet, and if anyone had asked why, Ian Thomson would have muttered "Simply wasn't done, don't need to" by way of explanation, if at all. However, since no European would have noticed it anyway and no Asian would have challenged such disparity of treatment, Inspector Ian Thomson was allowed to go on thinking that his cordoning off of the Asians, with the exception of the English-educated Straits Chinese, was entirely natural and in keeping with the scheme of things out in the East. Like thousands of his kind in the colonies, he subscribed to the use of ropes and canes for Asians and believed that these, together with red carpets, guns, drums and gold braids, were the essence of power, vital to maintaining public order in a colonial society.

"Carry a big stick and use it if you have to. The cane is something that all coolies understand."

"That so, sir?"

"Why, Hennings, none of them speaks a known tongue."

"I did pick up a few words of Mandarin before coming out here."

Thomson chortled. "Old chap! Trouble is, these fellows don't speak it. It's mostly gibberish with them."

"Look over there, sir. Who might that be?"

"Why, that's Sir Hugh Low, Resident of the state of Perak. This man single-handedly tamed the Malays."

"Those Malays beside him must be nobles. They're splendid-looking in their rich baju and sarong."

"Indeed they are! Look at them now. Wealthy beyond their wildest dreams. Pax Britannia did it."

"I heard that these fellows are going with his excellency to a conference in Kuala Lumpur."

"The poor sods! They wouldn't understand a thing. If not for chaps like Sir Hugh Low, none of these royal buzzards would've known the meaning of conference! Why, they'd still be slitting each other's throats."

"But sir, shouldn't we teach the natives to govern themselves?"

"Good Lord, Hennings! What made you say a thing like that? It's contrary to their race and history!"

He stopped when he saw the Honourable Ong Boon Leong coming towards them.

"Good morning, Inspector Thomson."

"Good morning, Mr Ong. This is Sergeant Hennings."

"Pleased to meet you, Sergeant."

"Any news on the Exchange, sir?"

"The price of tin is showing signs of rising even higher on the London Exchange. It's good news all round, gentlemen. Have a good day."

"Same to you, Mr Ong."

They watched him walk over to the Straits Chinese delegation of traders and compradors. Like him, they were smartly attired in dark morning coats and silk cravats, looking much like their English counterparts from the Chamber of Commerce.

"Now that's a civilised western oriental gentleman." Thomson chuckled. His lobster-red face shone like a grotesque mask in the sunshine.

Tuck Heng, squeezed behind the rope cordon amongst the Asian traders, tried to catch the eye of the inspector. Clasping his hands together, he bowed several times. To his great mortification, Thomson did not acknowledge him with so much as a nod.

He was filled with shame. Dressed in the traditional robes of a Chinese mandarin, he had been conscious of his high rank. He had observed the ease with which Boon Leong had greeted the Englishman, as though they were equals. Self-contempt followed by resentment against his brother swept through him. Outwardly he remained a picture of calm and dignity. He glanced at his companions from the White Crane and wondered if any of them had noticed his humiliation. Fool! he berated himself. Only a fool would stoop so low as to bow to a low-ranking red-faced foreign devil such as Thomson! And just so that he could keep up the pretence that he was doing as well if not better than that English-speaking swine! Brothers in name and by adoption, they were like a chicken and a duck, each strutting in his own corner of the farmyard pretending the other did not exist.

He'd snorted before at the sycophancy of the likes of Boon Leong and his Straits Chinese British Association. He'd laughed at their ridiculous foreign attire, but he had also half-wished, especially on public occasions such as this, that he could speak the foreign devil's tongue as fluently as Boon Leong and move among them with ease. He realised with a deep sense of failure that, despite his wealth, he could never speak like a high-ranking English gentleman. His English was that of a foul-mouthed sailor's. A member of the lower classes. The riffraff despised by those of high rank, Boon Leong had told him in a moment of unthinking derision years ago. That barb had remained lodged in his heart to this day.

His ship chandling business had brought him into constant contact with English seamen and masters of vessels. In due course, he'd acquired a sailor's rough speech. In those days, due to his ignorance of English society and manners, he'd been very proud of his achievement, uttering the seamen's words in a clipped Cantonese accent.

He recalled with agony the day when he, like a vainglorious cockerel, had crowed in his newly acquired tongue in an attempt to impress Boon Leong and his brothers. Oh, how they had choked and doubled up in laughter when they heard his sailor's talk! That was when he'd realised with intense shame that his speech was of such a low kind, no English gentleman would have uttered it. His shame was all the more heart-wounding for he'd always prided himself on being the son of a gentleman and a poet. From that day onwards, he'd studiously avoided Boon Leong and his brothers. "River water shouldn't mix with well water," he told his wife, and they stopped visiting Roseville, Boon Leong's mansion.

That was years before. But his heart had never stopped yearning for recognition as a gentleman and not as the trader and shop proprietor he had become. The mandarin robes, the silk hat with its peacock feather and the jade beads he had donned for this occasion demonstrated the high rank he had attained, unfortunately not by a scholar's learning. Merchant's gold had turned him outwardly into a scholar-mandarin.

The band of the infantry regiment struck up. The governor was making his way through the crowd to receive their gifts and good wishes on behalf of the British monarch. Heart thumping, his excitement and expectation mounting as his excellency drew nearer, he stood stiffly at attention, eyes fixed on the representative of the British Crown, and waited like hundreds of others in the tropical blaze for his turn to touch the white god's hand.

Chapter Twenty-eight

"*H*ome!" he said to his gharry driver in Malay.

Inside his small carriage, he sat for a long time without changing his position, his angular face and unseeing eyes turned away from the window. But when his gharry had left the crowded streets behind, the calm mask fell and his face betrayed anguish and bewilderment. Self-loathing and anger fought for primacy. He had looked forward to the ceremony for months, so proud that he'd been selected for what everyone had regarded as a great honour, and yet here he was, feeling empty and belittled. Was it for this that he'd spent a thousand taels of gold to buy the high rank of a mandarin? So he could appear in silken robes and be counted among the lesser beings? If it hadn't been for Wong-soh, he wouldn't be wearing the silk robe and peacock feather of the Qing dynasty which had killed his father. "To be a mandarin official is the highest honour a son can bring to the family, an honour which will bless all your descendants. This will be so, Qing or Ming, as long as the Son of Heaven sits on the dragon throne. You're the only Wong left in your family and upon your shoulders rests the honour of the Wongs." How could he fight that? And so he'd agreed. But his rank had meant nothing to the white gods. And his adoptive brothers. The gulf between them was as wide as the Western Ocean. They stood on the red carpet and he, behind a rope.

Shame and anguish bit deep into his heart. Imagine what Boon Leong would've said had he heard him muttering his miserable speech to the governor—ten words he had rehearsed again and again. And the great white god didn't even spare him a glance. He gripped his knees till his knuckles turned white. The more intense his shame, the more he wanted to hit out and hurt that cockatoo who had turned up his nose at him and referred to him disparagingly as a China-born bumpkin.

Boon Leong and his brothers had turned against him after the death of Tai-kor Wong. And when Baba Wee, their grandfather, passed away, the entire Wee clan had excluded him from their circle. Envy. That was the only reason he could think of. This moneyed family of arrogant English-speaking cockatoos couldn't bear the thought that a China-born had more business acumen than any of them! Was more wealthy than any of them! Old wealth jealous of new! Envy gnawed at their entrails! They sneered at his inability to speak English, Malay and Penang Hokkien. But money is louder than words anyway. As the towkay of a ship chandling business, an import-export company and a tin mine, why should he care what they thought of him? The Wees for all their pride were on the decline. Didn't someone tell him recently that one of Baba Wee's daughters-in-law was reduced to selling beaded slippers she'd sewn herself?

A thin dry smile spread over his bespectacled clean-shaven face. He adjusted his well-oiled queue and silk hat and smoothed out the creases of his robe. A thousand thanks to his ancestral gods! He was no longer an impoverished clerk slaving for the Wees but a respectable merchant and leader of the China-born immigrant community, the Tai-kor of the White Cranes and someone to be reckoned with!

The steady clip-clop clip-clop of his fine horses down the tree-lined avenue, the sighing of the breeze among the angsana trees, the comfort of the plush seats in his carriage and thoughts of the wealth he'd accumulated began to have a soothing effect on his spirits. He looked out and waved to the naked urchins staring in awe at the fine carriage.

"Generosity" and "gratitude". These two characters should be engraved in his heart. He was not some ungrateful wretch who'd crossed the river and destroyed the bridge. No, he could never forget that it was Baba Wee who'd adopted him as his grandson and given him the chance to work and acquire wealth. True, he wasn't a grandson on the same footing as Boon Leong and his brothers. More like a poor dependant.

After the death of Tai-kor Wong, Baba Wee had given him work and shelter in a two-storey shophouse fronting the boat quay. That became his home for twelve years. At first he was employed as a junior clerk and spent his days hunched over the counter with a Chinese brush and ink, filling in the large ledgers under the supervision of the senior clerk. The shop serviced many merchant ships. His quick mind soon grasped the nature of the work and he rose to supervisor when he was twenty-two. Later, when none of his sons showed any inclination to take over the shop, Baba Wee entrusted him with the day-to-day running of the business.

He mastered very quickly the art of getting orders from the ships and he made sure that his coolies delivered the supplies on time. He even went out of his way to court the English merchant ships and ships of the Royal Navy which paid better than the Asian vessels. After years of shameless hustling, he became one of the few Chinese on Penang's waterfront who could parrot the English seaman's tongue. At first his fellow workers and coolies guffawed at the sight of him, pigtail swinging, trotting after the hairy six-footers, hollering at the top of his voice in what sounded like gibberish. But as more and more orders came his way, their jibes soon yielded to a grudging respect and they began to refer to him as the young man with the silver tongue.

Then Baba Wee died and the business suffered because of constant squabbling among the heirs. One day, in a fit of bad temper and rage, Baba Wee's eldest son sold the shop to him for peanuts, amidst much acrimony from other members of the family, in particular Boon Leong's mother. Siok Ching accused him of taking advantage of the Wees. "Thief!" she hurled the label at him as though it was he and not her brothers who had raided the family coffers. "Interloper!" "Marauder!" The others joined in the name-calling. Their bitter words rankled to this day. Siok Ching's dislike of him sprouted into open animosity when he bought over the ship chandling business. "Big eyes, small stomach! Let's see how much he can chew!"

To prove her wrong, he started to acquire land and properties that belonged to the Wees. If Baba Wee's sons were more interested in women, opium and gambling, then he was at liberty to buy up whatever they would've squandered away or sold to strangers anyway. At least he was half kin, even though they refused to recognise him.

Boon Leong and his brothers, Boon Haw and Boon Pin, kept away from him too. Not that they were ever close to begin with, even though the young Boon Pin had once taught him how to eat durians. A whole world and a foreign tongue separated them. Boon Leong and his brothers had been brought up as English-educated gentlemen, the sons of the land. Siok Ching made sure that, like her brothers, her sons would be the scions of a Straits-born family and subjects of an English king. She even changed their surname from the Cantonese "Wong" to the Baba-Hokkien "Ong", so that although the written character remained the same, the pronunciation didn't. A betrayal of their Cantonese ancestors, he thought. Over the years he'd watched in dismay as Boon Leong and his brothers became more and more like the English. They dressed like them and even cut off their queues and prayed in church, the followers of a man who had allowed his enemies to nail him to a cross! What madness could've possessed Siok Ching to permit her sons to forget their father and ancestors?

Could anyone blame him then if he assumed the duties of an eldest son? He wasn't out to usurp Boon Leong's place. But Tai-kor Wong must be honoured, if not by his own flesh and blood, then at least by the son he'd adopted. He set up Tai-kor Wong's memorial tablet next to his parents' so that Tai-kor Wong would continue to receive the incense and offerings of his descendants. And he'd done this quietly without accusing Boon Leong and his brothers of betraying their father. That they should continue to treat him as an outsider he could only put down to their arrogance and ingratitude.

"Slow! Slow!" his coachman shouted, reining in the horses as his carriage swept into the driveway.

How grossly inadequate his once spacious bungalow appeared to him now. The house, a simple squat building of brick styled like a Malay kampong house and raised above the ground by eight stone pillars, had belonged to Baba Wee's youngest son. It had eight windows on each side, eight rooms and eight stone steps leading to the front and back entrances— eight being an auspicious number for the Cantonese, sounding much like the character for "prosperity". This feature had caught his fancy and he'd bought the bungalow when its owner was strapped for cash.

At the time of its purchase, he was still foolishly nursing hopes of being accepted by the Wee relations; he'd thought that owning one of their bungalows would enhance his status, especially since he had saved it from falling into a stranger's hands. But instead of appreciating what he'd done, they had castigated him as a China-born marauder and vulture who had preyed on their weakness. The very people who'd praised him as a diligent boy years ago and seemed eager to help him rise in the world slandered him now. Even his wife, Choon Neo, chosen for him by Baba Wee, thought he wasn't good enough for her. He would show her one day who was good enough! He frowned as he alighted from his carriage.

"Papa is home!" Kok Seng called out.

"Uncle is home!" his son's little cousins echoed.

"Children, out of the way!" The amah shooed off the little ones and scooped up the youngest toddler before greeting him, "Towkay!"

Old Mr and Mrs Khoo, his parents-in-law, came out to greet him. His brothers-in-law, sisters-in-law and their children crowded onto the verandah. Standing just behind them was Dr Lee.

"They've all come to offer their congratulations," Choon Neo whispered as he came up the steps.

She was a slim handsome woman who wore her long hair in an elegant chignon held in place by several gold hairpins. He noticed that she was wearing her best sarong and kebaya embroidered with a design of flowers and leaves for the photo session he'd arranged.

"Father is so very proud. He hasn't stopped talking about you the whole morning," Choon Neo purred.

"It's a good start, a very good start! You never know what this might lead to." His father-in-law came up and shook his hand warmly. A thin sprightly man in his sixties who still adhered to the fashion of his clerical days, he wore the colonial clerk's white tunic, white trousers and black leather shoes. "Did his excellency shake hands with you?"

"I … I shook his hand, Father-in-law."

"There, Dr Lee! I told you they'd shake hands!"

"Aah, what an honour, Old Khoo, for your family," Dr Lee murmured.

"Mr Paterson also shook my hand when he said goodbye. Very nice man, you know. Never failed to wish us good morning or good afternoon whenever he met us. I was his clerk for fifteen years before he went back to London. He gave me a book before he left."

And they had to listen once again to his father-in-law talk about the time he had worked for the English trader.

"The photographer is waiting to take our picture. Tua Koh, are you ready?" Choon Neo asked him, using the Hokkien honorific, "elder brother", to address him. He couldn't fault her for lacking in wifely respect in public.

"Are the children ready?" he asked, looking round the room, his face showing no trace of the disappointment he had felt earlier.

"Kok Seng! Gek Lian! Gek Kim! Come out!"

"Here's something for you. Put them on before we sit for our photograph."

As her parents and relatives looked on, Choon Neo tore

open the red packet. A pair of gold bracelets encrusted with jade and diamonds glittered in her hand.

"So very pretty!" his mother-in-law exclaimed.

"Must've cost a lot of money, Brother-in-law!" Choon Sim exclaimed, her eyes full of envy. She had not married as well as her sister and the thought pleased him. It meant that in marrying him, Choon Neo was regarded as having made a good match.

"Choon Sim, the things you say sometimes! Of course they are expensive! Just look at the jade and diamonds!"

Old Mrs Khoo helped Choon Neo put on the bracelets and went on in a loud voice, "Such a good husband, so kind and generous. Where to find one like him?"

He smiled at that. His mother-in-law liked to talk in this manner. But she wasn't like this in the early days. Choon Neo thanked him and was pleased with his gift. It gave her much face and she certainly ought to be grateful.

"Seng! Come in with your sisters!" he called out to his twelve-year-old son.

"Come, Boy-boy! Let Grandma look at you."

But the boy was awkward and shy.

"Towkay, if you're ready, we can take the pictures now." The photographer bustled in with his camera and stands.

Everyone got up and started to move out of the way.

"Mak! Pa! Please be seated. No need to get up," Choon Neo called out to her parents.

"Please remain seated," he too called out. "Take the seats in the centre, Mak."

"Cannot! You should be in the centre. You're in your official robes."

"Mak, Tua Koh really wants you and Pa to sit in the centre. There on the rosewood chairs, right or not?" Choon Neo turned to him.

He nodded and invited his parents-in-law once again to take the place of honour.

"Please, Father-in-law, I beg you not to stand on ceremony."

He led Old Khoo to the rosewood chair and then insisted that his mother-in-law should take the other seat. Despite their protests, his parents-in-law were very pleased. "They are respectable but not rich." This was what Baba Wee had told him when the match was arranged. Choon Neo's father, a distant cousin of the Wees, was a clerk in one of the English shipping companies which used the chandling services of Wee & Sons. Old Khoo had obtained the match for his daughter. A China-born son-in-law with good prospects was much sought after by the poor Straits-born.

And he had not disappointed his in-laws. In the beginning, Old Khoo, who spoke English fluently, had laughed at him when he heard him on the waterfront, shouting, "Yesee, sir! Can do, sir! Can do, sir!" Uttered with such eager-beaver cheerfulness that Old Khoo had immediately dubbed him "Yesee sir". But as his business prospered and expanded, Old Khoo dropped the absurd name and referred to him as "Towkay Wong, my son-in-law".

And he, in turn, accepted the change of name as his due. But to show that he was pleased, he appointed Chong Beng, Choon Neo's brother, as the manager of his ship chandling trade and properties in Penang.

In his quieter moments, he would admit that he had been lucky. With thousands of Chinese immigrants pouring into the Malay Peninsula, he'd found opportunities and success, married two women and crowned his glory with an official rank bought from the Qing government in Kwangtung. Thousands of coolies had died still wearing the same tattered tunic they'd arrived in.

"Towkay Wong, we're ready," the photographer came up to him, bowing and smiling all the while.

"Where shall I sit?"

"Over here, Towkay. And Towkay-neo, please sit over here. Now, everyone! Please look front and don't move!"

The photographer disappeared behind his black cloth to peer at the company assembled before him.

Old Khoo and his wife sat on either side of a small rosewood table, a porcelain spittoon beside the table. Tuck Heng and Choon Neo sat stiffly on either side of them, he in his mandarin silk robe and she in her batik sarong and kebaya of embroidered organdie, pinned down the middle with three large kerosang of gold and diamonds. Kok Seng wore his school uniform of starched white tunic and trousers. His sisters wore embroidered blouses over pink ankle-length skirts. Their Uncle Kim Hock sported a hat and wore the fashionable colonial clerk's outfit, a white tutup with a high stiff collar and a row of metal buttons made from Siamese coins, and a pair of white twill trousers. Uncle Chong Beng wore a Chinese merchant's long gown and a short silk jacket with frog buttons. Their aunts were in embroidered kebaya and sarong, like their mother.

Dr Lee busied himself with the young children and, with the help of the amah, sat them in a straight row at the feet of their elders. Then he stepped back to admire his composition.

"Very nice, very nice!"

Neither he nor the photographer raised their brows over the family's sartorial mismatch. Malayan society was fast changing and this was reflected in its fashions and customs, one of which was to have a photograph taken to mark an important family event.

"Towkay, Towkay-neo, ready? Children, please don't move. Look straight here, into the camera. Don't move. Don't move." A blinding flash!

"My heart nearly dropped!" his mother-in-law exclaimed. "I hope the photo is nice!"

"Very nice, madam, very nice! Good fortune and blessing on your family!"

Chapter Twenty-nine

A week later, the family was seated round the dining table having breakfast.

"Tell Papa about your promotion, Seng."

"What promotion?"

He looked at his son seated opposite—a stranger, twelve years old, his age when he'd lost his own parents in the fire. At twelve he was living like a gutter rat, a fugitive from the law. Here was his own son, well-fed, soft-haired and fair, a typical Baba boy doted on by his mother and his amah. The boy had never eaten bitterness nor felt the sharp claws of hunger and misery. None of his children had. And he was proud of it.

"I passed the school examination, Papa."

"So you're a young scholar now?"

"No, Papa. I'm only in Standard Five."

"The English schools are different from the Chinese," Choon Neo began in the polite and well-modulated voice she used whenever she had to explain English things to him. The men in her family spoke the language of the white gods and had worked for them for years. "They follow a different standard. Boys must study many more years before they're called scholars. Not like the Chinese schools. Any boy in school only, they call him a scholar!" She sniffed.

He bristled at the haughty edge in her voice.

"Dr Lee said our Seng is clever for his age."

He put down his chopsticks and bowl of porridge.

"Not important what others say about him now. More important what he does later on in life!" he hit back at her. "So many Baba sons we know go to English schools. But only know how to waste their father's money. I didn't go to an English school! But I've got a head for business. Because I work hard and learn hard."

He knew he'd made his point when Choon Neo didn't contradict him. He turned to Kok Seng. "Continue to study hard. With every step, rise higher and work harder. The next mountain is always higher than the one you're on."

"Papa!"

"Gek Lian! Didn't I teach you not to interrupt your elders? Other people will think that your mother didn't teach you any manners!"

"All right, all right, no need to scold her. What is it?"

"You're spoiling her. Like this, she'll never be ladylike. Eleven already, but she still refuses to thread beads and embroider a pair of slippers."

"But I hate sewing."

"How can a girl from a proper family grow up and not learn how to sew? The first thing a mother-in-law will look at is your embroidery!"

"My Wong-ma never learned how to embroider slippers. She grew vegetables and ploughed the land back in Sum Hor! Deep in manure right up to her knees!" he chuckled. There was a perverse streak in his nature. The more Choon Neo wanted to forget that she'd married a China-born, the more he wanted to remind her of it.

"But, Papa, I don't want to grow vegetables! I want to go to school like Joo Bee!"

"Girl! What are you talking about?" Choon Neo threw up her hands in exasperation. "Haven't I told you time and again, your brother goes to school because later he's got to go out and work! Girls should stay home and learn all the things a young woman should know."

"But Joo Bee is a girl and Uncle Boon Leong allows her to go to school. They're taught by English women from the

Missionary Society." Gek Lian prattled the name in English before deftly switching back to their Hokkien dialect. "Joo Bee also told me her teachers said that nowadays women from good families also can go out to work."

"Who's Joo Bee?"

"Joo Bee is your niece." Choon Neo looked at him with exasperation. "Surely you can remember that she's Boon Leong's daughter?"

"You brought my children to Boon Leong's house? Don't you know how I feel about going there?"

"Tua Koh, I know how you feel about the family in Roseville. But Boon Leong is still your children's uncle whether you like it or not. His wife is their Second Aunt. Also my cousin. Their children are our children's cousins. And cousins should meet, right or not? Surely you don't expect me and the children to live in Penang as if we've no relations? No, please let me finish first." She raised her hand to stop him from interrupting.

"You've got your other family and relatives in Ipoh. Why can't the children and I have ours here in Penang? We live like we're all alone in this world: you're not home most of the time. Besides, everyone knows we're related to the Wees and Ongs. If we don't visit them at least once a year, where do you want me to put my face every New Year? So when Mak Siok Ching said to me, bring your children, I did!"

She was sobbing into her handkerchief by now.

"All right, all right! Bring them if you want to! But don't go empty-handed. Bring some ginseng and herbs."

He knew he would regret it but Choon Neo had a way of making him feel that she'd suffered at his hands and that he owed it to her to let her have her way. But what had his family in Ipoh got to do with things in Penang anyway? He treated his two wives equally—the one chosen for him by Baba Wee and the other, by Wong-soh. Other women whom he'd chosen for himself and installed in houses elsewhere did not count as his wives although they served him in a way Choon Neo never did. Yet he was a considerate husband and accepted that females had their moods and there were times a man should not go near them.

His treatment of his wives was a vast improvement over what Tai-kor Wong and Baba Wee had done. Even if he had to sing his own praises. Hadn't he established separate households for all his women so that his wives and mistresses need not suffer under the thumb of one dominant wife? A less considerate, less forward-looking man wouldn't have done that. Separate households were expensive! But he'd wanted to treat his women well. He understood their need to be mistress of their own home. Surely this counted for something? A man ought to be measured against the standards of his community. And by his community's standards, he was kinder than most men. Choon Neo should open her eyes and look around and see how many husbands had done what he had, he thought irritably.

He turned to Kok Seng. "So you want to visit your Uncle Boon Leong and grandma?"

"Right, Papa," the children answered, sober and quiet, fearing another argument between their parents.

Choon Neo poured a cup of tea and handed it to him.

"Tua Koh, I give Mak Siok Ching herbs and ginseng whenever I visit her." Then after a pause, she added, "I know I should've told you earlier, but I didn't want to trouble you with such small matters."

He picked up his chopsticks and began to eat again to show that he was pleased by the change in her tone. He had to admit that Choon Neo had done the proper thing in bringing the children to Roseville. Especially during the Lunar New Year. Siok Ching would always be his Second Mother. He couldn't run away from that.

Choon Neo poured out more tea. She knew she'd won. No longer was there any need to hide their visits to Roseville. They could go as often as they liked. And Kok Seng would grow up with his cousins and acquire the self-assurance that only the sons of the rich moving in the right kind of society could acquire. In Roseville, Choon Neo was sure that Kok Seng would have many opportunities to mingle with the sons of those who mattered in society—English-educated lawyers, doctors and people who were well-bred and well-connected. Some day her son would go to London and return as a barrister or a doctor like his uncles.

"Papa, can I go to school like Joo Bee?"

"Gek Lian!"

"But Mak, I want to study!"

"Choon, didn't you say you learned to read at home?"

"I did." Her haughty tone returned as she described how she was tutored at home by a nun who had wanted to convert the family. "My father also tutored us whenever Sister Mary was too busy to come. Every night we children had to read to him. He didn't go out with his friends to drink or play mahjong like other men."

He heard the mild reproach in her voice. From the start, he had been a busy father. Tomorrow he would be leaving for Ipoh and Kuala Bandong and would be away for several months.

"Study at home like your mother, Gek Lian."

"But girls go to school nowadays, Papa. Even long ago in China, Zhu Yingtai went to school disguised as a boy."

"You've been watching too much opera." Nevertheless he was pleased that his daughter knew the famous legend of Liang Shanbo and Zhu Yingtai.

"I want to be like Zhu Yingtai."

"But she was so heartbroken when Liang Shanbo died, she killed herself by jumping into his grave. Do you want your life to be that sad?"

"What a thing to say, Seng!" Choon Neo clapped a hand over her heart and quickly muttered a short prayer to ward off the evil omen.

"Wash your mouth, you naughty boy!" Gek Kim, the eight-year-old, giggled.

"Papa, the convent school in Light Street is very good. All girls, no boys!" Gek Lian pleaded.

"Can I go to school too, Papa?"

"No, you can't!" Gek Lian glared at her younger sister.

"Both of you can't! You're girls!" their brother exclaimed.

"Girls go to school nowadays! Stupid!" his sisters shouted at him across the table.

"Stop it! You sound like market hawkers! Even if girls go to school these days, they don't talk with their hands on their hips."

"But Mak, Uncle Boon Leong says the world is changing."

"That doesn't mean you don't have to act like a lady. Your Mak is not blind. I can see that the world is changing. Dr Lee's granddaughters and your uncles' children are studying in the convent. Even Mr Tan, Papa's accountant, sends his daughters there. Now your Papa knows more about what's happening in the world than us. So you girls wait for his decision and don't pester him. Understand?"

She poured out another cup of tea and handed it to him. He glanced at her as he sipped his tea. It wasn't so rare these days for a girl to go to school. The world was changing. Choon Neo was right, as always, on such matters.

"Your Mak and I know that education is very important," he began slowly, weighing each word. "The world is changing and girls do go to school nowadays. We're living in modern times, in the twentieth century, not like the days of long ago.

"Look around you today. The foreign devils have built roads and railways here. They even have a telegraph service between Penang and London, and Singapore and Hongkong. Nowadays no need to wait months for news. When I was a boy working in the tin mines, I never knew the world was going to be like this!"

His voice rose steadily as he spoke. Seldom had Choon Neo given him the opportunity to appear so knowledgeable. At the same time, he suspected that his talk was part of his wife's master plan. Yet, despite his misgivings, he felt himself growing more enthusiastic as he described the wonders of the modern Western world to his children and spoke about the importance of school and education.

"Wealth and fortune, you can waste, but an education you'll keep all your life. And you'll learn many new things in school. Every week I read the Chinese newspapers from Singapore.

Something new all the time. Dr Sun Yat-sen's wife, Soong Ching-ling—do you know she's a graduate from an American college for women?"

"She went to university, Papa? A girl?"

"Not every China-born is old-fashioned, you know. So you see, Seng, these days even girls from China go abroad to other countries to study."

"And boys? What about the boys, Papa?"

"Even more boys go abroad. The governor of Kwangtung Province has just sent twelve young men to England to study shipbuilding."

"Papa, we can go to school?" the two girls asked.

"Let Papa finish what he's saying first!" Choon Neo served him yet another cup of tea, proffering the teacup with both hands this time. That's the way it should be. He was, after all, one of the most progressive men in these parts, a man in tune with the thinking of the new age.

"Choon, you can send the girls to the convent school."

"Oh Papa!" the girls squealed and danced round the room.

When they had quietened down, he took out a Chinese newspaper a clansman in Hongkong had sent him. He put on his glasses and read from it.

"Our scholars and officials should learn and adopt Western methods and principles of government for the sake of the people. Many scholars do not know that the science of government in the Western countries has rich and varied contents. Its chief aim is to develop the people's knowledge and intelligence, and to enable their countrymen to earn a livelihood in order to better their lives."

"I never knew that the Chinese newspapers publish things like this!" Choon Neo exclaimed. "I always thought they only write about old-fashioned things."

"How can you know? You don't read the newspapers."

For once he had shown Choon Neo that the China-born knew a thing or two about the modern world. He stuffed his papers back into his bag and took a sip of tea. A tiny smile played on his lips as he savoured it.

"Those young men who were sent to England, did they learn to read and write English, Papa?" Kok Seng asked.

"Surely they have to! You children remember Uncle Koh Hong Beng? We met him in Uncle Boon Leong's house. He went to England. He's the first man in Malaya to have a degree in English Literature."

"Mak, I remember, I remember!" Kok Seng was wriggling in his seat with excitement. "He's the one who played the piano in Uncle Boon Leong's house. Papa, when I grow up, I want to go to England to study too and then I will cut off my queue."

"Are you mad?"

The sudden silence round the table made his voice seem louder than he had intended.

"Our queue tells the world that we're Chinese!"

"But Tua Koh, all our relatives have cut off their queues."

"Your relatives! Not mine!"

"But what about your brothers? Boon Leong, Boon Haw and Boon Pin cut them off long ago!"

"That's their business! We Chinese don't cut off our queues!"

Chapter Thirty

The next morning, when they were seated in the gharry driving into town, Tuck Heng studied his son's face and wondered if he'd done the right thing in letting Choon Neo enrol the boy in an English school. "All his cousins are studying there. If Seng has no English, he'll get nowhere," she'd argued. But what's the result? The boy wants to cut off his queue!

He glanced at Kok Seng's head and was comforted that the boy was wearing his queue down his back like a Chinese gentleman.

Their gharry was driving past shophouses, five-foot ways and lanes lined with hawkers' wooden stalls. People from a thousand nations thronged the open market along the road. Penang was not Sum Hor. He sighed. Not Kwangtung Province, not China. It's a barbaric island on the margin of the Middle Kingdom where no queues adorned the heads of others. So why should he care what his son wore? Hadn't he married into a Straits-born Baba family full of English-educated men?

The world was no longer what it was when he was twelve or thirteen. Who could have predicted then that he would end up a rich towkay with a Nonya wife and Baba in-laws? Truly, a man's destiny is written in heaven, he thought, staring at Kok Seng till the boy, uncomfortable under his gaze, turned away and looked out of the window.

The world was tilting westwards. Even the Son of Heaven had begun to send bright young men to Britain to study engineering. And some of them had returned from abroad without their queues, sporting false ones under their felt hats to avoid trouble with the authorities. He recalled reading in the newspapers something Dr Sun Yat-sen, the president of the Revive China Society, had said in Hongkong. "Restore Chinese rule and expel the Manchus. Cut off your queue. It tells the world that we Chinese are a conquered people!" This was hard for him to accept. The Chinese had worn the queue for three hundred years. To cut it off was like chopping off an arm or leg. But things were changing fast. A man's head could turn giddy just thinking of the changes sweeping through China. Professors and students in the universities were openly defying the Qing government and calling for a revolution. What a time for a boy to be growing up!

He glanced at Kok Seng. What could a father say? He took out his silver pocket watch, looked at it and poked his head out of the window.

"Samy, faster!" he yelled to make himself heard above the noise in the street.

He couldn't wait to get away from Penang Island and return to the mainland and his business. A father must provide for his sons. And his daughters, he added as an afterthought. He'd just built a mansion in Ipoh and was waiting to move his second family into it. And on the way, he planned to stop in Bandong to look at a piece of land he'd been eyeing for a long time. It belonged to Musa Talib. The impoverished trader would be glad to get some money for it. He would build a huge Buddhist temple and monastery on that land in memory of the brave souls who had fought and died in the Bandong wars. He dreamed of developing Bandong into a big town, a modern town with brick houses, shops, schools, water piped into the homes and, some day, electricity. As a man of vision, he'd drag Bandong into the modern world and turn the sleepy village into a town. Then he'd be its number one citizen with streets and schools named after him.

He glanced at Kok Seng and envied the boy the future that awaited him. He was going to bequeath to his sons what he himself never had—land. A bit of earth in one's hand would turn a boy into a man.

His gharry had reached the waterfront. Ahead of him was a half-day's journey by steamer to Port Weld, and then another half day by train to Kuala Bandong, one night's stopover in that village and then on to Ipoh where his second family lived. Kok Seng looked up and muttered what sounded like "Have a safe journey, Papa."

"Study hard."

Then he opened the door and got off the gharry.

⋄⋅═◎═⋅⋄

Kok Seng leaned out of the window and watched till his father was lost in the crowd. "Go, Samy! Faster!" he yelled.

St Xavier's Boys' School was not too far from the sea front. Kok Seng jumped down from the gharry the minute it arrived at the gate. The morning bell had not sounded yet. Most of the boys were talking in little groups here and there on the playground. The more boisterous ones were running and chasing one another and getting all hot and sweaty. Hock Hin, his best friend, was waiting for him.

"I've got it, Seng! It's in my bag," he announced the moment he saw him.

Kok Seng nodded; his face was solemn and determined. This was the day and he was going to do it. He'd been planning this for weeks, and yesterday, when he tried to bring it up, his father had bawled at him. It'd be useless trying to talk to his father about it again.

"You can get disowned, you know, if your father finds out. I heard my uncle telling my father that this sort of thing happens among the old-fashioned China-born. Even in Singapore."

"I know, I know." He hated it when people lumped him with the China-born. Only his father was a China-born; he was a Straits-born, he reminded Hock Hin.

"My uncle said that one China-born towkay in Singapore disowned his son. Called him barbarian and foreign devil and chased him out of the house."

Kok Seng looked at the groups of boys on the playing field. Those fellows, like Hock Hin, had no pigtail. They wore their hair short like their English schoolmasters while he had to wear his long like the Chinese coolies. Why couldn't he be like the rest of them? He pushed his pigtail under the silk cap to keep it out of sight and grinned at Hock Hin. His heart was beating faster on account of what he was planning to do. "Be resolute in one's actions," Brother O'Brien had told them during assembly and he took comfort in those words.

"Give me the parcel. I'll hide it in my bag."

"You'd better keep your promise. My father will kill me if he finds out that I helped you."

The school bell rang and the boys filed into the hall. Brother Director and the teachers were already waiting for them on the stage. As he walked into the hall and took his place in the rows, he felt their eyes on him as he passed them. He didn't dare meet their eyes. His head felt heavy and so did his school bag with the parcel stuffed between his books. His throat went dry. He could hardly sing the Ave Maria and the school song. The gaze of the saints hanging on the walls burned into his head. He looked up at the grim-faced St Francis Xavier, the serious St Ignatius of Loyola, then the cheerful St Francis of Assissi and the bearded founders of the school in their dark soutanes. No queues, he thought. And yet these men were not bandits although his father called them foreign devils. Saints, not devils, he contradicted his father and felt the sudden rush of blood to his head. He was getting bold. And he liked it. His heart was beating so loudly by now that he could hardly hear what Brother Director was saying. All he could think of was his plan and what he was going to do after school.

His plan loomed large in his mind, filling his childish imagination with all sorts of terrible images. He could be thrown out of the house for this, he thought. He could be made homeless. But he had to do it. Awed by his own boldness, he could hardly wait for school to end. He had spoken to no one at home so nobody would be responsible for what he was about to do. He and only he would be responsible. For a man should carry the burden of his own action, he thought, repeating a saying he had so often heard his father utter.

He had told Hock Hin only because he needed his friend's help in purchasing the wig, but he alone had decided on what course of action to take. He felt faint with the headiness of his own decision and then a quiver of fear shook him for he knew not what the consequences would be if his father found out. He stole a look at his schoolmates. They seemed to be deep in prayer. He smiled, reassured. No one was looking at him. They were pretending to listen to the Brother Director. He leaned forward in his seat and tried to catch Hock Hin's eye, but his friend was looking elsewhere. Would he be able to do it, he wondered. What if he lost his nerve? And what if he failed? Or was caught by his amah, or worse, his mother? Would she take his side against his father?

Brother Director was reading something to the school, "… and therefore a man shall leave his father and mother and cleave …" The words startled him and sent his thoughts into a wild spin. Was he cutting off his father and mother? Was he becoming a man and leaving his father?

He closed his eyes and clasped his hands as the hall resounded with the Lord's Prayer and a Hail Mary. The closing, "now and at the hour of our death", comforted him. After the final "Amen" had died away, his head felt clearer. He followed the other boys and they filed out of the hall. The rest of the school day passed, but he couldn't remember what they did in class.

After school he went home and locked himself in his bedroom, pleading that he had homework to finish. Alone, he stood resolutely in front of the mirror, a pair of scissors in his hand. His reflection showed a sturdy lad of medium height, blessed with the soft Baba features of his maternal grandfather. He had his grandfather's pale *langsat* skin, small intelligent eyes and slender hands. The firm chin, bone structure and broad dark brow, however, were his father's and so was his look of obstinacy as he raised the scissors.

His father was wrong. Everyone knew their ancestors. It had nothing to do with the length of a man's hair. His grandfather and uncles wore theirs short like the English. And Grandpa had told him that their forefathers came from China more than three hundred years ago. Two of his great-great-granduncles had served in the court of sultans and princes and one of them was killed by the Portuguese when the latter conquered Malacca.

Of his father's own family in China, he had only a vague notion that they had been physicians and that all but his father had perished in a great fire. His father had never spoken of it. He'd only picked up bits of the story, listening to the adults who assumed that all children in their midst were deaf.

He looked into the mirror and snipped off a lock of his hair. A thrill of fearful elation coursed through his trembling hands. What if his father should disinherit him and throw him out of the house? What if …? What if …? But he was a Straits-born, not a China-born. Not a *ching chong cheena geh*. An English-educated boy, that's what he was! He snipped off another lock of hair. He would not grow up looking like an illiterate coolie. He snipped again. Another lock fell. Then again and again. Hair fell around him. Bold and light-headed, he went on cutting. He wanted to be an engineer, a builder of railroads, steamers and trains. A man of the modern world! A man of science and new knowledge! Wait till those fellows in school saw him! They would have no tail to pull! They couldn't call him *tow chang kia*, "pigtail boy", any more.

He gazed at his new image in the mirror. Hair touching his shoulders like one of the outlaws in the *Tales of the Water Margin*. He smiled at his new self. His amah had told him that Chinese men without queues were outlaws in their homeland. But this was Penang, not China. He wondered what his mother would say at the sight of his hair sticking out like a wild man's. He ought to go down the lane, wait for the Indian barber and get him to trim his hair and style it like an Englishman's.

His palms were sweaty as he tore open the parcel from Hock Hin. Inside was a silk pumpkin cap with a fake pigtail. He put it on and pushed his own hair under the wig. Then he looked into the mirror. He could look like a China-born at home, but in school he would take off his fake pigtail and look like the Baba boys. In this way he figured he could be both a Straits-born and a China-born. A boy with two identities. He grinned at himself in the mirror.

Chapter Thirty-one

*I*brahim stepped off the boat to the stirring beat of kompang drums. The jetty was crowded with villagers who had come to greet their penghulu, the headman of Kuala Bandong. He returned their greetings and thanked Allah for his safe arrival.

"*Assalamualaikum!* My old eyes are glad to see you," Musa Talib said.

"*Waalaikumussalam!*" he returned his old friend's greeting of peace.

"Datuk, you've brought great honour to our village and district," Haji Hamid declared. "Welcome home!"

"Welcome home!" the other men echoed his sentiment.

Haji Hamid was a highly respected reader of the Holy Book during the Friday prayers. Sometimes he assisted the Imam and recited the prayers aloud, filling their village mosque with the resonance of his strong clear voice.

"Welcome home, my honoured Father," Omar bowed respectfully, his lips lightly brushing his father's outstretched hand.

Ibrahim beckoned his twelve-year-old son to walk beside him as he talked to the villagers. He knew that Omar was eager to hear what he had to say about his trip to Kuala Lumpur, the capital of the Federated Malay States, a new political entity created by the British.

The young men started to beat the kompang drums in a stirring tempo and the villagers walked in procession from the jetty to the compound of his house, the largest in the village, almost a replica of the one destroyed by the English soldiers. The villagers crowded onto the verandah.

"Our journey by train was wonderful! Faster than the fastest bullock cart! We travelled with His Royal Highness, the chiefs and their advisors to Kuala Lumpur by this new train."

"Tok Penghulu, what's Kuala Lumpur like?"

"Kuala Lumpur is a big town. Very big. So many roads and people, and so many carriages, rickshaws, bullock carts and gharries on the roads that I lost count! The number of shops and big houses was astounding; I almost got lost!"

"Who own these houses? Who own them, eh?" Musa Talib was tapping his cane impatiently on the floor.

"Alas! Not us, Pak Mus. They belong to the white men, the Chinese towkays and some of our wealthy chiefs. But let me tell you about the Rulers' Conference," he quickly added. "It was held in a grand building. Bigger than a sultan's palace. All the important white men like the tuan besar governor were there. His Royal Highness, Sultan Idris, gave a long speech. A most eloquent man. He asked them to put more Malays in important positions in the government. My heart was filled with pride listening to him speak to the white men."

"Did they really listen to him?" Musa's querulous voice rose above the murmurs of the men.

"They listened to His Royal Highness with the greatest of respect, Pak Mus."

"Did the Chinese people listen to him too?"

"They were not there."

"But Kuala Lumpur is their city, is that not so? Built by their Kapitan China, Yap Ah Loy?" one of the men said.

"Don't talk nonsense! Chinese people don't own towns!"

"Pak Mus is right. Kuala Lumpur is not owned by them. It's the headquarters of the tuan besar governor of the Straits Settlements, also resident general of the Federated Malay States. Our Negeri Perak is part of the Federation now."

Patiently, he went on to tell his people about the beauty of Kuala Lumpur. Most of the villagers had never been out of Bandong, much less ridden on a train, which they called *kereta api*, "the fire car". Their world was the world of rice fields, rivers and forests. As their penghulu, he'd used every opportunity to widen their knowledge of the world, but habits of mind and the ways of the forefathers were too deep and narrow for one headman to change in a lifetime.

"According to the calendar of the white man, this is the year 1903, the year of the second Rulers' Conference. A very grand and special event for all our states. The sultans of Negeri Perak, Selangor, Pahang and Negeri Sembilan and their chiefs and advisors met to discuss important affairs with the tuan besar governor."

Seeing the villagers' uncomprehending looks, he switched to another topic he knew they would appreciate. He told them of the grandeur of the governor's palace.

"The dining table alone can seat sixty guests comfortably. Their women ate with the men. There were silver forks, silver spoons, silver knives, all from the white man's country. Everybody had to eat in the white man's way, using knives and forks. Including our sultans."

A loud gasp rose from the villagers.

"Did the white men wash their hands?" Imam Leman wanted to know.

"How strange to use forks and knives to eat!" Haji Hamid declared. "My own hand, I know where it has been. But other people's forks and spoons, I don't know where they have gone to! How can I be sure that they have not been wiped with a dirty rag?" he asked amidst loud laughter.

"But what did His Royal Highness say to the tuan besar governor in Kuala Lumpur?" a village elder asked.

"Many things, Pak Salim, many things. He asked the tuan besar governor to train more Malays so that we can join the government service."

"Asked? Why asked?" Musa Talib was indignant. He glared at Ibrahim as if it was his fault. "Do you people know it used to be the other way round? The white men asked the sultan and waited for his reply! Now the world is upside down! The sultans have to ask the white men! For advice! For money! For ... for ... for!" The old man coughed so vehemently that he had to stop speaking.

Ibrahim could tell that Musa Talib's cough was the hard dry cough of the habitual opium smoker. He averted his gaze. He pitied and despised the old man. For years old Musa and his sons had been ensnared by the Chinese parasites who operated the opium and gambling dens in Bandong Valley. They had lost heavily at the gaming tables of the vultures and owed the bloodsucking moneylenders vast sums of money, like so many chiefs and their families in Perak and elsewhere.

The decline of Musa Talib's fortunes was a sign of the times. The old Malay world of his childhood had passed away. The white men had taken over the running of the country. The chiefs, who used to let Musa trade on their behalf, had become poverty-stricken after their right to collect taxes had been stripped from them and they had to live on the small stipends granted by the white rulers. And many of them, like Musa's sons, had foolishly dreamed of increasing their small incomes at the gaming tables of the Chinese crocodiles.

"Pak Mus, you're tired. Let Zam and Din see you home."

He knew the signs by now and was determined not to let the old trader's tirade against the white men mar his homecoming. "We'll talk again after the Friday prayers," he told the villagers.

Musa Talib struggled to his feet. A spasm of coughing shook his large sagging frame as Zam, a young farmhand, helped him down the steps. The other village elders took their leave too, followed by the rest of the men.

Ibrahim stood on the steps and watched his people depart. He'd not done too badly, he thought. Though not as rich as the Datuk Panglima Kinta of the Kinta Valley, which had the big town of Ipoh as its crown jewel, he'd managed to remain Datuk and a penghulu of Bandong Valley. He wasn't rich, but at least he wasn't destitute like so many other members of the nobility, he consoled himself.

His father had been wise to send him to the white man's school. His six years in the Penang Free School, with fees paid for by Baba Wee, had helped him learn the white man's language sufficiently to communicate with the district officers. Then he'd returned to Bandong to marry the girl chosen by his mother and the government had appointed him the penghulu of Kuala Bandong. After the war, the white men had abolished the position of menteri of Bandong Valley and divided the tinrich valley into several districts. Although nothing was said, he knew that the abolishment of the menteri's post was a punishment for his father's part in the murder of Birch and the revolt against white rule. After the white man's victory, there were no powerful chiefs left in Perak. Sultan Abdullah was exiled and all the chiefs who had taken part in the revolt were hanged.

At first he'd found his job of assisting the English officers a very bitter pill to swallow. He was, after all, the son of the former menteri of Bandong who'd had hundreds of slaves at his beck and call. Mr Douglas, the district officer, was a commoner whose skin turned red as a boiled prawn in the sun and whose speech and manners had not endeared him to the Malays. But Ibrahim had learned to keep such thoughts to himself. He was a man of the world and he realised it had changed irrevocably. It had become a white world!

It had turned white the day the son of Perak's most powerful chief threw in his lot with the white men. Seri Adika Raja had fought like a tiger against the British. But the great chief was killed when he tried to escape from British reprisals after the death of the much-hated Birch. A few years later, his son, Wan Mat Salleh, did the unthinkable! Before the shocked eyes of he Malay nobles, Wan Mat Salleh agreed to work in the British Resident's office! And so the great chief's son became the first of many Malay nobles to work for the white man. In 1885, Wan Mat Salleh even helped the white rulers to settle a dispute with Pahang's royal family. At first he was castigated by many chiefs for his betrayal of the Malay cause. However, in 1894, and Ibrahim remembered this with great pain and clarity, when the white rulers appointed Wan Mat

Salleh to Perak's Legislative Council and returned to him his rightful title of Seri Adika Raja, every Malay aristocrat in the land began to change his tune. They praised Wan Mat Salleh for his political astuteness! The mousedeer had fooled the crocodiles! What cunning! What cleverness! Better the humility of the mousedeer than the loud roars of a toothless tiger! Royal families began to send their sons to work for the white men.

No fool himself, he'd watched and learned. Over the years, he'd seen how once powerful chiefs were thrown out of office by the victorious white men. Without their tax collection and slaves, noble families were reduced to destitution. His own mother had wept when she discovered how her relatives and friends had demeaned themselves by working as manual labourers in road and railway construction gangs simply to keep body and soul together. His mother had told him such horrendous stories that, as a young man growing up in Penang, he'd vowed he would succeed at all cost by adapting to the requirements of the white man's rule and save his family from such shame.

With a pragmatism that belied his youth at the time, he stopped moaning for those bygone days. Who could bring back the past when even the sultans and their great chiefs seemed happy to forget that they were once the supreme rulers? Ibrahim willed himself not to be bitter.

"Stooge! Where's your courage, son of Bandong?" Musa Talib had taunted him more than once for accepting the minor appointment of penghulu. But he forgave Musa. The old trader was loyal to the old ways. There was nothing wrong with that, he thought. Musa Talib had the courage to go on opposing while others had stopped.

But Ibrahim knew it took more than courage to oppose the white men. Once, two chiefs from Negeri Sembilan had foolishly petitioned a visiting admiral from Turkey to remove the white men from their country. Not only were the chiefs dismissed from their office by the British Resident, they were also rebuked publicly by their sultan. This incident had sent a shock wave among the chiefs all over Malaya, and Ibrahim realised then that the sultans were against opposition to the white men.

With heavy heart and steely determination, he had settled down to his work as a native assistant to the district officer. A minor appointment; yet he could not help but feel proud that he was one of the few Malays considered good enough to be appointed to the Malayan Civil Service. This was an elite service dominated by the white men and from which even the sons of some sultans were excluded. Out of one hundred and fifty-nine officers in the civil service, he was one of only five Malays appointed. Sultan Idris had announced this dismal fact during the Rulers' Conference.

Ibrahim thanked Allah for His mercy. He was glad that he had listened to the imam in the Penang mosque where he'd attended Friday prayers during his lonely student days. "Vengeance is an accursed emotion," the imam had told him, his voice gentle and wise. "It should be left in the hands of Allah. Take care of your people and walk the path of right-eousness and peace. Allah in His mercy will be just."

"Praise be to Allah," Ibrahim murmured as he went into the house where his wife, mother and children were waiting for him.

⊷══◉══⊶

Across the Bandong River, Musa Talib was making his way home with the help of two farmhands.

"Easy, Pak," Din said kindly as he brought his sampan close to the riverbank. "Watch your step."

"Thank you, thank you." Musa coughed and wheezed. "I've got to clear the disgust clogging up my lungs!" He spat a thick green gob into the river. "Our penghulu ..." He wheezed and stopped. It wouldn't be right for him to tell Zam and Din what he thought of Ibrahim's smugness. "Nah!" He changed his mind. "The tiger cub has grown into a kitten."

"What?"

"Kittens! We're all kittens now! We were tigers once! Remember? Lord of the jungle! Nah! What do you ignorant fools know?"

"Hey, Pak! We row you across the river and you insult us?"

"Insult? What do you frogs know about insult? For years you've been living under a coconut shell! The insults of the white men are everywhere, but you don't smell a thing!" Musa tottered out of the boat.

"Din, we go back! The old man's crazy!"

"Go! Go away! What do you youngsters know about insults? We Malays can't even carry our own kris into town nowadays! And this is our country. And didn't you hear? His Royal Highness has to beg the white chief to let us work in the government! But we were the government!"

"Shh! Pak! The whole village will hear you."

"Who cares? If I were young again, I'd wear my kris in my sarong and … and …" he coughed and sputtered, and had to stop to catch his breath.

Din walked with him to his house. Its wooden supports had been eaten by white ants so one side was lower than the other.

"Thank you, Din, thank you! I used to carry the sharpest kris in Bandong. Aye, we were kings and warriors in those days! The Datuk's father and I used to fight the English dogs! We burned their ships and dumped their bodies into the sea! Now we beg them to give us work! Phui!" He spat.

He just couldn't understand it. How could things have changed so much with the death of one miserable English dog? Birch! That very name filled him with hatred. Heroes had died because of that dog! And yet neither their blood nor their cannons had stopped the greed of the white men. And they had come and spread their rule like a billowing shroud over the land! And no one seemed to mind. The peasants lived as before—like dumb oxen in the field. And the sultans and their princes? They lived even better than before—like birds in golden cages.

"I should've run away to be a pirate." He sighed. "Too late, too late."

Musa dismissed Din wearily and went up the steps of his house. It was time for his evening meal.

"Som!" he called out to his wife as soon as he entered the covered verandah.

"Pak Musa, good evening!"

"Che' Wong! What brought you here?"

"Ah, Pak Musa, a good wind! Your health, good, ah? I've brought you a little something. Very small."

His eyes lit up when he saw the bale of Indian muslin on the floor and the box of cigars which Tuck Heng was holding out to him with both hands.

"Thank you, my friend, thank you. You're very generous, my friend, very generous to think of an old man like me."

"I think of you sometimes, Pak Musa."

He found Tuck Heng unusually solicitous, enquiring about his wives and his good-for-nothing sons.

"Aye, we're well, thanks be to Allah. Please sit down, Che' Wong."

He re-tied the knot of his sarong before sitting on the mat. Then he reached for his *sireh* box, took out a betel leaf on which he spread some lime, sprinkled some cinnamon powder and bits of arecanut, and folded the leaf over this mixture before stuffing it into his mouth. He pushed the box towards his visitor.

"You chew sireh, Che' Wong?"

"No, thank you, Pak Musa."

"What can this poor man here do for you, Che' Wong?"

"Pak Musa, how can you say you're poor? You're sitting on a goldmine! Your land by the river is worth lots of money!" The laughter sounded false to his ears, but all the same he listened attentively as Tuck Heng launched into a long speech in fractured Malay about how land sold off at the right time had made many Malay chiefs rich. "They know how to seize chance to make money. Like a hawk seizes its prey. Many white traders looking for land to buy. And the government sells. Thousands of acres of Malay land to the white traders. But Malay landowners are getting cheated by the white men!"

"What can I do?"

"I can help you and the chiefs. Sell your land. Chinese buyers pay you and your friends many money. Better price!"

"But I don't want to sell my land."

"Pak Musa, your land brings you money. Money good."

"I know! But I didn't say I wanted to sell my land!"

"Ahem! Pak Musa, I … I've something to tell you. You know our mutual friend, Merchant Lim Ah Teck? He gives this letter to you."

Tuck Heng handed him the letter written in a fine Jawi script by a Malay letter writer on behalf of the Chinese merchant. He gazed at the letter for a long time without saying a word. Finally he roused himself and yelled to his wife, "Som! More light!"

His old woman brought in an oil lamp, placed it on the floor and left. He held the letter in his trembling hands and read it.

About three years ago, I addressed my friend on his debt to Inche Chan Ah Kow and Inche Wong Tuck Heng and my friend in reply promised to settle the amount. This, Inche Wong informs me, has not been settled and the full sum remains still due. I trust that …

He crumpled the letter in his hand; he couldn't go on. But there was no need to read to the end anyway. He knew the rest of its contents. It was a proposal urging him to sell his land to his creditors.

He felt the keen eyes of the vulture upon him. He refused to look up. He shifted the weight of his old body, making the floorboards creak painfully with age. He coughed and finally he spoke, but he still didn't look at the vulture.

"I'm just a poor old man. Insya Allah, I will die poor but never have to sell my land to anyone! You understand? Never!" He spat the red sireh juice out of his mouth and it splattered upon the mat near the vulture's foot. He knew that he was being extremely rude. But there was no need to be courteous to a vulture waiting to peck at his bones. Where's honour and friendship these days? The friendship that Baba Wee and Tai-kor Wong had shown him? The friendship of those days when

Tai-kor Wong was his partner and blood brother? The days of honourable men who dared to fight the white dogs! Not greedy men driven by money and profit!

"Ahem! Pak Musa!"

He refused to look up. Even his sons were waiting to feed on his corpse! He spat again and lapsed into a resentful silence. Let his creditors hound him! Let those vultures do what they like! When British guns and cannons turned Malay dragons into earthworms, he crawled under a coconut shell to hide his grief and shame. Let them call. Let them knock! But he'd stay inside his shell.

⟡

It rained heavily the next day. Loud incessant torrential rain fell upon the attap roofs. Storm clouds rolled down from the distant hills and thunder rumbled ominously above the valley. The storm unleashed such tempestuous winds that several trees were uprooted in the night. The winds whipped through the valley and ripped off the flaps of sodden attap which hung perilously from roofs.

Runnels of brown mud ran between the stilts of the huts and his legs as he stumbled, hatless and soaked to the skin, down to the wild grass and lallang along the riverbank. What a comfort the storm was! It came every year, the monsoon rains. Unvarying and yet always changing. Always forceful! Temperamental like an angry spirit of the forest, roaring fear into the hearts of men. Smashing into pieces the boats of the English dogs on the high seas! Old friend and enemy rolled in one! He ran into the heart of the storm as howling winds tore at his baju. The rain slashed at the waist-high grass and jungle trees. A hard and merciless rain that pelted his flesh and stung his eyes. But he made no effort to shield himself. His soaked baju and sarong clung to him as he stumbled blindly like an aged elephant running amok. Amok! Amok! He was amok! The end of the world was at hand. The light had dimmed. He could not see where he was going as he pushed his way through the underbrush. The earth was calling out to him, *bumiputera,* "son of the soil"! He heard his name as high winds shrilled and lashed at the trees. A large branch crashed down upon him and sent him sprawling into the foaming brown mud. He thrashed about like an overturned tortoise. But he was past caring who saw him. This mud was his, handed down to him by his father and grandfather. The mud of his land. The land of his ancestors who had come from India. Mamak, the Malays had called them since the time of Tun Perak! They were Mamaks from Kedah! The descendants of Mahathir, advisor to the raja of Patani and menteri of Bandong! He sobbed for his line. For what he was about to lose. It was the end! But this mud was still his! His mud! His land! His river! His flood!

The river burst through its banks. Floodwater rushed into his throat and nostrils. His screams were drowned out by the howling wind. A swelling undertow of roiling killing mud pulled him into the river. He clawed at the slippery earth beneath him and clung to the drowning foliage even as the swirling floodwater swept him further and further away. Finally, exhausted, he gave himself up to the river's wild embrace. The true son of the earth returning to the earth.

But no one moaned his passing. No one knew of his last moments on earth. No one knew that only his undying belief in the power of the past and in a bit of earth upon which he had lived his poor life had sustained him to the end. And no one protested when, one month later, his sons sold off his land to Towkay Wong Tuck Heng.

Chapter Thirty-two

"*T*he Chinese trader killed him!"

"How can you say that?"

"I saw the crocodile going into Pak Mus's house!"

"It's the opium!"

"It's a broken heart. Broken by his good-for-nothing sons!"

"Why Pak Mus ran amok, only Allah knows. Great is His name and great is His mercy," Ibrahim said.

What he didn't say was his worry about the sale of Malay ancestral land to the Chinese traders and white planters all over the country. It was a disturbing trend and he looked to the British administration to do something about it. He saw it as his duty to report the sale of Musa Talib's land to Mr Douglas, his superior in Ipoh. For the next few days, he spent hours drafting and writing a lengthy report.

"I'll go to Ipoh and deliver it personally to the senior district officer," he told his wife.

Musa was his last link to an era that had seen better days. Just thinking about the sale of his land almost broke his heart. How could he sit idle and watch his people being cheated by the Chinese opium traders and gambling den operators? That Musa Talib's sons owed those crocodiles huge sums of money was besides the point, he thought. He blamed the Chinese for setting up gambling and opium dens in Bandong in the first place. Those sons of snakes were greedy and ungrateful! They'd come from across the South China Sea, poor as vermin, dirty, ragged and landless, like the worst of the Malay peasants eking a living at the jungle's edge, but after they'd prospered, they'd forgotten that it was Malays like his father who'd been the first to offer them the golden opportunity to dig for tin in Bandong! Had it not been for his father's open-handed ways, would Chinese traders like Wong Tuck Heng become rich towkays? Tuck Heng's name crossed his mind several times as he wrote his report. He remembered the uncouth and ignorant youth. Now that ignoramus had become the owner of some of the choicest land in Bandong Valley.

"'Bang, you've not touched your rice and curry. Is something troubling 'Bang?" Miriam asked him.

The lamplight cast a warm glow on his wife's frowning face. His family was seated on the matted floor of their covered verandah for the evening meal. Round the dinner mat were his four children, his wife and his mother, who still looked regal despite their reduced circumstances.

In the compound, gathered round a small wood fire, were their former slaves, twenty or so old men and women who had wailed when they were told to leave the family. They'd nowhere to go and so they stayed on and he fed them. Every one of them living on his meagre salary as a penghulu.

"Better to let our children lifeless lie than let our ancient customs die." Citing an ancient proverb, his mother had lectured him when he'd protested at first that it was against the white man's law to keep their former slaves. But his mother didn't care for the white man's law. All she knew was that one could never replace the traditions of one's race once they were discarded. And loyalty and honour were part of their tradition. So were duty and obligation to one's dependants.

"'Bang, your curry is getting cold," Miriam urged him to eat.

"In the name of Allah the Compassionate, the Merciful," he murmured and began to eat.

After their meal, Miriam asked him, "'Bang, did Imam Leman speak to you about Aziz? Our son should be going to the village school like his elder brother."

"I know it's time for Aziz to go to school."

"He can learn to read the Holy Book together with Omar," Miriam added.

"No, I've other plans for Omar. He's twelve this year, time for him to leave Imam Leman's school and go to Pulau Pinang to attend the English school where I studied. You heard me, Omar?"

"I heard you, honoured Father."

But the boy looked unhappy in the lamplight. Ibrahim was reminded of his own unhappiness when he had to go to the English school in Penang too. Not that he had any regrets going; he had learned a lot from the white teachers and he wanted Omar to reap the benefits of an English education.

But looking at his son, he remembered how extremely difficult it'd been for him to leave family and home after his father's death, to live among strangers and learn the white man's tongue! If only Omar could study the white man's language in Bandong, he thought. That was when it struck him that his son need not leave home if there was a school in Kuala Bandong. It could prepare the boys for government service and fulfil the hopes of the Malays to have more people in the government!

"I'll talk to Mr Douglas about setting up a school in this district when I go to Ipoh to hand him my report," he said to Miriam. "But first I'll talk to the village elders. See how they feel about it. A school to teach the Holy Book and the English language! Why didn't I think of that earlier? If our people know the white man's language, they'll be able to work in their government like me." And the more he talked about it that night, the more excited he became. "Tomorrow I'll go and see Imam Leman and Haji Hamid. Omar, bring out your books and show me what you've copied for the imam while I was away."

"Honoured Father … must be tired. Tomorrow …"

But he was firm. "Bring me your copybook."

"Father, forgive me. I've not copied out any verse from the Holy Book."

"Didn't Imam Leman hit you for being lazy?"

"He did not, Father."

"Bring me the cane!" he shouted to the servant girl.

The servants who were having their dinner in the compound crept up to the house. Mak Som's eyes were pleading with him to spare her favourite. She had looked after Omar ever since the boy was born.

"My beloved one, my little one," the old nanny kept murmuring to no one in particular. A slave was not supposed to address her master unless she was spoken to; although Mak Som was no longer a slave, she was too ingrained in the old ways to change. To this day, she'd stop in her tracks and crouch by the roadside to let those of the noble class walk past first. Once Ibrahim had tried to tell her that she need not do that but it was useless. Mak Som went on doing what she had been taught from young.

When the servant girl brought out the cane, Aziz, his younger son, hid behind his grandmother. His two daughters stopped their chattering and sat as still as mice beside their mother. Omar knelt before him, his back straight and stiff as though he was expecting some very hard blows.

Ibrahim raised the cane and let it fall on the boy's back three or four times. Secretly he was pleased that Omar was taking his punishment like a warrior—without flinching. He had to teach Omar what he himself had been taught. That learning was important in their family. Imam Leman should've beaten the boy for his laziness, he thought with some irritation. But the old imam, like old Mak Som, still clung to the ancient ways so he would never cane the son of a chief.

The next night, before the family's evening meal, Ibrahim took out the book that had been the subject of much talk in Kuala Lumpur. It was a beautifully bound copy of the *Hikayat Abdullah*, an autobiography written by the late Munshi Abdullah, the special assistant of Sir Stamford Raffles.

He had invited Imam Leman and Haji Hamid to join them for the reading of the *Hikayat* at his house. Because of the presence of male visitors, his mother, Miriam and their two daughters sat behind a screen. For this evening's reading, he chose a chapter in which Munshi Abdullah described his school days:

> Every day I used to go to school in the morning and I was taught by my father at night. Many times I was beaten and slapped. Many writing tablets were smashed in pieces when they were used to hit me on the head. Many canes were broken over my body. Time after time my mother used to weep because I suffered such frequent chastisement. Sometimes my fingers were beaten till they were swollen because I had made mistakes in writing. Mark well how difficult it is to aspire to knowledge, wisdom, skill and learning. Soon my heart was filled with hatred, anger and spite against my teacher. Many were the prayers I offered for his speedy demise, to release me from the pain of study so that I could go out and play whenever I liked. At that time I was very fond of flying kites. My father used to beat me frequently and hang the kite round my neck, ordering me back to my studies. I was highly delighted whenever my teacher was too ill to give me lessons for then I could go out and play; if during a lesson he or anyone else ordered me to go anywhere, even to dangerous places, I was thankful to go just to get away from study. If I had the slightest feeling of bodily discomfort I purposely made myself ill to avoid lessons. I would rather look on the face of a tiger than that of my teacher …

Omar kept his eyes on the mat, his finger tracing its intricate weave as he listened to his father's rich clear voice. His heart began to grow a little lighter as his father read on. That the Munshi who was respected as a great teacher had felt the hardship of acquiring knowledge and learning made his own burden seem more bearable. He turned to Aziz and winked. Even the grave Haji Hamid and Imam Leman were laughing heartily over his father's reading of certain parts and they were joined in their laughter by the women and girls behind the screen.

The teachers had power to inflict any of these punishments in the school. Even if the children were the sons of rajas and rich men, the teachers still did not mind. They could cane them in school even until blood was drawn and no action would be taken against them for they taught well.

Ibrahim closed the book and called Aziz to his side. Turning to Imam Leman, he made the formal speech all parents made when they entrusted their child to a teacher.

"Tok Imam, I hope you will grant me this favour in your kindness. Here is young Aziz, my son. I place him in your care so that he may be taught to read the Word of Allah."

He took the tray of betel leaves, arecanuts and sweetmeats from the servant and presented it to Imam Leman with both hands. Next he took the cane beside him and presented it to the imam.

"Tok Imam, let me present you with this cane. It's a rod of correction. Please use it should Aziz show indifference to your teaching. Please use it to show him the way through the Holy Book. Short of breaking his bones, all things are permitted to you. Please accept my son as your disciple, Tok Imam."

"Honourable Datuk, I accept Aziz as my disciple. May Allah in His mercy bless him and lead him to learn the little that I know."

The servants brought in trays of curries and rice, and jugs of water and basins for the washing of hands. Ibrahim invited his guests to eat. During the meal, Ibrahim broached the subject of building a modern school.

"When I was in Kuala Lumpur, I heard and learned many things from other chiefs. Some of them, like my late father, think that we should let our sons learn the white man's tongue by setting up schools in our districts," he began and looked to Haji Hamid for support.

"Aye, that is true." Haji Hamid nodded. "I've travelled to many parts of Perak and Pulau Pinang, Tok. I too heard that many chiefs are beginning to see the importance of learning the white man's tongue. But you, Tok Imam, should continue to teach the Holy Book in our village as always. Our young ones must commit the Holy Book to memory and recite it every day," Haji Hamid assured the old imam. "See for yourself, Tok, the fruit of an English education before us, our Datuk Penghulu. I can see in him that the fruit is good."

"Thank you, Haji."

For the next several days, Ibrahim's head was full of plans. He knew that there would be problems ahead. Many of the villagers were conservative and few among them cared about education. The men had been farmers for generations.

Word about the English school soon spread. By the time Ibrahim met the men at the mosque after Friday prayers, he could sense their unease.

"Is not the Word of Allah good enough for us all?" Pak Dewa asked.

He was a newcomer in the village, but he spoke with great confidence for he had studied in a *pondok* school in the state of Kelantan. The villagers respected the graduates of these small religious schools.

"Better that we learn the Word of Allah and the teachings of the Prophet first than the words of the infidel!"

Loud murmurs of agreement followed. Then some men spoke about the evil ways of the towns.

"Blessed be the name of Allah and His Prophet," Imam Leman murmured piously as he looked around. Faced with Pak Dewa's opposition, the old teacher was uncertain of his own stand now.

Ibrahim felt his anger rise as he listened to the men. In the old days, no villager would've dared to question his decision. He prayed for patience before he spoke.

"Allah most High, most Just, most Compassionate, help us," he began. "When I was in Kuala Lumpur, I heard and saw many new things I had not even dreamed of. Things that would've frightened me! Take the train, for example. It eats fire and belts out smoke. Before I boarded the train, the talk of other men scared me. Many said that the fire-breathing train would kill us. But look, I'm still alive. And a journey that used to take seven days by boat and elephant now takes only one day. And do you know what else I found out?"

He paused and looked at the faces of the men before him. Then fixing his eyes on Pak Dewa, who was a native from the state of Selangor, he went on.

"I found out that the Selangor Malays have their own schools already. Now we know what they are like. Didn't Raja Mahmud of Selangor help the British in the war against us and save that white man, Frank Swettenham, in Pasir Salak? After that, didn't Frank Swettenham turn a blind eye when Raja Mahmud and his Selangor Malays burned and looted our valley? There's something else that I found out! When Frank Swettenham was our Resident in Perak, he didn't want us to get an English education."

"It's not important what the white man wants or doesn't want!" Pak Dewa shouted defiantly.

"I didn't say it's important, Pak Dewa. I merely want to share with all of you what happened in the past. My father was killed by the white men with the help of foreign Malays from other states!"

And Ibrahim gave the word "foreign" the desired emphasis so that all the villagers knew he was referring to Pak Dewa's foreign origins.

"Foreign Malays helped the white men to defeat us in Perak! That's one point I would like to make. The second point is this: Inche' Frank Swettenham didn't think it was safe to teach us the white man's language. Now I have this information from the most reliable source—his Malay clerk who can read the white man's writing! Can you see how unsafe it is for the white men to have a Malay who can read his language? What will happen if our children were working in the white raja's office? Will the white men be safe from us?"

The villagers roared. They were beginning to see his point.

A pair of Malay eyes in their midst! Heh, heh, heh!" Tok Samat cackled.

"Now we see what our honourable Datuk Penghulu is getting at." Che' Mat stood up. "Learn to understand what the white man is saying and writing about us behind our backs!"

"I heard that there're many Englishmen who can read and speak our tongue! And they can sweet-talk our chiefs and sultans and persuade them to do things. So we must do the same!" Haji Hamid added. "What *si buaya*, the crocodile, does, *si pelanduk*, the mousedeer, can do too!"

"But beware the crocodile!" Pak Dewa warned them. "Still as a log it lies in the water and bites you when you least expect it."

"But we Malays are as nimble as the mousedeer!" Haji Hamid declared.

"Besides, the crocodile might not be the white man," Ibrahim added. "Si buaya might be a Chinese crocodile. The Chinese people, my friends, have sent many of their sons to the white man's schools in Kuala Lumpur and Penang. They want to give their children a better life."

"Then we'll send our sons to the new school to give them a better life too!"

"Build us a new school!"

"Very good! I'll make the journey by river and see Mr Douglas myself."

His vision of the new school filled his imagination. He could see it producing future Malay officials who would join the white man's government service, and one day these Malays would regain the power and influence their fathers had lost.

Chapter Thirty-three

Bandong is life;
Bandong is plenty.
Bandong ponds filled with prawns;
And Bandong streams full of fish.
Bandong skies full of birds;
And in our valley, life is sweet.

*H*e was in an expansive mood on the morning he set out for
Ipoh accompanied by Omar. His valley after the season of rain
and thunderstorms was as fresh and innocent as a pubescent
girl. The rice fields were flooded and jewels gleamed on the tips
of young rice shoots in the morning light. The air smelt fresh.
Brown sparrows and padi birds twittered and teased the water
buffaloes wallowing in the mud. The women and children were
in the streams catching haruan fish. Some men, up early, were
sharpening their axes and parangs before going into the jungle
to chop wood—chengal, merbau, meranti and teak which had
given their village these elegant houses on stilts. What a gem
his village was! An emerald, green and precious!

"The English school won't be ready for you so you'll still
have to go to Penang, my son. But first we go to Ipoh. It's
time you see something of the world outside Bandong. One
day you'll be a penghulu like me. And if Allah wills it, even
a menteri like your grandfather."

"Datuk! Wait! Wait!"

A breathless Haji Hamid came up. With him was a stocky

young man of robust build, an unsmiling face and thick dark eyebrows.

"This young man asked you to please help him find his Chinese father."

There'd been many mixed unions in Bandong Valley, especially in those villages near the Chinese tin mines. No one had minded the children of such unions. All life came from Allah. But this was the first time anyone had come to him with such a request.

The young man bowed and kissed his hand as a mark of his deep respect. "My name is Nawawi."

"Nawawi and his mother used to live here. During the Bandong War, his mother fled. She settled in the Chinese jeweller's village, Pasir Salak, remarried and had seven other children. She passed away last year. Before she died, she told Nawawi about his Chinese father. A miner who used to be with the White Cranes in our valley, one Inche Chan Ah Fook."

"My mother gave me this," Nawawi handed him a beautifully carved kris.

"It's made by the famous Pawang Duhamat," Haji Hamid explained. "He gave it to Nawawi's father for saving his life. Look at the fine markings and these ridges on the blade. A man would kill to possess such a fine weapon."

"How can I be of help?"

"Che' Wong Tuck Heng, our towkay, lives in Ipoh. Since you're going there, why not bring Nawawi to see him? He might be able to help Nawawi find this Chan Ah Fook. Poor lad, he's been wafting like a feather since his mother's death."

"Why do you seek your Chinese father? Are you not happy in Pasir Salak?"

"A man likes to know his origins, like the river its source. Forgive me, Datuk, I'm a durian among cucumbers at home."

Nawawi's eyes were restless as he spoke. Not a good sign. Reluctantly he agreed to take the young man with him, but only because Haji Hamid had made the request and he did not want to disappoint the good haji. He doubted that a Chinese father would acknowledge his Malay-bred son.

Nawawi proved to be very useful on the river. He was a skilled boatman and seemed to know instinctively where the rocks and shallows were as he guided their sampan downriver. At first he spoke little. But alone with Omar, he began to talk and told stories that made the boy laugh. Ipoh was in the next valley and the journey by land and boat would take three days so Ibrahim took the opportunity to speak to his son.

"Our family has a proud heritage. Our bloodlines are joined to the Bugis of Celebes and Tun Perak of the great Malacca sultanate. White men are ignorant of our nobility. They've little regard for a man's heritage. They took Bandong Valley from us even though it had been bequeathed to us forever by His Royal Highness. They took it not because we're a bad people, but because your grandfather was fiercely loyal to the sultan and our land. Don't hate them because of what I told you. If you do, then they win. Hatred and anger will only destroy our hearts. No, my son, better to learn from them and take back what's rightfully ours than let our hearts be consumed with hate. Insya Allah, one day you will get back Bandong and the title of menteri."

"But Nenek said our family had always fought the foreign invaders—the Dutch and the Portuguese. She said we're warriors."

The boy's grandmother had been filling his head with nonsense again.

"There's some truth in what she said, but a warrior is a thing of the past. Useless in these days of white rule and gunships. Become an administrator, Omar. Learn the ropes of government. Government officials in the Malayan Civil Service have better prospects."

He had to make Omar understand that Malay society was not what it was before. Even a former great warrior like Raja Mahmud of Selangor had to act as a native guide to the white rulers in order to survive.

"My son, it's true that we're the descendants of warriors. But what Nenek forgot to tell you is that there're two kinds of warriors. Those who fight with their hands and those who fight with their heads. We can be like the rhinoceros and use brute strength. Or be like the mousedeer and fight the enemy with cunning and intelligence. Our Creator, blessed be His name, gave us a brain so we can learn new things. We're not born full of knowledge. But we learn as we grow up. And learning, especially learning something foreign, is never easy. Your heart must be humble and open. The warrior of today is one who has a humble heart and uses his head, not his kris."

Omar nodded solemnly.

"How lucky you are," Nawawi blurted and then turned a dark crimson.

"Nawawi, you can speak freely in my presence."

"Forgive my rudeness, Datuk. I've heard that no Malay chief can become a district officer."

"That is so. The white men introduced so many new laws into our land that only their own officers can understand them."

"Didn't we have our own laws, Father?"

"My son, Perak has ninety-nine laws handed down from ancient times. They were adopted so that we have the law of Allah and the law of the Edicts. Before the white men came, people in Perak had to obey them."

"The Chinese jeweller said that His Royal Highness and the chiefs left the Chinese people to their own laws and headmen."

"True, Nawawi. Very difficult to control the Chinese. So it was wiser to let their own Kapitan China control them. And don't forget, they speak a babble of tongues. Impossible for us Malays to understand them—even when they speak our tongue."

Nawawi chuckled at this and regaled them with imitations of Chinese people trying to speak Malay.

⊶≡◉⊜≡⊷

After three days, they arrived in Ipoh. It was still very much a Malay kampong when he had visited it as a child. But since then it had grown into a thriving centre of the Kinta Valley with three major roads lined with Chinese shophouses of brick and stone. The senior district officer's quarters and office, the municipal and administrative centre, a small hospital, a police station, a fire station and a recently built railway station were signs of the town's growing importance.

To Omar, the main roads and shops were a display of wonders. Leather shoes for men, black and brown, polished to a shine. He looked down at his bare feet and wished he had shoes on them.

"Cost many Straits dollars," Nawawi told him. "Only the white men and Chinese towkays wear leather shoes. See the Chinese shopkeepers? Not so rich so they wear cloth ones. And those Indian moneylenders, they wear sandals. Poor coolies and people like us go barefoot. When I find my father, I'll be rich enough to buy leather shoes."

"You really think that your Chinese father is rich?"

"I hope so. I've worked all my life since twelve. Ran away from home because I hated my stepfather's whip. The Chinese jeweller let me work for him so I stayed in his house. He told me about my father, Chan Ah Fook. When I find him, he'll give me money."

Nawawi's eyes shone. The Chinese are rich, he told Omar. Richer than the Malays. If he could find his Chinese father, his life would change for the better. But Omar was listening to him with only half an ear. The noise and chaos of the roads crowded with horse-drawn buggies and gharries, rickshaws, bullock carts and pony carts fascinated him. He had never seen so many different types of vehicles before. And the food hawkers along the sides of the roads. What strange and unfamiliar smells were wafting out of wooden tubs and brass pots brewing on wood stoves.

"Hurry, Omar! Your father is leaving us behind."

Ibrahim was striding ahead, in no mood for idle chatter and dawdling. The town's a foreign country to Malays like him, he thought bitterly. Where's the village he had known as Kampong Paloh? This is a monstrous labyrinth crammed with Chinese bodies and dwellings. Their shophouses, little red shrines and temples and the wood-and-attap huts, homes to squalid families who squabbled and spilled onto the sidewalks and back lanes, pressed upon him. Every way he turned, he was confronted by Chinese faces, Chinese buildings and Chinese squalor. The shrill cries of hawkers assailed his ears. The very air was full of their smells and odours. He felt choked and suffocated. He missed the fresh breezes of the open rice fields and wondered how these Chinese could live in such dank warrens, toiling away day and night like beetles on a dunghill. The clamour of the pedlars and the large red signboards everywhere left him dazed and disoriented. He hurried along, dragging Omar with him while the hapless Nawawi trotted after them.

He made for the open space at the edge of the town. Wide open waste ground belonging to no one and where his eyes could travel to the jungle and the hills in the distance without being blocked by a shophouse or hut. He took in a deep breath to calm himself. Aaah! What wouldn't he give for a whiff of the aroma of freshly cut wood, the pungency of spices drying in the sun and the tang of mud freshly turned by the farmer's plough. His ears longed for the cries of the padi birds and the croaks of the padi frogs. The call to prayer from the turret of the village mosque would be music to his ears. He muttered a short prayer for forgiveness for his heart was pounding with a fierce resentment against all foreigners. Foreigners who had changed the face of the earth he knew so well from childhood! The Malay ancestral plots and elegant houses on stilts. All had given way to dirt and squalor.

"Honoured Father, are you not well?" Omar asked.

Chapter Thirty-four

*T*uck Heng rose earlier than usual on the morning deemed auspicious for moving into his new mansion. Lai Fong brought him a basin of warm water. He washed himself and began, as was his habit, to turn his mind to the day's affairs, little knowing that what he proposed the gods in heaven would not dispose.

"Is everything all right downstairs?"

"Yes. The amahs and servants know that we have to move into the mansion at the appointed hour."

"Good. The white gods are coming to see the electric lights. The whole of Ipoh is waiting to see our mansion light up tonight. I want everything to go well."

"I'll tell the head servant to send for the engineer to check the lights again."

"Good. Please tell Small Dog to come in now."

As was their custom, he and Lai Fong spoke politely to each other like friends at a distance. It was as if daytime had drawn to a close their intimacy of the night before.

Small Dog, the barber, was summoned. He bustled into the bedroom with his razors, brushes and a basin of warm water he had fetched from the kitchen downstairs. His hardened scrawny body, covered with the welts of past floggings at the hands of mine supervisors, scraped and bowed before his benefactor. Tuck Heng had saved him from the brink of death.

"A good morning to you, Towkah. An auspicious morning it is for Towkah! A good fortune day! In the market they're calling you Kapitan already!"

Tuck Heng was cheered by Small Dog's news. "Towkah" sounded good in his ears, but "Kapitan" was even better. Tonight's celebration was a double happiness event to celebrate his move into his new mansion and his appointment as Kapitan China of Ipoh. Why, not too long ago, he was "Mr Yesee sir" on the wharves of Penang. Now he'd be as important as the Right Honourable Ong Boon Leong, addressed as "Towkah" by the Hakka and the Cantonese and "Towkay" by the Hokkien and the Straits-born.

"The honourable Kapitan China," Small Dog said with a flourish of his towel.

"All the same whatever name."

"No, not the same! Towkah is respected as a leader and a man of learning. A forward-looking man."

"In Penang, my wife's relations think I'm just a rich Chinaman." But one day he'd show them that he was not a man to be ignored. As he leaned back into his reclining chair, he chuckled at the thought that Mr Douglas, the senior district officer, had asked him specially to invite Inspector Ian Thomson and a lady reporter from London to see the light-up.

"Towkah, your mansion is the first building to use electric lamps in this country. You're ahead of your time."

"So begin and don't waste time, you chattering dog!" He laughed.

Small Dog made a lather while he asked about the rumours making their rounds in the coffee shops. As was their habit over the years, they started with the gossip and rumours, went on to the prices of tin, pork and other commodities, then moved on to politics in China and the great world before returning to the state of affairs in Ipoh, and once again the gossip Small Dog had picked up at the big houses in town where he was the regular barber. Consequently the process of lathering and shaving was prolonged, for every time he spoke Small Dog had to stop shaving.

"Tin is doing very well on the Exchange. Some people say that rubber will do well too. What do you say, Towkah?"

"That's the crop with a future. The white gods are promoting it. And what they promote here is what their people want back in London."

"But what for? You can't eat rubber. You can't make anything out of it."

"That's what you think, Small Dog. But our eyes can't see as far as the eyes of those English. Did you read the papers from Singapore?"

"Towkah, you're laughing at me again. Those words in the papers know me, but I don't know them!"

"The newspapers say that the English people will use rubber to make wheels for motorcars."

"Motorcars?"

"Carriages with engines, no horses. But can go faster than horses. On rubber wheels."

"First electric lamps, now this! I was just telling my friends, 'Tonight you'll see wonder. Electric lamps can make the night as bright as day! No need for oil or kerosene lamps any more!' You're a forward-looking man, Towkah. Nobody can keep up with you."

"We Chinese must learn from the West. Just look at their machines. Have you seen them?"

"No, but I heard that they can dig a thousand times deeper. How do they build such machines?"

"It's their schools, Small Dog. They learn to use their heads and hands. Not like our scholars. So busy memorising long useless poems and essays written thousands of years ago that they don't think any more. If our scholars had spent their time thinking about China, why, they might've overthrown the Manchus long ago!"

"Towkah, it's true what you've said! Is it true then that you're going to build a modern school in Ipoh? They say that you want teachers to teach in Mandarin and open the school to all Chinese."

"Right! A good idea, isn't it?"

"If we've a school for everyone, don't care what dialect he speaks, then maybe we Chinese won't fight so often, right or not? As I've said before and I say it again, we need a forward-looking man like you in this town."

"Aye, you praise me sky-high, Small Dog. Now you and I are old friends for more than ten years so I don't mind telling you. Only in Ipoh am I regarded as forward-looking. Over on Penang Island, my half-brothers think I'm a backward Chinaman." He laughed.

"What? They've no ears, ah? You can speak the foreign tongue too. All that yeh-see, yeh-see."

"I don't speak English that well. Also I wear a queue. So my wife and her family over there think I'm backward. The Babas, they cut off their queues. Especially those who studied in the English schools. Dr Sun Yat-sen and all those who have studied in Western countries wear their hair like the foreign devils. These new scholars are against our Manchu dictators."

"Brave men!"

"You think they're brave?"

"As brave as we Hakkas. We're fighters. Never kowtowed to dictators. Our heroes in the Taiping Revolution scared the shit out of those sons of bitches in the Forbidden City. Now if I were a learned man like Dr Sun, I'd cut off my queue too."

"Small Dog, I was thinking the very same thing myself."

"Towkah, I talk only. You know what this town is like! A thousand tongues will wag! Especially the Save Our Emperor League!"

"Let them say what they want. They look backward, I walk forward."

But Small Dog was hesitant. He'd never cut off a man's queue before. Though he had spoken confidently, he was anything but confident when he brought his scissors towards Tuck Heng's queue. He had never given anyone a Western-style haircut before. But he'd seen how it was done down at the Indian barbershop where the foreign devils went to get their hair cut and trimmed.

"Small Dog, a queue, just hair."

Later Small Dog would tell others that he'd had a premonition that fateful morning. That he'd felt that it wasn't an auspicious thing to do. But Towkah Wong was insistent, so what could he do?

"Cut it off, Small Dog. It's getting late."

His good name and standing in the community mattered to Tuck Heng. That he was regarded as backward in Penang vexed him more than he cared to admit. If the queue was a symbol of backwardness in the eyes of the English-educated, he'd cut it off. And since the queue had become also a symbol of support for the Qing emperor on the Dragon Throne, all the more it should come off.

"Cut it off, Small Dog! We Chinese are adaptable. The world has changed, so must we! Like the Monkey King, we can change our appearances."

"Right, Towkah, please keep still."

He laughed as the strands of hair fell around him. He felt light-headed and renewed. "Good, Small Dog! Carry on! Cut!"

"From now on, the English barbarians will not think of you as backward. You're a great man of vision, Towkah!"

If he felt the barb in Small Dog's words, he brushed it aside. If the thought that he might be doing this out of a need to be accepted by the English-educated had occurred to him, that too would've been brushed aside.

"Is Towkah going to wear a shirt and trousers from now on? Like the rich foreign devils?"

"As the saying goes, 'A man is first respected for his attire before he's respected for his character'. So I'll wear clothes to suit the occasion. If I'm going to the kongsi, I'll wear my silk gown and jacket. If I'm going to the English devil's office, I'll wear a shirt and trousers. Flexible as the bamboo that I am, eh, Small Dog?" He chuckled, pleased with his own answer.

He'd lived in this part of the world far too many years not to realise that a man had to be a cultural chameleon in order to get by.

"Towkah, do you like it?" The barber was standing back to admire his own handiwork.

"Not bad, not bad at all."

He peered into the mirror and saw himself with hair cut short and swept back behind the ears.

"Now I shall go downstairs and show myself to the women and hear what they have to say."

"Towkah, if you don't mind, I'd like to get out of here before your Wong-ma whips me."

"Wong-ma will hold her tongue and whip today. It is not any other day."

But the barber gathered up his things quickly and left by the backstairs.

The sun had risen above the shanty huts beyond Tuck Heng's house. Their ugliness sickened him each time he looked at them. He would tear them down and rebuild. He would change the face of Ipoh and Bandong. In his imagination he was already looking at a town much like the one he had known in China—one of civic grace and elegance with broad streets and tree-lined avenues, with shophouses and townhouses, with schools, medical halls, shrines and temples and clan associations. A town alive with pedlars, letter writers, storytellers and newspaper readers who would read aloud the daily papers to the illiterate coolies and charge them half a cent each. It would be as lively as the town in Sum Hor where he grew up. The thought filled him with longing and made him all the more determined to build it. That was what land was for—to be owned and built on. All men strived to own a bit of this earth; to pass it onto their flesh and blood. Land is identity, stability and family. The reason for slogging.

He heard Lai Fong coming up the stairs and braced himself for her reaction. His second wife was chosen by Wong-ma who had brought her over from China. But after two sons and two daughters, he and Lai Fong were still strangers. She was not fond of speech and was reticent to a fault. Whenever he came home from his trips, she had nothing to tell him. He knew little about her except that she had grown up in an orphanage run by some English missionaries in Kwangtung, and she had even studied in a Chinese school for girls. Not that he was complaining for he was pleased with the way she kept his household and his aged Wong-ma in good health and harmonious balance.

To many people, Wong-ma's choice of a daughter-in-law was fated. After Tai-kor Wong had banished her from Penang, Wong-ma was befriended by a young Chinese Christian on board the ship to China. During that terrible voyage, their ship had nearly sunk and Wong-ma, depressed and suicidal, had almost lost her life. The Chinese Christian had saved her and raised her spirits. He gave her a sense of direction in her life and tried his best to convert her. But Wong-ma had refused. "No, thank you," she told her Christian friend. "I don't want to go to a different heaven after death and be forever separated from my ancestors."

But the kindly missionary did not give up. When he found out that Wong-ma was utterly at a loss in Kwangtung, he took her to the missionaries' quarters where they gave her food and shelter and helped her to return to her native Sum Hor, thereby earning her eternal gratitude. That experience had opened Wong-ma's eyes. For the first time, she saw how the foreign devils could be kind. In choosing Lai Fong, who worked in the missionary centre, Wong-ma was being shrewd. A wife who had had some contact with the English foreign devils would be an asset to her son who lived in a country ruled by these same foreign devils.

"Aiyah!"

"What do you think?" he asked, a little self-consciously.

"You ... look very different," she sputtered, and for the first time since their marriage he glimpsed mischief on her face. "I better go and prepare Wong-ma for your new look. She ... ah ... she might not recognise her son."

Chapter Thirty-five

"Ma, I've told Ah Lan-chay to go into the carriage with you and the children. To keep them quiet. The whole morning they've been jumping like grasshoppers. Especially Kok Wah."

"Bring my little precious to me. I'll look after him. Tell everyone to be ready by noon."

"Please don't worry, Ma. Have some tea."

Wong-ma sipped her tea and watched as Lai Fong poured out three cups of rice wine and placed them carefully in a row on the altar. In dress and demeanour, her daughter-in-law was a plain woman who eschewed jewellery, her only ornaments being a pair of jade earrings and a jade bangle. Her samfoo was well-tailored but looked modest next to those worn by the wives of other rich men.

"Humble and sensible, that's my daughter-in-law. It's true, she's from an orphanage. But what's more important? Character or family background?" she asked her listeners.

Even in her old age, Wong-ma continued to pooh-pooh the conventions of her day and urged Lai Fong to do the same.

"Under my roof, my daughter-in-law must use her head. And her mouth too. Listen to me, Fong. We're the women-generals in this new country. We've got to take charge. Of course a wise woman won't let her husband know that. With a man, you can't show your true self. I tell you this even though Tuck Heng is my son."

And for that, Lai Fong was grateful to her mother-in-law.

Theirs was not a relationship of blind obedience and submission. It was more a collaboration with the older woman showing the way. Unknown to Wong-ma, however, she had had another teacher.

Miss Higgs, the plainly dressed and plain-speaking missionary from Yorkshire, had saved her from her father when he attacked the orphanage to force her to return to their village to marry a dolt. Speaking Cantonese with a quaint accent, Miss Higgs had taught her that a woman should be free from male tyranny. "No man should force a woman to marry against her will." Miss Higgs brooked no nonsense from the men whether English or Chinese. She ruled her orphanage with a firm hand.

And Lai Fong, following her example, managed her husband's household with a firm hand too. Every dollar spent by the cook and the head servant had to be accounted for, thrift and honesty being the hallmarks of a good servant, according to Miss Higgs. Those who shirked their duties or abused Lai Fong's trust found her punishment swift and sharp for they were instantly sacked. Not even an appeal to Wong-ma could change her mind.

Once Wong-ma had pleaded for a servant and Lai Fong had replied with a quote from the Bible which Miss Higgs had taught her to read in Cantonese. "If a man is not faithful in safeguarding what is another man's, who can trust him?" Wong-ma had concluded that her daughter-in-law was quoting a saying of the Great Master. She repeated it to her friends, saying it was from Confucius.

But Lai Fong didn't correct her mother-in-law. Had she pointed out the mistake, Wong-ma would've lost face and perhaps a crack in their relationship would've been created. Was it always necessary to demonstrate one's knowledge and honesty? Had she not camouflaged her true feelings during her years in the orphanage, the Christian missionaries might not have accepted her. During her stay with them, never once did she reveal her disbelief in their strange god who had allowed himself to be killed on a cross.

From a very young age, she'd learned that questioning authority openly did not pay. Frankness led to caning. Growing up in an extended family of sixteen children with dozens of busybodies living under one roof, she had learned the art of concealment.

When she was twelve, her father sold her off to a sixty-year-old landlord to be his thirteenth concubine. A week before her marriage, she hid herself in a farmer's wagon and made her way to the Christian mission in Kwangtung. She had heard that the Christians were determined to stop this heinous practice of forcing girls into concubinage. When her father and the landlord, backed by a horde of furious men, stormed the mission, Miss Higgs had called in the soldiers of the English embassy.

Defeated, the men left. But they had not forgotten. Years later they returned with a vengeance. That was the year she met Wong-ma in the orphanage. By then she was twenty-one and well past marrying age. Trouble was brewing in the Kwangtung District and the local warlords and Qing officials were mounting attacks on the Christian mission. Anti-Western feelings ran so high that the mission was burned down. When she looked back on those turbulent days, she realised that it was necessity that had forced her to marry Tuck Heng.

"Ma, I … ah … I've something to tell you. It's Tuck Heng Kor! He … he's cut off his queue this morning!"

"Aiyah! Why did he do that? And today of all days!"

"Ma, please don't worry. It's the modern style."

"What modern? What style? All Chinese men wear queues! Only criminals and Christian converts have no queues!"

"Ma, many men in Penang have already cut them off."

"They're just the Straits-born. They follow the foreign devils! They don't count. His Nonya wife! She must've put him up to it!"

"But Ma, Tuck Heng Kor didn't cut his hair in Penang."

"Aiyah, Fong! Those women are clever. They can twist a man round their little finger. Never trust them!"

Chapter Thirty-six

Cries of wonder rose from the townsfolk when the electric lamps were switched on. Wong Mansion was transformed into a magnificent jewel heralding the age of scientific wonders in Ipoh. Its light could be seen for miles.

"Wah! Night into day! Just like that!"

"Keeps the ghosts away!"

"Keeps the robbers away too! So bright like this, who dares to rob you?"

Inside the mansion, Tuck Heng's guests were just as dazzled, both by the electric lights and their host's new hairstyle.

"New hair, new house, everything bright and new! I congratulate you, Kapitan!" Chan Ah Fook's voice boomed across the drawing room, filled to overflowing with guests and well-wishers. He took out his silver pocket watch, stared at it for a moment and exclaimed again, "So bright, my poor old eyes can read the time! Very good, very good!" He slapped Tuck Heng on the back.

"Thank you, Uncle Ah Fook, thank you!" He was relieved.

As the proprietor of the Medical Hall of a Hundred Prosperities and the president of the Chan Clan kongsi, Old Master Chan Ah Fook was Ipoh's most respected and influential resident. His eyes might have dimmed with the years, and a stiff gait might have slowed his walk, but his voice was as strong as twenty years ago, still capable of rallying his White

Crane clansmen. His approval was important.

"Clansmen, our new Kapitan is to be congratulated! We're proud of him and happy for him that the foreign devils hold him in high regard."

Loud applause greeted Ah Fook's speech. His gold teeth flashing in the glare of the electric lights, he ended it by declaring, "I'll install electric lamps in my house too. All my piglets are here to see your lights, our Tuck Heng!"

He waved his cane and pointed to his children, one of whom was just six. After the loss of his Malay woman, he had returned to China and married a farmer's daughter who had blessed him with six sons and four daughters.

"My piglets and I wish you bright success and bright fortune, our Tuck Heng!" Then dropping his voice to a melodramatic whisper, he asked, "Young dog, why did you cut your hair like this? Are you declaring your support for Dr Sun's anti-Manchu party?"

"Why're you whispering to my son? Come and sit down." Wong-ma pointed to the seat beside her. "My Tuck Heng owes you much for teaching him how to survive in this country. Even as he rises, he should seek your advice before embarking on anything. Even the cutting of hair!"

"Ma, your old friends have arrived." He tried to distract her from the subject of his hair.

"Right, right! Old Fook, at our age, it's so good to see old friends again. Even Big Tree and Big Dog and their families are here."

"May good fortune and bright success enter this house!"

"Aiyah, Loh Pang, no need for such formality. I see your wife every other day. And why such a big gift? Your presence is enough!"

Wong-ma's face was wreathed in smiles. Tonight she was the quintessential matriarch, charming, hospitable and gregarious as she greeted her former White Crane comrades. All of them had settled in and around Ipoh and had prospered with the town. Many of them owned shops, tin mines, factories and trading firms of one kind or another. Big Tree and his brother were the town's rice merchants and Old Lee, the butcher, had become the owner of several pig farms in the countryside.

"Our good wishes, Wong-ma. May good fortune and blessings enter this beautiful mansion! Many thanks for inviting us," Big Dog greeted her as he led his children to bow with clasped hands before her.

"How tall they've grown! And they've kept their queues! Ah, fine young men! Chinese to the bone!"

Tuck Heng ignored her barbs and the stares of his elders, sidestepping their questions about his haircut. "And your daughters, Big Dog? Any good match yet?" Talk of marriage was bound to distract them.

"You girls are all waiting for a good husband, aren't you?"

"Look, Wong-ma. You're making them blush."

Big Dog's daughters fled into the inner chambers where Lai Fong found them giggling with merriment. Meanwhile their brothers crowded round Tuck Heng and plied him with questions about his hairstyle. Their admiring looks and murmurs made their elders frown. But there was little that the older generation could do to stop the spread of new ideas and fashion sweeping into Kinta Valley. Young men returning from Penang and Singapore were already sporting Western-style cotton shirts, jackets with coin buttons and twill trousers. Many too had started to wear their queues hidden beneath their felt hats, walking with a swagger as they swung their walking sticks in imitation of the English foreign devils.

"They're just restless. The best thing is to get them wives," Mrs Chan Ah Fook said.

"I can be your children's matchmaker."

"And a better one you'll not find in the whole of Ipoh," Wong-ma declared, patting Aunt Loh, her friend of many years.

"Our Wong-ma is drunk with happiness tonight! That's why she's praising me to the sky!"

"Look at her. Smiling till you see only her teeth! May our Wong-ma grow old and prosperous like Laughing Buddha, surrounded by grandchildren and great-grandchildren!"

"Thank you, thank you!"

Wong-ma dabbed away a happy tear. Watching her, it struck Tuck Heng that her face was no longer the dried-up bittergourd that had confronted him years ago in a dim red hut in Bandong. Like the rest of her, it had filled out with the good years although the lines of bitterness were still etched on her cheeks.

"Thank you, thank you, my friends," she was murmuring, poised between weeping and smiling. She was the proud mother of the Kapitan China of Ipoh. "Our gods have ears even in this foreign country! I know they've heard my prayers!" she declared with such certainty Aunt Loh was to remark later that her words might have challenged the Malay spirits that night. "Why else would the Malays cause trouble?" she asked.

But for the moment, no one in the mansion was thinking of troublesome spirits or the Malay partners of the White Cranes during the Bandong wars. The old comrades were reminiscing and their memories were personal, communal and therefore highly selective. As tales of past battles, terror in the jungle, betrayal by friends and defeat by foes flew back and forth across the room, Wong-ma was stabbed by the memory of her banishment from Penang.

"Here, he drove in his knife! When he forced me to leave my Tuck Heng, the son I'd waited for more than twenty years! Right here!" She clapped a palm over her breast. "To this day I can still remember how he asked me to leave Penang! And I vowed to return some day. Every night I pray. Lord Buddha, I say, don't let him be reborn! Let him wait till I join him in the next world! So I can tell him to his face how I felt all those years! And when I join our ancestors, I will be buried next to him in Penang! As we say back in Sum Hor, 'Alive I'm his wife; dead, I'm his ghost!' Then the sons of his Penang wife will have to bow before my grave!"

"Choy! What a thing to say!"

"Chieh, at our age, what're we afraid of? If it's our time to go, we go. If it's not our time yet, even if we want to die, we can't. That's why I'm still here and Tai-kor Wong is not. So what's wrong with a few words about the grave?"

"Choy, choy," Mrs Chan looked distraught as her eyes sought her husband's for help.

"Wong-ma! No more talk of unhappy things! Trot out your little piglets. It's ages since we've seen them."

Ah Fook gave the others a wink. Her grandsons, Kok Kiong (Nation's Strength) and Kok Wah (Nation's Prosperity), were her two most precious gems.

"Fong! Bring out my piglets!"

"Yes, Ma."

The children came in.

Yoke Foong (Jade Phoenix) and Yoke Lan (Jade Orchid) greeted their elders in the restrained manner little girls from good families were trained to assume in company.

"But here's the most important piglet!" Big Tree pointed to Kok Kiong.

"How old are you? Eleven?"

"Almost twelve, Granduncle," Kok Kiong replied. He was a serious-looking boy with the grave features of his mother.

"Have you mastered the Three Character Classic yet?"

"Master Lao is already teaching us the Four Character Classic, Granduncle."

"Excellent! Excellent! A scholar in the making, I say, Wong-ma."

"I can say the Three Character Classic too, Granduncle!" Little Kok Wah tugged at his silk jacket.

"Don't boast! You can only recite three pages!" his sisters protested.

The little boy drew himself up to his full height and puffed out his chest. "But I'm only three years old! One year one page!"

The whole company burst out laughing and the boy scampered to hide among the folds of his grandmother's samfoo.

"Are we shy now?" Wong-ma hugged him.

Yoke Foong and Yoke Lan tried to pull him away, but he clung to his grandmother. "Go away! I'll stay with Grandmama!" He stamped his foot.

"No need to be rude. You can sit on my lap while your sisters show us their needlepoint."

Yoke Foong blushed as she brought out the phoenix she was embroidering. The girl was fair like her mother. Her nose was finely chiselled and her almond-shaped eyes were like her mother's too. Next to her, Yoke Lan, who took after her father, looked like a peasant child, with none of her older sister's delicate features.

"I don't like needlework. I want to go to school, Grandmama."

"Your Papa said he's going to build a school here for everyone. Right or not, Tuck Heng?"

"Right, Ma." But his eyes were fixed on the doorway.

"Are you looking out for Old Buffalo and his family? They should be here soon. Last month I sent our servant to his farm. It's out in the middle of nowhere."

"How are his wife and daughters?" Aunt Loh asked.

"Haven't seen them for years. Old Buffalo never lets them out of his sight."

"The older he gets, the worse he becomes! His girls have never been to town, you know? Old Buffalo guards them like a miser guards his gold."

"Don't worry, he'll be here." He got up.

"Where're you going, Tuck Heng?" Wong-ma asked.

"I've to go outside and wait for the senior district officer and his party. He's bringing a foreign woman to watch the lion dance."

"Didn't I tell you our Tuck Heng will go far?" Ah Fook asked. "Look at those lines and that mole. Signs of fame and prosperity."

⊷═◎═⊶

He felt he was standing at the summit of success as he scanned the sea of faces in the garden. The gates of the mansion had been thrown open for this auspicious occasion and the townsfolk, drawn like moths to the free food and bright lights, were crowding into the grounds. Coolies who were members of the clans and kongsi were streaming through the gates and helping themselves to the food laid out on wooden trestles.

"Scrambling like hungry ghosts," Mr Lam, his manager, grumbled.

"Once in a lifetime, let them be."

He was prepared to be a generous host. All he asked from the gods was to let everything run smoothly tonight, especially the senior district officer's visit. Who knows what this might lead to? Perhaps an appointment to the Legislative Council which would place him on the same footing with the Right Honourable Ong Boon Leong. That would be something to look forward to.

Beyond the gates of Wong Mansion, the open grounds had been transformed into a fair, lit by the oil and kerosene lamps of hawkers who had seized the chance to make some money. Throngs of men with wives and children in tow, miners, amahs, rickshaw pullers, labourers and office clerks with their parents, grandparents, aunts and uncles, cousins and the entire extended family had come to view the wonder of the electric lamps. Snapping at their heels were hustlers, hawkers, pedlars, medicine men, snake charmers and even beggars on crutches who hobbled out to the fairground to rattle their tins at the crowd.

"Watch this miracle!" A man sliced the air with his sword. t drew the crowd.They gathered round him and his assistants.

"A snake! Look, it's a python."

He slit the belly and drank its blood.

"Good, ah! Good, ah!" The crowd clapped.

"Now watch this!"

His tongue stuck out. His sword sliced it.

"Eeee! Ma!" Children covered their eyes. Their mothers screamed. Blood dripping from his mouth, the man raised his bottle.

"Miracle snake blood," his assistants announced. "One dollar! One dollar!"

The man took a gulp and the tongue stopped bleeding. Loud applause followed.

"See! No blood! Cured immediately!" The medicine man went round the circle of people, displaying his miraculously healed tongue. The men rushed forward.

"Here! One bottle!"

"One bottle for me!"

"Over here, two bottles for me!"

"Only fifty bottles left!" the medicine man yelled.

At this, the crowd pushed and fought its way to the centre, hollering for bottles of the snake blood.

"Twenty bottles left! No more! No more!"

Men fought each other as they tried to grab at the last few bottles of this miraculous medicine. Their women screamed and cursed at the mob and tried to protect their daughters. Old Buffalo waded into this sea of angry men with his wife and daughters.

"Son of a pig! Keep your bloody hands to yourself! That's my daughter you're touching, you swine!"

His wife clung to their three daughters. Her arms tried to shield them from contact with the beasts. "Don't let them touch you!"

The girls were terrified. They had never left their farm before. They floundered and squirmed in the sea of bodies. The noise overwhelmed them. The babble of foreign tongues confused them. They clung to their mother and struggled to keep up with Old Buffalo who was charging through this heaving writhing sea. Never had they seen so many people before! Their farm near the silent hills was miles from the nearest dwelling. Aaah! A black beast with red teeth! The girls recoiled from it. The ragged bundle spat at them. "Blood! Blood!" The girls shrieked and backed away from his stream of red sireh juice. They fell over each other. Huge shadows loomed. The oil lamps hissed and sputtered. The multitudes pressed in. They felt trapped. A thunderous clap of firecrackers made them jump.

"The lion dancers are here!" the crowd roared.

Vigorous beating of drums and firecrackers greeted the arrival of the senior district officer and his entourage which included Inspector Ian Thomson, Mrs Winters, a writer for a magazine in London, the chief engineer and the surgeon general. They had arrived in two gharries accompanied by a small contingent of Sikh guards.

"Welcome, welcome, very honourable sirs and lady!" Tuck Heng greeted his guests and bowed with hands clasped before him. "Tank you! So very, very much tank you! Please to come in!" He spoke in his clipped and heavily accented English. Flustered by the presence of so many important white people, he scraped and bowed and chatted incessantly above the noise of the drums and gongs.

So much face for him, he thought. Aye, so much face! He could think of nothing else except the prestige and privilege of entertaining them. He bowed and smiled, and bowed and smiled, as he led his white gods and goddess to the dais, specially erected so that they could sit apart from the mortals. His only regret was that Ong Boon Leong was not there to witness his glory.

"Please, sir, ah, you sit! Lion dance, begin soon. Very soon."

"Oh, how quaintly he speaks," Mrs Winters whispered to Mr Douglas. A burst of firecrackers greeted her words. This was followed by the roll of drums and the clang of gongs and cymbals. "Oh, how delightfully exotic and colourful! I shall be able to write a wonderful piece about this."

A pair of lions led by the bigheaded clown pranced in front of them. The black lion of the Hakka Black Flags trotted round the red lion of the Cantonese White Cranes. It cocked its head, eyes blinking with mischief, and raised its tail and hind leg like a dog peeing. "Good-ah! Get him!" The crowd guffawed and cheered again and again. Inside the mansion, guests from the Cantonese and Hakka clans raised their glasses and toasted Wong-ma and her son, "Good health! More wealth and prosperity!"

Cymbals clanged. The bigheaded clown flung copper coins into the air. Free money! The crowd surged forward. The lions pranced and fought for the red packet of cash and green lettuce of victory dangling enticingly atop a bamboo pole. "Higher!

Higher!" the crowd roared. The pinnacle of a lion's success and proof of a lion dancer's skill was to be the first to snatch away the red packet and lettuce. The black lion kicked up its front legs. The red lion fended off its attack. "Move back! Move back!" The White Crane and Black Flag members shoved away the urchins and beggars picking up the coins. A Sikh guard's moustache twitched with consternation. His fellow guards held on to their wooden truncheons. Memories of riots lingered in the police force. Again and again the bigheaded clown teased the prancing lions with his fan and flung more copper coins into the air. "More! More! For good luck!" the crowd roared. Two red strings of firecrackers went off.

"God of Thunder!" Old Buffalo's wife let go of her daughters' hands and covered her ears.

"Ma! Ma!" her terrified daughters screeched. They had lost her. Other bodies pressed against them. Mouths leered at them and eyes winked at them. The girls covered their breasts. "Turn back! Turn back!" But their shouts went unheard. Their way was blocked by the bodies surging towards the lions and the hail of copper coins.

"Pa! Pa!" Hysteria gripped them.

"Eaters of shit! Watch your bloody hands! Daughters! Where are you?" Old Buffalo bellowed. "Daughters!"

Young Omar squeezed past him. Wedged between the thousands of arms and legs, he craned his neck this way and that way as he pushed under the mob. He wanted to see everything. He elbowed his way through the throng, trying to edge closer to the lion dancers. "Wait! Wait!" Nawawi went after Omar. His own head was giddy with anticipation. His Chinese father was in the mansion. He was sure of it. All the White Crane miners would be there, the shopkeeper in the town had told him. Hurry! Hurry! His heart pounding, he fought his way towards the electric lights.

"Nawawi!" Ibrahim called after him.

"Datuk! He's in there. My Chinese father is there!"

"How can Che' Wong tell you which of his friends is your father?"

"I'll show him my father's kris!"

He reached into the folds of his sarong. Out came the kris which flashed menacingly in the lamplight.

"Malay devil with knife!" Old Buffalo's daughters screeched.

Heads turned. People started running. "Malay devil with knife!" The cry was taken up and repeated throughout the fairground. "Amok!" another cried. Panic seized the crowd. Blind fear rippled through their hearts. A child stumbled and wailed. "He's got a child!" Mothers grabbed their children and ran. Fathers tore through the multitudes. Some stalls were overturned. The oil lamps ignited and burst into flames. The fire spread to the other stalls. "Kill the pigs!" Chinese hawkers lunged at Malay pedlars, blaming them for the fire. Fist fights broke out. More stalls were overturned. Black Flags and White Cranes raced out of the mansion and leapt into the fray. Some of them swooped down upon Ibrahim. They felled him with a mighty hand chop on his neck.

"Pig-eaters!" Nawawi rushed to Ibrahim's defence. He fought back with a vengeance and knifed a White Crane.

"Watch out! The Malay devil is armed!"

"Police! Police! Quick! Over here!"

The Sikh guards parted the mob and fell upon Nawawi. A truncheon hit him on the head. Then a burly Sikh pulled him up by the hair and tried to wrest the kris away.

"You son of a pig!" Nawawi clung to his precious kris. He kicked out at the guard.

"Father!" Omar stumbled among the legs. A kick in the stomach sent him sprawling. "Father!" he screamed in pain.

"Omar! Omar!" Ibrahim raced towards his son. The monsters and their truncheons danced all round him. "Omar! Omar!" Still the blows fell upon him. Before his horrified eyes, he saw Nawawi mercilessly bludgeoned. He tried to stop them.

"Mistake! Please stop!" But his pleas went unheeded.

The grounds of the mansion was a sea of confusion by now. Mrs Winters had fainted on the dais. Mr Douglas and the chief engineer shielded her body from the crush of coolies swarming all over them. Inspector Thomson fired his pistol into the air. It set off a stampede. Like a herd, the crowd made for the gate. Several people were trampled on. More women fainted. Children wailed. Thomson raced to a gharry and ordered the Indian syce to bring it round to the dais. He fired his pistol again and again to clear a path for the vehicle. The shooting sent those inside the mansion scampering for cover. Tables and chairs were overturned. Veterans of the Bandong wars thought that a battle had broken out.

"Children! Into the kitchen!" Wong-ma's voice was hoarse with fear. Gunshots kept ringing inside her head. Visions of the Bandong dead clouded her aged eyes. Their ghosts shrieked and flew round and round the room. The walls wavered and caved before her. She missed a step. "Aaah!" Headlong down the steps she fell.

"Grandmama! Grandmama!"

Chapter Thirty-seven

*T*he messenger from Ipoh came to the house just as the muezzin in the mosque was calling his faithful to prayer. Choon Neo received him in the front room.

"Towkay Neo, so very sorry to wake you up so early."

"Has something happened? How's Towkay?"

"Towkay is fine and in good health. But Towkay's mother has joined her ancestors."

Choon Neo sank into an armchair as Ah Ting recounted the whole story of that inauspicious night. As she listened, a dark jealous anger filled her heart. How humiliating that she'd to learn about this new mansion through a servant! And only because his mother had died. Her head swam, and with great difficulty she tried to follow what Ah Ting said. Slights and gestures, real or imagined, filled her head. How could he treat her this way?

"Towkay is bringing the coffin home for burial."

"Home?"

"He's bringing the coffin here."

"What? He's bringing his mother's body for burial next to his father?"

"Yes, Madam. He asked you to make the necessary arrangements and follow the Cantonese customs."

"Gods in heaven! What's he thinking of?"

"I can't say, Madam. Tomorrow the hearse with the coffin will be here. Towkay said to let the family in Roseville know.

He said Masters Ong Boon Leong, Ong Boon Haw and Dr Ong Boon Pin are Tai-kor Wong's sons, so also Wong-ma's sons and mourners. They should observe the proprieties and pay their respects to her. Towkay also said to ask your brother to arrange for the wake and funeral. Hold the wake in this house, he said. Don't think about money. Just get the best."

"Oh, what am I to do?"

"And Madam, there's also good news. Towkay is now the Kapitan China."

"Thank you, Ah Ting. Go into the kitchen and get something to eat. I'll send for you later."

Her head was spinning. What madness could have seized Tuck Heng? The whole of Penang knew Siok Ching as Tai-kor Wong's first wife. Why was he stirring up trouble by bringing Wong-ma here for burial? The blow to Siok Ching's pride would be so great that she couldn't even bear to think of it. Roseville and the entire Wee clan would turn against him. And her. Boon Leong and his brothers were men of high standing. And the Nonya pedigree and Baba heritage of their mother was impeccable. Who was Wong-ma, for goodness sake? The woman's family were coolies with feet deep in muck and dung!

She sent for the amah to help her dress. She had to alert her brother, Chong Beng, about the funeral arrangements and then hasten to Roseville to break the bad news to them.

"A rat! That's what he is!" Her mother didn't mince her words. "You tell him I'll not attend the funeral!"

"Mak, please don't make things worse."

"Choon!" Chong Beng snapped at her. "A slap on Aunt Siok Ching's face is a slap on our mother's face! Now he's so high up, the Kapitan China of Ipoh, you can afford to ignore your relatives' feelings, is it?"

"Did I ask him to do this? Did I?"

"Then send someone to stop him!"

"You're his manager! Why don't you send someone? I've already told you that he wants you to make the arrangements for the funeral! Are you going to do it or not?"

Chong Beng gave her an angry glare. Then the fork-tongued snake turned to their mother. "Mak, if you say no, I won't do it. I'd sooner lose my job than stab you and Aunt Siok Ching in the back."

"My son, good jobs are very hard to come by. Do what you have to but do it as his manager. Not as his brother-in-law. It's good I can still tell you what to do. As for other people, they're already married out. So I'll shut my mouth in case they say I interfere too much."

"Mak, I didn't even think that! I was going to ask you to come with me to Roseville to break the news to them."

"You know what your husband's plans are! You go and tell them yourself!"

"Mak, I didn't know anything till this morning! He's built a mansion for his Cantonese family in Ipoh! And he didn't even tell me!"

She rushed out of the house and slumped into the seat of her gharry and sobbed, "To Roseville!"

She dreaded to think what her mother-in-law would say. Siok Ching was known for her sharp tongue. Warm and hospitable when in good humour, she could be cold and cutting when crossed. She'd never tolerated any slight from anyone. Her mother had told her the story of how a grief-stricken Siok Ching had berated the White Crane elders over plans to bury Tai-kor Wong; how she had fought off the claims of Wong-ma and told the elders in no uncertain terms that Tai-kor Wong should be buried in Penang and not Sum Hor as Wong-ma had demanded. "His sons are here in this country! He should be buried here so they can sweep his grave on Remembrance Day! In Sum Hor, who'll sweep his grave? His China wife is barren! And in case you all forget, I'm his first wife! I'll be buried next to him when my time comes!"

The elders had backed down. They'd never expected the tiny Nonya lady to oppose them. No one dared even suggest that she follow the traditions of Sum Hor after that. Besides, at that time, Wong-ma was stuck in China and expected to grow old and die quietly there. Who would've thought that the stubborn coolie woman would return to stir up trouble even in death? It would be such a scandal. Her thin shoulders shuddered at the thought.

Her heart was pulled in several directions. One minute she was enraged by her husband's deception, the next appalled by his stupidity and blindness. How could he ever hope to succeed in raising his coolie mother above a highborn Nonya? Everyone would treat them as pariahs.

Tears welled up again. A cold fear gripped her. Never again would Kok Seng and his sisters be welcomed in Roseville. The threatened loss of privileged company, opportunity for Kok Seng to mix in good society and good prospects for her daughters made her review her situation.

Years ago, when she'd discovered that her husband had started other families elsewhere, she'd decided not to depend on him to do what was right for his children. So over the years, she'd learned to clutch her heart, bite her tongue and put on a smiling face when he came home. And it had paid off. He bought her gold trinkets, jade and diamonds as if to salve his conscience. She'd hoarded these as her savings against an uncertain future. Like her grandmother, mother and aunts before her, she knew that the wife of a man with other wives must look out for herself and look after her own future.

All the way to Roseville, she looked her future in the eye and saw it firmly tied to her son. If Kok Seng did well, then she would live well. She mustn't compromise his prospects for a grandmother he'd never met.

Chapter Thirty-eight

*F*ortunately Boon Leong had not left for his office yet. He, of all persons, must not be left in doubt as to which side she was on. She was ushered into the dining room where the family had just finished breakfast.

"Please forgive me, Mother-in-law!" She went down on her knees.

"What's this, Choon? Tell me what it is! No need to kneel!"

"Please let me finish."

As she had expected, Siok Ching almost threw a fit.

"That evil woman! Even in death, she gives me trouble!"

"Mak, please, no need to shout like this."

"How not to shout? You all tell me! That China woman and her son are out to smear our name! Stop him, Boon Leong! He can't bury that woman next to your father!"

"Mak, listen. That woman is also Father's wife. And you know how these Chinamen are. Their clans will fight for her if Tuck Heng asks them."

"Isn't there a law to stop him? Do you want people to laugh at me? I won't bear it! I'd rather die!"

"Mak! Calm yourself. And Sister-in-law, please get up."

Boon Leong was so distressed that he literally pulled her to her feet.

"Brother-in-law, you're the only one who can stop my husband from doing this."

"This is terrible, just terrible." Kim Neo, her sweet and gentle sister-in-law, wrung her hands helplessly.

"Mak, please have some tea. Forgive me, I'm married to an ingrate!"

When Siok Ching accepted her cup of tea, she was relieved.

"You'll ruin your health if you cry like this, Mak," Boon Leong tried to soothe his mother. "Kim, send for my brothers. Tell them to come over as soon as possible. We've got to handle this like a family."

His stress on family pleased Choon Neo. She searched his face for signs of displeasure. But neither anger nor annoyance had ruffled the smooth lines of his regal face. He was speaking to his mother in calm measured tones.

"You won't lose face, Mak. You've said many times that Grandfather chose my father to be his son-in-law. So Father married into your family, not you into his."

His mother was crying softly now, but she was listening.

"According to custom and tradition, my late father's wives are my mothers whether my brothers and I like it or not. If we don't take part in the rituals, people will accuse us of being unfilial and disrespectful to the dead and you of not bringing up your sons properly. And yet," he put his arm round his mother, "you're right in feeling wronged. Our father had already said that you're his first wife. According to the customs of China, only first wives are buried beside their husbands, others are buried in separate graves."

"The witch is trying to claw her way into the plot next to your father. Over my dead body! Do something, Boon Leong!"

He got up and stood by the window, looking out at the green lawn for a long while before he turned and spoke again. He was waiting till his wife and Choon Neo had calmed his mother down. As he listened to them, it suddenly struck him that the situation was grotesquely funny. Fighting over a hole in the ground! He hid a smile. His own mother fighting with a dead woman! Over who should be buried next to the dead man they'd so reluctantly shared!

"Mak, you're right to feel outraged," he lied. "Tuck Heng

should be stopped. And yet ..." he paused and searched for the right words, waiting till he was sure that his mother was listening, "if we challenge him, we'll fall into the very trap he's set for us. He'll use the chance to tell people how you've used your father's wealth to push aside a poor coolie woman. People will turn against you. And the gossips will wag their tongues and side with him and his mother."

"Let them say what they want! I've no ears to listen!" His mother burst into tears again.

"But Mak, please consider again. Do you want to give Tuck Heng this victory?" using the one word which would make his mother think carefully. "Do you want Grandfather's name to be dragged into the mud? And do you really want my brothers and me to fight Tuck Heng?"

"I don't know, I don't know what to do any more," his mother moaned. "My son, I ... I ..." Tears were streaming down her face again and it took all his strength to continue speaking in the calm measured tone he often used in the courts to argue his cases. "The only way to avoid this cunning trap is to be generous and be seen as generous."

"What? Give in? Let him do what he wants?"

"No. Let big hearts prevail over small ones. Show how gracious a well-bred Nonya can be," he flattered his mother, adding that it was to his mother's advantage to err on the side of generosity by not opposing Tuck Heng's plans. "Treat him as Father's son, an errant son accepted by you, the long-suffering mother. Offer him Roseville for his mother's wake."

Everyone was shocked.

"But Brother-in-law, you're a Christian! And it'll be a Chinese funeral!" Choon Neo protested.

"Precisely because we're Christian, we should be tolerant and charitable towards Tuck Heng, shouldn't we?"

The enigmatic smile on his face left Choon Neo puzzled and worried.

"I'd rather die," Siok Ching moaned.

Chapter Thirty-nine

"Cannot! We Cantonese of Sum Hor have our own customs. The wake must be in the house of the eldest son. Thank my brother for me, but I cannot accept his generous offer." After Boon Leong's servant had left, he turned to Choon Neo. "In my own house I can do what I like, in his I've got to defer to him. Right or not?"

She kept a pained silence. She resented the invasion of her home by a horde who spoke a dialect she could hardly understand. Her head reeled under the unfamiliar faces who had taken over her sitting-room, her dining-room, her hallways and passageways, her bedrooms and the entire kitchen! Worse, that other woman had brought her sons and daughters!

"He's moved them into my room," she complained.

"What? They're sleeping on your bed?" Her sister-in-law, Kim Neo, was shocked.

"I was smart. I quickly got my two girls into bed first. Her children are sleeping on the floor. I'll scratch her eyes out if she dares to insist on the bed."

"Did she serve you tea? Greet you properly?"

"She can't even speak Hokkien. Just a nod if we happen to meet."

"Oh, Choon, you must be feeling terrible. How can Brother-in-law be so callous?" Kim Neo's usually soft voice deserted her.

"It's only a small thing to him. Tuck Heng is too busy with arrangements for the funeral."

Tears burned her eyes as she said it. She brushed them off, annoyed that such a small thing could affect her so.

"All the aunts and uncles have been talking about nothing else but the grand show your husband is putting up. Boon Leong says he wants to show how important he is in the Chinese community."

By the second night of the wake, her house was so crowded she had to step over several sleeping bodies to get to her bedroom where her daughters slept huddled under the mosquito net. At the foot of the bed lay the children from Ipoh. Choon Neo took a good look at the two sleeping boys. She did not doubt that her husband had fathered other sons elsewhere. He was that kind of Chinaman, she thought bitterly. If only her own father had been rich enough to match her with Boon Leong. Her cousin's elegance and forbearance had made her husband seem all the more vulgar in her eyes.

With an angry shove, she pushed open the shutters. The heat was killing. Her clothes were soaked. She went out to look for Kok Seng, but her son seemed to have disappeared into the company of the gamblers under the tent erected in the garden. Guests and mourners alike were taking the opportunity to play mahjong and card games till the wee hours of the morning, all in the name of keeping the dead company.

And the deceased, lying in her grand coffin of teakwood, was never in want of company. Relays of grey-robed priests chanted prayers every night. During these rituals, the Cantonese women from Ipoh were loud and domineering. They took over everything from the keening for the dead to the cooking for the living. When they were not wailing, they were sitting around the coffin, folding incense paper and trading stories about Wong-ma. By the third night of the wake, they had shaped a story that took the town by storm and fired the imagination of all who heard it. Within a day or so, even the rickshaw riders who ferried visitors to the wake were retelling the story in the marketplaces.

According to the story, Tuck Heng was the heroic filial son who'd brought his downtrodden mother back to Penang to reclaim what she had lost to a highborn Nonya. Every downtrodden China-born wife who had arrived in Malaya only to discover that her husband had already married a local woman could identify with Wong-ma's story and sang praises of the filial son who was reinstating her. The women had stories of their own to tell too and in their retelling of Wong-ma's story, they added their experiences. Before long, Wong-ma's story reached epic proportions in the marketplaces, coffee shops and teahouses where the town's gossips congregated. Friends and relatives of Siok Ching, Boon Leong and his brothers hit out against the storytellers and added their side to the tale. Not to be outdone, Tuck Heng's supporters in the White Crane added the story of how this humble son of a poet, beheaded for his dissident views against the Manchus in China, had escaped death, had come to Malaya and risen steadily from poor coolie to impoverished clerk in a shop of the wealthy Wees, to become at last the Kapitan China of Ipoh.

"Wah! Good! Good!"

It was the stuff of every immigrant's dream. The whiff of success in the opium dens and the hope which drove the rickshaw coolie to ply his fare day and night, in rain or shine.

Crowds started to converge upon Choon Neo's bungalow daily to catch a glimpse of Tuck Heng. They gawped at the rows of wreaths and banners lining both sides of the road from end to end. These were lavishly embroidered with Chinese characters in praise of the deceased and offering condolences to her famous son.

Such expressions of support from the clans and societies were not lost on Boon Leong who came to the wake every night with his brothers and their families. Braving the stares and whispers of the Cantonese crowd, they took their places beside the coffin for the ritual keening. On the first night, Boon Leong and his brothers apologised for their mother's absence. Siok Ching had taken ill and had to stay in bed on doctor's orders.

"How very convenient," the gossips hissed.

Choon Neo glanced at Boon Leong and wondered if he

noticed the knowing sneers, but he appeared oblivious. Even Tuck Heng's triumphant smirk seemed to have gone unnoticed.

She was glad that Boon Leong held his head high. He knelt when Tuck Heng knelt and kowtowed when Tuck Heng kowtowed. He and his brothers did everything filial sons would do during the rituals except hold joss sticks.

"They're Christians," she told Tuck Heng, but he wasn't impressed.

Her uncles and aunts and relatives of the Wees and Ongs also came to the wake out of courtesy to Boon Leong and his brothers. But they were appalled by the loudness and pushiness of the rich Chinamen and their wives.

"So loud and so blunt, most uncalled for!" Uncle Wee Thiam muttered under his breath. "And they cut you off before you've finished talking."

"Just a while ago, I was trying to help two of them decide how we're going to arrange ourselves for the funeral procession tomorrow. But then this ... this Big Dog fellow was so loud. Good gracious! He shouted into my face! So I quickly got out of there," her aunt complained to Choon Neo.

She patted her aunt's hand and made sympathetic clucking noises. She was grateful for their presence. It helped to ease her sense of isolation among the Cantonese women. At least there was someone to talk to in between the prayers and rituals. Otherwise she would have nothing to do for the Cantonese women had taken over everything. They were doing things according to the Sum Hor customs she knew nothing about. She was an outsider.

"There's no order in their ways. Everything so slapdash! Just look at their food," she whispered to her aunt.

She shuddered at the sight of their steamed pork buns, far too big for one to bite into without making a mess! And the platters of fried noodles had huge pieces of pork and chicken floating in thick brown gravy. The vegetables they served were not sliced but broken off so that the rough edges of the stalks were still there. How they could've served visitors such rough and ready fare was beyond her comprehension. We Nonyas, she thought, would have sliced the pork into thin slivers, shredded the chicken and served the fried noodles garnished with finely chopped spring onions, thinly sliced chillies, a sprinkling of fried onions and a dash of pepper. If a woman's cooking reflected her degree of refinement, these Cantonese women had none at all.

⌐≡◎◎≡⌐

The day of the funeral began as a sweltering morning with a clear cloudless sky. By noon the mourners were soaked and their clothes clung to their bodies. The coolies tied white towels round their heads to prevent beads of sweat from getting into their eyes. The family mourners took their places behind the hearse, thickly clothed in sackcloth that made the heat all the more unbearable. So it was a great relief to all when the sky suddenly darkened and the tropical storm, which had been building up all morning, broke over their heads. The squall, short and sudden, drenched everything.

"Not a very good sign," a banner bearer muttered under the weight of his soaked banner.

The first hint of trouble came when news reached the family that Siok Ching had tripped and fallen down the stairs. She had hit her head and was unconscious. Boon Pin and Boon Haw left the procession at once to attend to their mother. Their action was loudly condemned by the Cantonese women although Boon Leong was staying on for the funeral procession through the town.

Then, while the mourners were still talking about the shocking news of Siok Ching's fall, a fight broke out among the Chinese bands. They had been arguing over who should lead the procession.

When it looked as if the fight might get out of control, Boon Leong sent a messenger to the chief of police. He was taking no chances. Not with hundreds of coolies, rickshaw pullers and members of *tongs*, secret societies, taking part in the funeral procession.

"I don't want a riot in town. I've a duty to protect you, the children and all our relatives," Boon Leong explained.

A riot squad of Malay policemen arrived, armed with rattan shields and truncheons. Several band members were hauled away. That quietened the bands, but the onlookers were shocked. So were the clan and kongsi elders. They felt Tuck Heng had lost face. Doubts had been cast on his ability to control his clan members.

"What bad luck! Very unfortunate," people started whispering.

The presence of the riot squad at the funeral had befouled the air. The British authorities had never disrupted a Chinese funeral before.

"Betrayer! Running dog!" Tuck Heng spat.

Choon Neo said nothing. The next day, news came that Siok Ching had passed away. Boon Leong and his brothers immediately took off their mourning clothes to don fresh ones for their own mother. Tuck Heng, his wives and their children were forbidden by Sum Hor custom to take off theirs, and because they were already in mourning, they couldn't attend Siok Ching's funeral. It was just as well because Boon Leong announced that his mother had died a Christian, having been baptised by an Anglican priest just before she died. Instead of being buried in the Chinese cemetery next to Tai-kor Wong and Wong-ma, Siok Ching was buried in the Christian cemetery of the Anglican Church.

"Very clever, her sons! Like this, their mother won't lose face!" Lee-soh sniffed.

"It goes to show that our Wong-ma has won. She's finally with Tai-kor Wong in death," Aunt Loh said.

But one week later, when they were having breakfast, the amah came running into the dining-room.

"Towkay! Many policemen at the door."

"Find out what they want. We're eating."

Minutes later the servant returned, looking very worried.

"Towkay, they want to search the house."

"What?" Tuck Heng stood up. "Do they know who I am?"

he yelled. "I'll go and see what these running dogs want!"

The police party was headed by an English inspector. A young Chinese interpreter asked in Hokkien, "Are you or are you not Mr Wong Tuck Heng?"

He was seething with rage and refused to answer the running dog who was a Straits-born Baba. He looked the young man up and down, disdain burning in his eyes. Seeing this, the English inspector asked, "Are you Mr Wong Tuck Heng?"

He gave a sullen nod. The inspector took a letter out of his pocket. The young man stepped forward and translated into Hokkien what the inspector read out.

"The authorities are in possession of information which allege that you, Wong Tuck Heng, are involved in the illegal trafficking of opium and women and in the operation of opium dens and brothels. It is also alleged that as the head of a secret society, you have harassed the Malay natives and you are illegally involved in the buying and selling of native land. We are duly authorised to conduct a search of your premises and to remove any evidence found therein."

"Let lightning strike dead that running dog! He's still mourning for his mother and yet he's doing this to me! May the Thunder God strike him dead!"

"Tuck Heng Kor, how do you know it's Boon Leong? Do you have proof? Maybe it's …!"

"Bitch!" He slapped her across the face before she could finish.

"Don't think I'm blind! Half your heart's given to him."

That night he left Penang, taking Lai Fong and her children with him.

IV

IN THE GROUND OF
OUR DAILY LIVING
1912

Chapter Forty

"Zam! Here! Here can!"

His Malay chauffeur stopped some way from the temple gate and he got out of his open-top Bentley, one of the first on Malayan roads. That was still his passion—to be among the first of the rich and powerful.

His hand reached up to sweep back his windblown hair. The years had flecked it with grey although his thin serious face had retained its unsmiling smoothness and the eyes behind their wire-rimmed glasses were as keen and hungry as a newly arrived immigrant's. His nose still twitched at the whiff of a risk or a chance to increase his stakes in a venture. No stranger to adversity, his nerves had been steeled by setbacks and opportunities won and lost in the cutthroat world of doing business in the Federated Malay States, where British traders were trying to break the Chinese stranglehold on tin mining.

He had tried to fight off the encroachment of the foreign devils whenever he could, but in the process, he had antagonised several big dogs in the government and many of his projects were blocked. He was no idiot, however, and one day, he wised up to the colonial game. *Teh susu!* A "tea-and-milk" company. Me, the tea and he, the milk! As any tea-drinking Chinese would tell you, tea is of the essence, not milk. Only the white man is stupid enough to dilute his tea with milk, he mused.

The next day, he invited the retired Inspector Ian Thomson of the police force to sit on the board of his tin mining company and Thomson, eager to increase the size of his retirement egg, readily agreed. With a white man on his flagship company, his fortunes rose steadily. He soon gained the trust of foreign banks and ready access to the English officials in the Land and Mines Department. Eventually he was able to acquire several thousand acres of rubber plantations, more tin mines and mining rights and a stake in the highly profitable opium revenue farm in Perak as well.

"My troubles in Penang taught me a lesson. Never forget who's the new emperor of Malaya," he said to Ah Fook.

"Don't forget the poor buffaloes you left back in the mines," Ah Fook chided him. "Thousands of Old Sticks are stuck in those dung holes."

"So you think the gods are sending me a sign? Wong-ma's death was a sign?"

"Better read it as a sign than regret later, right or not?"

He believed Ah Fook was right. So when his mourning period for Wong-ma ended, he vowed to Heaven that he would set up a medical hall in every town and village in the country. From Ipoh to Kuala Lumpur to Singapore, he would see to it that coolies and their families would be able to buy herbs and medicine cheaply and consult a physician at no extra charge. Word was sent to Sum Hor inviting poor physicians to work in Malaya.

"On my last trip to Singapore, I met some of them. All Hokkien-speaking. Old-fashioned clods still clinging to their pigtails! And they think I'm half a foreign devil because I've cut mine off!"

"So why keep a Hokkien woman in Singapore?"

"I need someone to teach me to speak Hokkien!"

That had so tickled the Cantonese bone in Ah Fook that the old man had roared and ribbed him about how pretty Hokkien girls were some of the best teachers in the world. That was five years ago and it was the last joke they'd shared before the old man joined his ancestors.

He passed through the moon gate of the temple and stopped to admire the pair of green dragons sitting on its roof. The glazed green tiles had caught the light of the setting sun, but within these high walls a deep sea green silence shaded the courtyard, broken now by the soft patter of the grey-robed priest hurrying down the steps to welcome him. He caught the look of mild surprise in the old priest's eyes. The temple was not due to open till next week.

"*Si-fu*," addressing the priest as "highly respected teacher", he bowed. "I didn't mean to disturb you. I just want to walk around a bit and pay my respects …"

"Towkah Wong, no need to apologise," the old priest's soft Cantonese voice stopped him in midspeech. "If not for you, there'd be no temple here. Please feel free to come any time, I'd be only too happy to attend to you and your family."

"No, no, Si-fu. I didn't mean to trouble you. I just want to visit the ancestral hall and walk around a bit before the grand opening. It's quiet and peaceful now."

"I understand. Please follow me, Towkah Wong."

"Si-fu, no need to trouble yourself. I can find my way. Please accept this."

He pressed some money into the old priest's hand.

"I'll light the lamps and announce your gift to the gods, Towkah."

And with that, the old priest left him to find his way through a side gate, past the shrubbery and into the ancestral hall lined with rows of memorial tablets of the White Crane coolies and miners. He lit three joss sticks, planted them in the brass urn and kowtowed three times. That done, he entered a much smaller chamber dominated by an elaborately carved altar of blackwood. The memorial tablets of his parents, his adoptive parents, his son, his comrades and former White Crane elders gazed down on him. He lit three joss sticks again and planted them in the brass urn just as the deep tonal chimes of the temple bell announced his offering.

Kneel.

Kowtow.

Stand.

Move on to the next tablet.

Kneel.

Kowtow.

Stand.

But he could not bring himself to kneel before the small wooden tablet bearing his son's name. Little Kok Wah would be fourteen today if he had not forced his family to leave Penang so suddenly: the little fellow had a high fever. But after the police had searched his house so unceremoniously, he couldn't bear to stay another day longer on the island. Consumed with shame and hate at the time, he could think of nothing else except vengeance.

Forgive me, Wong-ma. Little Kok Wah was your favourite. Is he with you now? Or has he been reborn as someone else's son? Someone who's a better father.

He wished he could talk to his wife, but not a word of blame had escaped Lai Fong's lips. Her self-control had mocked him. His lack of new sons after Kok Wah's death pained him. If he'd had a few more sons, the loss of one wouldn't have made such a difference. Kok Wah's death had left him with Kok Seng and Kok Kiong.

Bad luck comes in threes, he sighed. Wong-ma, Siok Ching and Kok Wah had died within the same year. No wonder his fortunes had plunged to dangerous depths. Fortunately he had friends and benefactors in the brotherhood and also among the dead.

Uncle Ah Fook, I can never thank you enough. In life and death, you've helped me. Please don't worry about your sons and daughters. I will personally see to it that they are well-settled. I regret to report that their mother is ill. Ah Fook-soh has not been in good health for many months. When the gods decree that she joins you in the next life, everything will be done to ease her passage into the next world. I, Wong Tuck Heng, kowtow and pay my respects to you, Uncle Ah Fook. May your spirit rest in comfort and continue to bless and protect your descendants.

He knocked his head lightly three times on the cool tiled floor. Then he got up and moved down the row of memorial tablets till he came to Old Stick. He got down on his knees.

Old Stick, I hope you've received the three baskets of gold and silver I asked Lai Fong to burn for you on the fifteenth of last month. I was away on business in Ulu Tilang. And I visited Old Buffalo and his wife. I had reported earlier that their three daughters went missing on the night of the terrible riot. Old Buffalo and his wife had searched for them everywhere. No news of them for years. At the time I had my own problems so I couldn't help them. Then last month, out of nowhere, one of the daughters went home to see them. Old Buffalo said she looks like a Malay woman now. She was big with child and brought along three of her six children. They were brown and half-dressed. Her husband's a Malay fisherman. At first Old Buffalo wanted to kill her. But his daughter knelt and cried. One of her sisters had been raped and killed herself. The other was living in a brothel in Taiping and didn't want to go home. Old Buffalo and his wife wept. I told them, "Be glad. You still have one daughter, six grandchildren and one more on the way." Who would've thought that Old Buffalo, so very careful about his daughters, would end up like this.

He lit a stick of sandalwood incense.

Old Stick, I hope you'll be happy in this new temple. Please continue to watch over my business. Every year I'll bring you your weaknesses.

He took out the bottle of rice wine in his pocket and his eyes lit up as he poured a generous libation onto the floor and invited Old Stick's spirit to partake of it.

Drink up, old friend. I know you used to like Three Stars rice wine and I've even brought you your other weakness. Take it and enjoy it.

He placed the canister of opium in front of Old Stick's memorial tablet. Outside, the sun was sinking below the hills. He left the ancestral hall and followed the path to the tombs. He'd ordered a stonemason to build them in memory of his adoptive parents, Tai-kor Wong and Wong-ma. When the time came for him to join his ancestors, he'd be buried here too, the site of the White Cranes mining settlement.

Once he'd dreamed of returning to Sum Hor in his old age, but his last visit home in 1910 had proved disappointing. When he arrived in Sum Hor, he was surprised that nothing had changed and yet everything seemed to have changed. Unchanged were the brigands and warlords who continued to pillage the countryside. Unchanged was the corruption and greed of the officials and landlords who ruled the peasants' lives. The floods, droughts, plagues of locusts and other calamities of heaven and earth had continued to claim lives. What had changed were the people he knew as a child. They were either dead or had left Sum Hor for the South Seas or the Gold Mountains in America. Only the very old, very young and women had remained behind. After more than thirty-seven years in Malaya, he found that he had no family to return to in Sum Hor. His close relatives had all been killed because of their ties with his father. Those who called themselves his relatives were mostly strangers who treated him as a goldmine. At first he didn't mind for they were so poor. He distributed gifts of cash and goods, rebuilt their houses and donated to schools and temples. But the more he spent, the emptier he'd felt. Emptiness hung about the mountains, rivers and rice fields. When he was slogging in the Bandong mines, he'd dreamed of revisiting these places of his childhood. Yet when he returned, he realised that the past was a country he could only revisit in his memory.

So what had changed? he'd asked himself again and again. He or Sum Hor? He stooped to pick up a clod of earth and crushed it between his fingers. Bits of sand fell to the ground. Thirty-seven years was a lifetime away from China. Could he have transferred his feelings from the land of his birth to the land of his adoption?

He walked past clumps of bamboos, willow trees and the pagoda. The temple grounds gave way to bush and thicket. As he waded through the lallang, their sharp blades cut his skin and the sting reminded him of his youth. Once again he was the fleet-footed deer who'd dashed through the wild lallang to warn the White Cranes of the Black Flags' ambush.

A cool breeze came up from the river. He took a deep breath. The scarred land of the opencast mines, the earth devoid of any vegetation except scrub and lallang, greeted him on the far banks. From the mines to the banks of the Bandong River, he could see the distance he'd travelled since those days when he was a fifteen-year-old mongrel fighting for food in the mines. Bandong was where he had started out, and Bandong was where he'd returned to build his temple to honour his ancestors. When he first arrived, he was a refugee, an exile without a country. Bandong gave him refuge and a new life. Bandong was where he became a man with two mothers—one gave him life, the other gave him an upbringing. To whom should he be more grateful? Both sides of a man's hand are of the same flesh.

The murmur of rushing water drew him to the riverbank. The Bandong River had carried him to safety and danger. He had sailed its waters and found work and friendship in the mines. He had almost drowned in its waters when he was shot by the Black Flags. Bandong River had flowed steadily between its banks, marking the rise and fall of kongsi and kampong, Chinese kapitans and Malay rajas and the death of Datuk Long Mahmud and Tai-kor Wong. Abruptly he turned back. Musa Talib had drowned there.

Large drops started to fall and the sun had dipped behind the trees. Quickening his pace, he ran through the lallang, but age had slowed him down. By the time he reached the main hall of the temple, he was soaked. The brief tropical twilight had ended and the sky was dark.

"Aiyah, Towkah, come in, come in." The old priest ushered him into his lamp-lit quarters at the back of the temple.

"Looks like I'll have to wait out the rain, Si-fu."

"You'll catch a cold in those wet clothes. If you don't mind, you can change into these dry ones and have dinner with me. I seldom get visitors."

He liked the old priest and accepted his invitation to stay for dinner. He changed out of his wet shirt and trousers and put on the loose cotton pants and tunic the priest had lent him. Having stripped off the trappings of his modernity, he squatted on the wooden bench like a coolie and began to eat.

"Sweet potato porridge and salted eggs. Aah, it's been years since I've eaten such good food."

"If the company is good and the conversation excellent, even a drink of plain boiled water will taste like heavenly wine." The old priest chuckled.

"How true, Si-fu. But good friends are difficult to find in this world. And we trading people have too many worries and too few friends."

The old priest refilled his bowl with more sweet potato porridge.

"How many sons does Towkah have?"

"Only two, Si-fu, only two."

"Better than only one, right or not?"

"That's true, Si-fu." He sighed and lapsed into a long silence. The old priest ate slowly and did not try to engage him in conversation.

"How very different from each other, those two," he began after some time. "Like a duck and a chicken."

"Mmm?" The priest was surprised.

"My son, Kok Seng, attends the English school, speaks the foreign tongue and thinks like a foreign devil. Like he's got no Cantonese bones and Cantonese blood. But it's my fault, Si-fu. I've stayed away from Penang and don't see the boy often enough."

The old priest nodded encouragingly.

"Kok Kiong, my other son, is better. Quiet, serious and filial. I've sent him to Canton for further studies. Just to make sure that he'll be Chinese. He's coming home soon to help in the family business."

He drank more tea and glowed with pride as he spoke of Kok Kiong and how a good modern education was a nation's strength.

"Some people say that I'm wise. One son educated in English and another in Chinese. It's like having one foot in China and the other on the foreign devil's land." He chuckled softly.

The old priest plied him with more porridge.

"Thank you, Si-fu, thank you. When Kok Seng comes over from Penang, I'll ask him to be a merchant like me. But an English-speaking one. Then he'll do even better than me and outfox the white men, I hope. The English are full of trickery. In China, they sell opium to us. Even bombed Kwangtung when we refused to let them bring it in. Here in Malaya, where they're the rulers, they pass laws forbidding us to sell opium."

"Is this not the right thing to do?"

"But Si-fu, the English government makes money from opium too. And also gambling. These English hypocrites condemn us with one side of their mouth and use the other side to sell even more opium to China. That's why, Si-fu, I won't give up the opium farm. But I'll use my profits to open more medical halls. It's hard enough being a coolie in Malaya, away from home and family. They need a bit of sweet smoke to get by each day."

"Coolies are arriving by the shiploads each day," the old priest added as he fanned away the mosquitoes buzzing round them.

"Tin and rubber prices are high now. So the foreign devils want coolies and pass laws to make it easy for plantation owners to bring them in. But when prices fall, they'll kick out the coolies and send them back to China like pigs and cattle! These English are very clever at changing the law to suit themselves!" He snorted, blew his nose and stood up. "I should know, Si-fu. My adopted brother in Penang is an English-educated lawyer. His tongue is slippery as a snake's."

"May the peace of Lord Buddha be with you, Towkah."

"Thank you. The rain has stopped. I must get going. Very good dinner. Thank you."

"Come any time, Towkah."

"Thank you. I hope everything will be ready for the opening ceremony."

"Don't worry, Towkah. The chief abbot of Bright Hill Temple will be here."

"Good, good! I want everything to go well."

His eyes resumed their hard glint behind the wire-rimmed glasses. He insisted on changing back into his shirt and trousers still damp from the rain and was all businesslike once he was dressed. Even his speech became brisk.

"Good luck, good fortune! The more I make, the more I give you." He snorted and blew his nose.

Chapter Forty-one

"Assalamualaikum, Tok Penghulu!"

Ibrahim pressed the brakes of his bicycle and came to a halt next to the Bentley.

"Waalaikumussalam!" he returned Zam's greeting of peace. "Waiting for your Towkay?"

"Ya, Tok. He's visiting the new Chinese temple."

"Looks like you're going to miss prayers at the mosque."

"That's so, Tok. I pray Allah in His mercy forgives me."

"Allah is infinite in His mercy."

Ibrahim cycled away, pedalling furiously past the red and green monstrosity. Its foreign architecture, hideous dragons and sword-wielding gods offended his aesthetic sensibility. Nothing could be uglier. Except their spirit huts by the roadside and dilapidated shrines housing their foreign gods. He pedalled faster. The sky was a dark angry orange. Rain clouds were rapidly covering the horizon. Large cool drops started to fall. On his face. His back. Come, rain, come! Fall. Fall upon the rice plants. God willing, let this year's harvest be bountiful.

His publication, *Tanah Melayu*, "Malay Land," was in dire need of contributions and subscribers. If the harvest was good, people would have money to buy his magazine. The bimonthly was his life's work. Even though few read it. People were too busy trying to make ends meet. Better to focus on making money like the Chinese. That was how he thought sometimes in his despair, but, God willing, he would make *Tanah Melayu* into the kind of periodical the educated Malays were already publishing in Singapore and the Javanese and Sumatrans, in the Dutch East Indies. Bandong was a lifetime behind those places.

Things had not turned out quite the way he had envisioned for his people ten years ago. The terrible riot in Ipoh had nearly killed his son. And Nawawi, that scoundrel, had slipped away from Ipoh. Not a word of thanks or an apology for all the trouble he'd caused!

After the riot, Mr Douglas had rejected his proposal to build an English school for Malay boys in Bandong Valley. But he'd refused to let the white man's rejection douse his hope of awakening his people. So he took to writing and publishing. It had not been easy to sustain the initial excitement of those early years when his journal was launched. It had caused quite a stir. He was forthright in his editorials and allowed his writers to say what they wanted. But he was careful too. He made sure that he was not contravening any state laws in his writings. Some white men like Mr Hennings had studied the Malay language and kept an eye on Malay publications. They had also banned many Chinese societies by simply labelling them secret societies. Chinese leaders thought to be troublesome were jailed or banished. Few Malay writers would wish for such a fate. Who could forget the sad case of Sultan Abdullah and his chiefs in the Perak uprising? The English had banished them to some faraway island in the South Seas; they were as good as dead to their families.

He stopped outside the community hall next to the mosque and leaned his bicycle against the wall. He mopped his balding pate. His face was lined, but his eyes had retained their lively intelligence. Several men were inside the hall. He did a quick count. Twenty-five. The audience was larger than he had expected and he recognised some graduates from the Malay College in Kuala Kangsar.

"Good evening, Tok! Assalamualaikum!" they greeted him.
"Waalaikumussalam!"

He took his place at the table. The chairman introduced him to the members of the Bandong Society for Malay

Advancement, mostly young clerks and clerical assistants in their twenties. Most had passed the Junior Cambridge Examination and were employed in government departments like public works, agriculture, mines and survey. The storm broke overhead just as he started to speak. The rain drummed upon the zinc roof above him like loud background music.

"My young friends! I thank you for inviting me! When your chairman told me that many of you are proud holders of the Junior Cambridge Examination Certificate, I realised that I'd be addressing the members of an elite Malay club! There're not many of you in this country! But, Insya Allah, you'll be like the chilli padi that will make the whole curry hot and spicy."

His audience laughed and applauded, pleased with his flattering description of them.

"We Malays in Bandong have come a long way. From being ruled by a menteri to being ruled by a district officer! That's the price we've paid for our progress!

"Bandong is a modern town connected by rail to Ipoh and the royal town of Kuala Kangsar. A town that boasts of two rice mills, a bank and shops. But they're owned by the Chinese! Bandong has a bus service. Again owned by the Chinese! A rickshaw depot. Again owned by the Chinese! A railway station. Owned by the white rulers but controlled by an Indian station master! A post office. Again owned by the white man and controlled by an Indian! A police station. In the charge of a Sikh police inspector! O honourable sons of Bandong, our small town has many government departments! But all in the charge of Englishmen assisted by Chinese and Indian chief clerks! But that's progress—or is it?"

They sat stiffly in their rattan chairs and gazed at him with impassive faces. The rain drummed on and on. Part of the zinc roof sprung a leak and someone got up and placed a pail to catch the drip. The chairman shifted uneasily in his seat. Then a young man stood up, bowed stiffly to the chair and Ibrahim.

"Honoured Tok, I seek your forgiveness first before I speak."

"Please go on."

"Like you, Tok, we've found jobs in the government. Before the white rulers came, we were padi farmers. Today we're respected government servants."

"That's true," he answered in a kindly voice, addressing the young clerk as an equal. "Many of us have found jobs in the government. But, honourable Tuan, I think there're too many of us in the government."

"Too many of us?" They looked at him.

"Look around you. Bandong has too many Malay punkah pullers, Malay gardeners, Malay constables, Malay postmen and Malay junior clerks! In the whole country, there're too many Malays in jobs like peons and road sweepers. Inside our hearts, we want to have a fair share of higher appointments in the government service. You who've passed the English examination, don't you want to be trained for a higher post?"

But the holders of the Junior Cambridge Examination Certificate were wary. Yes, they agreed with Tok Penghulu. But that depended on what their superiors thought. Better to be humble. Besides, life was safe and peaceful under the white man. Without them, the Malays would be like fatherless chickens hunted by hawks and eagles. Other powers would take over their land if the British moved out. He could almost hear the thoughts racing through their heads as they waited for him to finish his speech.

"We want, Insya Allah, to take charge of our own country! We Malays are now poor people living in a great country!"

"Begging Tok's pardon." The chairman was very apologetic. "We can't talk about politics here. We don't want the government to think that we're a political or secret society."

Cowards! Their English education had changed them into mincing little courtiers dancing to the tune of their masters, lowing like cows led by the nose ring! Please, Allah in your mercy, don't let Omar become one of them.

He stood up and, raising his voice to make himself heard above the persistent drumming on the tin roof, declared, "Tonight I'm here not to talk about politics but to talk about my acre of earth and my place in it!" He picked off the clump of mud that had stuck to his trousers and held it up for all to see. "Look, this bit of earth belongs to you and me."

Chapter Forty-two

"*H*old the lamp higher, lah!" Omar whispered.

A branch snapped underfoot. Kok Seng froze. Mr Chelvalingam almost fell against him.

"Sorry, sir!"

"It's all right, old chap, just carry on."

Outside the pool of light from the hurricane lamp, everything was dark and still. Omar was leading them to a place where the wild rambutan trees, ripe with fruit, were said to be attracting flying foxes. Bound to be plenty of them, he had promised Mr Chelvalingam.

"Nearly there, sir. Higher, lah, Seng."

Kok Seng held the lamp higher.

"Now look out for clusters of red eyes," Mr Chelvalingam whispered into his ear. "Up there in the trees. Can you see them?"

"Er, yes, yes, I can see them now."

He hung his lamp on a high branch. More red eyes among the trees. Those fruit bats were everywhere!

"Shoot when I give the word."

He had no great love for shooting, unlike Omar who had won several awards in school for marksmanship. But a gentleman ought to know something about shooting and hunting, Uncle Boon Leong had advised him. On the wall of his uncle's study were several trophies, the largest of which was a wild buffalo's head his uncle had shot during a hunt with the lieutenant governor of Penang.

"Seng? Ready?"

"Yes, sir."

They raised their double-barrelled guns and took aim at the myriads of tiny red eyes gleaming among the masses of shadows. The blast shattered the jungle which broke into frightened twitterings. Dark things scuttled underfoot. Shadows shook the branches above them. The red eyes scattered and reassembled to their left. They took aim and fired again. The red eyes flew to their right and they shot again!

"Right, fellas, I'm sure we've enough meat for the curry Mrs Chelvalingam promised to cook for us."

They lit two more lamps and searched the undergrowth for their fallen prey. A family of gibbons in the treetops called out to one another in piercing melancholic cries as they retreated from the light of the lamps.

They each had a sackful when they emerged from the jungle into a clearing of lallang that reached up to their shoulders. Bathed in bright moonlight, nothing seemed more beautiful and serene than this lake of wild grass as a night breeze sent ripples through it. The three of them plunged in, forcing their way through swathes of sharp blades that cut the skin where it was unprotected. Two hours later, they were back in town.

"Hello! Hello! Back from the hunt and laden with meat!"

Mr George Nambiar came out to meet them. He was the Chelvalingams' other house guest. A highly respected lawyer from Madras who had read law in Oxford, he was in Taiping for a few days to address the Indian Association.

"Mary, you'll have to cook us flying fox curry tomorrow!" Mr Chelvalingam called out to his wife.

"I've never eaten flying fox curry before."

"But Seng, you Chinese cook it as a soup and drink it as an aphrodisiac."

"The curry is delicious and just as efficacious! Is that the right word, sir?"

"That's the right word. Always learning new English words, that's our Omar. You'll make a fine magistrate some day."

"Thank you, sir. But right now, I'm just a humble junior clerk."

"So you're in the Malayan Civil Service?"

"No, no, Mr Nambiar. We Malays join the Malay Administrative Service."

"Just like in India, one service for the white men, another for the natives. And the more highly educated we natives are, the more insecure the white men become." Mr Nambiar cocked his head and, dropping his voice to a conspiratorial low, he added, "They want to keep us down at the lower rungs. They believe, and they're right, of course, that educated Indians are discontented Indians! But what they're really afraid of are thinking Indians."

"Oh, George, do let the poor boys sit down for a cup of coffee and some supper before you start lecturing them about Indian politics!"

Kok Seng was relieved. He was famished. Mary Chelvalingam bustled in with plates of *roti prata*, curry and a large pot of steaming coffee. Dressed in a long skirt and long-sleeved cotton blouse, her ample girth and cheerful voice exuded warmth and good humour. Kok Seng liked her. She was a Sunday schoolteacher and the choir mistress of Taiping's Tamil Methodist Church. Like her husband, she'd been educated in English mission schools in Ceylon where her grandfather and father were barristers. When she was eighteen, she had married John Chelvalingam and settled in Penang where he taught history and geography till his retirement. They had six children, two boys and four girls.

"All married and settled in various parts of Malaya," she said. "John's a lawyer in Kuala Lumpur and Paul's a pastor in Kulim. Our third daughter, Sarah, has married the pastor of the Anglican Church in Singapore."

"See, boys, where education can lead you? To the church."

"Oh George, do be serious!"

"I'm serious, Mary." George laughed. "Ignorance is always

a barrier to advancement. Schools in the great British Empire train us to carry out orders, not question them. Did they teach you that in Penang Free School?" George Nambiar turned to him and Omar.

"Now George, my young friends have had a long day. They're ready to retire." Mr Chelvalingam laughed and gave them a wink.

"Don't worry, John. I'm just sharing some views with my new friends here. What're you doing, boys?"

"Omar is working and I'm waiting to go to Oxford."

"There you are! Omar is already a government clerk and Seng will be a lawyer like me! What harm will it do them to know the underside of colonial rule? Sooner or later they'll find out anyway."

"Oh no, sir! I've got to study first."

"And so you will. But first, you've got to know certain things, views that John wasn't allowed to utter in your history class when he was your teacher. In English schools, the Empire comes first, not the truth." George Nambiar chuckled.

Kok Seng was wide awake now and had little desire to retire.

"What's this truth, sir?" he asked.

"Like the truth about what the British did to your people in China." George Nambiar looked at him, expecting him to say something. "Young man, the British forced the Chinese emperor to admit opium into your country! And China was only allowed to impose a two per cent tax or some such trumpery! A crying shame and a disgrace if you ask me! Don't you agree?"

He nodded as undoubtedly this was the only response expected of him, for George Nambiar was speaking as if he was in the pulpit. His moustache quivered and his dark eyes rolled upwards as he denounced Britain as a nation of wicked men.

"When a nation forces such an evil drug upon another nation, it is a blot upon its name and history. A great blot upon the English name, I say!"

Kok Seng glanced at Omar and was comforted that his friend appeared just as astonished as himself. In all their school years, they'd never heard anyone make such a scathing attack on the English. Their years in Penang Free School had taught them to admire the English for their sense of honour, gentlemanly conduct and sportsmanship. That Britain could have behaved so dishonourably towards another nation was something that had never occurred to him, and glancing at Omar, he didn't think Omar could've thought about it any differently.

"Don't be surprised by what he says." Mr Chelvalingam chuckled. "George is a member of the Indian National Congress."

The name meant nothing to him. Mr Nambiar told them that as early as the nineteenth century, English-educated Indians were already questioning the presence of the British on Indian soil. Omar's eyes lit up and he asked many questions about the Indian National Congress.

"George made quite a stir in Penang when he spoke against Mr Roberts last year," Mr Chelvalingam told them.

"Mr Peter Roberts, our headmaster?"

"Yes, the very same Peter Roberts who wrote in the *Penang Chronicle* that there was no unity among Indians in India. His conclusion was obviously based on his two years of teaching in Madras. I couldn't contain myself after reading his letter. I wrote to the Editor to let the English public know that all Indians supported the Bengalis against the lieutenant governor who forbade them to sing their national anthem, *Bande Mataram,* or 'Hail Mother Country'. The lieutenant governor's action is contrary to all established principles of British law and equity. The *Penang Chronicle* printed my letter in full the next day. You should've printed it in your newsletter, John."

"Sorry, George. I really don't want our church to be caught up with politics in the Indian subcontinent. Our members are all in government service. And believe me," Mr Chelvalingam lowered his voice, "the government does monitor our actions. There's such a thing as the Malayan Political Intelligence Bureau here."

It was the first time he was hearing such talk, and the more he listened, the more confused he became. He listened quietly as Omar asked George many questions.

"India belongs to Indians, China to Chinese. So Malaya belongs to Malays," Omar muttered.

"But things have changed, Omar. This country is under the British. We're all British subjects now," Mr Chelvalingam corrected him. "Seng, are you a British subject?"

"Yes, sir."

"Not a Chinese subject?" Mr Nambiar was surprised.

"No, I'm born under the British flag in this country. I'm a Straits-born Chinese. Not China-born but Malayan-born!" he rattled off the words and phrases that seemed to have come from somewhere inside his head, somewhere he'd never known existed.

"Malayan-born Chinese? A new hybrid! Born of China's poverty and Malayan tropical fecundity! Let's drink to that!" the effusive Mr Nambiar proposed and everyone including Omar raised their coffee cups and toasted the new hybrids, Malayan-Chinese and Malayan-Indian.

"Who knows, eh? One day these names will be accepted in this country! Right, Omar?" Mr Nambiar pressed him.

But Omar's smile gave nothing away.

⋅⊷═◉═⊶⋅

The next day, they left Taiping and took the train to Bandong and Ipoh. He shielded his eyes from the sunlight streaming in through the train's open window. The noise, the heat and the swaying of the carriage had lulled him and Omar into a lethargic silence. He felt uneasy. Perhaps he was being overly sensitive, but it seemed to him that the nearer to Bandong the train chugged, the less inclined for talk he and Omar became. They were friends, he and Omar. Had been so since they were a pair of gangly fifteen-year-olds. What held them together in school was hockey, especially during the year before the Senior Cambridge Examinations when they'd captained the hockey team to great success under the guidance of "Chelvie", their affectionate nickname for Mr Chelvalingam. Life was less worrisome then. School was where no one talked about politics and no one was worried about how he fitted into society. The nearest thing to a political act he remembered doing was cutting off his queue when he was in St Xavier's, a year before Uncle Boon Leong had him transferred to Penang Free School. He'd wanted to be known as a Baba boy and not a *Cheena geh*, a China-born bumpkin with a pigtail. He looked round the carriage. He was the only Chinese without a queue.

Omar was dozing beside him. Their third-class carriage was hot and crowded. The women, talking at the top of their voices, had plonked themselves in the middle of the aisle with their baskets and crawling babies. He regretted his decision to travel third class. But Omar could not afford a first-class train ticket. No Malay could unless he was a member of royalty. Even wealthy Chinese would hesitate to travel first class on trains. Only the English-speaking Babas were at ease in a train carriage full of Englishmen. Besides, the English had once considered barring Asians from travelling first-class on the trains. But a strong protest from the Straits-born Chinese had stopped it. Boon Leong, president of the Chinese British Association, had sent a sternly worded letter to the governor about justice, equality and the King's Chinese.

The train stopped at a small station. More passengers swarmed into the carriage like a flock of quarrelsome mynahs. Those who couldn't get in were thrusting bags and baskets through the windows into the arms and faces of the people inside. Others shoved and pushed their luggage between the seats to stake out a space on the floor where they made themselves comfortable as soon as the train pulled out of the station. Once settled in the aisle, they refused to move and blocked everybody's way. They took out boxes of food and began to eat. Then they chewed sireh and splattered the space under the seats with red betel juice.

"Omar, wake up! We're nearly there!"

"I'm awake! I'm awake!" Omar opened his eyes.

"How can you sleep like this?"

"I wasn't asleep. Just don't want to see the mess, lah."

"Look over there. Can you see the green roof of the pagoda?"

"Ya."

"That's my father's new temple."

"I know, lah! Your father owns the land by the river. It belonged to a Malay family before your father bought it."

"Lots of Chinese buy land from Malays, what!"

He regretted it the moment he'd said it. He hoped Omar wouldn't take his words as a boast. He didn't mean them that way. He thought of saying something more to try and explain himself. But he changed his mind. The less said, the better.

Omar was looking out the window at the passing hills and jungle beyond the River Bandong.

"I grew up here. When I was a boy, this was all jungle. Now ... look." He pointed to the orange-tiled roofs of the Chinese shop houses coming into view. "You Chinese work very hard to buy and own land. Then you sell. It's like what you own, you also disown. We Malays are different. We're part of the land. We can't disown it and it can't disown us. Just like the forest cannot disown the trees."

Their train crossed the Bandong Bridge and more rooftops of Chinese townhouses and shops came into view. Passengers were taking down their bags from the luggage racks above the seats and getting ready to disembark. Omar, who was getting off at Bandong Town, tapped him on the shoulder.

"Good luck in your law studies, Seng."

"I haven't told my father about my plans yet."

"He'll surely agree. Not easy to get into Oxford. You're lucky your uncle has connections."

"I hope you'll get that government scholarship and join me next year."

"I hope so too, Insya Allah."

The train pulled into the station. Omar reached down for his bag under the seat.

"Good luck in your new job. Write to me?"

"Sure, lah! Old friends must keep in touch. And you don't forget it, Cap!" Omar gave him a sudden jab in the ribs.

"Adoi, you monkey!" He returned the jab, just like in the old days in school after their hockey matches.

"Don't forget to write."

Chapter Forty-three

*I*t was evening by the time his train arrived in Ipoh.

"Built by tin and the China bumpkins! Tin, opium and prostitutes!"

But Mother had her own reasons for hating the town. Father had fled there after the troubles and the death of his two grandmothers. The reason was never openly discussed. He knew it was something between Father and Uncle Boon Leong. He was twelve at the time, too young and too playful to understand everything. But he was there when the police searched their house. When Father slapped Mother. That was the night he left Penang. And stayed away for ten years.

Mother crumpled and Uncle Boon Leong had to step in. Gek Lian and Gek Kim were sent to the convent school in Light Street. He himself was taken out of St Xavier's and put into Penang Free School so he wouldn't have to endure the taunts of schoolmates. Making friends with Omar in the new school was a welcome relief. Being Malay, Omar had no inkling of what was happening in his Chinese world.

Mother cried every day. The whole of Penang was gossiping about Father and the closure of his shops and shipping business by the colonial government. Secret society leader! Mother was so ashamed that she shunned company and lived like a poor widow although they were not poor. Father sent them money from Ipoh.

He was fifteen when he saw his father again. That year he

learned about little Kok Wah's death and saw Second Mother shedding silent tears in front of the family altar.

Second Mother's haunted eyes followed him during his brief stay. Half a son was better than none so she tried to befriend him. But his Cantonese was miserable and their conversations seldom went beyond the social niceties. Over the years and many visits later, when his Cantonese grew better, they were able to talk. About her sons. Her hopes. She cried each time he had to leave and looked forward to his visit each year. And each year, without fail, she cooked him his favourite food and special dishes to tease his palate. And he, in turn, tried his best to eat all that she piled into his bowl. Her maternal love had gone into the hours spent cooking for him and so his affection for her went into the eating of all that she'd cooked.

"Second Mother insisted on waiting for you. We're having a special dinner to wash off Kok Kiong's dust."

"Eh?"

His father gave him a wry smile and went on, "Washing off the dust is our way of welcoming a traveller home. And Second Mother wants you to meet your brother."

From the tone of his father's voice, he gathered that Second Mother's insistence on waiting for him must be of some significance and a measure of her feelings for him.

"When did Kok Kiong return?"

"Two days ago," his father replied, lapsing into Penang Hokkien dialect as they walked out of the Ipoh railway station.

They got into the Bentley. The ride through the town was exhilarating for the car was still a novelty and many people stopped and stared. Zam tooted noisily as he manoeuvred expertly among pedestrians, rickshaws and the slow-moving bullock carts. Passersby waved. His father was pleased with the attention that the Bentley was getting. Tomorrow he would broach the subject of doing law and going to Oxford, he decided.

"Towkah! Towkah!" The servant came running to the gate. Zam stopped the car. "Master Kok Kiong has rushed to the coolie depot. Big trouble over there!"

"What trouble?"

"Coolies fighting with English foreign devils!"

"Zam, to the coolie depot!" his father shouted in Malay. Then switching back to Hokkien, he said, "Seng, you'll have to act as interpreter."

A large crowd was gathered inside the courtyard of the two-storey building. The police had surrounded it and an Englishman was barking orders. A young man ran up to them.

"Kiong, your brother, Seng."

The young man looked at him and bowed. "Kor," he addressed him formally as "Elder Brother", but there was no time for other niceties.

"What happened?" Father asked.

"They're holding the Englishman hostage. Our own coolies, Father."

"Towkah Wong, do something. The White Crane's name is blackened! The foreign devils will blame us!" Mr Kong was a fifty-year-old rice merchant and one of the White Crane elders.

"How did this happen?"

"Coolies accused labour contractor of cheating them. Refused to go back to the mines. So this Harlow from the Chinese Protectorate, he ordered them to go back. He told them, 'You signed contracts. So must go back. That's the law!' He didn't want to listen to Ah Loong. So they argued. And this Harlow slapped Ah Loong. Right in front of everyone. Now Ah Loong is the leader. How can he lose face? So Ah Loong pushed Harlow. They fight. Coolies locked the door. Ah Loong won't let Harlow and his people leave."

"Father," Seng spoke for the first time. "Do you want me to find out from the Englishman over there what they're going to do now?"

His father nodded. Seng got out of the car and pushed through the crowd.

"Stop!" A Malay policeman barred his way. But before he could explain, something else happened.

"Open the door if you don't want to die!" a man acting as

interpreter for the Englishman was shouting in the yard.

A coolie came out to the balcony.

"We'd rather die than go back to Three Miles!"

"Let Mr Harlow go or the police will shoot!"

"Shoot, lor! Never fear die!"

The chief police officer raised his hand. His men fired. The coolie pitched forward and fell headlong into the street below. A gasp rose from the crowd. The police stormed the building. Five shots were fired. Minutes later, thirty-two coolies emerged with their hands on their heads.

"Move along! Go home!"

The crowd scattered. By the time Seng reached the car, the sky was dark.

"One dead, three wounded. Thirty-two taken to the police station," he reported in halting Cantonese so that Kok Kiong and his father's friends could understand.

"Towkah Wong, you and your sons go home. Lam and I will find out what's going to happen to our coolies," Mr Kong said.

"After that, please, you and Lam come for dinner. Simple meal only. Washing the dust from Kiong."

"We'll certainly come."

In the car, Seng shook his half-brother's hand.

"Welcome home, Kiong," he said in simple Cantonese.

"Thank you, Kor."

Silence after that. He couldn't think of what else to say. Many questions crossed his mind—questions phrased in English, which he could hardly express in Cantonese, but which he would've liked to ask Kiong. Brotherly things like: how was college? Did you make any good friends? Girls? What're the girls like in Kwangtung? But he didn't have the words.

During the entire ride home, no one spoke. Father was seated between them, staring straight ahead, looking as if he was thinking of something else. Did Father realise that he had to act as their interpreter? Or perhaps Father didn't care. How could he get to know Kiong who spoke only Cantonese and Mandarin?

He observed his half-brother closely that night. Kiong came down to dinner dressed in the dark tunic and trousers of his college in Kwangtung. The quintessential Chinese student. Courteous. Deferential. Bowing with hands clasped before him when he was introduced to the family's friends and relations. During dinner, Kiong's face glowed. From the occasional translations from his father, he gathered that Kiong was telling the family and guests about the momentous events sweeping across China. Especially in the colleges and universities. He was almost envious as he watched his half-brother. Kiong was not more than twenty, yet he spoke with confidence and conviction.

"We the youth of China will fight the Empress Dowager. She's a puppet of the Western powers."

Kiong looked round the dining table and gave each elder a respectful nod.

"Father, Mother! Uncles, Aunties! We the youth not only have to fight against the West. But also old thoughts, old ideas and old ways of doing things. We must free our minds."

"Well said, well said," Mr Lam murmured. "If we want to be a modern nation, we must fight against the old thinking."

The servants brought in a large platter of sweetmeats. His father, beaming with pride and brandy, invited everyone to eat.

"My friends! My future son-in-law and his honourable parents—our respected Towkah Chang and Mrs Chang. Uncle Big Tree and Aunt Yee-ma! Mr Kong and Mr Lam! Thank you for coming to this small meal. Tonight we welcome home my son, Kok Kiong. He has returned from his studies in Kwangtung College! My elder son, Kok Seng from Penang, is also here to welcome home his brother."

"Congratulations, Towkah Wong! Congratulations, Mrs Wong!"

They raised their cups and drank a toast.

"You've been blessed with filial sons, Mrs Wong."

"And we thank the gods and our ancestors for their blessings." Lai Fong wiped away a happy tear. In a few months' time, her elder daughter, Yoke Foong, would marry Mr Chang's eldest son. And if all went well, Yoke Lan would go to the women's college in Shanghai next year. She'd see to it that her daughter would not be deprived of a chance to study. No illiterate herself, she'd been following the new thinking and philosophy in China.

"Kok Seng! Kok Kiong! Your granduncle toasts you both!" Big Tree, seventy years old, raised his glass of brandy. The men joined him.

"What are your plans for them, Towkah Wong?" Mr Chang asked.

"Naturally I hope the two of them will enter the family business. These past few years, the gods in heaven have tested us sorely. Three years I was hiding in Singapore. Fong had to manage the medical hall almost single-handed. Then I had to travel to raise funds for the war back home."

"You've certainly devoted a lot of time and money to this worthy cause, Towkah, and we all respect you for this. Our best respects to Towkah!" Mr Kong raised his glass.

"Our best respects!"

"To Dr Sun and his revolutionary brotherhood! May the Kuomintang defeat the Manchus!" Kok Kiong raised his glass.

His elders looked at him. They had not expected him to propose a toast as if he were on an equal footing with them.

"To Dr Sun and his brotherhood!" his father said hastily. Everyone drained their glasses.

"To think that the Manchu devils nearly kidnapped Dr Sun while he was in London!" Mr Lam chuckled as he picked at his fish with his chopsticks.

"Ha! The English did something good for once. If they hadn't rescued Dr Sun, no Kuomintang today, lor!"

"Thanks to the English devils, our Dr Sun is famous now!"

Peals of laughter round the table. Even Second Mother was giggling.

"And to think that the English authorities here say he's a criminal! Now that even London has recognised Dr Sun as a respectable leader, the governor must be feeling like a donkey."

"But Dr Sun was a secret society leader," Granduncle Big Tree chuckled.

"Tell us about it," Kok Kiong urged him.

"Dr Sun's brotherhood started as a secret society before he formed the Kuomintang! If it hadn't been secret, the Manchus would've killed everyone. In 1906, the brotherhood was still illegal. And the government here banned it. All those who opposed the Manchus were regarded as shit stirrers. And it's easy to be branded a troublemaker! You're one if the English devils didn't like your face. Luckily they liked mine."

"Our respects to you, Uncle Big Tree! To your health and long life!" Everyone laughed.

"Yam seng!"

"To Dr Sun's Three Principles!" Kok Kiong raised his glass again.

His elders looked at him again. No one said a word. Then Mr Chang scratched his head.

"To this day, I've never quite understood the Three Principles. How can we have a China without an emperor?"

"Min yu—the people's right to have! *Min chih*—the people's right to govern! And *Min hsiang*—the people's right to happiness! These are Dr Sun's Three Principles. Same as Lincoln's, the American president. Government of the people, by the people, for the people," Kok Kiong rattled off.

"Right! Sons of China have the mandate of heaven!"

Father thumped his fist upon the table, his face flushed with brandy and heady talk. "Our homeland will be free!

"We drink to that!"

Kok Kiong recounted the struggle to free China from Manchu rule and foreign domination. His voice was strong and powerful like one used to speaking to large audiences.

"China does not need an emperor to be a great nation. We're weak at this point in our history. So the foreigners bully us. Look at how the English treat us in this country. A few hours ago, the chief police officer ordered his men to shoot Ah Loong because he had hit an Englishman. The English don't want Chinese people who can stand up to them. They want submissive buffaloes to work the mines. If our homeland is strong today, no English foreigners will treat us like this."

"Right, ah! Right, ah!"

More dishes were brought in. More glasses of brandy were drunk.

"Please help yourself to the food," Second Mother urged.

Uncle Boon Leong's calm voice floated into his head like a counterpoint to Kok Kiong's stridency. Years of after-dinner chat over coffee and cigars in his uncle's study had attuned him to the principles of English law. He could see things clearly from the colonial administrator's point of view.

"Father, the coolies broke their contract and took the law into their own hands. The chief police officer had no choice but to uphold the law. Otherwise Chinese, Indian and Malay coolies will just do what they like. We're living under the English flag so we must respect English law."

He was sticking out like a nail on the table. But he had to speak out as a British subject and a native son of the Straits Settlements.

His father's wry smile as he translated his words for the |rest of the company told him that he was with the wrong crowd.

"Please understand. Kok Seng has studied in an English school. He's lived with Englishmen all his life," his father said.

"We understand, Towkah. It's unfortunate but we understand."

Damn it! What's so unfortunate about his education, he wanted to ask. But he held his tongue. Not out of fear but out of a lack of words. A lack of Cantonese to say what he wanted.

Dinner went on, but he'd lost his appetite. Second Mother filled his bowl with the choicest meat. He left them untouched. She was too taken up with Kok Kiong, however, to notice.

A warm night breeze blew through the house, fluttering the curtains and bringing the muezzin's call to Isyak prayers, the last prayers of the day for the Muslims. He thought of Omar and wondered if his hockey vice-captain would ever write to him.

Chapter Forty-four

*H*e slipped out of the house for a breath of fresh air. The moon had risen and the garden with its ornamental carp pond was bathed in a cool silvery light. Fragrance of jasmine wafted by, awakening childhood memories of *pontianaks*—Malay ghosts which announced their presence with sweet floral fragrances, beautiful sirens which haunted the cemetery and other dark lonely places at night.

A sudden plaintive cry rose from the bush. He waited for an answer from the shadows beyond, but the night remained silent after that lone birdcall. A warm breeze brought the fragrance of jasmine which seemed to grow stronger the longer he lingered in the garden. Cautious, and perhaps superstitious about this midnight fragrance and the spirits associated with it, he retraced his steps back to the house.

From the window of his study, Tuck Heng watched this stranger of his flesh cut across the moonlit path and enter the house by a side door. He made no attempt to call after him although he would've liked to speak with his half-foreign son about tonight's dinner. He moved away from the window.

A gulf, wide as the Kinta River, yawned before him each time he felt the impulse to talk to this son. He listened to Kok Seng's footsteps fade down the hallway.

The traitor had Seng in his clutches now. The blackguard who branded him troublemaker and undesirable. How could he make Kok Seng see what Boon Leong had done? How could he teach him love of nation and homeland? He'd left Seng's education to his mother. A very grave mistake. The boy had grown into a man who upheld the English flag and English law. Not Chinese.

"Father, forgive me! Kiong is your only grandson who loves China the way you did."

This was plain to him now. Sooner or later, Seng would follow his uncle's footsteps—go to England, study English law and English ways and become a running dog lawyer. He slumped into his armchair.

What a burden a man's son is to him! Kok Seng means "Nation's Success". But China will never be Seng's nation. He sighed and thanked the gods for Kok Kiong—Nation's Strength. In him, China had gained a son. He lit a cigar, savouring the spicy fragrance of the Javanese cheroot.

Too restless to sleep, he smoked deep into the night. When your horse dies, get down and walk. Great Master Mencius once wrote, "When Heaven is about to place a great responsibility on a man, it first tests his resolution, wears out his bones and sinews and frustrates his efforts in order to stimulate his mind and toughen his will. For only when a man falls can he rise anew." Hadn't he risen anew?

Was he not one of the richest men in Ipoh? Hadn't he opened more tin mines in the Kinta Valley than any Englishman and planted more acres of rubber, coconut and sugarcane than any other elder in the White Crane? Then why was he so full of fears? Fear that these would slip from his grasp. Fear that the English authorities would take his land and give it back to the Malays.

He snuffed out his cigar irritably. Would the English with one sweep of their pen take away what he'd worked so hard to gain?

Chapter Forty-five

His Majesty has been pleased to confer upon you, Sir Boon Leong Ong, the Most Distinguished Order of Commander of the British Empire. Your family have been British subjects for many generations, and their names are well-known in the colony for the interest they take in all matters pertaining to the colony and …

*T*hree months after his return from Ipoh, news of his uncle's knighthood sent them flying to Roseville. Mother herded them to the mansion to congratulate their uncle. Everyone was there. Messages of congratulations poured in. Penang was proud of her native son.

"A first for the family!"

"And it won't be the last, mark my words," Granduncle Botak declared.

"We're all so excited for you, Auntie Kim-kim!"

"Not Auntie Kim-kim! Her Ladyship, Lady Kim Neo." Gek Lian giggled.

"Lady Kim Neo!" his cousins bowed and curtsied before all of them doubled over in laughter on the sofa.

"Oh, Auntie Kim-kim, look dignified when you go out! Nose in the air! A ribbon for your hair." Gek Kim moaned.

"Don't forget a hat. Ladies wear hats."

"Adoi! Making fun of your aunt? Where're your manners, girls?" Their mother wagged a finger at them. "Of course Auntie Kim will be dignified!"

Choon Neo sat down, complaining to her son that her legs were killing her. Kok Seng handed her a cup of tea.

"Thank you, Son. Now go and congratulate your uncle."

She sipped her tea and watched as Seng joined his cousins in the garden. The years had left their mark on her once slim figure. She'd grown into a stout matron.

"Choon, you're not joining us for the photo-taking in the garden?" Lady Kim Neo came up to her.

"Sister-in-law, it's very kind of you to include us. But really, you shouldn't bother. It's a joyous occasion for your family."

"Boon and I have always regarded you as part of Roseville. The family photo won't be complete without you and the children. If you're not out on the lawn with us, Boon will ask for you."

"Yes, Auntie. Papa will ask. If you don't join us, how can Seng, Gek Kim and Gek Lian join us?" Tommy, her nephew, pointed out.

"Yah, lah! Auntie Choon, come! All in the family, what!"

"But Seng's father is not here."

"Aiyah, Choon, you're here. That's all that matters."

She agreed to the photo-taking in the end. But everyone could see that she wasn't pushing herself forward. When news of Boon Leong's elevation reached her, she'd immediately cast herself in the role of a social inferior. Not one who was materially poor, of course. She would've been shocked if anyone had suggested that. How could you say that? she would've pestered the unfortunate speaker. Kok Seng's father is not poor, you know. He's got land, tin mines and houses elsewhere. He's not like his half-brother, Sir Boon Leong. But he's a rich towkay. Thank the gods! One must be contented with what one has. Not everyone can have such a good life like my cousin, Lady Kim Neo!

If her own marriage had proved disappointing, Choon Neo wasn't about to admit it to outsiders. She wore the badge of a Chinese tycoon's wife as proudly as she could in the social milieu of Roseville. Only Lady Kim Neo, her sweet patient cousin to whom she'd confided most of her bitter feelings, knew that her universe and standards of success were those of the British Empire. For her, the height of social grandeur was the annual Christmas Charity Bazaar followed by tea with the governor's wife. An event graced by the ladies from the very best families in the colony. English-speaking naturally. No China-born wives or China-born towkays were ever invited. What was a wealthy China-born towkay compared to a Knight Commander of the Order of the British Empire? Aah, many, many rungs below the imperial hierarchy.

She glanced at Lady Kim Neo, who was a picture of grace, but Sir Boon Leong, greying at the temples, was the more dignified. Pinned on his dark morning suit were British Empire insignias and the sash that went with his title. He was standing beside his wife seated on the wicker chair with her plump hands folded on her lap. Lady Kim Neo was dressed simply for the photo-taking. A peach satin skirt and a samfoo jacket with embroidered frog buttons. Looking down at her own kebaya dress, she was secretly pleased. Her baju panjang, reaching down to her knees, was of the finest voile, embroidered with an intricate border of flowers, leaves and butterflies. Her sarong was of the finest batik, specially ordered from Medan. Jade and diamond hairpins held her well-oiled and well-scented chignon in place. Rings on her fingers, gold and diamond bracelets on her wrists and kerosang brooches down the front of her baju. She was every inch a highborn Nonya dressed in full regalia. Ready to be presented to His Majesty the king himself if fate so decreed. But alas, her poor fate. She patted her chignon. The photographer clicked! Envy and regret was frozen forever for posterity.

⋅∻≡◎⟸∻⋅

Penang rejoiced. Roseville was feted. The mansion was at its grandest. Sir Boon Leong's dinner party was the talk of the town for weeks. Glittering chandeliers and strings of lights and paper lanterns were strung across its spacious grounds, turning it into a fairyland of lights. Gharries, carriages and cars of every important person on the island swept up the gravelled path. Horses trotted down avenues between cultivated lawns graced by palm trees and rose bushes. A cool sea breeze fanned the guests. The mansion, built upon a grassy knoll, commanded a splendid view of the sea. When the guests reached the white portico, they were greeted by Indian servants smartly attired in white cotton tunics and loose cotton pants. Then their affable host conducted them upstairs. The spacious verandah was brilliantly lit for the occasion. Lady Kim Neo and her sister-in-law, Choon Neo, welcomed the arrivals.

"My dear Lady Kim Neo! How charming you look!"

"Why, thank you, Sir John! How nice of you to grace us with your presence, Lady Jane! This is my sister-in-law, Madam Choon Neo."

"What a lovely dress, Madam Choon Neo!"

"Thank you, Lady Jane." She beamed at the wife of the secretary of the Legislative Council.

Downstairs at the portico, the Indian coachmen clung to the neighing high-spirited ponies as one of the newfangled motorcars throttled to a stop. More guests arrived. The spacious verandah upstairs was filled to overflowing. Introductions were made. Compliments were exchanged. The gentlemen were invited to help themselves to sherry and bitters on a sideboard. Members of the Straits Chinese British Association and those from the legal and medical professions wore Western-styled dinner jackets. Their wives were immaculately coiffed and beautifully attired in sarong and embroidered kebayas. Some wives wore silk cheongsams with mandarin collars. All of them were English-speaking and they chatted with the English guests who included Mr and Mrs Scott, Mr Bowers of Bowers Trading, Sir Richard Harcourt of the high court, Reverend Johnson, the vicar of St George's, and his wife. Several prominent members of the Malay, Indian and Arab communities were also present.

Choon Neo kept a sharp eye on the servants and amahs who took care of the young ladies, mostly relatives of the Wees and the Ongs. The girls, bright-eyed and excitable in their silks and chiffons, flitted among the more sombre-clothed gentlemen. She looked around for her two daughters. Such a dinner party was the right occasion for Gek Kim and Gek Lian to be seen. Someone might seek their hand in marriage. Wasn't this what every good mother hoped for?

At eight o'clock, the dinner gong sounded. The guest of honour, the governor of Penang, and Lady Kim Neo led the way down the stairs.

The dining-room had been transformed overnight. Like everyone, Choon Neo was impressed with the prized Coronation china and the variety of silverware on the tables. She was conducted to her seat and was overwhelmed by the honour. Lady Kim Neo had seated her between the vicar and Sir John.

Chinese servants in white livery stood behind each chair. Before each guest lay an exquisitely embroidered white napkin and a plate of fancy bread. Large silver tureens had been placed on the long white tables. Then Sir Boon Leong, in deference to the vicar of St George's, invited Reverend Johnson to say grace.

As soon as grace was over, the head servant gave a light clap. Soup was served. Napkins were unfolded and the elegant silver clattered amidst the guests' polite chatter. Fish cooked with a tangy sauce was followed by English beef, smoked duck, Yorkshire ham, dutch potatoes and brussels sprouts. Wine flowed liberally and the servants were kept busy with glasses and bottles. The faces of the men reddened and those of the ladies attained a lovely rosiness as the meal progressed. Towards the end of dinner, the Hainanese head servant proudly brought in a huge cheese.

"Part of a fresh consignment newly arrived from London," Sir Boon Leong announced.

"Oohs" and "aahs" rose from the white throats of his English guests as they savoured the prized cheese in tiny nibbles. The look of satisfaction on Sir Boon Leong's face was that of someone who knew he had passed some vital but ill-defined test for a gentleman. To be accepted into the best circles of colonial society in the Straits, it was not enough for an English-educated Baba to have studied in London. He must learn to appreciate what an English gentleman in London would have appreciated. And this rare Stilton showed that he did.

"More wine, Ah Loke."

"Yes, Tuan Besar," his head servant murmured.

When the last course was over, Lady Kim Neo rose from her seat. The governor and his wife took their departure. Choon Neo and all the ladies followed suit. They retired to the drawing room on the upper floor, attended by amahs bearing pots of tea and coffee.

The men relaxed. The servants cleared the tables and brought in liqueurs, coffee and cigars. As the cigars were lit and puffed, the men's voices grew more voluble and excited. They turned to the hot topics of the day. The phenomenal price of rubber and tin on the London Stock Exchange. The Chinese revolutionaries' takeover of Shanghai and Nanjing. Kok Seng, eyes aglow, followed the conversation round the table with great interest.

"Dr Sun's forces have the upper hand! But there'll be total chaos if the imperial forces fail!"

"Stocks will fall!"

"Total collapse!"

"The whole of China is a bloody mess! Warlords are at each other's throats! Enemy one day and allies the next! Caution, gentlemen, caution!"

"But Mr Bowers, begging your pardon, sir! China is a vast country. Very rich. I've been up the Yangtze River. Full of opportunities, gentlemen! Opportunities for men with daring and imagination." Mr D'Rozario went on in his eager high-pitched voice. "There're profits to be made, sirs! Huge profits! Provinces inland, away from Shanghai, are ready for the tapping. First to get in, first to get rich."

D'Rozario's voice rose even higher, excited by the prospect of cheap labour producing cheap goods for a mass market. His heavily accented English speech dominated the table. He seemed to be speaking to the Malay, Arab and

English traders all at the same time. It was simply dizzying, watching him switch from one language to another with the greatest of ease as he answered the eager questions of the men. He was said to have mastered several languages— English, Malay, Hokkien, Cantonese, even Cristang, the patois spoken by the descendants of the Portuguese conquistadors of Malacca. Because of this, it was rumoured that he had established a strong base in Portuguese-controlled Macau at the tip of China, and was building a trading empire which would cover Siam, the Malay States and the Dutch East Indies. He was a handsome, dark-complexioned man with wavy hair and bright close-set eyes beneath bushy brows. His eagerness to please the authorities had become something of a private joke among the more stolid members of the European community, especially among those who prided themselves on their own less adulterated bloodline and heritage. However, whatever the European traders might have thought of him in private, they were more than willing to do business with him. D'Rozario was one of the most influential traders in the Straits, with impeccable connections to the wealthy Baba merchants and the Malay royal families. But more importantly, he was also a client of Sir Boon Leong. That, for many of the English traders, was good enough.

"Well, Rozario, surely you've something new to tell us about the Chinese troubles. I've just heard that our coolies are leaving. Literally hundreds, maybe thousands in Penang, Singapore and the Malay States are returning to China to fight against the Manchus."

"Who's paying for the voyage of these poor blighters?"

"Why, the rich towkays in our colony! These towkays and coolies are alike. They come here to make money. But their loyalties are with China."

"Once a Chinese, always a Chinese!"

"Well, Sir Richard, if you mean the China-born immigrants in our colony, then you're absolutely right. Unlike us, these China-born are loyal to China, their homeland. But we Straits-born Chinese are British subjects."

Sir Boon Leong signalled to the head servant to bring more wine. As the glasses were being replenished, he went on, "And for the record, Sir Richard!"

At this, his guests burst into merry laughter. They looked expectant. They were going to be entertained by a mock courtroom debate between the two men.

"Here, boy!" they called to the servants. They quaffed more wine and asked for their glasses to be filled.

"We Babas have been in Malaya since the fourteenth century. Anybody who doubts that can take a look at the graves in Bukit China in Malacca. We, their descendants, call ourselves Baba or Peranakan or Straits-born, Sir Richard, to distinguish ourselves from the China-born. You'll not find any local-born Babas sailing to China to fight. Our loyalties are with His Majesty and the British flag."

"Hear! Hear!"

"To the king!"

"The king!"

"And here's to Sir Boon Leong!"

"To your good health!"

"It appears several merchants in the colony are raising money to buy arms for the Chinese forces," Sir Richard announced darkly.

"Good God! It's gunrunning, isn't it? Is the government doing something about this?" Mr Davis was a fervent believer in the power of the courts and an advocate of stricter laws to control the activities of the Chinese immigrants. He was all for breaking their hold on tin mining.

Everyone looked to Sir Boon Leong for a response. But he got up to ring the bell and when his head servant reappeared, sent the man for more coffee.

"Mr Davis, sir! It's not gunrunning!"

All eyes turned to him. Kok Seng felt the sudden rush of blood to his face. He was dizzy, but he steadied himself and went on.

"Many China-born like my father want to end the Manchu domination of their homeland. They want to free their country from foreign rule."

They looked at him.

"What my nephew said is true, gentlemen." His uncle came to his rescue. "They've lived and worked in freedom under our British flag. Naturally they would like to see their own countrymen back home enjoy the same freedom as they do here in this colony."

"That's a noble sentiment we can all share."

Pious murmurs of "aye, aye" went round the table.

"But gentlemen, let us not forget that these same Chinamen have fought among themselves for years. I won't put it past them to take advantage of these troubled times. They'll use this colony as a base for their private gang wars back in China! Our police and courts ought to exert some control over their political activities. In the state of Perak alone, there're more than ten thousand avowed revolutionaries among the coolies and tin miners! Supporters of Dr Sun's revolutionary forces."

"Are you sure, Davis?"

"Ask Bowers! He's got a mine there and he can't find coolies to work it. Where're these damn coolies? Off to fight their wars!"

"This is preposterous! Something's got to be done!"

Several people clamoured to be heard at once. Sir Boon Leong glanced at his nephew. Kok Seng caught his uncle's eye.

He stood up, excused himself and went out to the great hall.

"Play!" He ordered the band to strike up a Viennese waltz.

Upstairs, the women who had been waiting in anticipation all night for the dancing to begin, came trooping down the stairs.

"Gentlemen! The ladies are coming down!" Sir Boon Leong announced. And he deftly led his guests out of the dining room.

Chapter Forty-six

nothing could make the known and familiar
more beautiful than the knowledge
that one will be leaving them soon ...

*H*e was bored after the dinner party. Vague longings and a restless energy drove him to cycle all the way to Tanjong Bunga beach and back. Some evenings he cycled to Ayer Itam village and trekked up the stony path to the Kek Loksi Buddhist Temple from where he could look out at Penang Hill, but the view failed to soothe his restless spirit. He cycled round the island, stopping at the places of his childhood like the fruit orchards that had once belonged to his great-grandfather Baba Wee.

Leaving for England soon. Must study and pass my Latin. Must do a lot more reading in Uncle's library. Mother keeps pestering me to go for fittings for shirts, trousers, waistcoats and a winter coat.

"Must buy your woollens. Today we go to the Indian tailor in Bishop Street. Very good tailor, especially winter coats for men. All the ang moh go to him before they go back to England. Sir John goes to him also, you know. So he must be very good!" I wish she'd stop using the English as a yardstick for everything!

Omar wrote to him:

> I am busy editing a Malay magazine. My friends and I are trying to set up an organisation to help poor farmers in the rural areas. All we had was our land. And land is what others are taking from us. Bit by bit.

Omar's dedication shamed him. Who am I? A self-centred muckworm. Wriggling in the dark. Not knowing who he was. Who am I? He asked himself.

My mother's son. My father's son. My uncle's nephew. Graduate of Penang Free School. The truth was he was a neither-here-nor-there person who swayed with the wind. Proudly defended British law and the British flag in his father's house in Ipoh, in front of all those China-borns. But in front of all those Englishmen, he'd felt that he ought to speak up for the China-born Chinese in this colony. Why did he feel compelled to speak? And make a fool of himself? It wasn't as if he was loyal to China.

He dawdled over his Latin. Procrastinated going to the tailor's. Frustrated his mother's efforts to outfit him. Then on 15 December 1911, he fled to Roseville. News of Dr Sun's triumph shook Penang. Whole streets exploded in wild jubilation, firing off string after string of firecrackers. Headlines in the Malayan papers screamed "Man of the Moment! The Manchus have been defeated! The sons of China have won!"

He waded ankle-deep through piles of red debris when he went for his usual game of tennis with James and Tommy.

"They say Dr Sun's going to be president."

The three of them were discussing this great piece of news when his uncle joined them and surprised them with a story of his own.

"Your father is one of those who helped Dr Sun spread his revolutionary message in these parts. Even when the authorities forbade such political activities."

"He did?"

"He could've been deported if he were caught."

"That's why I worried about him and your family all these years. Sometimes family members get deported too."

"Was our Uncle Tuck Heng a revolutionary?" James asked.

"That I can't say, James. All I know is that he helped Dr Sun when Dr Sun was here. In 1894, Dr Sun joined a secret society in Kwangtung. Its aim was to overthrow the Qing dynasty. It had eighteen members. Of the eighteen men, seventeen were eventually beheaded by the Manchus. Dr Sun was the only one left to carry on the great conspiracy. He went everywhere to spread his message of revolution. America, the Dutch Indies and French Indochina. When Dr Sun came to Malaya, the Chinese government tried to get the authorities to expel him. They failed. Because China-borns like your Uncle Tuck Heng helped him. With their assistance, Dr Sun visited various parts of the Straits Settlements and the Malay States. It was said that he wore old clothes, was unshaven and went from town to town like a rag-and-bone man selling knick knacks in a pushcart."

"Incredible!"

"Seng, it's time you knew that your father was very active in Chinese revolutionary politics."

"Is he still active?"

"I believe he is. Your father is still courting grave danger. His shops and medical halls harbour all sorts of riffraff. I've long suspected your father of belonging to some secret brotherhood. When you were about thirteen or so, your father was embroiled in a big fight in Ipoh. His faction came out against the faction that supported the emperor. Your father didn't actually fight, of course. But his people did. That's why your mother was always so anxious when you visited Ipoh."

"I didn't know that."

"How could you? We never talk about such things here."

"We can talk now because Dr Sun is no longer a revolutionary?"

"The most important thing is for the British to regard us as loyal subjects. Our lives are peaceful and safe here. Why should we get mixed up in the politics of China? That's why that night at the dinner, I had to make it clear to Sir Richard

332 • A BIT OF EARTH

that we Straits-born are different from the China-born. China is not my country. Neither is it yours, Seng."

"I know, sir."

⊷══◉◉══⊷

Dr Sun was proclaimed president of the Provisional Government of China. Shophouses and buildings of clan associations hung red banners, red bunting and the blue and white revolutionary flags. Outside the headquarters of the White Crane, the imperial dragon flag was ceremoniously burned in front of a large cheering crowd. Everywhere, the Chinese people were jubilant.

He waited anxiously. But still no word came from his father. London was beckoning meanwhile and the thought of walking through Trafalgar Square or studying in the hallowed halls of Cambridge quickened his blood. He'd dreamed of this ever since he was twelve.

The days before the Lunar New Year were especially busy for him. Since this was going to be his last New Year celebration at home before his departure for England, his mother wanted everything to be special. She'd planned a big reunion dinner for the second day of the Lunar New Year which, traditionally, was the day when his father would join them. Father celebrated the New Year with two family reunion dinners. The first dinner on New Year's eve was with his family in Ipoh and the second dinner was with them in Penang. Strings of firecrackers welcomed the gods of wealth, happiness and prosperity. But that year, the gods deserted them.

His father telegraphed. He would not be joining them because of a special celebration of the White Cranes in Kuala Lumpur. The family didn't know what the celebration was. By the time they found out, it was too late. Violence had erupted and a government commission was set up to investigate its causes.

Chapter Forty-seven

*T*uck Heng arrived in Kuala Lumpur for the greatest, most important celebration of his life. Men of high standing and great repute had gathered to hear him speak in the great hall of the White Crane. The tide had turned at last for China. And for him.

"Great rejoicing this New Year! Everywhere all over Southeast Asia, Chinese people are letting off firecrackers. China belongs to the Han people again! Today the White Cranes celebrate the first year of the Chinese Republic!"

An explosion of cheers. His voice rose as he spoke. Towkays, merchants, traders, labourers, coolies and rickshaw pullers standing elbow to elbow stamped their feet and applauded him.

On the stage with him were the White Crane elders, distinguished by the red rosettes pinned to their black silk robes.

"Yam seng!" punctuated his speech every so often. Some rich towkays had donated a thousand jars of rice wine for the celebration and the coolies were helping themselves to it.

"Yam seng, my brothers! My countrymen! At last we Chinese can look the foreign devils in the eye as equals! We're no longer slaves of the Manchus. Walking with our heads bowed in perpetual kowtow! Today we walk with our heads up! Drink to the glory of our new republic! To Dr Sun Yat-sen!"

He swept back his short grey hair and raised his glass to acknowledge the cheers of the audience. His face was flushed with drink and happiness. How he wished his poor father were alive to witness this great event! An event that he had helped in no small way. Dr Sun himself had acknowledged his contribution in a letter to the White Crane kongsi, appointing him chairman of the Malayan branch of the Kuomintang.

He caught a glimpse of Kok Kiong in the crowd, talking to the young men of the clans. A wave of happiness washed over him. His son was doing what his father had done. Kok Kiong, the returned scholar from China. Bone of his bone. Flesh of his flesh.

"This glorious moment in our history is engraved in our hearts forever! We will live to tell our descendants and the descendants of our descendants that we the coolies and towkays of Malaya helped to free our homeland!"

His audience of Cantonese and Hakka men went wild. They cheered and hooted. Many had used their life's savings for this journey from the mines to witness the rebirth of their homeland. Old men cried. They might never see China again.

"You've made sacrifices. You who have the strength gave of your strength! You who have the money gave of your money! You supported your revolutionary brothers at home! And the revolution has succeeded! The Republic of China belongs to all of us!"

"To all of us!"

His audience stomped and yelled.

"Yam seng! Tuck Heng Tai-kor! Yam seng!"

"Thank you, my brothers, thank you! The Son of Heaven is no more! His lackeys are gone. We don't have to wear the queue and kowtow to the Manchu dogs any more! What is our queue?"

"A pig's tail!"

"The tail of a slave!"

Roars of laughter and jeers.

"Right, my brothers! Those damn pigtails are a sign of our enslavement! For three hundred years, Chinese people wore the queue. Why?"

"We were slaves!"

"Downtrodden!"

"Conquered!"

"No! We wore it to stay alive! We wore it to save our heads! To save our families! But three hundred years is a long time, my brothers! Three hundred years grew into a habit! A habit into a custom! We forgot what the queue was for! To mark a slave! Our fathers and great-grandfathers wore the queue as a sign of defeat and submission! But we're free men now! No more queues, I say! Right or not?"

"Right!"

"No more kowtows to foreigners! Right or not?"

"Right!"

"Are we free men today?"

"We are! We are!"

"So let us act as free men, my brothers! Cut off your queues! I call upon all those who haven't done so! Cut them off and hold up your head! Show your loyalty to President Sun Yat-sen!"

Thunderous applause broke out. The lion dance troupe beat their drums as the men chanted, "Cut! Cut! Cut!"

They drank toast after toast to Dr Sun and the glory of the new republic. Shouts of "Yam seng!" filled the hall. The Cantonese and Hakka revolutionaries started to rail against the conservative Teochews and Hokkiens who supported the reforms to save the Emperor.

"They supported that imperial arse licker Kang Youwei!"

"How could they support that bastard?" A stout coolie jumped upon a stool and addressed his question to the crowd. Drums and firecrackers drowned out their answers.

"Are they worthy men of Tang?" another coolie asked.

"Pui!"

The men spat and quaffed more rice wine.

"Snakes and worms! That's what they are!"

"Are they sons of our republic?" the stout coolie on the stool thundered.

"NO! We spit on them!" his audience roared.

"Save your spit!"

"Take out your scissors! Help them to become the sons of the new republic!"

"Good idea! Cut off the bastards' tails!"

"Right! Cut! Cut! Cut!"

They took their rallying cry to the streets. Packs scattered to hunt down the rats' tails. All those still wearing the offending queue fled before the raging drunken mobs. Amidst cries of "Imperial reformist bastards!" unfortunate passersby were dragged into the White Crane building and their locks forcibly shorn off. Gangs of short-haired coolies banging on drums and gongs roamed the town.

"Manchu arse lickers!"

They smashed down doors and forced their way into the townhouses and shophouses. Fist fights broke out when they met with resistance. The stubborn, the old-fashioned and the plain ignorant were beaten up and left for dead.

Kuala Lumpur's residents, especially the English and other non-Chinese, scrambled indoors, fearing for their lives and properties. The small police force was harassed by mobs wielding sticks and knives. Some policemen opened fire on a brawling crowd outside the White Crane building. Ten people were killed and hundreds were injured in the melee. A building belonging to the Hokkien clan was torched a few hours later. Packs of men armed with bamboo sticks fought in the streets and alleys. Several gharries were overturned and torched. Their bonfires chilled the hearts of many families as they cowered behind closed doors.

Masked marauders raided several homes in the outskirts of Kuala Lumpur. The next morning rumours flew and scattered like leaves in the wind. Some Teochew women had been raped. Vengeance! the clans vowed. Old scores were recalled and settled in bloody battles in the streets. Drunken fist fights in the coolie houses of Chinatown left hundreds wounded and dead.

Tuck Heng, fearing reprisals from the authorities, summoned the elders of the White Cranes. They tried to rein in the coolies. But the spark of passion and vengeance had been ignited. Once fanned, it turned into a raging bushfire, wild, ugly, evil and uncontrollable. The residents and public officials of Kuala Lumpur watched in dismay till the fire burned itself out.

The governor of the Straits Settlements, a strong-minded Englishman, sent in armed troops to quell the violence. A three-day curfew was imposed and hundreds of Chinese were thrown into the city's jails. But the people were unappeased. The English residents were indignant. Over the next few weeks, English language newspapers in the colony were inundated with letters. Stern government action must be taken against the Chinese mobs and their leaders.

> The Chinese should never be permitted to disrupt the peace and commerce of our colony. The freedom they enjoy under the British flag is exceptional, but they should be sternly reminded that they are sojourners in a land which belongs to others. Those of us who have the interests of this colony at heart must remember that the Chinese are here to make money out of it. In times of danger they can hardly be relied upon. It is the English who are responsible for this colony's peace and well-being and it is upon the English that the defence of the colony will fall in the hour of its peril.

"That's so unfair!"

Kok Seng had rushed to Roseville with his mother and sisters as soon as he heard the news.

"Aren't the English merchants making money too? If they can't make money out of tin and rubber, they wouldn't be here."

"And I'm in the Royal Volunteer Corps to defend king, flag and country!" James added. "Those blokes in the papers are tarring us all with the same brush. I'm going to write ..."

"You'll do no such thing!" Sir Boon Leong's curt voice silenced any further protest from the young men.

"Those letter writers are not talking about us. They're talking about the Chinese aliens. Like Seng's father! About China-born sojourners who stir up trouble on our soil!"

Kok Seng was downcast. His uncle was right. A Straits-born Chinese would never think of himself as a China-born immigrant. He sat glumly beside his sobbing mother and tearful sisters. Uncle Boon Haw had just arrived from Kuala Lumpur with bad news. Their father had been thrown into a police lockup.

"I'm so sorry for you and the children." Auntie Kim took his mother's hand in both her own.

His mother, choked with tears, could not speak.

"I knew this would happen sooner or later," Uncle Boon Leong growled. "I'll take the train down to Kuala Lumpur tomorrow and see what I can do. The White Crane isn't what it used to be during our grandfather and father's time. All sorts of bad hats are in it. It's really a secret society now."

His uncle pulled up a chair, but the sight of a sobbing woman discomfited him. He was visibly agitated as he went on.

"I … I'm trying to state my position clearly, Choon, so that there'll be no misunderstanding between our families. We're related after all, Tuck Heng and I. He's my father's adopted son. Seng is my nephew and your two daughters are my nieces."

"Seng and his sisters are born here. They won't be deported because of their father, right or not?"

"To tell you the truth, Choon, I can't answer your question now. All I can say is that an immigrant is considered an alien and under the laws and regulations of this colony, he can be deported back to his country of origin. Nothing is said about the children of an immigrant. We'll have to wait and see."

Chapter Forty-eight

"My whole life married to him, I always have to hide my face. Remember the troubles when his mother died? And now this! If not this trouble, it's that trouble! It never ends! When he first came to this country, he was in trouble with the law already. A fugitive from China with a price on his head. You know that his father went against the government? Now the son is going down the same road. What's going to happen to my Kok Seng? The boy is going to England to study law. So we must uphold English law, right or not? If the government says Seng's unsuitable for law studies, his father's to blame! What am I to do?"

"Choon, we don't know what's to happen yet."

"Easy for you to say, lah! Seng's father is not like Boon. His clan and his politics always get him into trouble. How many times have I asked him to cut off ties with the White Crane? Let the Chinese in China deal with their own problems, I always told him. But he refused. He knew the authorities didn't like it. He knew that they'd deport him. But he didn't care! Now he's caught! How will this affect his daughters' chances of making a good match? Such a thought never crosses his mind, I can tell you! And just before this trouble happened, he wrote to Gek Lian. Gave her permission to take up nursing! Nursing is the most degrading work a girl can do. Even if Gek Lian herself doesn't know any better, he, the father, should know better, right or not?"

"Tuck Heng's thinking is very different from yours, Choon."

"Different, I don't mind. But have some concern for the girl's future, lah! What else have I got besides my children? Nothing else ... In the early years, I was a very devoted wife. I helped to raise his standing among the good families in Penang. But how did he repay me? With shame and disgrace! Sure, he bought me jewellery. But do you think gold and diamonds are enough to take away my hurt? I scraped and stretched his money in the early days. Always kept his house open, his table well laid and his guests well supplied with food and drinks. But he's got a hole in his memory! A big ... big hole!" She broke down and sobbed.

"Choon, please don't cry. You'll only make yourself sick."

"Did he think of me when he went to the call girl? Just after the birth of his son! Did he think of me when he took a concubine? First in Taiping? Then in Gopeng? In Malacca, in Kuala Lumpur and the latest one in Singapore. A woman in every place! But still not enough. He sent for his mother and his China-born wife. Built a mansion for them! Ten times bigger than my bungalow!"

"Lie down and rest for a while. You won't be able to sleep on the train."

How could she rest? Kim had a good marriage. A good life. So it was easy for her to talk. Sir Boon Leong never looked at another woman after marrying her. Theirs was a good Christian marriage. Boon Leong's brothers, Boon Haw and Boon Pin, also Christians, each married one wife. She envied these wives of Christian men. Tuck Heng would never ever see the goodness of a rich man having only one wife. "Such a man is a fool," he said. "One man, many wives. As natural as one teapot to many cups." But not to her! Not after what she'd seen in Roseville. There was a better kind of marriage than this! Why should a woman share her husband with others?

She wept and was angry with herself for weeping. She shouldn't cry and fret for Tuck Heng after all these years. Better save her tears for herself. She sat up. Opened her suitcase and started to re-pack for the coming trip to Kuala Lumpur.

If the gods had been kinder to her and if her father richer, she would have been the wife of Sir Boon Leong today. She could not think of him even now without some memory of their younger days creeping in. They played hide-and-seek in the garden, fed the carps in the pond, rode in pony traps to Baba Wee's orchard in Ayer Itam. In the orchard they were allowed to roam and pick rambutans in the long hot lazy days of the fruit season. When she was about sixteen, Boon Leong had peeled a rambutan, kissed it before giving it to her. He did it not once but twice, and those were the sweetest rambutans she had ever tasted.

The memory brought a sudden hot flush of colour to her face and left her drenched in a cold sweat. In three hours she would be leaving for Kuala Lumpur with Sir Boon Leong and Kok Seng, travelling in a first-class carriage by themselves. What could she possibly say to him during the long journey? Thirty years of small talk across the dining table in Roseville, always in the presence of others, had built a monumental mound beneath which lay buried the feelings she had once harboured for him. Her heart had died the day he married Kim Neo. It was a match which her own father, a poor distant cousin of the Wees, could not make for her because he was just a clerk from a poor family.

She brushed away a tear, closed her tired eyes and tried to get some sleep. But her heart was beating too fast. Instinctively she put her hand on her breast and tried to still the chaos which threatened to overwhelm her. A storm was brewing in her mind. The wind was blowing asunder the closed pages of her past, sending the leaves fleeing before her as she stumbled after them, now with the sun in her eyes, now with the shadows and dust, half-blinding her to the present. She clutched at her bitterness. Struggled in vain to drag a millstone over the memories of her girlhood and what-could-have-been, till finally, exhausted, she fell asleep on the bed.

Chapter Forty-nine

*T*he misty silence of the country lane shattered in a hail of pebbles under her horse-drawn gharry, hurtling towards the temple in Bandong. The grey sky was tinged pink. She leaned out of the window and took a deep breath of the cool clean air. Fragrance of ripening jackfruit. Patchworks of young rice plants in the fields. A lone buffalo lowed its sad notes. *Nam moh or li tor fatt,* "Lord Buddha bless us," she prayed. Her husband's fate was hanging over the family like an executioner's sword.

Her eyes feasted hungrily on the scene rolling past her window. She might never see this again. For who could tell what the days ahead would bring. The rice fields, fringed by coconut palms, banana trees and brown huts on stilts were different from the rice fields of Sum Hor. She would love to see Sum Hor again. But not as a deported criminal.

"Mistress, drink this. You haven't eaten anything."

"I'm not hungry."

Ling placed a silk cushion behind her head and served her a cup of tea. If she had remained in China, she'd never be able to have a maid to serve her tea, not even in a hundred lifetimes. Here in Malaya, she had two maids and five amahs to see to her comfort. What more could a woman want?

She'd travelled ten thousand li across the ocean to marry a stranger in a strange land. A lifetime ago. What did she hope for then? Two bowls of rice and a roof over her head. But expecting little, she'd found much. A home, a family, respect, abundance and so much more than she had ever dreamed was possible in a woman's life.

"Take charge of the medical hall."

"Cannot, cannot! I'm a woman."

"This is the twentieth century. Young women in Kwangtung and Hongkong are already studying and teaching in schools."

"But I've no education."

"You know how to read and write."

"But I've no experience."

"No experience, can learn. Ah Weng, the accountant, can teach you. I can teach you."

She smiled. At the heart of each man sits a teacher who likes to teach women. And because she'd shown timidity, Tuck Heng had encouraged and taught her the rudiments of running a business.

"The world is changing. Those who can't change won't survive. Clinging to tradition will make us lag forever behind the foreign devils. We have to aim high to help others."

How could she disagree with his noble sentiments? Tuck Heng was forward-looking in some ways and backward-looking in others. Like the fingers of her hand, his faults and virtues were of different lengths. A wife, if wise and patient, accepted her husband's hand and did not seek to cut off one of his fingers. Marital fidelity was not in the nature of man. Marriage was about mutual dependency, duty, loyalty and devotion.

"Here're the ledgers and accounts. Ask Ah Weng if you don't understand the figures."

She took the books and sat down with the accountant. A few days later, he asked, "What do think of Ah Weng? Can he be trusted?"

Surprised that he sought her opinion, she told him what she thought. The next time, he asked her about a house he wanted to buy. One thing led to another. Sometimes he spoke of his doubts and misgivings. Sometimes he sought her advice. And so, gradually, without either of them noticing it, the countless infinitesimal exchanges of small talk between them turned into a friendship.

A friendship because they seldom came together as man and wife. And how did she feel about this? Feelings were clouds across the sky. They would change and pass. It wasn't important how she felt. It was more important what she could make out of her life in this country.

She began to pay attention to the men's talk, the traders and merchants who visited Tuck Heng. She served them bowls of bird's nest and shark's fin soup, all the while listening to their talk to pick up useful nuggets about the trading world. Through long hours of patient listening, she gathered, in minute fractions, knowledge of how things worked in business and details about life in other parts of Malaya. In this way, without moving out of Ipoh, her knowledge of Malaya grew. None of the men minded her presence. She was quiet and unassuming and was no trouble to them. Nothing could be gained by asking questions or appearing too eager. Seeming indifference, deference and patience got her what she wanted to know.

Soon she was able to show Tuck Heng a healthy profit from the medical hall. Then she started a letter-writing and reading service for illiterate coolies and amahs. For a very small fee, an illiterate coolie could send a letter home to China or have a letter read to him. She liked to sit behind the counter for a few hours each day and watch their faces light up when their letters were read out. It was magical and wonderful that she, a woman of humble origins, could help these people. Just like a man.

She became bolder. She found out that the coolies were reluctant to enter a government post office because the clerks spoke only English.

"Ah Weng, we help them send money and letters home."

"Mistress, it's against the law. Only the government can open a remittance service."

"Ah Weng, your ears need cleaning. I said we help our friends to send money home. Helping friends is not against the law, right or not?"

Ah Weng grinned. Soon coolies and amahs knew where

to seek a friend's help. Would she be able to do these things if she were back in China?

The sun had cleared the mists covering the hills. Her gharry stopped outside the temple gates. The old monk ushered her into the inner sanctuary of the Hall of Ancestors and lit the oil lamps to announce her offering to the gods. She kowtowed and poured out several libations of rice wine upon the floor.

"Parents-in-law, I beg you to protect your son and grandchildren from banishment and deportation. A good horse never grazes on old pastures. Let him stay and prosper in this new land."

The old monk shuffled in with a pot of tea.

"Si-fu, help me. Save my children's father. He's in great trouble with the red-haired foreign devils."

She knelt before him.

"Mrs Wong!" Gently he raised her and helped her to a seat. "Mrs Wong, I've been praying for him ever since I heard the news."

"Thank you, Si-fu. What should I do now?"

"Master Tuck Heng's destiny has brought him to this part of the world. Your destiny brought you to him. Pray and trust in the Lord Buddha."

"I'm taking the train to Kuala Lumpur tonight with my son and two daughters. My husband's adopted brother is in Kuala Lumpur. He doesn't speak Cantonese and I don't speak the foreign devil's tongue. What am I to do among all these foreigners?"

"Mrs Wong, since I came from China many years ago, I've met men and women of many tongues. But as the Lord Buddha is great and merciful, all of us, even the foreign devils who speak in strange tongues, have hearts capable of goodness."

"I'm worried, Si-fu."

"Heaven will not block all his routes. Your husband has friends and relatives. They will help him …"

"Si-fu, please don't judge me too harshly if I complain. My heart has too many secrets."

"What you tell me will remain within these walls."

"Thank you, Si-fu."

"Have some tea, please."

She sipped her hot tea meditatively. After a while she plucked up courage again and asked the monk, "Si-fu, is it wrong to want to stay on in this country? Am I betraying my ancestors in wanting to stay?"

The old monk shook his head.

"Betray is a very strong word, Mrs Wong. We have a saying in China, 'Enter earth, sprout roots.' Do you understand my meaning?"

"Are you saying that I've entered the earth of this land and sprouted roots, Si-fu?"

His eyes twinkled with gentle humour as he gazed at a weeping willow he had planted next to a coconut palm. Then speaking in a low soft voice, he turned to her.

"From sunrise to sunset, from one day to the next, till our black hair turns white, we eat, we sleep, we bear children and we watch them grow. We watch them get married and in turn bear children of their own. How time flies, we say to ourselves. Then one day, we look down at our feet and we're surprised. Roots have sprouted in the ground of our daily living."

Chapter Fifty

*T*hey were herded into two cells in the Kuala Lumpur Central Police Station. Tuck Heng was squeezed into a cell with nine other men. Their cell was foul and stuffy. A small skylight in the ceiling let in air and light. Below that was the wooden tub with a broken lid which served as their toilet. Out of respect for him, the coolies gave him the floor space farthest from the wooden tub. Still the stench at the end of the day was unbearable for they were not allowed to empty the tub till the next morning.

"What's going to happen to us?"

"The White Crane won't desert you. Someone will come."

But no one came. No police officer showed up. Only the Indian peons came round with mugs of tap water after they'd banged on the door of their cell.

"Quiet! Drink up and sleep!"

He looked at his pocket watch. They had been held for more than twelve hours.

Then one of the coolies started to sing softly to himself an aria from a popular Cantonese opera, *Lament of a Scholar Imprisoned by the Mongolians*.

"Louder!" a voice in the next cell yelled.

So the coolie sang louder, his rich baritone rising to the ceiling. Another coolie joined in. And another. Then a member of an amateur opera troupe sang the part of the boastful Mongolian king.

"The Mongolian doesn't know what boastful is! Wait till he meets the red-haired barbarian here!"

He recognised the voice. "Low Yau! Are you here too?"

"Tuck Heng?"

"Those devils nabbed me when I was trying to settle a fight in Peng Street!"

"Always making peace! But the bastards won't believe a word you say!"

"And you think they believe you, Mr Editor?"

"Chieh! We in the Yat Poh Press never cared a damn what the devils believe! Wait till I write about this!"

"Quiet!" the Malay guard shouted.

But no one heeded him. To pass the time, they sang and told each other stories of ancient Chinese heroes and their own village heroes.

"Who doesn't know that Towkah is the son of the Brave Poet of Sum Hor?"

"How many scholars have his courage to speak up?"

"But it takes only a few to turn the tide. See what one man, Dr Sun, has done."

Just before sunset, they were given their first meal, a tin plate of rice and slop and a mug of sweetened black coffee. As their cell grew dark with the coming of night, the talking ceased. Surrendering himself to the darkness, he lay down on the hard concrete floor and tried to sleep. But cockroaches crawled all over him and the stench from the toilet and the humming of insects kept him awake. It reminded him of his days in the Bandong mines. He flapped his arms. But it was useless. The pests returned as soon as he stopped. He cursed under his breath. He'd done nothing to deserve this incarceration.

The next day a group of White Crane elders visited him and the coolies.

"Send a telegram to my family in Penang and Ipoh."

"We've already done that. We've also written and presented a petition to the governor."

The petition began with the usual fawning phrases:

> We, the undersigned British subjects and Chinese merchants, humbly present this petition to His Excellency, the Governor of the Straits Settlements. We deeply regret and humbly apologise for the disturbances which broke out during the Lunar New Year celebrations. It was unforeseen and unfortunate. The Chinese people have always been peace-loving and law-abiding.
>
> When your petitioners reflect on the thousands of Chinese who arrive like ants each year at Penang, Malacca and Singapore, they see that the fame of Your Excellency's government and the paternal protection which the people receive under Your Excellency's government have made the Chinese brave the stormy oceans to come to these shores to seek a livelihood. They know that in this country, protected by the British flag, they will find ...

The flourish of brushstrokes expressing the standard phrases of flattery had been honed to perfection by centuries of petition writers who had had to appease the emperor and his dreaded mandarins in the Forbidden City. But the petition writer of Kuala Lumpur, writing on behalf of the Chinese merchants, had added a little sting.

> Your petitioners have long enjoyed the fair and just rule of Your Excellency's benevolent government. However we fear that people of bad character have misinformed Your Lordship about the disturbances. Their misguided actions have led Your Lordship's police to imprison most unjustly the Honourable Wong Tuck Heng, a highly respected leader of the Chinese merchants.

The very phrase "imprisoned most unjustly" shone in the darkness as he tried to get some sleep on the second night. But sleep eluded him again in the hot crowded cell. He was still furious with the English inspector who had stood at the doorway, holding a white handkerchief to his nose while he tried to verify the number of coolies in each cell. Everyone including the editor of the Yat Poh Press was classified a coolie. What had irked him most, however, were the Inspector's cold grey eyes. They said that the prisoners were the muck stuck to his boots.

He flicked away something which had landed near his ear and sat up. Voices were coming from the office down the dark passage, but he couldn't make out their words. Then silence regained its hold and his restless thoughts returned once again to plague him like the horde of mosquitoes buzzing in his ears. He flapped his arms several times. Each time, the pests returned undeterred. Finally he gave up and lay down.

As the night dragged on and his irritability subsided, a niggling apprehension rose to the surface of his mind. First like a nebulous cloud on the distant horizon, inching nearer as the hours crept in the dark till he felt a rat's nipping. What had he done with his life? His father was beheaded for writing about the suffering of the peasantry, for refusing to recant and lick the ass of the mandarin lord.

What have you done?

Damn pests! He flicked at the whining mosquitoes. Nothing as noble as his father. What's fund-raising and speechifying compared to poetry? Even the English press had belittled him as "John Chinaman upset with pigtail!" and called the riots "the Chinamen's pigtail brawl"!

When his clan leaders had shown him translations of the papers, he had fumed. Liars and hypocrites! The Inspector had accused him of being a political activist and had threatened him with banishment and deportation. If it was just a matter of the pigtail, then the punishment was weightier than the crime.

Like a newly caught tiger in a cage, his thoughts paced up and down. Was it a crime to express one's support for one's homeland? Hadn't the English foreign devils expressed similar patriotic sentiments for king and country, carousing into the early hours of the night, their drunken soldiers knocking on doors and waking up entire neighbourhoods on New Year's Day and Empire Day? Snakes and hypocrites! He was born a son of the Chinese earth, how could he not rejoice in the liberation of his homeland? He accepted foreign rule in this country, but he could never accept foreign rule for his China.

He stared at the dark ceiling above him. His keen mind had caught a whiff of sweet-smelling inconsistency. "But Malaya is not the same as China," he muttered under his breath, mouthing his thoughts aloud as if to reassure himself. He sounded loud and hollow in the silence occasionally punctuated by the sudden snorts of his sleeping cellmates. He cocked his head and listened, but all he heard was the soft scuffling of rats among the rafters.

Rats! The first to leave a sinking ship or a house in flames. For some unfathomable reason the image of burning houses returned to plague him. His home in Sum Hor and the Datuk's house in Bandong were burned by rats. Yellow or white, they were all rats!

Struck by the similarity of these two events, he became superstitious and believed that the gods were trying to tell him something. He was certain without quite knowing why that his future was somehow tied to his adopted homeland as well as to China, his original homeland. Hadn't his adoptive father, Tai-kor Wong, risked and lost his life to help the menteri of Bandong fight the English? Had it not been for Musa Talib sitting on him like an elephant, he would have killed the English rat who shot Tai-kor Wong! And that would have been the end of his life in this country! He recalled how he and Ibrahim had stood side by side watching in helpless anger as the English soldiers set fire to the houses of Bandong village. Flames and heart-rending wails, and yet … he sighed and closed his eyes. Since then he'd lived a comfortable life, offering little resistance, like a fallen leaf floating with the currents down the Bandong River.

A lifetime of river water had flowed under the bridge since he last visited Bandong village, and he wondered what had happened to Ibrahim and his family since Musa Talib's death. A death he recalled with shame and guilt as though he had been the one to push the old man into the river. Was he being punished now, he wondered, for his grasping callous greed?

A sliver of moon shone through the tiny window of his cell. Strange, how the moon seemed brighter now that he was behind bars.

The White Crane elders had mentioned that the governor

had set up an inquiry to look into the cause of the riots and that some English-speaking Chinese had been asked to sit on the panel of advisors. Always English-speaking. He slapped his arm. Something had bitten him in the dark. It felt like a hard-shelled beetle. He spat on his finger and rubbed the spit onto his arm. Spit, the cheapest balm for bites in the mines.

When at last dawn came, he was curled like a prawn on his side in the same way that he had had to sleep in the overcrowded sheds in Bandong. The Malay policeman unlocked his cell door.

"Wong Tuck Heng!"

Chapter Fifty-one

"*F*ather!" his two sons greeted him, their eyes sick with worry.

"Uncle Boon Leong is here to take you home," Kok Seng said.

He saw his brother talking to the Malay sergeant. The policemen saluted them on their way out. The letter with the chop of the governor's office had impressed everyone.

"Goodbye, honourable Tuan-tuan."

"Thank you," he and Boon Leong answered in Malay. An instinctive response. Something which his two sons had yet to acquire.

He got into the horse-drawn carriage and sat next to his half-brother. Kok Seng and Kok Kiong took the seat facing them. He shook his brother's hand warmly.

"Thank you."

That Boon Leong should've gone out of his way to get him freed! Why?

"Where're we going?" he asked.

"To my townhouse."

Kiong appeared ill at ease in the presence of his English-speaking uncle and was silent throughout the journey.

"Where's Uncle Boon Leong's house, Seng?"

"Near the Lake Gardens, Father."

Just like Boon Leong to buy a house near the foreign gods, he thought. When they reached the house, he was even more surprised to see Choon Neo and Lai Fong. With them were

Yoke Foong and Yoke Lan. The girls came running down the steps towards his carriage.

"Papa! Papa!" They crowded round him as soon as he alighted. Mindful of Choon's feelings, he asked about her daughters.

"They cried and cried when they heard the news and Gek Lian pestered me day and night. 'Let me come with you! I'm going to be a nurse,' she said. 'If Papa is sick, I can help to nurse him.' But I don't think a prison is a fit place for a girl to visit. If Gek Lian and Gek Kim come, more gossip and more scandal!"

"Quite so, quite so," he murmured although he would have liked to have seen his daughters. Then turning to Lai Fong, he asked in Cantonese, "But you didn't mind prison? You brought your two girls?"

"Foong and Lan were so worried about you, how not to bring them with me? Time they learn about the world like their brother, Kiong."

Such a stark difference in their replies. Lucky for him neither understood the other's dialect well.

"Go upstairs, change and wash up. Breakfast is served in the dining room," Choon Neo announced and tried to take charge of him. "Don't stand out here. Go inside."

"Some friends and associates are coming to discuss your case later," Boon Leong told him.

"My case?"

"It's become far more important than you think."

He wondered what else Boon Leong had in store for him, but he could see that this was not the time to ask. Lai Fong was also urging him to go and change out of his clothes at once.

"Prisons are unclean places. Murderers and thieves have died there. So yesterday I went to see the priest, and he recommended a special bath." When they reached the landing, Lai Fong turned round and spoke in a hushed voice. "The old priest warned me. Our family will suffer misfortune if we don't act harmoniously."

She led them into the bedroom.

"This priest is highly respected as a soothsayer. Very accurate in his predictions. Please take off your clothes. I'll take them to the temple later and burn them."

Lai Fong chatted on. Choon Neo was strangely quiet. She took out a fresh suit of clothes for him and laid them out on the bed.

"Wear these after your bath," Lai Fong said. "They've been specially blessed by the priest."

He glanced at Choon. She wasn't the kind to let another woman take charge. She left the room after laying out his clothes. Is this the new harmonious order, he wondered, as he took off his clothes. Lai Fong helped him into the hot tub. Gingerly he lowered himself into the water infused with herbs and pomelo leaves. Lai Fong poured jugs of warm scented water over his head as he closed his eyes and sank deeper into the tub. When he came out, warm and relaxed, she helped him to dress.

"Everything bad has been washed away. Today is your good-luck day."

"Thank you."

Choon Neo returned.

"For you to ward off evil," she said.

Dutifully, he placed the pomelo leaves in his pocket and wondered what to make of his wives. Did they agree to make peace at last?

"Go down for breakfast. I'll join you later."

Lai Fong gathered up the soiled clothing, pleased with how things were turning out. Harmony. At least on the surface. The ancestral spirits should be pleased.

She had seized the initiative the moment she stepped into Sir Boon Leong's house. The silence between her and Tuck Heng's first wife had to end.

"Elder sister, please accept this cup of tea."

Swallowing her pride, she had offered Choon Neo the customary cup of tea with the respect due to a first wife. Then without a word to anyone, she took things into her own hands and went to the soothsayer. She had great faith in the power of the gods and even greater faith in the power of human action to change the decisions of the gods. But to do that, a woman had to be practical. No point kneeling and crying all day. The gods were the officials of the heavenly Jade Emperor and these heavenly officials were no different from the earthly ones. They could be bribed with suitable offerings or placated by obedience and submission.

"Seng, come with me to see your mother. I must tell her what the soothsayer said."

Much to her surprise, the opposition she had anticipated did not arise. Choon Neo had listened quietly.

"Family unity and harmony must come first. We must stand strong in the face of trouble. I'll do what's necessary," she promised.

Lai Fong had even pleaded unashamedly for Sir Boon Leong's help.

"Only someone like you who knows the ways of the English lords can help Tuck Heng," she had flattered him and wept in his presence.

And her brother-in-law was moved. Not a difficult thing to do if a woman knows how to use her tears. And she'd have used anything, almost anything, to protect her fragile tenure on Malayan soil. She saw in a flash that she and "that Hokkien woman in Penang" (for that was how she had referred to Choon Neo before this) must ensure that their tree would not fall.

"Please go down for breakfast with Elder Sister. I'll join you when I've cleaned up. We mustn't keep Brother-in-law waiting."

"We'll go down first, Choon."

A little smile lit up Choon Neo's face. Small courtesies like this mattered to her. As first wife, she should take precedence in all matters, however small, and if "that Cantonese woman" (for that was how she referred to Lai Fong in her heart) had done the right and proper thing years ago, they wouldn't have become bitter rivals.

But she'd no time and no inclination to recall past hurts and slights now. Such matters paled beside the weightier issue of Tuck Heng's possible banishment and deportation. What could be more humiliating than to be deported like a common criminal?

No, she must not think of it yet. Thank the gods that Boon's standing was high and he knew all the right people. He'd never allow the family's good name to be sullied. And for the sake of the family, she'd do anything. Well, not quite anything. The ritual bath was one of those things she wouldn't do. Wash a man together with another woman? Not the right and proper thing for first wives to do. She'd felt the hot rush of blood to her face when Lai Fong had broached the subject, and in that very instant all her prejudices against China-born women had returned. All the prostitutes in Malaya were China-born immigrants, she'd thought, disregarding the fact that dire poverty might have something to do with it.

She muttered a prayer, "Please, Guan Yin, Goddess of Mercy, help Boon to bring Tuck Heng to his senses! My mouth is locked. I cannot speak."

"Come, let's eat," Sir Boon Leong called out.

On the large table was a motley spread of breakfast food. Rice porridge and condiments for Lai Fong and her children; half-boiled eggs, bread, butter and apricot jam for Sir Boon Leong, and nonya cakes for Choon Neo.

"Kor, please sit."

Tuck Heng was taken aback. Boon Leong had not addressed him as "Elder Brother" for years and he wondered what he had done to deserve such brotherly respect.

"Please treat this house as your home and stay here as long as you like."

"You've been very kind to my family."

"My duty. We're family."

"Our Brother-in-law has gone out of his way to help us. He went to see the governor himself," Choon told him.

"The governor? None of my visitors told me that."

He felt his anger rising. The White Crane elders had missed out on something when they ought to be the first to know what was going on.

"It's like this, Father," Kok Seng hastily explained. "Uncle sent a telegram to the governor before we came down to Kuala Lumpur together."

"Aah, so you know the superior man himself." And he half-wished that he was not so beholden to someone who had betrayed him once before.

"Kor, what happens to you affects us all. If we're not careful, the whole family will be pulled this way and that. A bundle of sticks is always stronger than one."

"Right, right."

How could he quarrel with that kind of logic with its whiff of self-serving preservation? He picked up his chopsticks and began to eat.

Then it struck him that by staying in Boon Leong's house, his movements could be monitored by someone trusted by the English authorities. Was the snake actually serving the authorities by appearing to help him? He must tread carefully. Still smiling, he turned to his brother and thanked him once again for his hospitality.

"No, no, Kor. My duty, for we're family. Now we've got to see what we should do."

"Who's coming later?"

He reached for a bit of salted egg.

"Boon Haw and Boon Pin."

"The others?"

"Tan Ee Peng."

"Proprietor of Tan Ee Peng Medical Hall. A member of your Straits Chinese British Association?"

He'd met his business rival on several occasions before and knew Mr Tan as a dapper dresser of Western suits who had travelled extensively in Europe. His villa in Singapore was said to be chockful of imported Italian marble statues of naked men and women.

"Ee Peng is a member of the Federal Council. Highly respected by the English. But most important, he knows you so he'll speak for you."

"He will?"

He was wary of these Straits Chinese British Association types. Always sucking up to the foreign devils. But he was puzzled. Why should these lapdogs come forward to help him?

"Chan Chee Pak and Lee Kong Meng are coming too. Now you've known Mr Chan for many years and he told me confidentially, er, just between him and me, that both of you were underground members of Dr Sun's Tung Meng Hui."

"He told you that?" He almost choked on his porridge.

He had not expected a man like Chan to whisper such things to anyone. Least of all to Boon Leong. The Revolutionary Brotherhood was an anti-Manchu revolutionary society. Members had risked deportation and banishment when the society was formed in Singapore at a time when the British government still supported the Qing dynasty.

"Please don't be alarmed. The authorities will find out about such things sooner or later. They've been monitoring your movements for years through the Chinese Affairs Secretariat. They knew you helped Dr Sun."

He nodded and smiled. But inside he was seething with rage and anxiety. All branches of the Revolutionary Brotherhood were unregistered. They could be prosecuted for being members of an illegal organisation.

"Don't worry. Dr Sun Yat-sen is president of China now. Britain has formally recognised him. The authorities here will certainly not punish his supporters. That is, if they don't stir up trouble."

"True, true."

He picked up his chopsticks and began to eat again, chewing on his food cautiously.

"Here, have some salted fish and black beans." Lai Fong sat down beside him. "How's it going? The talking good or not?" she asked in Cantonese.

"Don't know yet. Wait and see."

Then switching back to Hokkien, he laughed. "You might be right, Brother! I've nothing to fear, right or not?"

Boon Leong fixed his eyes upon him.

"Kor, please understand. Dr Sun is not the president here.

The English have their own laws. Tell me about your activities so that I can help you."

"Tell you what?"

He put down his chopsticks and was about to continue. Sensing trouble brewing, Fong stopped him.

"Please tell Brother-in-law, eat first and talk later."

Her eyes appealed to Choon Neo for help.

"Right, right." She turned to Sir Boon Leong. "Brother-in-law, talk after breakfast. Better that way."

Ever the affable host, Boon Leong agreed and urged the younger members of the family to eat. But they had little appetite. Kok Seng was grim-faced. Kok Kiong and his sisters hardly touched the porridge. Their mothers too were silent as they ate and so breakfast ended very quickly.

Then the two brothers disappeared into Boon Leong's study.

Chapter Fifty-two

*B*oon Leong took the leather armchair behind the desk, poured out two cups of coffee and pushed one towards Tuck Heng.

"I will come straight to the point," he began tersely in Hokkien.

A glance from him made Boon Leong stop. Conscious that he'd made a mistake, Boon Leong gave a thin smile.

"Kor, we're concerned about your case," he began again. "Not just me but all of us, family and community." Boon Leong's voice was low and less officious this time round. "The elders are meeting here in two days' time to prepare for the government inquiry next week."

Tuck Heng sat up stiffly, wary of what he was about to hear. He tried to make out the expression on Boon Leong's face, which was in the half-shadows for the room had only one window looking out into the courtyard.

"Who called for the meeting?"

"I suggested it."

"Who's coming?"

"All the clan and kongsi leaders, representatives of the Straits Chinese British Association and even the members of the Emperor Protection League Society."

"You invited those bastards? Those lapdogs supported the emperor!"

"Please, Kor! This isn't the time to quarrel among ourselves. We must speak with one voice before the governor."

"Since you know the governor, you speak to him! Some people have two mouths! One mouth says this. Another says that!"

He had always been blunt. Let the lawyer be careful with his words. He reached for his cup and took a loud satisfied sip of the fragrant Malaccan coffee.

Boon Leong compressed his lips and looked out at his prized roses in the courtyard. He had expected this. His good relations with the English had always aroused Tuck Heng's envy. But he was prepared to be patient with China-born like him. His half-brother had always struck him as rather churlish, without the civilised graces and objectivity of an educated man. He recalled his late mother saying that it had to do with his years in the tin mines and mixing with the crude miners.

"I can assure you that this governor's more willing to listen than the previous one. At least he released you on bail."

"Don't talk to me about the old governor. That buzzard supported the imperial reformist bastards."

"Sir John Anderson is a very strict man. He didn't hesitate when he had to apply Clause Four of the 1888 Banishment Ordinance."

"What clause, what ordinance, I don't know. But this I do know! That foreign devil hauled Dr Sun into his office one day. Ordered Dr Sun, a Chinese, not to interfere in Chinese politics! What kind of shit is that? Can these foreigners honestly say they didn't interfere in China's politics? Wait, wait. Don't tell me." He held up his hand.

"Let me tell you! Against the will of every thinking Chinese, they supported a court we hated. So they could gain from China's weakness! Can't you see through their cunning? You, a cunning lawyer yourself!"

Boon Leong refused to be baited. Dr Sun Yat-sen's case was well-known throughout Malaya. In 1908, Sir John Anderson had threatened to expel Dr Sun. The editors of several Chinese language newspapers were also severely warned. They would be banished under the Straits Settlements Societies Ordinance if they published articles advocating intrigue or sedition against the Manchu government. Two years later, the governor had ordered Dr Sun to leave Penang. According to the English language press he had made "inflammatory speeches to incite his coolie audiences to overthrow the Manchu regime".

"I'll be plain with you, Kor. This new governor will listen. Up to a point. But he's not going to be all that different from the previous one. The English government doesn't want people living here to be involved in politics. If the commission of inquiry finds that the riots were started because of politics, then there'll be big trouble for you. You'll be deported. Your family might suffer the same fate."

Tuck Heng was silent for some time. Caution restrained him now. He was not unaware of the dangers that Boon Leong had pointed out and he appreciated his brother's bluntness. But his brother was also part of the English-speaking Chinese in the colony and such persons, in his view, were ultimately the lackeys who served the interests of the English barbarians. He said nothing.

"Next week, many leaders of our community will be called before the commission of inquiry. The governor wants to hear their views and seek their advice. Now, some of us have thought of a plan to help you."

"Why are you doing this?"

"Father adopted you. Like it or not, we're family. Then some leaders also want me to speak unofficially to the governor."

Tuck Heng's brows drew together. His eyes behind their wire-rimmed glasses narrowed.

"Why?" he asked.

"The clan leaders are anxious. Worried that the riots have put the Chinese people in a bad light. They don't want the government to … to suspect them of doing anything wrong. Good relations with the government … good for trade … good for all Chinese living here, right or not?" Boon Leong struggled with his Hokkien.

"What did you and the others plan to do?"

"Very simple. Make sure … make sure that the authorities

see you as a respectable merchant. Not a leader of coolies and gangsters. So don't tell the commission... don't say that you're an elder of the White Crane."

"But they will ask."

"Tell them ... say that you've left the society. That you joined it when you were young. But you're no longer with the society."

"Why say that?"

"You've got to show that you ... you're a leader. Of traders and merchants. Not coolies. Then the government will respect you."

"But I was in the White Crane hall."

"Just say you were the guest of honour that day. Tell the commission that unruly coolies and gangsters took advantage of the New Year celebrations and started the fighting and looting. Not your speech."

Tuck Heng baulked at "gangsters" and said so.

"Say coolies then. No difference to me. Say that you and other leaders tried to stop the violence but could not. Then before you finish, remember to tell the governor that you, er, you appreciate the way that the government and the police have handled the situation. And you, er, you appreciate the freedom and peace here. Say you're loyal to the English king. The other leaders will support you."

Tuck Heng couldn't take his eyes off his brother's face. What a piece of shit, he thought. This twisting and turning to stab others in the back. How typical of Boon Leong to speak with a forked tongue!

"So! Actual events are not important. Truth is not important. To save their own skins, the clan leaders have agreed to lie."

Boon Leong's eyes had a glint of triumph when he said, "They've given me their word to support you."

"What good is their word? They're also elders in the White Crane! Like me! We've taken the blood oath."

"I'm aware of that, Kor."

"I've sworn loyalty to my White Crane brothers. I am part of the White Crane!"

"I know that too. But you've got to think of yourself and your family."

"So you want me to lie?"

"Why're you making a fuss? All China-borns lie when they see a policeman, right or not?"

The eyes before him held something like amused contempt. He noted the well-groomed hair, the fashionable white shirt and white trousers and the expensive black leather shoes which completed the attire of the English-educated Straits-born gentleman. Long-suppressed feelings of having been slighted, despised and scorned as a lower species of the human race stirred in his heart once again.

"So that's what you think of us, eh? You and the English bastards! That we lie whenever we open our mouths? You think that coolies are dirt! And you want me to blame everything on them!"

"Calm down."

"No, Brother! You look down on us, the China-born! Because we poor sods came over here packed like pigs in coolie ships! But I tell you, Brother, that from these pigs, you get traders, merchants, shopkeepers. And you're right! Lowdown coolies too! Thousands and thousands of them. But without them, who'll mine your tin? Pull your rickshaws? Build your houses? Grow your food? These pigs slog in the sun so that you and I can live in the shade! Let me tell you more! They're not the only pigs who come to Malaya. Among the pigs are newspaper editors, reporters, teachers, letter writers, clerks, herbalists and physicians! Thinking literate people like you! These are the people the governor wants to deport! Because they can rally the coolies."

Once he had started, he could not stop. His Hokkien speech was fluent, fluid and fiery like a native of Fujian Province and that was his advantage. He was in his element and if Boon Leong had tried to parry his words, he'd have reduced him to a hen floundering in water.

"Coolies have become towkays and have founded news-papers, schools and reading rooms, temples and hospitals all over this Malay land! Coolies have parted with their hard-earned dollars to help their homeland! Coolies have fought against Manchu rule for generations! The uprising in Kwang-tung last year claimed seventy-two martyrs. Do you know that thirteen of them are coolies from this country? They shed their blood to free us and you want me to call them gangsters and ignorant bastards before the foreign devils?"

An uneasy silence followed. Then Boon Leong put his hands together in a deliberate gesture of mock applause. Clap! Clap! Clap! A hard light had come into his eyes and the words which came were slow and measured as if he wanted to make sure that their significance sank in.

"It's very noble of you to think so highly of others, Kor. I applaud you and I'm humbled by what you said. But I hope you will think again. This government does not regard the riots lightly. If the inquiry thinks you've broken the law, the authorities will banish and deport you and confiscate all your properties."

"I know that. Each man's deed is each man's load."

"Well said. But one man's deed is also many men's trouble."

Boon Leong reached for the small bell on his desk and rang it. Moments later, the rest of the family entered.

One by one, they came into the room and studiously avoided his questioning eyes. They sat on chairs placed round the room, eyes downcast. Lai Fong sat between her two daughters and held their hands. They looked uncomfortable. Seng sat next to his mother and handed her a handkerchief. Choon looked as if she would burst into tears soon. Kok Kiong was the only one who appeared untouched.

"What's this?" He turned to Boon Leong.

"I think the family might help you to see things more clearly."

"I don't understand."

"Whether you like it or not, Kor, your decision is going to affect all of us. Your wives and your children. My wife and my children. And my two brothers' families too. Boon Haw and Boon Pin have wives and children too. Their daughters are of a marriageable age and I've heard from Second Sister-in-law," Boon Leong nodded in Lai Fong's direction, "that your eldest daughter, Yoke Foong, is already betrothed to the son of a very good family in Ipoh. Boon Haw's daughter is betrothed too. How will your imprisonment and deportation affect them? Boon Pin has a son in government service. My son, James, and your son, Kok Seng, are going to England to study law soon. Your action will affect their future. Your other son, Kok Kiong, is a fine young man. But if you're deported, he'll have to bear the burden of being head of your Ipoh family. Is he ready?"

Tuck Heng did not answer him but turned instead to gaze at the roses in the courtyard. Most of the blooms were fading like much of his idealism, he thought. He knew that his family was waiting for him to speak, but what could he say to them? His tangled feelings and memories were pressing upon him and the constriction in his throat would not go away. He had been young when he had had to bear the consequences of his father's single rebellious act. And the result? His father beheaded. His home torched. His mother, brothers and sisters burned to death. His life destroyed. What good came out of his father's sacrifice? Nothing. His father became a hero, it was true. But at what cost to himself and his family? As a boy fleeing the Manchu sword, he had turned against his father in his heart and condemned his father's act more than once, blaming him for all that he had lost. Was this what he wanted to bequeath his children?

Boon Leong waited patiently. This was not the moment to hurry a man. Years of legal work had given him an unerring sense of timing, of sniffing out the moment before a man caved in to spring his questions. He watched and waited. Then he leaned forward. His eyes held the other's with a piercing gaze.

"Kor, we all want to do the right thing. But what is the right thing?"

He waited for the question to sink in like a grain of sand dropped gently into a well. Its light weight buoyed by the body of water. When he spoke again, choosing his words carefully, almost as though he was debating with himself aloud, his voice had a quiet insistence which was difficult to ignore.

"Who comes first? Our family? Or people outside our family? If you're deported and separated from your wives and children, do you think they can depend on strangers for help? Then there're our ancestors. Will their spirits be at peace? And what about your land and properties? All that you've worked for will be lost. Have you thought about that?"

Boon Leong's low grave voice sounded reasonable, patient even, for he was not forcing his listener to accept his views. This was important for the shrewd lawyer knew that Tuck Heng would never let himself be pushed. He glanced at the others and it struck him that the Ongs and Wongs were a fragmented lot. Not everyone had understood what he said. Kok Seng was translating his words into Cantonese.

He nodded in Kok Seng's direction to mark his approval and encouragement. He had always treated his nephew as one of his sons and was pleased when the young man chose to join the legal profession instead of his father's business.

"Even if you think your wives and children are willing to leave Malaya with you, are you very, very sure that you will have a good life in China? Don't forget there's still fighting going on in many provinces even though China is now a republic. Let's say, for the sake of our discussion here, you go back to China alone and your family remains here. Are Kok Seng and Kok Kiong ready to take over your business, tin mines and shops?"

A long pause during which Tuck Heng cast his eyes round the room, looking at each face, waiting, fearful, their eyes avoided his gaze. No one else spoke.

Boon Leong continued, "Let's say, you think they're old enough or able enough to shoulder the burden, there's still another consideration. One which is beyond yourself and your family." Boon Leong's grave but insistent voice droned in his ears.

"In law, every act has a consequence. You do something, something else will follow. If you, a towkay, gets deported because of politics then you set ... er ... a precedent." He paused and struggled to find its equivalent in the Hokkien dialect. "It's, er, it's like throwing a rock impulsively into the pool, without thinking, and that first rock will cause many ripples in the calm pool. Think of your friends and associates, Kor. Which one among them is not involved in China's politics? Secretly or openly. And all have families and businesses to protect. Are you going to sacrifice your friends, associates and family because you can't be a blade of grass and bend a little?"

He waited for the question to sink in before going on.

"I know it's a matter of personal honour. But this whole affair might make the English government question the loyalty of every Chinese living under the British flag. Now I can tell you're a practical man. A man of the world. A man of business. And you know that poor relations with the government will affect the lives of all Chinese living here, towkays and coolies alike. If the towkays do poorly, won't the coolies suffer too? So please think again, Kor."

Boon Leong had prepared his speech and his questions well and he delivered them flawlessly. Every possible lever was being used to sway Tuck Heng to his point of view.

"You do the honourable thing and sacrifice yourself and your family, but the world remembers one day and forgets the next. Your family, my family, on the other hand, will have to live with the result of what you do. So what you choose to do will affect us all."

There was a pause as though the very thought of that had overwhelmed him. Then he went on, "If you accept full responsibility for the riot, are you so sure that it will not be useless? Are you a hundred per cent sure that one man can save those coolies from deportation?"

Boon Leong's eyes went round the room and looked at each face in turn, drawing each member of the family to himself and his cause with the assurance of a man who knew that he already had their support.

"Let me explain to you some of the English laws here. Seng,

you'll have to explain what I'm going to say to your father and the others. I'll have to use English when I talk about the law."

Kok Seng nodded. He was honoured by his uncle's inclusion of him in the attempt to make his father come to his senses, as his mother had described it.

"Explain to your father that the government has a number of laws at its disposal to control the Chinese in Malaya. A Chinese can be deported and sent back to China under the Banishment Act of 1888 or the Secret Society Ordinance. Appeals are useless in such cases. If the government thinks you're a troublemaker, you'll be sent back to China. Like any criminal. Besides these two laws, the government has another law—*ius sanguinis*, the law of blood. Under this law, a Chinese is a son of China and he can be repatriated to China if the government doesn't want him here. It doesn't matter whether he is born or has ever set foot in China."

Kok Seng did his best to explain what his uncle had said and a profound silence settled on the room as he spoke. His Cantonese was terse.

Tuck Heng sat rigidly in his chair. A thin blue vein throbbed at his right temple as he listened. He sat for a long time and said not a word after Kok Seng had finished. The others shifted uneasily in their seats as the full weight of English law descended upon them.

Then Kok Kiong stood up as though he refused to be weighed down by the foreign devil's laws. "Father," he said.

Tuck Heng turned to him.

"I don't understand all that Uncle said. But I'm not afraid of returning to China. Our young republic needs her youth."

His eyes were bright and he spoke in Mandarin, the national language of the new China.

"Sit down, Kok Kiong. When it concerns you, we'll talk about you. Right now it concerns me!"

Kok Kiong sat down. The light and colour had drained from his face. He did not look up or speak to his father again.

Then his younger sister, Yoke Lan, stood up. She strode deliberately across the room and took the seat next to her brother. Her bold support for Kok Kiong was not lost on the rest. Yoke Foong, meanwhile, burst into tears, fearful of losing her chance to make a good match. Lai Fong patted her daughter's hand. Her lips were pursed in a way Tuck Heng knew from habit showed she was angry with him.

"Seng, what about you?" Tuck Heng turned to the Penang branch of his family.

Kok Seng knew that he was being called to take a stand. He summoned his courage and spoke for his mother and sisters as well.

"Father, you've our respect and we're mindful of your difficulties. But my sisters and I are born here. We don't want to live in China."

Chapter Fifty-three

On the morning of the inquiry, he entered the august chambers of City Hall and took his place next to Boon Leong. His brother's face held an expression of studied objectivity as he riffled through the sheaf of papers on the table in front of him. In the row of seats behind them were members of the White Crane who had been accused together with him of starting the riot. He looked around the chamber and saw Kok Seng in the public gallery, but the rest of his family was nowhere in sight. His stomach muscles tightened. He'd expected them to be out in full force. Had they begun to distance themselves already? He felt his son's eyes on him and the young man's words, we don't want to live in China, almost rattled his resolve.

The governor and the six officials of the Commission of Inquiry came in and took their places at the table facing the public gallery. He was dismayed. They were all Englishmen, including the secretary for Chinese Affairs and the head of the Chinese Protectorate. He'd never faced so many foreign devils before. Stern inscrutable faces. Cold grey eyes. Red beards. Brown moustache. Sharp noses. Barbarian, barbarian, barbarian, he repeated the word inside his head like a secret mantra as he was conducted to a seat set aside for those to be interrogated by the commission.

"Your name," the Chinese interpreter asked in a loud officious voice.

"Wong Tuck Heng."

"Raise your right hand and repeat after me. I swear to tell the truth, the whole truth and nothing but the truth, so help me God."

"I swear by my ancestors that I will tell the truth and not betray my brothers," he said in Cantonese. Cheers and applause from the gallery.

"Do you want me to repeat the oath?" the flustered interpreter asked.

"No need. Tell the foreign gentlemen that since I don't believe in their god, I shall take the oath by my gods."

"Anything the matter?" one of the Englishmen asked.

"No, no, sir. Everything's fine."

He saw the man in charge of Chinese Affairs whisper something in the governor's ear and the governor nodded.

"Tell His Excellency and the commission about the riots," the interpreter told him.

"I, Wong Tuck Heng, greet Your Excellency, the Great Prince who rules the Straits Settlements and the Malay States. I greet too your honourable officials who help Your Excellency to govern the country," he began in his best formal Cantonese.

"I'm emboldened by Your Excellency's patience and willingness to listen to so many people during the past several days. Therefore I shall speak frankly and without fear, for you are respected by all Chinese as a just and fair-minded man."

He saw the flicker of a smile from the head of the Chinese Protectorate.

"His Excellency says to go on," the interpreter whispered.

"Your Excellency, the riots during Lunar New Year are not anti-British. The coolies were celebrating the new year and the liberation of China from Manchu rule. For after three hundred years of foreign domination, China is free."

He stopped, watching their faces as the interpreter translated. He could feel Boon Leong's eyes burning through him, but he refused to look at his brother.

"I beg Your Excellency to hear me out. The China I came from, the China ruled by the Manchu dogs, has suffered a great deal. Wars, plagues, starvation and corruption! Every coolie has a sad tale to tell about official corruption in the old China. So Your Excellency can understand why we support the new Republic of China. We Chinese hope that the new China will be free of official corruption like the Straits Settlements under your enlightened rule."

"Hear, hear!" The foreign devils clapped. He turned and looked in Boon Leong's direction. His brother smiled for the first time.

"It is my firm belief that Your Excellency's a just ruler. You will not deport someone because of his patriotic feelings for his homeland. If so, Englishmen must be deported from this colony too. Because on Empire Day, they show their love for their country and they get drunk! The coolies have been unruly. True! They have fought and they've cut off the queues of others. But must they face the terrible fate of deportation for the excessive expression of patriotic feelings? What will happen to them if they return to China?"

He paused and looked at his brother. But Boon Leong was examining his papers again.

The interpreter finished translating and hissed, "Go on."

"Let me tell Your Excellency. If they return to China, they will face wars and starvation. Poverty, hunger and shame. All their hopes and dreams for a better life will die on the ship back to China. Starved of hope. Robbed of dreams. And faced with the prospect of unemployment and certain hunger. You are sending them back to a withering death. I beg Your Excellency, can they not be punished in some other ways? Lock them up in your jails. Send them to hard labour in your mines. But don't send them back to China."

Shouts of "Right! Right!" came from the crowd in the public gallery. Boon Leong looked alarmed. His fists were clenched till his knuckles turned pale. Kok Seng's expression was one of bewilderment. This wasn't what Uncle Boon Leong had rehearsed with his father.

"Among the people here today whose fate depends on your justice are Chinese who've resided here for years. They're respectable persons in the community. They have a business or several businesses. They may be married and settled here and they regard this colony as their adopted country. To deport such traders, towkays and merchants will raise many fears and questions about the justice and fairness upheld by so many learned gentlemen in Your Excellency's government. Therefore I urge Your Excellency and Your Excellency's officials to ponder this very carefully. Thousands of lives depend upon your justice and compassion."

The governor and the members of the commission sat stiffly in their seats. Their faces were inscrutable as the speech was being translated for them. Never in the history of the colony had a Chinese made such a speech in their presence. This was unthinkable audacity! The highly sensitive issue of the governor's immense power to deport anyone without trial was being brought out into the open by a Chinaman! Englishmen in the colony were just as unhappy as the Chinese with the deportation law. It gave the governor too much power and it violated the Englishman's sense of justice and fair play. But it had never occurred to the English that a Chinese was capable of questioning that very law.

"Your Excellency, in the mines, the plantations and the towns, life would be impossible without Chinese coolie labour. Do you need to dig a drain or a cesspool? Chinese coolies will dig it for you. Do you need to dig tunnels for waterworks or collect nightsoil in the towns? Chinese coolies will do it. They will do anything to earn a living. All the things which other people don't want to do, they'll do. It's true, we've among us many troublemakers and gangsters too. But let me assure Your Excellency that although we Chinese are some fingers long, some fingers short, on the whole we're law-abiding and very grateful for the opportunities we've found in this country of our adoption."

Cheers erupted from the public gallery. There was a loud crash. It seemed to have come from outside the chamber. Shouts of "Mrs Wong is here! Mrs Wong is here!" rang in the corridors leading to the chamber.

Chapter Fifty-four

The pounding of the steam engine and the howl of the wind drove out his thoughts. Kok Seng strained to look for signs of land ahead, but there was no telling where land, sky and sea met in the vast darkness.

"Do you remember when you were a boy, you wanted to cut off your queue? I refused to let you. But you did it anyway. Your thoughts were well ahead of mine."

He strained to look at his father's face, but the night was too dark for the moon had not yet risen.

"Why so solemn, Seng? I'm just deported."

"You're leaving us, Father."

"I'll find a way to come back. Heaven will not block all my roads. To live is to change."

Courageous words. To live is to change. But there've been too many changes already, Kok Seng thought. He was still dizzy from the changes of the last few weeks. His mother had cried till her eyes, dry with a dark anger, had turned away from his father when they were at the harbour saying their last farewell. Choon Neo's heart had hardened. "Your father thinks only of himself and his name. What about us, eh?"

"When I'm gone, remember this," his father spoke into the wind and noise. "Two very different animals united to produce you. The monkey and the horse."

"Eh?"

"Your mother's family is Baba. They're like the Monkey

King. Highly adaptable. Their ancestors left China and settled in this country a hundred, maybe two hundred years ago. Maybe longer. Married local women and adapted to the life here. They can change themselves seven times seven like the Monkey King. When the Malay kings were powerful, the Babas spoke Malay, wore Malay clothes and hungered for Malay titles. Then the English barbarians came. The English were more powerful than the Malay kings. So your mother's family changed again. They learned to speak English and do things the English way. Just look at your Uncle Boon Leong."

Kok Seng remembered the dinner, the lights, the wine and the dancing in Roseville when they celebrated his uncle's knighthood. Now it all no longer seemed as magical and grand as before. Like a broken mirror, the cracks would always be visible even after careful repair. He would never again be able to enter his uncle's world of English law without noticing those cracks.

"Mark my words. When China becomes powerful, your uncle and his family will change again. They'll learn to speak Chinese and return to China. The Monkey King is smart. He's a survivor."

Intrigued, he asked, "Who's the horse?"

"The Wongs of Sum Hor. We'd rather leave good pastures and starve than stay to serve a bad master. My forefathers gave up high positions and great wealth in the capital city. Moved south to the village of Sum Hor and settled there. They became humble village physicians, loyal to the Ming emperor. Courage and loyalty, my son. These are the traits of the horse. It's not afraid to throw off a bad rider."

A passing steamer sent their vessel rolling and rocking with the waves, his father clung to the railing. The roar of the engines seemed to fill the silence between them. When his father spoke again, his voice was tense.

"Boon Leong's advice was good. I should've moved away from the White Crane coolies so I wouldn't get into trouble with the government here. But if I did that, I'd be breaking my White Crane vows. Vows I swore when they accepted me.

378 • A BIT OF EARTH

The White Cranes in China saved me from my murderers. They risked their lives and those of their families. Should I repay their courage with cowardice? If I'd moved away from the coolies to save my own skin, my aunts and uncles, who were all members of the White Cranes, who'd died for me, would've died for nothing. And I'd be leaving you nothing but a legacy of fear. Fear of losing one's head, one's wealth and one's possessions. What kind of heritage is that?"

He could almost hear the rising pain and anger in his father's voice as he spoke of that horrific past in his childhood.

"Father."

"No, let me finish. We might not have another chance to talk like this. You're my eldest son and I've never talked about such things with you before. I always regretted my father didn't talk to me. I was angry with him when I was a boy. He died a hero for nothing. And our whole family died with him. For what? I used to ask myself. One day you and your sisters might think like this too. I've lost nearly all our properties to the government. For what? You might ask one day. But compared to my father, what I did is nothing. To be banished and deported and lose all that I own. It's nothing when you think of being beheaded and torched, right or not? These English barbarians won't behead me. They won't do anything bad to you or to your mother and sisters. Although they're foreign devils, they're civilised and fair-minded. So why should I act in fear? We guard and protect ourselves all the time against loss. Afraid of losing what we have. Yet when disaster strikes, we're defenceless. A disaster or a war comes, you lose everything too. Who can foretell such things?"

The moon came out from behind the clouds. Its light fell upon his father's face, softening its angular features. He looked more of a scholar now than the harsh grasping trader that Choon Neo had made him out to be.

"Land and properties, you can lose. But if you lose your spirit, then you lose the very thing that makes us human. Courage and loyalty. That's part of our spirit as human beings. Many times I came close to losing that. Do you know why?"

His father turned towards him and held his eyes by the light of the paraffin lamp which a crew hand had just lighted.

"Family," his father went on and for a brief second, his father rested a hand on his shoulder. The ship lurched and his father's hand moved away. Years afterwards he would recall this moment as the closest his father had come to showing him affection.

"Not my land. Not my tin mines. Not the shops and plantations. But our family. I've thought about every one. Uncle Boon Leong, Uncle Boon Haw and Uncle Boon Pin's families. They're also part of my big family. Your family."

His father looked away to gaze once again at the dark silvery sea all round them. They were halfway down the Straits of Malacca and should be reaching Singapore soon, he reckoned.

"Your uncles' father, Tai-kor Wong, adopted me. Their grandfather, Baba Wee, was very kind to me. I didn't want to harm the families of those who'd helped me. But I knew that what I said and what I did at the inquiry would affect your uncles and our family. They might be deported too and lose their properties. I too was scared of losing what we have. We're Chinese so we're scared of losing."

How odd, he thought. What has being Chinese got to do with it anyway?

"We Chinese have suffered terrible loss in our long history of wars, disasters and corruption. And loss has made us greedy. And afraid. That's why we guard against loss all the time. We marry many wives so we can have many children. If we lose some, we still have others. We're afraid to lose, so we eat faster. Work harder. Sleep less. And grab more. So we won't lose out to others. But life is more than being better, faster, harder. Did they teach you this in the Christian school?"

"They did, Father."

"Good. We're part of an unending chain. Generation after generation. While in prison, I thought to myself, what will I pass on to the next generation? Not money, not land. These don't last, I tell you. Baba Wee's wealth didn't last. His sons squandered it after his death. I thought of Tai-kor Wong, my adoptive father. He was not a wealthy man, but his loyalty shines to this day. The Malays of Bandong still talk about him. Tell stories about how he remained loyal to Musa Talib and the menteri of Bandong. He knew the Malays would lose to the English. Yet he risked his life and the lives of his men to bring supplies to the menteri. Because the menteri was his friend. Don't forget Tai-kor Wong is also your grandfather. And he's a White Crane hero."

This was the first time he'd heard of his grandfather's death spoken of in this light and he was proud of his own lineage. He listened intently to what his father was saying till a feeling almost akin to pain gripped him. He might not see his father again. He wanted to say something to him, some words of comfort, assurance or respect but no words came.

"Courage and loyalty are immeasurable. They give meaning to our lives. Who knows when a man is called to join his ancestors? So you tell me, could I have moved away from the coolies and done what your Uncle Boon Leong and mother wanted me to do?"

Years into the future, on a cold dark night in London, just before he plunged into the struggle for national independence, Kok Seng would look back and realise this was the moment he understood the father he hardly knew, the man stripped of his properties and deported by the British authorities.

"There's a price to be paid for speech. Mine is a small price. A grass hut on a mountain where I shall live."

He was about to speak, but his father stopped him.

"Don't feel bad because you don't want to come with me, Seng. You're different. You're born in Malaya, not China. Your feet were rooted into this bit of earth the day you were born. Just remember, you come from a noble family, blessed with the divine spirit of dissidence. A descendant of those not afraid to question the emperor!"

His father's eyes shone with pride and mischief as a low rumbling chuckle rose from his belly and turned into a full-throated roar as he shouted into the wind.

"Your Second Mother is a roaring tigress. A roaring tigress, you hear that?"

They clung to the railing of the ship and laughed at the memory of Lai Fong at the head of the women's brigade.

"Father, did she tell you beforehand?"

"No! Not a word!"

"Incredible!"

"I know! She's Hua Mulan's daughter!"

The Sikh guard couldn't believe his eyes as Lai Fong pushed past him at the head of the horde which had suddenly descended upon City Hall that morning. Red-faced English officers rushed down the corridors at the head of long lines of police guards, wielding batons and rattan shields.

"Faster, sisters, faster!" Second Mother had led them towards the chamber where the hearing was taking place. "Faster!" Her voice screeching above the shouts of the women. Many of them were carrying babies and toddlers. Five-year-olds were clinging to their mothers' hands and running alongside the adults. Children as young as seven were helping their grandmothers to keep up with the rest.

They crashed through the barrier of rattan shields. Bringing the babies and children was Lai Fong's idea. She had lived long enough in the missionary centre in Kwangtung to know that no Englishman would hit a baby or an old lady. "Englishmen respect God, queen and women," Miss Higgs had said. "Faster! Sisters! Faster!" The English officers and their guards retreated before this onslaught.

No one to this day believed that the storming of City Hall was the work of one woman. One woman who rallied the amahs, the wives and relatives of the imprisoned coolies.

"Second Mother still has her medical halls. She'll look after your mother and sisters while you're away in England."

"Yes, Father."

"Study hard."

"Take care of yourself, Father, and come back soon."

"I will."

A sly smile crept into his father's face.

"I will return. The White Cranes will give me another name and identity. The English barbarians can't tell one Chinese face from another. I too can be the Monkey King. For what is life but a succession of change; of one thing after another; painful beginnings, fearful setting out into the unknown, leaving what we are for what we have not yet become. We sail forth boldly, keeping a steady keel and a keen eye on the horizon, to reach islands, land whose fragrance we sniff at at the edge of our dreams; and so we sail on, hoping that the next landfall will be our own bit of earth."

Then his father thrust a scroll into his hands.

"My gift. Ask Second Mother to translate for you."

SECOND FRAGMENT

什么是故土？
植入
希望、生命、
梦想和回忆的
一撮土。

What is homeland
In which we planted
Our hopes, lives,
dreams and memories?
A bit of earth.

AUTHOR'S NOTE

A Bit of Earth is a work of fiction based on fact sculpted by the imagination. A footnote in a history textbook about the adultery of a tin miner's wife had excited my teenage imagination, and I have been interested in the history of Chinese tin miners in Malaysia ever since.

Bandong is a fictional village in the Malaysian state of Perak. The Bandong war in the novel is based on the tin mining wars in nineteenth century Perak, which was colonised by the British. Malay resistance led to the murder of James Birch, the first British Resident of Perak.

British rule brought thousands of Chinese to the tin mines and rubber plantations of Malaya. These Chinese coolies were treated as dispensable workhorses. They could be easily deported under two laws upheld by the British—*ius sanguinis*, "the law of blood", and *ius solis*, "the law of the soil". The law of blood asserted that any Chinese could be deported to China, regardless of whether he was born there or whether he could speak Chinese. The law of the soil, on the other hand, stated that a person was a native and a citizen of his place of birth. In their dealings with the Chinese in Malaya, the British applied either of these two laws, depending on which gave the colonial government greater advantage and legal expediency at the time.

REFERENCES

Hill, A.H. "The Hikayat Abdullah: An Annotated Translation", *Journal of the Malayan Branch of the Royal Asiatic Society* 28: 1–354, 1955.

Leech, H.W.C. "About Kinta", *Journal of the Straits Branch of the Royal Asiatic Society* 4: 21–33, 1879.

Moore, Donald and Joanna. *The First 150 Years of Singapore*. Singapore: Donald Moore Press Ltd in association with the Singapore International Chamber of Commerce, 1969.

Ong Siew Im, Pamela. *Blood and the Soil*. Singapore: Times Books International, 1995.

Roff, William R., *The Origins of Malay Nationalism*. Kuala Lumpur: University of Malaya Press, 1967.

Song Ong Siang. *One Hundred Years' History of the Chinese in Singapore*. Reprinted with an introduction by Edwin Lee. Singapore: Oxford University Press, 1984.

THE AUTHOR

Suchen Christine Lim is an award-winning author of novels, short stories, children's stories and a non-fiction book. She was awarded the Southeast Asia Write Award in 2012 for her body of work.

Photo by Russel Wong

Fistful of Colours, winner of the inaugural Singapore Literature Prize, is cited as a classic Singapore novel. Later *A Bit of Earth* and *The Lies That Build A Marriage* were short listed for the same prize. Her debut novel, *Rice Bowl*, is considered a landmark novel on post-independence Singapore. *The River's Song* was chosen as a "100 Best Books of 2015" Kirkus Reviews (USA) and Book of the Month in *The Sunday Times*, Singapore.

Awarded a Fulbright grant, she was a Fellow in the University of Iowa's International Writing Program, and later its Writer in Residence. She was a Fellow in Creative Writing at the Nanyang Technological University, Singapore, and has held writing residencies in the US, UK, Australia, South Korea, the Philippines, Vietnam and Myanmar.

OTHER WORKS BY
SUCHEN CHRISTINE LIM

NOVELS
Rice Bowl (1984)

Gift From The Gods (1990)

Fistful Of Colours (1992)
(awarded the inaugural Singapore Literature Prize)

The River's Song (2014)

Dearest Intimate (2022)

SHORT STORIES
The Lies That Build A Marriage (2007)
(shortlisted for the Singapore Literature Prize)

NON-FICTION
Stories Of the Chinese Overseas (2005)